D0191668

Cathy Bramley is the *Sunday Times* Top Ten best-selling author of *A Patchwork Family*, *My Kind of Happy*, *The Merry Christmas Project* and *The Lemon Tree Café*. Her other romantic comedies include *Ivy Lane*, *Appleby Farm*, *Wickham Hall*, *Conditional Love*, *The Plumberry School of Comfort Food* and *White Lies and Wishes*. She lives in a Nottinghamshire village with her family and a dog.

Cathy turned to writing after spending eighteen years running her own marketing agency. She has always been an avid reader, never without a book on the go, and now thinks she may have found her dream job!

Cathy loves to hear from her readers. You can get in touch via her website www.CathyBramley.co.uk, on Facebook @CathyBramleyAuthor or on Twitter @CathyBramley

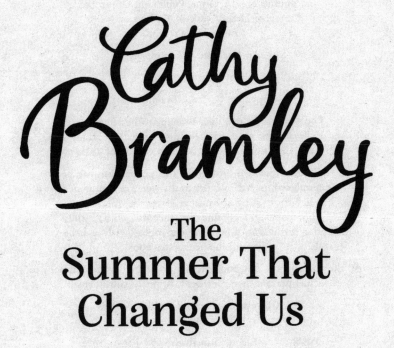

Cathy Bramley

The Summer That Changed Us

ORION

An Orion paperback

First published in Great Britain in 2022 by Orion Fiction,
an imprint of The Orion Publishing Group Ltd,
Carmelite House, 50 Victoria Embankment,
London EC4Y 0DZ

An Hachette UK company

1 3 5 7 9 10 8 6 4 2

A CIP catalogue record for this book is
available from the British Library.

ISBN (Mass Market Paperback) 978 1 4091 8682 3
ISBN (eBook) 978 1 4091 8683 0

Typeset by Born Group

Printed and bound in Great Britain by Clays Ltd, Elcograf S.p.A.

MIX
Paper from
responsible sources
FSC® C104740

www.orionbooks.co.uk

For Phoebe, who makes me proud every day
love Mum x

Hello, dear reader!

Of all the books you could have chosen, you chose mine and I'm very grateful, so thank you!

While you're here, I thought I'd take the opportunity to tell you a bit more about myself. I was brought up in Birmingham, but now live in a pretty little village in Nottinghamshire. Our two daughters have flown the nest (although there still seems to be a lot of clutter in their rooms), but we love having country walks on our doorstep, as does Pearl, our dog.

Despite being slap-bang in the middle of the country I LOVE the sea and visit the coast as often as I can. Waking up to the sound of waves is probably one of my favourite things, along with going to the cinema, cooking for friends, and finding the perfect dress (an endless quest, but still, I try).

I've always been a fan of reading, but I didn't turn my hand to writing novels until 2013 and I haven't looked back. I write about love, family, friendship and community, and how life can be so much brighter when people look out for one another. The pages of my books are stuffed full of women who are determined to make the best of the hand they have been dealt, and the sort of women I'd be proud to call my friends.

My novels can be read as standalone stories, but now and again, you'll see people and places crop up from previous books. For example, readers of My Kind of Happy will recognise the florist's and several of the customers from reading The Lemon Tree Café and A Patchwork Family. Well, that's enough from me for now, I'll leave you to enjoy your book in peace; I hope it brings you happiness!

Best wishes,

Cathy

xxx

Chapter One

In Merle Bay, a small seaside town on the north-east coast of England, two seagulls were squabbling on Katie Small's kitchen roof. She flung open the window and threw out her toast crusts into the cottage's tiny backyard.

'Stop fighting, you hooligans,' she yelled.

The squawking stopped instantly, and two enormous white and grey birds swooped down to collect their spoils and flew off above the rooftops.

Peace at last, thought Katie, swallowing the last of her coffee.

The seagulls didn't bother her anymore; she was used to their boisterous antics. Unlike her auntie, she laughed to herself, remembering how Auntie Jean used to yelp and duck down if one of them ever came near, convinced they'd attack her if they got the chance. Vicious blighters, she'd mutter darkly.

The yard, deserted now, was bright with spring sunshine and the terracotta pots her dad had filled with cheerful primulas yesterday caught her eye. Good old Dad. He and Mum had come up from Nottingham to spend the weekend here at the cottage. Allegedly to relax before flying off on holiday last night, but Dad had hardly taken his coat off before he was wielding a screwdriver, oiling squeaky hinges and tidying up the garden. He was always the same when he was here. Auntie Jean had been his older sister and he'd worshipped her, but now she was gone and the cottage belonged to Katie, he'd taken up the role as official handyman. Mum was as bad: washing everything in sight, from the net curtains (which really had to go, Katie thought with a sigh) to the cushion covers, right down to the skirting boards. Never knowingly without a damp cloth in her hand, that was his Josie, Dad had said fondly about his wife, teasing that that would be the epitaph on her tombstone.

Breakfast over, Katie quickly shoved the butter and milk back in the fridge, tossed the bread in the bread bin and ran hot water in the Belfast sink. The kitchen was tiny, a single storey addition to the terraced cottage. It was the only room which had been redecorated since Katie moved in with her auntie ten years ago. With its cream and pale blue colour scheme and beach-themed artwork, it was the room Katie felt most at home in. She washed her mug and her toast plate, drying them up with one of her auntie's tea towels, which she noticed was looking a bit threadbare these days. Another thing to add to the list, she thought. But not right now, because it was already eight o'clock and she wanted to put a new window display in the shop before she opened up.

Katie went through to the living room to collect her keys and all the props she'd prepared for the window. She was filled with a sudden rush of warmth as she recalled one of a series of conversations she and Auntie Jean had had when it became obvious that the old lady's days behind the counter were numbered.

'Let's talk shop, our Katie,' she'd say, making herself as comfortable as her advancing illness would allow. 'The shop window is our biggest advert. It's our customers' first impression of Auntie Small's. Always make it a good one.'

Katie swallowed a lump in her throat at the memory.

The crocheted blanket draped over her aunt's wingback armchair in front of the gas fire, the collection of china figurines on the shelves of the dresser, the hessian bag bulging with sea glass in the corner next to the plastic case full of Jean Small's seventies disco vinyl records . . . Despite it being over a year since she'd died, her presence was evident in every nook and cranny of the cottage.

'Right,' said Katie determinedly, scooping up her shoulder-length chestnut hair and securing it into a bun. 'I'm off to make a good impression.'

She picked up a wooden crate and a black sack full of willow twigs and stepped out onto Merle Bay's high street, a steep hill lined with a mix of cottages, shops, tea rooms and a pub or two. She gazed downhill as always while she locked the door, marvelling at the view: a shimmering blue-green sea, under an endless sky.

Her heaven, her haven. She was happier here than anywhere else in the world.

Still with keys in her hand, she moved uphill a couple of paces to the next door and unlocked it. Her five-second commute was over. It was time for work.

Forty-five minutes later Katie climbed down off her chair and fanned her face, glad to be out of the direct sunlight. She studied her new spring window display critically. *Not bad at all.*

After her parents had left yesterday, she'd spent the evening making flowers from tissue paper. Now they were suspended with coloured thread from branches of twisted willow. She'd taken a rustic wooden crate that had been lurking in the shed full of Auntie's gardening paraphernalia and brushed it clean. Now it was stuffed with armfuls of tulips and anemones and bluebells – artificial of course, she didn't want to have to touch the window again for at least another four weeks.

She leaned back into the tight space and adjusted one of the mannequins. *There. Done.* The new spring lingerie collection at Auntie Small's was officially on sale: cotton prints, sleek satin and pretty lace in pastel shades of yellow, pink and aqua – something for everyone. Well, nearly everyone. She pushed up the sleeves of her oversized shirt and remembered the utilitarian plain white garments beneath. She favoured sports bras: supportive and comfortable with the added bonus of strong compression which made her boobs look smaller than they were. Not in the least bit flattering, and neither were her big knickers, but as it had been two years since she'd allowed anyone close enough to see her in her undies, what did it really matter?

'Why can't you wear something a bit more sexy?' her last boyfriend, Gareth, had complained. 'Even my mum wears smaller knickers than you.'

It was the last time Gareth saw her underwear, or her for that matter, because she dumped him on the spot. That sort of comment made Katie's skin crawl. It wasn't that she was a prude, but she wanted a partner who respected her choices, not ridiculed them. And shortly after that, Auntie Jean's leukaemia worsened, and Katie had taken over the running of the shop. As much as she loved living here, the average age of residents was nearer sixty than thirty. There might be plenty more fish in the sea, but not many of them seemed to have made their way inland to Merle Bay. And as for internet dating, the thought of putting her profile online brought Katie out in a cold sweat.

The bell above the door chimed as the first customer of the day walked in and Katie abandoned thoughts of her dismal love life with pleasure.

It was Mel who owned the hair salon at the top of the high street.

'Hello!' said Katie, surprised.

There were only about six hundred people who lived in Merle Bay all year round (some of the houses were second homes, or holiday lets with no permanent residents); a good proportion of the women bought their underwear here and Katie was familiar with a lot of people's vital statistics. But until now, not Mel's. As far as Katie could remember, Mel had never bought anything from Auntie Small's.

'Hi.' Mel hovered at the door, twirling a lock of her dark hair around her fingers. 'Have you got anything that will make me feel like a million dollars, but ideally only cost me about twenty-five pounds?'

'You're in luck, loads of things fit that request,' said Katie.

Nula, the shop's only member of staff knew everyone. Katie remembered her saying that Mel's husband had left her just after Christmas out of the blue. Which might explain why Mel looked as if she had lost quite a bit of weight since Katie had last been into the salon for a trim.

'Is it for a special occasion?' she added.

'I wish,' Mel said flatly. 'No. I looked in my underwear drawer yesterday and was greeted by a sea of grey. It was depressing.'

'Grey is a lovely colour,' said Katie, 'I wear a lot of grey myself.'

'Maybe, but most of mine were once white. Anyway, I fancy something bright and beautiful.'

'Something just like you then,' she replied, causing Mel to pull a face. 'I mean it. Look at you. You manage to look glamorous in jeans and a ponytail.' She gestured to Mel's outfit.

'You are kind.' Mel ventured further into the shop. 'Sorry. The last thing you want to hear is my whinging.'

'If you want to get something off your chest,' Katie grinned at Mel, 'pardon the pun – feel free, you can tell me anything. I promise, I won't tell a soul. Coffee?'

Mel accepted her offer and Katie poured them both a small cup from the machine. Freshly brewed coffee was something she'd introduced recently. Not only did it smell wonderful, it made everyone feel like a special customer – which to Katie, they all were.

Katie sipped her drink and waited.

'My ex came to collect the kids for the day yesterday and after they'd gone, I moped about feeling sorry for myself. I just felt . . . ' Mel sighed.

'It's OK to feel whatever you feel,' Katie encouraged her.

She chewed her lip, saying finally, 'I felt obsolete. Oh God, it sounds so lame and pathetic.'

Katie had a sudden flashback to coming home from sixth form one day to find her mum hastily drying her tears. *I used to look forward to having more time to myself once you'd grown up*, Mum had admitted sheepishly, *but now it's actually happening and you're so independent, I miss being needed.* But Katie had needed her, and at twenty-eight, still did. Even though they lived three hours' drive away, her parents were her support system.

'Mel, I doubt your children could manage without you for very long. Not to mention your clients at the salon. Can you imagine the state of our hair if anything happened to you?' Katie tugged at her own thick mane. It had a bit of a kink to it – neither straight nor curly – and she felt it looked messy whatever she did with it.

Mel managed a lopsided smile. 'True. And by the way, I don't remember seeing you in the salon for a while.'

6

'I know, it's on my to-do list, promise.' Katie hated sitting in the hairdresser's chair feeling exposed when surrounded by so many mirrors and bright lights. 'What I'm saying is, you're a long way from obsolete. Why not see it as an opportunity for some me-time?' she suggested. 'Do the things you don't get a chance to do when the kids are with you.'

Mel drained her coffee. 'Good coffee and good advice. Thanks.'

'You're welcome.' Katie ran her eyes expertly over Mel's body and made a quick assessment of her new size.

Katie might be young to be running a well-established lingerie shop, especially one which catered to the needs of an ageing and ample population, but she'd been doing this job for ten years and she was good at it. Half of her customers came in wearing the wrong size and were amazed how much better they looked with a narrower strap or a bigger cup.

'Now, why don't you go and undress while I select some options. We'll have you feeling like a goddess in no time.'

'OK.' Mel gave Katie a wobbly smile on her way to the changing rooms. 'The window looks very enticing, by the way. I love spring colours, so much nicer than all that red stuff for Valentine's Day. Which I totally ignored this year, for obvious reasons.'

Katie sympathised; she tried to avoid Valentine's Day herself, but it wasn't that easy in her line of work. More men came through the door of Auntie Small's in the run-up to February the fourteenth than in the rest of the year put together. Whatever her views on their purchases were, she couldn't deny it was good for the shop's takings.

'We celebrated Galentine's Day here too,' Katie said diplomatically. 'And it wasn't all red.'

'Hmm. You don't splash out on fancy knickers for the *gals* though, do you?' said Mel from inside the cubicle.

'No,' said Katie firmly, 'we do it for ourselves. Because we're worth it.'

Mel popped her head back out of the changing-room door. 'Thanks for listening. I have people in and out of my hairdressing chair all day long telling me about themselves. It's nice to do the talking for once. But you won't mention my woes to anyone, will you?'

Katie shook her head. 'Wouldn't dream of it. Nula and I are keepers of many secrets; from nursing bras to naughty nights away, there's not much you can hide from us at Auntie Small's.'

Mel's eyebrows shot up. 'Blimey, I never thought of that. Who's been buying sexy undies?'

'Couldn't possibly say,' Katie said primly, with a sparkle in her eye. She slid a froth of satin and lace through a crack in the door. 'Here, try these on. Trust me,' she said, as Mel started to argue that she'd given her the wrong size. 'I'm an expert.'

Ten minutes later, Mel had left with an Auntie Small's bag containing some pale pink satin wrapped in scented tissue paper. Katie had made her promise faithfully not to save it for best and in return for a discount, Mel had booked Katie in for a trim free of charge.

For the next hour, Katie sat in the small space she'd carved out as an office at the rear of the shop, working through her admin jobs methodically, whilst keeping an ear trained for the sound of customers at the door and enjoying the peace. Nula started at ten o' clock and was a complete extrovert. The job in the shop was absolutely perfect for her; she was great at putting customers at ease, but Katie found concentrating on the accounts quite tricky when her employee was in full flow.

At five to ten, Katie stood, stretched and put the kettle on ready for Nula to brew her ginger tea as soon as she arrived.

The shop had originally been called Merle Bay Lingerie when Jean Small had set it up in the eighties. She had been the sort of grown-up you called 'Auntie', even if you weren't a blood relative, because she made you feel like you were family. She was warm, welcoming and had turned the mundane act of buying new undies into a celebration. After a year of everyone referring to the shop as simply Auntie Small's, Jean had given in and renamed it.

Katie missed her aunt terribly; her death had been Katie's first taste of grief. Discovering that Jean had left her the cottage and the business in her will had been a real shock. She was honoured and grateful but also a little overwhelmed by the responsibility. But it had been Auntie Jean's wish that her only niece inherited her modest empire and with her parents' support, Katie was trying her best. She hadn't managed to make the cottage her own yet, but the shop, she had to admit, was thriving.

'Well, doesn't that display look a sight for sore eyes!' Nula exclaimed, staring at the window while peeling off a handknitted cardigan from her plump arms. If Jean Small had been everyone's auntie, then Nula was everyone's nanna. She'd been a dinner lady at the local primary school before working here and Katie just knew she'd have been the type to give children extra portions when no one was looking.

'Why thank you,' said Katie, pouring hot water into her assistant's favourite mug and handing her her first tea of the day.

'You should have waited; I like doing it.' Nula stopped at one of the mirrors, patted her grey curls into place and gave Katie a look of rebuke.

'I know you do, and your displays are far better than mine,' said Katie, 'but I need the practice.'

Besides, it was a point of honour with Katie: whenever she found something challenging, she'd grit her teeth and persevere until she got the hang of it.

Nula blew on her tea. 'And how are Josie and Brian? Full of the joys of spring, I hope?'

'Very well, thanks,' said Katie. 'They'll be in Malta by now, sunning themselves. Dad will be halfway down his first ice cream.'

Katie loved having her parents to stay. She also heaved a sigh of relief when they left. When they weren't doing practical jobs, they were on some campaign or other where Katie was concerned; this time it was that she should clear Auntie Jean's things from the cottage and move into the biggest bedroom, not stay cooped up in the little single that she'd been staying in since she was a child. They'd even offered to help her. She would do it, she promised them, soon. It was comforting somehow, keeping it like it was; erasing Jean's presence seemed too final.

'They'll like Malta,' said Nula authoritatively. 'They've got a Marks and Spencer.'

The door opened again.

'Post!' declared Alice Jennings, the post lady.

While Nula crossed to the counter to check the diary to see if they had any fittings booked in as she did every morning, Katie waited as Alice sorted through her bag for their usual bundle of letters.

'You'll be wanting some new lingerie now that you're famous,' said Nula.

Alice batted a hand. 'Oh, give over.'

The post lady had made a delivery to a pregnant woman on the far side of town two weeks ago only to find herself delivering a premature baby single-handedly.

'I read the article in the *North East Gazette*, Alice,' said Katie. 'Lovely photo of you with the baby.'

'We got three copies,' Alice smiled coyly and pulled a newspaper cutting out of her jacket pocket. 'Graham's got one to show his buddies and we've got one in a frame. It's the most exciting thing to ever happen to me.'

'Not just to you,' said Nula, 'I don't think anything that exciting has happened in Merle Bay for years!'

Which was one of the things she loved about it most, thought Katie: its gentle pace of life.

Nula managed to get Alice to put her bulging post bag down and peruse a rail of jersey camisoles. Katie took the pile of letters through to her office, intending to sift through them later, when her eye fell on a hardbacked envelope addressed to Catherine Small with 'personal' written in capitals across the front in red pen.

She frowned; usually her private mail was directed to the cottage next door but this one definitely had the shop's address on it. And no one called her Catherine anymore, that name was part of her old life. She slid her finger under the flap and pulled out the contents.

The shock of what she saw made her heart stop. She stared in horror as a tremor of fear shot through her. A large black and white photograph of a naked young girl with wild chestnut hair, too much make-up around her wide eyes, lips parted in surprise.

A handwritten note had been paperclipped to the picture: REMEMBER THIS?

All at once the room spun and she swayed on the spot,

her fingers fumbling to get the photograph back in the envelope.

'Katie?' Nula's face loomed large in front of her and she touched Katie's arm. 'Are you OK, love? You look like you've seen a ghost.'

'Yeah, yeah, I . . . um,' Katie forced a smile. 'Can you hold the fort for an hour? I need some fresh air.'

'Of course, love,' said Nula, full of concern, 'you take your time.'

Fresh air and space to think or maybe scream out loud where no one would hear her. There was only one place that would do: Sea Glass Beach.

Chapter Two

Grace slowed down as she approached the next junction, rapidly scanning the place names on the faded signpost, hoping to see her final destination amongst them. Ah, there it was, Merle Bay, five miles. She indicated and turned left, rather late in the day according to the driver behind her who honked a horn angrily at her.

'Grace?' said Zoe via the car's speaker system. 'Are you still there?'

Grace was beginning to regret ringing her sister hands-free after leaving the motorway. She'd never done this journey before and the roads had become narrower and windier as she'd got closer to the coast. She and Myles had always split the driving on long trips but now her bum was numb and her shoulders stiff with tension. The satnav couldn't give her verbal instructions now that she and Zoe were speaking, and she was a bit worried she was going to miss some vital turning. On the plus side, the scenery with its wall-to-wall green fields under wide skies was gorgeous, and it felt like balm to her weary soul.

'Yes, bear with, almost missed the sign for Merle Bay and this road is virtually single track. Not far to go now, I'm only a few miles away.'

Zoe sighed heavily. 'I'm really not sure that you're doing the right thing, you know.'

'Really?' Grace smiled to herself. 'If only you'd mentioned it.'

'Ha ha.'

'Trust me on this one, Zo,' Grace tried to soothe her younger sister for the umpteenth time. 'Right now, I need some space. I need to be somewhere new, where there isn't a memory of him imprinted into every inch of the place.'

The line was quiet for a moment. 'I get that, I just don't understand why you have to be quite so far away. There must be millions of places closer to Birmingham, closer to *me*. I worry about you and I'll miss you. And the kids will miss their Auntie Grace.'

Grace swallowed hard, determined that her voice wouldn't give away just how vulnerable she was feeling. The grief she carried from losing her husband last November changed from moment to moment. Sometimes a weight on her shoulders, at others a tightness in her chest. Or like today, it brought more tears. She'd stopped at a motorway services and bought two takeaway coffees: a latte for herself and a flat white for Myles. Only to remember she was driving solo. Would always be driving solo from now on.

She'd leaned on Zoe a lot since Myles died; her sister had been her rock and she'd miss that support, but now, five months on, she needed a change of scene.

'I know you worry,' said Grace, 'but you've got enough on your plate without me adding to it.'

'Nonsense,' said Zoe dismissively. 'There'll always be room for you here, remember that.'

'Thanks.' Grace's heart melted with love for her sister.

Zoe was a single mother of two: Daniel, aged eleven, a quiet biddable boy, with strawberry-blond hair, nose permanently in a book, and flame-haired Ruby, just seven months old, and who looked set to crash through life creating the most noise possible. Zoe was divorced from Daniel's father, who'd been so unreliable with child support payments that Zoe had lost the will to keep chasing him for money. Nobody knew Ruby's father, including Zoe herself. After waiting years for her prince to come and give her the second baby she wanted, she'd visited a sperm bank and chosen a donor. She hadn't told Grace until after she'd had her twelve-week scan; Grace had never wanted children, but she couldn't help feeling proud of her sister for making her own dreams come true. And Ruby, born last September, had certainly been a ray of sunshine during the darkness of last winter.

Grace and Myles had always helped out financially when Zoe's pride would let them: baby equipment, trainers for Daniel's growing feet, two new tyres when Zoe's car skidded on black ice. Myles had even set aside a little nest egg for each of the children in his will.

Last month, Zoe had found a nursery place for Ruby and had gone back to work as a nurse on a men's ward of the local hospital. Grace admired her for juggling family life and a demanding job with zero help from the fathers but her sister's return to work had highlighted her own inactivity. So here she was, taking action.

'In Northumberland, where no one knows me, I can be as sociable or as antisocial as I want, *and* I can be just me, not the remaining half of "me and Myles". And then there's the future; I need to think about who I'm going to be without him.'

Grace gripped the steering wheel so tightly that she felt her rings cut into her fingers. Her wedding and diamond engagement rings, still sparkling after sixteen years, and her newest one, an eternity ring, Myles's gift for her fortieth birthday six years ago. But they hadn't had an eternity, they hadn't even managed another decade. Myles had died of a heart attack, aged sixty-one, just months after he'd retired. Grace wasn't just mourning the love of her life, she was mourning the future they'd never have: the fun, the travel, time to be spent together enjoying the fruits of their hard work.

'Well, looking on the bright side, at least you'll be free from Myles's kids for a while. Pair of vultures,' Zoe muttered. 'I hope you haven't given them your new address?'

'Austin and Liv aren't that bad,' Grace chided, not mentioning that of course she'd given her stepchildren her address.

Not that they were children anymore; Austin was twenty-nine and Olivia twenty-seven – which was the age she'd been when she'd met Myles. She'd sent them a message on the Byron family WhatsApp group and told them that she was renting a house for six months in Merle Bay and that they'd be welcome to visit anytime. No reply as yet, but then they were probably busy; she'd have been the same at their age. It would be a shame to lose contact with them, after all of these years watching them grow up.

Grace had never tried to mother them, but she'd always supported Myles in being a good father. It had taken a few years to earn their trust, especially from Olivia who was very close to her mum. But the four of them had always got along well together, had fun even. Mind you, if she never heard from his ex-wife again, she wouldn't lose sleep over it. Grace had tried hard to be civil to Julia, but she was a cold fish. It was as if she was jealous of Grace, which was silly because it had been Julia who'd left Myles and that had happened long before Grace came on the scene. Myles and Julia were the same age, fifteen years older than Grace. Julia had hinted that she thought Grace had been far too young for her ex-husband, but Myles had a theory that she was jealous that his second marriage was clearly happier than his first.

'Sorry,' said Zoe, not sounding in the least apologetic. 'But when I think about how much their father has already done for them and how grabby they've been since his funeral. Makes my blood boil.'

'They've lost their beloved father,' Grace continued smoothly, 'and don't forget he was in their lives long before he was in mine. It's normal for them to want to have his things as mementos; there are memories attached to some of his things that don't mean anything to me.'

Myles had been a demonstrative man, touchy-feely and never passed an opportunity by to give her a hug or a kiss. He taught her not only how to love but to be loved. It was the same with his children whom he adored and who idolised him in return. Grace had always been proud of the relationship he'd had with his kids. Most of her divorced friends complained about the lack of interest their ex-partners showed in their children, but Myles had always made an effort to stay involved in their lives.

Zoe sniffed. 'Funny how the only things they wanted were the expensive stuff: his Rolex watch, Tiffany cufflinks and his art collection.'

'Myles would be pleased they wanted them,' said Grace loyally. In truth, she had been a little shocked at how quickly his son and daughter had come round to claim what they saw as rightly theirs. But she had the benefit of age; at forty-six Grace knew that the most important things in life didn't come with a price tag. Without Myles, possessions were meaningless, nothing could possibly be as valuable to her as a heart full of happy memories of their life together. 'And if they bring them comfort, why not?'

Zoe made a disgruntled noise and Grace smiled to herself and glanced at the satnav screen.

'I'm almost there,' she said, her stomach giving an involuntary flip.

According to the map the next turning led directly to the sea and would take her straight to Sea Glass House. Maybe Zoe was right, perhaps she was crazy, but this was the first major decision she'd made since Myles died and she was proud of herself for getting this far. If she hated it, she could always go home. What was the worst that could happen?

'OK, I'd better let you go,' said Zoe, but there was warmth in her voice and Grace felt a tug of longing for her sister who'd been such a port in a storm for her since Myles's death. 'And it is only six months, I suppose.'

'Exactly.' Grace breathed a sigh of relief; the sooner her sister resigned herself to Grace's move, the better. 'Will you be all right? Back at work, Daniel, the baby . . . ?'

'Me? Always all right,' Zoe reassured her. 'It's you I'm worried about, rattling around in that big house with nothing to do and no one to speak to.'

'Don't you worry, I'll find something to keep me busy.'

Zoe's voice softened. 'Ah, Gracie, that's the girl I know and love. But not too busy I hope, be kind to yourself; you're meant to be having a break, don't go getting a job.'

'Oh, don't worry, I'm doing well if I remember to brush my hair at the moment, I certainly couldn't hold down a job.'

'Luckily for you, your hair never needs brushing,' said Zoe. 'I swear it doesn't even move in the night.'

Grace conceded a small smile; she was fortunate. Her mid-blonde hair was fine and poker-straight, cut into an easy-to-wear bob. Apart from a few stray strands getting stuck to her lipstick on a breezy day, she rarely had any trouble with it.

'Also, luckily for me, I don't need to work. No, I intend to sleep and think and be soothed by the sea while I decide what to do next.'

Grace had enough money in the bank to never have to work again if she was careful. Although that didn't give her the comfort it perhaps once would have done. She and Myles had decided to sell their construction company, Byron Homes, lock stock and barrel last spring. The money had only been in the bank for a month or two when Myles died. He never got further than planning the new life they'd dreamed of. It made Grace feel sick every time she thought of it. It wasn't bloody fair.

'All right for some,' Zoe said. 'I'm joking, before you start trying to chuck money my way again.'

Grace shook her head affectionately. She knew Zoe wouldn't want to swap places with her for the world.

They'd both done well, career-wise. Money had been scarce growing up in Birmingham, but they'd had love and support in abundance and their parents had been so proud to see both their girls head off to university. Grace to study architecture and Zoe nursing.

'OK, but anything you need, you only have to—'

'I know,' Zoe interrupted. 'And thanks, G. But what I need most is for my big sister to smile again.'

Grace took a quick look at her satnav screen again; she was a mere 500 metres away from her new home. The road began to slope downwards, and Grace got her first glimpse of the sea. The April sun danced across the glittering water, turning it silver, and the effect was stunning. Grace's nerves jangled; she was moving somewhere new, on her own. Right now, she'd give everything she owned to have Myles's comforting hand on her thigh.

'I will, I promise,' she said quietly.

She ended the call by sending love to the children and within seconds, she pulled up to the entrance of Sea Glass House. She parked next to a small white van, which presumably belonged to the person who'd be handing over a set of house keys.

Climbing out of the car, she stared in awe at the ultra-modern house. 'Bloody hell.'

The building was set at the top of a short slope. She could see straight down to a crescent-shaped pebble beach, deserted except for a couple of people and a dog skipping in and out of the waves.

Her back ached, she had the beginnings of a headache and cramp in her legs, but she ignored all that; she felt like a kid in a toy shop not knowing where to look first. If the breeze blowing straight off the North Sea hadn't already taken her breath away, then the sight of this incredible house certainly would have done.

Despite her underlying sadness, the architect in her couldn't help but be excited; the pictures she'd seen didn't do this place justice. A slim steel framework supported curved glass walls which offered an uninterrupted view of the bay below. It was sleek and sexy, bold and beautiful, but at the same time, it reflected its setting so well that it was almost invisible.

'Clever,' she murmured at the wide overhang around the perimeter, which would act both as a roof cover to the patio area and protect the interior from getting too much sun. She could easily downscale that feature to work on a more modest property. She stopped her train of thought and shook her head; she wasn't here to work, she was here to rest, she reminded herself.

The front door opened, and a man lifted his hand in greeting. 'Hello!'

'Hi!'

They strode towards each other and she took his outstretched hand.

'Rob Napier from Premier House Services,' he said, introducing himself. 'And you must be Mrs Byron.'

She nodded. 'Call me Grace.'

'Pleased to meet you. These are for you.' He held out a keyring from which dangled at least half a dozen keys. 'You're in for a treat; we manage over a hundred properties and Sea Glass House is by far and away my favourite.'

'I'm not surprised.' She looked across to the edge of the property where a series of connected terraces cascaded down towards the sea. She already felt uplifted; this place was going to work wonders for her, she could tell. She was going to press pause on a life that no longer felt like her own; a chance to catch her breath and reimagine herself.

'Shall I give you a tour, or would you rather investigate for yourselves?' He looked over her shoulder towards her car.

'Myself, I think,' said Grace, deliberately ignoring his mistake. 'I'm a real property nut, I'll be exploring every nook and cranny for hours.'

He lifted his eyebrows. 'Oh? Is it just you? Mr Ashcroft mentioned the Byrons being old friends, I just assumed . . . ' His voice petered out and a look of concern passed across his face.

'Just me.' She smiled faintly. 'My husband passed away recently. Ned – Mr Ashcroft – is a good friend of ours.'

'Mrs Byron . . . *Grace*.' Rob scratched his head. 'I'm so sorry, I wasn't aware. Please accept my apologies and my sincere condolences.'

'It's fine, honestly.' Grace rushed to reassure him. She was doing this a lot at the moment, consoling others who weren't sure what to say.

'Everywhere has been cleaned, top to bottom, the garden given a tidy up and Mr Ashcroft asked for us to stock up the fridge and the cupboards with the basics to keep you going,' Rob continued.

'Oh, he is sweet.' She felt a rush of warmth for Ned; he'd always been kind to her, and the last six months even more so.

He and Myles went way back; they'd been at college together on the same construction course before going their separate ways: Ned developing luxury waterside properties and marinas and Myles setting up Byron Homes. Ned had been trying to tempt Myles and Grace to make use of his new holiday home in Merle Bay since it had been completed a couple of years ago. He'd been excited to show it off and visiting it had been something she and Myles had talked about doing as soon as they had the chance.

He'd popped in to see her a few times since the funeral, even managing to drag her out for a coffee occasionally. It was during their last get-together in March that he reminded her that the offer still stood to stay at Sea Glass House.

'You'd love it there. It's standing empty,' he'd said. 'So really you'd be doing me a favour. Stay as long as you want, a week, a month, a year, whatever you need, Grace. Be my guest.'

And thinking that a change of scene might be just what she needed, she'd accepted and brought with her enough belongings to keep her going for a few months.

'Anything special I need to know before I unpack?' She smiled at Rob and jangled the keys; she couldn't wait to be alone and explore her new abode.

'Yes, right,' said Rob with relief. 'The manual for the burglar alarm is on the kitchen table. In fact, there's a manual for everything on the kitchen table. Mr Ashcroft is very organised.'

'That sounds like Ned,' said Grace, smiling, remembering how he'd always be the one to arrange get-togethers, booking restaurants and sorting arrangements.

'The small silver key unlocks the pool house where you'll find everything you need for the hot tub. The big one opens the gate to your private access down to the beach. And this bronze key . . . ' He tapped the relevant key for her, 'is for the wine cellar. Mr Ashcroft insists that you help yourself.'

'Ah, a glass of wine in a hot tub.' Grace sighed with pleasure. 'I think I can manage that.'

Rob smiled. 'OK, that's all the essentials covered. Now, do you need a hand carrying stuff into the house?'

She shook her head.

'That's kind of you, but I can manage.' She extended a hand to bring their exchange to an end. 'Thanks for everything.'

They shook hands and she removed two suitcases from the boot of the Range Rover as he headed back to the van.

Rob stopped. 'Oh, I almost forgot, some post arrived for you this morning. I've left it just inside the front door on the glass table.'

'Thanks.' She raised a hand to acknowledge his words.

Post already? She'd hoped to have at least a couple of days cut off from the outside world without the interruption of post. The amount of paperwork she'd had to deal with in the aftermath of Myles's death had felt endless. She waved Rob goodbye, wheeled the cases up to the house and pushed open the front door. Her gaze swept over the open-plan interior: pale wooden floors, modern log burner, a kitchen which the pickiest celebrity chef would drool over, sofas which begged to be curled up on, and of course, the star attraction: the sea, framed by every window. *Living art*, thought Grace, already looking forward to watching it change with the weather.

Oh Myles, my darling, you'd have loved this place. Why didn't we make the time to do this together? She hauled the cases over the threshold and spotted two envelopes on the glass table. One contained a card from her sister and the kids, wishing her happiness in her new home. The other bore the all too familiar logo of her solicitor. She slipped a finger under the edge and tore it open.

Roger Mathers, her and Myles's solicitor, had been an absolute star, helping her make sense of Myles's affairs, making sure she properly understood every single form she signed. He'd managed to strike the right balance between sensitivity and professionalism. He'd been brilliant with the will too. When Austin and Olivia had bombarded her with questions about Myles's wishes, Roger had stepped in and addressed all their issues himself.

Dear Grace,
I hope this letter finds you well. I'm so sorry to intrude so soon in your new home, but there has been a new development in respect of Myles's estate. I've received a letter from a solicitor acting for Austin and Olivia Byron informing me that they intend to contest their father's will on the basis that they feel that their share should be equal to yours. I had hoped that my most recent meeting with them had put a stop to this course of action as they have no grounds on which to contest. However, please can you let me know at your earliest convenience whether you wish to . . .

Contesting the will? Her body tensed as she read the whole thing through twice, her sense of dread deepening with every sentence. She could hardly believe what she was reading. How could Myles's own children do this to her, and why? They had each already been awarded twenty-five per cent of his estate each, Grace to receive the remaining fifty per cent. He'd been a wealthy man; both Olivia and Austin would be set up for life before they'd even turned thirty. But now, it seemed, they weren't content with that.

Roger needed her to make a decision: either she had to settle out of court and pay them an amount they were satisfied with, or they would seek to have the will overruled.

'Shit,' she murmured under her breath. She could cry, she really could. She put the letter down and shook her head. Myles would have been appalled with them.

She groaned and rubbed her eyes. She was tired after that long drive from Birmingham, but more than that, she was exhausted after months of coping with a world that no longer had Myles in it. She decided to postpone unpacking for now; a shower and a strong cup of coffee might help. Positive action was always a good plan.

Come on Gracie, chin up, you've got this, girl.

Chapter Three

Robyn woke to the sound of Finn in the kitchen. His customary half hum, half whistle carried up the steep stairs of their cottage along with the crash of pans, slamming of cupboard doors and the slosh of something being whisked vigorously. Her stomach fluttered with love for her husband. He loved cooking, always able to produce a feast no matter how slim the fridge's pickings. He'd only been off work for a couple of days and already she'd got used to being spoiled with three proper meals a day. As of next week, she'd be back to toast for breakfast and lunch.

The blind was partially open, and through the salt-spattered glass the sun dazzled in the sky. It was a beaut of a day. She sat up and strained to listen for the waves crashing against the harbour wall just a few metres away. The sea must be calm; all she could hear was the tinkling of masts and seagulls mewing in the distance. The winds could be brutal in winter this close to the sea but as soon as the weather was mild enough, she and Finn slept with the windows open. Falling asleep each night to a lullaby of waves and the scent of the fresh briny air was heavenly.

I am lucky, she told herself.

Sometimes, sitting in her attic studio looking out of the window at the sea, or on her way home when the chunky limewash walls and dark blue (Duchess blue; she'd googled it) windows of Admiral Cottage came into sight, she had to pinch herself. This perfect place was *her* home. Sometimes it felt too good to be true.

She was startled out of her daydream by a couple of seagulls landing on the roof, claws clattering on the tiles above the bedroom, even noisier than Finn. Finn wasn't a fan of gulls, they were a menace to fishermen, and they made a right mess of the small courtyard at the back of the cottage, but Robyn liked their jerky walk and the comical way they bickered amongst themselves and the sly tactics they used to steal food from unsuspecting passers-by.

A thought took her by surprise: maybe she could draw one? A jolly one with long legs and a plump body? She swallowed hard; for the first time in . . . gosh, she couldn't even remember, she reached for her notebook from inside the drawer beside her bed. She drew with urgency, her heart racing, determined not to think too deeply about it in case she gave self-doubt a chance to interfere. With a few strokes a cheeky-looking seagull appeared. Robyn studied it, pleased with herself. It would make a good character for a children's book, or even a design for a mug. She felt a stirring inside her, a surge of creativity, and gave herself a moment to savour it; how long had she waited for that to come back?

Right. It was a sign. Today was the day. No more procrastinating, no more *perhaps I should leave it another few days*. The sun was out, the light in her little studio would be perfect and look at her go, not even out of bed and she'd drawn something. How amazing was that? Yes, Robyn McGill, she told herself briskly, today you're going to be the woman you want to be: positive, proactive and perky.

Perhaps perky wasn't the best choice. *Anyway, moving on.*

She rolled her shoulders back, testing her chest muscles for tightness; only the tiniest of twinges, nothing to moan about. OK. First job: her daily gratitudes. Her counsellor had suggested doing this. Counselling hadn't lasted long. Robyn wasn't a great one for talking about her feelings, so she'd attended the absolute minimum number of compulsory sessions. And as for going to group sessions, she'd completely vetoed that. The last thing she wanted to do was sit around talking about the thing which united them all. She didn't like even thinking about that, let alone talking. But gratitudes she could just about tolerate. Preferably it should be written somewhere, but Robyn still felt like a plonker doing it and if Finn were to come across it, she'd be mortified, so she did it in her head instead.

Number one. Her new niece, Elizabeth Alice McGill. Third child to Finn's brother Callum and his wife Claudia. Robyn smoothed the duvet over her stomach with both hands, remembering how Claudia had lamented her wobbly bits yesterday and told her how lucky she was to have a body unravaged by childbirth. Robyn had counted to ten, wishing that Claudia would, just for once, engage her brain before opening her mouth. Anyway. Elizabeth, or Betty as she was going to be known, was a blessing. Tiny, dark-haired and already ruling the roost in her big noisy household, and because she'd arrived unexpectedly early, delivered by the post lady, no less, her daddy, Callum, was having some time off, which meant that Uncle Finn was doing the same because the two McGill brothers worked together in the family fishing business.

Number two: her boss, Morgan. Technically Robyn was self-employed, but all of her regular work was commissioned by *Our Eco Life* magazine, and so Morgan was as close to a boss as she had. Robyn had met lots of people since her surgery and heard all sorts of tales about unsympathetic employers. Morgan was an angel by comparison, allowing her the flexibility to work as much or as little as she wanted. And for the last year it had been very little.

Last but not least Finn, the love of her life, by her side every step of the journey which she was still on. She was very grateful to have a husband who cherished her and treated her as if she were made of porcelain. Although – she bit her lip, feeling disloyal – if she was really honest, sometimes she wished he'd come up behind her, wrap his arms around her, his body crushed against hers and breathe hotly into her neck, whispering how much he wanted her . . . Robyn frowned; somehow, she'd managed to drift off the theme of gratitude.

The eight o'clock alarm on her phone interrupted her stream of thought and she turned it off. There was just one more thing she wanted to do before getting up.

She slipped her hands underneath her pyjama top and laid them on her stomach. Despite what Claudia thought, the flesh beneath her fingers was pillowy and soft. Her hands drifted sideways to her hip bones; she'd never be classed as curvy, but she was no longer straight up and down thanks to a combination of losing her muscle tone from inactivity and the impact of medication which she'd been warned would result in weight gain. The last two years had given her wrinkles, her first grey hairs and a new nervous habit of nibbling the skin at the side of her thumbnails, but at least she didn't have the torso of a greyhound anymore – every cloud and all that.

OK, deep breath, Robyn. She placed her hands over her breasts. Inhale, exhale. She forced herself to register the sensation of the firmness beneath her fingers, the smooth shape of them.

Hello ladies. Thanks for being here. You still feel weird, but give me time, I'll get there. I know I did the right thing, but I miss the old ones . . .

'Good morning, gorgeous girl,' came a voice from the doorway.

'Finn!' Robyn pulled her hands from under her top and sat up quickly. 'Jesus! You made me jump.'

'Whoops!' He bit his lip sheepishly and she felt bad about her sharp tone. She watched him walk around the bed and felt a throb of desire for him. He was kind and patient, honest and hard-working, beautiful inside and out. She'd fallen in love with his quirky features the minute she'd set eyes on him: angular jaw, lopsided smile, a nose which looked like it belonged to a boxer, not a fisherman, and one grey and one green eye, which to Robyn looked like the sea on a stormy day.

To her relief it looked as if he hadn't seen what she'd been doing under her pyjamas; not that she was ashamed, but she there were only so many conversations about 'it' that she could manage in a day and if they started this early she'd reach her limit before lunchtime.

'One milky tea, just as you like it.' He put a mug on her bedside cabinet and sat down on the edge of the mattress.

'Thank you.' She held her arms out to him and he leaned closer, kissing her neck, her cheek, her mouth. He was infinitely tender but today she didn't want tender; she tightened her grip around his neck, pressing her body against his.

'Now, breakfast,' he murmured, pulling away gently. 'How do pancakes sound? Made with maximum taste and minimum cost.'

'I'm fine with toast, honestly.'

He pretended to look offended. 'That won't nourish your body, let alone your soul.'

'True.' She laughed softly. He'd added an extra challenge into his kitchen creations by trying to make nutritious food on a budget. She appreciated his dedication, after all money was always tight. 'You don't have to keep spoiling me, you know. I'm not an invalid.'

For the briefest of moments his brow furrowed, and she realised she'd hurt his feelings. But then he smiled and stood up.

'Make the most of it,' he said. 'Once Callum and I go back to sea, you'll be getting your own breakfast.'

'I love you,' she said, sipping her tea, which, as predicted, was exactly how she liked it.

'Glad to hear it.' He grinned and placed a soft kiss into her curls. 'Then take a shower while I make you the best blueberry pancakes you've ever had.'

She swung her legs out of bed, listening to the creak of the stairs as Finn headed down to the kitchen. A door slammed and he started to whistle.

Her reflection stared back at her from her dressing table mirror. On one level she knew she had a pleasant enough face: she liked her deep brown eyes, the freckles across the top of her cheeks which she'd never grown out of and her pointy chin. Today though, she only saw hollows under those eyes, an oily nose, sallow skin and a spot on her chin.

What had Finn said? *Good morning, gorgeous girl.*

He never used to talk to her like that. He was more likely to call her Thumper because of the way she marched everywhere in her chunky boots, or Pixie-face, or Hedgehog-hair . . . any number of jokey pet names, but never anything as gooey – or, in her opinion, as wide of the mark – as gorgeous.

It felt like he was trying too hard. And the thought of what that might mean made her want to cry.

Twenty minutes later, she was on her second pancake. They were thick and fluffy (because he folded in whisked egg white, Finn informed her) and despite not thinking she was hungry, she was really enjoying them.

'If you don't mind,' said Finn, pouring syrup over his stack of pancakes, 'I need to go down to the boatshed and see if I can sort out the software in the GPS system. The guy was asking silly money to come out and repair it, so I'm going to have a go myself first.'

'Fine with me. Actually,' she forked up the last piece of pancake and avoided his eye. 'I'm working today too.' She hadn't done much for Morgan for a while, but she'd email her this morning to ask if there were any projects coming up and then she was going to have another go at that seagull.

They locked eyes, both knowing that Robyn going back to work was a mammoth step forward.

'My talented wife,' he murmured.

'It's time,' she said softly. 'Besides, I need to earn my keep, it's important to me.'

Robyn had been brought up single-handedly by her mum, whose relationship with Robyn's dad had been over before she was born. Her dad had been an irregular presence in her life in the early years, but her mum's love had more than made up for his lack of interest. She had drummed into her only daughter the value of financial independence and practised what she preached, working as an accountant for a brewery. She gradually rose through the ranks, pouring her energies into her child, her job and her home. Robyn got used to letting herself into their house and following her mother's written instructions for making dinner, until one day, not long after starting secondary school, her mother was sitting on the sofa when she came home, waiting for her with bad news. Two years later, her mum died of breast cancer and Robyn's loving home died with her. She moved in with her father and stepmother. She didn't want to be there any more than they wanted to have her, and she'd counted down the days until she could save up enough to leave the house that she never thought of as home. She'd striven for financial independence ever since, wanting to be self-sufficient, to know that she had the money to fund her own decisions. Twenty years after losing her mum, she hadn't changed, except that now she and Finn were a team.

'You've had other important things to deal with.' Finn reached for her hand and squeezed it. 'Only take on what you feel you can manage. We'll always get by.'

Robyn felt a stab of guilt. Fishing was a tough business, both physically and financially. Finn had taken over the lion's share of the burden for long enough. The moment was broken by Finn's phone beeping. He picked it up and his face softened into a smile. He scrolled through the message and then handed her the phone.

'Aw, look at that.'

Robyn looked at the picture of Baby Betty in her Moses basket surrounded by an army of soft toys. 'Cute.'

'Callum says he left her for one minute and while he was gone, the other two kids decided Betty needed some company.'

Finn's eyes were shining as he took the phone back and Robyn studied him, trying to work out what was going through his mind: pride at his niece and nephew's kind deed, or envy of that perfect little girl, wrapped up tightly like a sausage roll, her tiny features peeking out from her blanket.

Positive, proactive, perky . . . That was today's mantra. Having children of their own was no longer an option. She was reconciled to it, and Finn claimed to be too. But was he telling the truth? Or was he just telling her what he thought she needed to hear? *Ask him, Robyn, just ask.*

She licked her lips, mouth suddenly dry and opened her mouth to speak. 'Do you—'

But down the hall the letter box opened and the post thudded onto the mat.

'Hold that thought.' Finn pushed his chair back, scraping it noisily on the tiled floor. 'I've been waiting for news from a finance company, it should be here this morning.'

He fetched the mail, dropped a pile of letters onto the table and sifted through them, pushing a couple with Robyn's name on them across to her.

'Excellent, it's here!' he said, tearing into a manila envelope.

Robyn opened her own post. The first was confirmation of a hospital appointment. She pushed it aside and opened the second, hoping it was more interesting. Inside was a remittance advice, notifying her of a bank transfer from *Our Eco Life* Magazine. A hundred pounds, a drop in the ocean compared to their monthly outgoings. There was a card pinned to it and she flipped it over. It was from Morgan.

Hey Robyn, I hope this finds you well! I have some sad news; I've been made redundant along with two others from the management team, so as I write this, it's my last day at the magazine. Our Eco Life *is getting a revamp editorially too and for the time being at least, they are pulling the illustrations. Hopefully this won't be too much of a disappointment to you, I know you haven't felt up to working much anyway. Keep in touch, all best, Morgan.*

Oh God. Poor thing, thought Robyn. The tone of the note was bright and breezy, but Morgan had been at that magazine since its first issue; she'd be devastated. And bang went her own plan to get earning again. Now what was she going to do?

It took her a moment to notice that Finn had gone quiet. His expression was grim, and he was shaking his head.

'Bastards,' he muttered. 'Greedy, ruthless bastards.'

Robyn stared at him. 'What's up?'

He passed her the letter and folded his arms. 'Last winter we asked for an extension of the loan we took out for the GPS system and now they've tripled the interest rate. The repayments are going to have a massive impact on profit.'

She got up from her chair and made a space for herself on his lap, wrapping her arms around his neck.

'I'm so sorry,' she said, kissing his cheek.

'Not your fault, love.' He returned her embrace and sighed. 'Mind you, probably not a bad thing that you're going to be working again.'

'Well.' Robyn felt sick. 'About that, I've had some bad news . . .'

Finn groaned. 'Oh no, not you as well.'

Her early morning mantra deserted her; instead, she was filled with guilt and sadness. She wasn't a mother, she wasn't an earner, she wasn't even the woman Finn had married anymore. She didn't know who she was and all at once she'd never felt so useless in her life.

Chapter Four

Katie rounded the headland and almost wept with relief when Sea Glass Beach came into view. If she could just get to the water, stand at the very edge where land met sea, then she'd be able to think clearly and try and process what the hell had just happened. She'd speed-walked here, and for the last twenty minutes she'd battled to keep that sickening image of her eighteen-year-old self, naked and terrified, at bay. She'd tried to focus on her physical sensations – the tight lungs, the coarse breathing and the race of her pulse. But it had been impossible, the shock wave was too seismic to ignore, and her brain fired round after round of questions at her.

What did this mean? What was the sender's intention? And why was she getting this photo now, ten years after it had been taken?

Katie wracked her brains to try and remember the name of the model scout back then: Roy something, maybe? She and her dad had tried to track him down themselves soon after the photoshoot but to no avail. The police had shown little interest and so Dad had suggested hiring a private detective. Katie had begged him not to; the sooner they could draw a line under the whole incident, she'd reasoned, the sooner she could start moving on with her life. And her darling father, who wanted nothing more than to smooth every bump in his daughter's path, had eventually agreed.

She could probably find out what happened to him a lot more easily now; there was a lot more information online these days than ten years ago. Not that she wanted anything to do with him, but now that he'd found her, it looked like she didn't have any choice. Would he get in touch again, she wondered? If so, she'd better prepare herself. Knowledge, however unsavoury, was still power. Assuming it was him who sent the photograph, that was.

But why? She was aware her thinking had come full circle, but she couldn't help it. She couldn't think of one possible explanation as to why whoever had sent it had done so.

She gripped the wooden handrail and concentrated on putting one foot in front of the other down the steep worn steps which cut through the rocks and curved down to the shoreline. It was the least accessible beach in the area, which was why it was her favourite; she was far less likely to be approached here by people she recognised than on the main sandy beach at the bottom of the high street.

The wind whipped around her ears and blew her hair out of its bun and into her eyes. She was glad she'd pulled her North Face jacket on before she'd left the shop. The sun might be out, but the breeze was bracing, the sea air scoured her skin and made her eyes water. At least that was what she was telling herself.

She jumped down the last step, her trainers landing with a crunch. Sea Glass Beach was shingle and coarse sand, and every now and then, the sunlight caught sharp-edged shells and stones, giving the beach a magical sparkling texture. Magic, she thought glumly, she needed a bit of that right now.

The beach wasn't long; she could walk the length of it in ten minutes, seven today, given the mood she was in.

She glanced left and right; at the far end of the bay, a man was throwing a ball into the waves for his two Labradors to chase after. A few metres away a woman was following the dark line left by the tide, her head bowed, and her hands clasped a camera which hung from a neck strap. Most of her face was hidden behind a long scarf, but short dark hair poked out of the top of it and chunky lace-up boots kicked through the seaweed and driftwood.

Katie looked away quickly to avoid any potential small talk and headed straight towards the water, pushing her hands deep into the pockets and tucking her chin into the neck of her jacket. There was something about being known as the bra shop lady that made other women feel comfortable in her presence and want to unburden themselves; she'd seen them almost naked, which inevitably created an intimacy between them. Auntie Jean had been brilliant at making people relax and Katie did her best to emulate her. She loved her job. She loved making others feel good about themselves. She enjoyed the challenge of listening to the hang-ups women of all shapes, sizes and ages had about their bodies and working out how best to help them.

More often than not, this connection with her customers extended beyond the boundaries of Auntie Small's. She found herself listening to tales of boob jobs and weight loss and details of new love affairs in the oddest of places. Women trusted her with their secrets, even though she never reciprocated and kept herself to herself. She had worked hard since being in Merle Bay to be professional, respectable, discreet. Would they feel the same, she thought, if they knew the truth about her?

A sob formed in her throat. Her life had spun out of control once; she couldn't bear it if it happened again.

And Mum and Dad, how would they cope a second time around?

She slowed a few paces from water's edge. Her feet were already beginning to sink in the wet sand, and she didn't want to have to walk back with sopping trainers.

The words on that handwritten note floated back into her head.

REMEMBER THIS?

'Course I bloody do. How could I ever forget?' The words slipped out unintentionally and Katie shot a quick glance over her shoulder. The man at the other end definitely wouldn't have heard from there, but the woman might have. But she was a short distance away, crouched down, raking through the shingle and not paying Katie any attention. Thank goodness.

Katie studied her properly now, realising who she was. Robyn McGill. As far as Katie remembered, she'd never been into Auntie Small's, but Merle Bay wasn't large – they were all connected in some way or other. Robyn was related to Claudia McGill who *did* shop at Auntie Small's, in fact she had flown into the shop last week looking for a feeding bra after giving birth early. The baby girl delivered by Alice the post lady.

Which brought her back to this morning's post: the photograph, the note.

Oh God. Katie shuddered. She turned and headed towards the far end of the beach away from everyone. She had to keep moving; even though the sun was out, it was only April and it was too cold to stand still.

She dragged her mind back to that day in the studio. The photoshoot had been of a different girl, vivacious and extroverted. Katie, or Catherine as she'd called herself then, was the school head girl, leader of the debating society, a county-level rower. An all-rounder popular with the girls and lusted after by the boys. She'd had offers from university to study law and had ambitious plans to spend her career demanding justice for the vulnerable. Her parents were full of pride for their only daughter who'd sailed through her teenage years without causing a ripple of trouble. She'd led a charmed existence – no, not charmed, she'd worked hard for her achievements – a *happy* existence. And life could so easily have continued that way. *If only . . .*

If only she hadn't been tempted to earn extra money to fund her studies.

If only she hadn't taken the opportunity to lessen the financial burden for her parents.

If only she'd taken the time to research the 'model agency' to check its credentials before heading off to London without telling a soul. Not her mum and not her best friend Rose, who'd never forgiven her for keeping it a secret.

If only . . . There were a hundred and one reasons to regret the worst decision she'd ever made in her life.

Stop. Just stop. Her head felt like a pressure cooker and she could feel anxiety building just as it had back then. Auntie Jean had been the only person to listen and not judge. To care but not try and take control. God, how she missed her. What she'd give to talk through this new development with her now.

For a moment she allowed the sounds of the sea to soothe her: seagulls mewed overhead, and gentle waves tumbled and frothed at her feet. She needed to pull herself together and get back to the shop; Nula would be wondering what had happened to her.

She turned her back on the sea and looked at the coast-line. Up to her left was the big modern house, a glass fortress, presiding over the bay. It was rarely occupied but today there was a black four-wheel drive parked outside; holidaymakers, she presumed. She was glad; the house was too beautiful to sit empty. A movement caught her eye: a wide glass door slid to one side and a person emerged to stand on the terrace. Hard to tell from this distance whether it was a man or a woman. Imagine waking up to this view every day.

Katie walked in the direction of the house until she reached the end of the beach and leaned back against the rocks, tilting her face up to the sky. She filled her lungs with the sharp sea air, pulled a bottle of water from her pocket and took a sip. The sky here was endless. Being under it made her feel free. Back in Nottingham the family home was in a perfectly pleasant suburb, but she'd shared the sky with three quarters of a million others and when her dreams disintegrated, she'd had a weird sensation of being on display, as if everyone could see through her clothes to her skin beneath. Gradually she'd felt herself fading away, as she tried to make herself invisible. Dropping out of school, stopping eating, ending up on antidepressants; a far cry from the life she'd envisaged.

Coming here had been a good decision. A temporary move that somewhere along the line had become permanent. Now she loved every inch of Merle Bay; she wouldn't want to live anywhere else – why would she? She was a grown woman, a *business*woman, a homeowner. If her past was catching up with her – and it looked like it might be – she wouldn't run again. Running away wasn't an option. No, she'd have to deal with it another way.

The click of a camera jolted Katie from her thoughts. It was that woman, Robyn. She was crouching down on one knee and she had the lens pointing in her direction.

41

Katie hated having her picture taken at the best of times; today anger spiked through her like ice.

'Excuse me!' she shouted, pushing herself up from the rocks and striding towards her. 'Did you just take a picture of me?'

At that moment a seagull swooped in front of her face so closely that she felt the air displaced by its wings and she jumped back, sloshing water down her front.

'I'm so sorry. I didn't mean to cause offence, or make you throw water all over yourself. And no, I didn't take your picture, at least not intentionally.' The woman lowered her camera and tugged her scarf away from her face.

She had the most beautiful green eyes, Katie noticed, but beneath them were dark circles which made her look hollowed out and tired.

Katie's anger faded as quickly as it had come; what had possessed her to yell like a banshee at the poor woman? She could kick herself.

'It's fine,' Katie said, feeling a tinge of shame rise to her face. She screwed the lid back on her water bottle and shoved it in her pocket. 'Please ignore me, I'm not myself today.'

'Ditto,' she replied flatly, slipping the lens cap back onto the camera. 'Actually, I'll rephrase that. I am *completely* myself. And therein lies the problem.'

What a sad thing to say, Katie thought.

'You're from the underwear shop, aren't you? I haven't been in, but your windows always look gorgeous.'

Katie smiled. 'Thank you so much, I'll tell Nula, my assistant – she's the creative one. I'm Katie, by the way, and you're Claudia's sister-in-law, I think?'

'Robyn, yes.' She nodded, wrapping her arms around her waist protectively. 'She was my best friend at school, and we married the McGill brothers, so now we're related. Look, I'm sorry, I disturbed you. You looked like you wanted to be alone and actually so do I, so I'll leave you in peace.'

Now Katie was intrigued. There were very few local women who didn't ever come into the shop and Robyn was one of them. She wanted to know more about her; besides, in her experience, people who wanted to be alone were often the ones who needed someone to talk to.

Aware of the irony in her own logic, she smiled at Robyn. 'I completely understand if you'd rather not, given how rude I was, but can I see the photo you took?'

Robyn shrugged. 'Sure.'

She turned the camera towards Katie so she could see the screen on the back of it. The seagull that had almost flown in her face had, moments before, been perched on the rock just behind her. The camera had caught the bird mid-hop, head cocked to one side and looking cheekily in Katie's direction; a sliver of her sleeve appeared in the shot too.

'Whoops, I did just get you after all,' said Robyn, pulling an apologetic face. 'Don't worry, I'll delete it.'

'Please don't, I overreacted,' Katie said quickly. 'It's a great picture. Are you a photographer?'

'No.' Robyn didn't speak for a long moment. 'Right now, I'm a nothing.'

Katie's heart squeezed for her. She sounded like she needed a hug, not that Katie would dare. Somehow Robyn managed to give off *don't touch me* vibes. Katie had already got off on the wrong foot with her; she needed to build bridges, not blow them up.

Katie smiled. 'That can't be—'

True, she had been about to say, but before she could finish her sentence there was a scream from directly up above them beyond the cliff. The path leading upwards was hidden from view and carved out of the rocks like the public right of way. Robyn and Katie looked up towards the glass house and then at each other. At the bottom of the path was a gate marked private which must lead directly to the property.

'Sounds like someone's had an accident,' said Robyn.

Katie nodded. 'I saw someone out on the terrace earlier. Should we investigate?'

'Shit a brick, my ankle!' yelled a voice. 'HELP! Is anyone there?'

The women darted towards the gate.

'We're coming,' shouted Katie. 'Just stay where you are.'

'I don't have a lot of choice in the matter,' came the voice again. 'Hells bells, this hurts.'

The gate came up to Robyn's chest and was very sturdily built from wooden bars with pointed ends. She rattled the chain which was looped around the frame and peered over the top. 'Oh no, there's a padlock on the other side.'

'Never mind, I think I can jump it,' said Katie. 'Stand back.'

It had been years since Katie had done any athletics but at one time, she'd been quite good at this sort of stuff. Plus, she was a great deal taller than Robyn.

'Please be careful,' said Robyn anxiously, taking Katie's water bottle from her.

Katie blew out a sharp breath and then took a run at the gate. She leapt into the air and using her hands to push off, she vaulted over it and landed relatively unscathed with a thud on a patch of sand on the other side.

'That was amazing!' Robyn's face appeared pressed against the bars of the wooden gate.

'I can't believe I just did that!' Katie grinned, brushing the sand off her hands and knees. 'Shall I go without you or . . . ?'

'No way,' said Robyn, slinging the camera and Katie's water bottle over the gate into Katie's waiting arms. 'Watch this.'

She leapt up at the gate, grabbed the top of it and flailed around with her legs to get some purchase.

'Try getting your toes between the bars,' said Katie. 'There's a cross piece here.'

She thrust her arm through the bars and guided Robyn's boots into place.

'Ta-dah!' Robyn heaved herself up to the top and grinned at Katie, panting from the exertion. 'Now all I need to do is get my leg over.'

'Said the actress to the bishop,' said Katie, who despite the potential seriousness of the occasion was quite enjoying the drama.

'Don't make me laugh,' Robyn gasped. 'I already needed a wee before I decided to straddle a five-foot gate.'

'I don't mean to sound ungrateful,' came the voice again, sounding more panicky than the last time. 'But if you could hurry up, that would be most appreciated. Thank you.'

It was a woman's voice, Katie decided. Poor thing. 'Hang on in there, we're on our way!'

The ground was higher on her side of the gate and by standing on a rock, she could just about reach Robyn. She helped haul her up by the sleeves of her jacket.

'I've got your top half,' she said. 'You deal with the bottom half.'

'This has got to be the most intimate I've been with a stranger in a long time,' Robyn spluttered.

'Lucky you.' Katie raised an eyebrow. 'This is a pretty standard Monday morning for me.'

With a bit of effort and a lot of giggling, between them they managed to get one of Robyn's legs over the gate.

'Who's actually there?' said the voice, panting in pain. 'Because I think I should warn you that I'm, what you might call, scantily clad.'

'No worries,' Katie shouted back. 'I'm, sure it's nothing either of us haven't seen before.'

'Maybe not,' chuntered the voice. 'But you haven't seen mine before.'

Katie looked at Robyn, who was still laughing but had gone a peculiar colour. 'You OK?'

'This is more painful than I thought it would be,' muttered Robyn. Beads of perspiration had popped up on her forehead. 'At least it's not wrought-iron bars, or I'd have had multiple piercings by now.'

The poor woman was balanced on a row of pointed boards, her arms tight around Katie's neck. That wouldn't be doing her nether regions any good.

'It doesn't look much fun, I agree. What do you want me to do?' Katie asked, clenching her lips together to prevent a bout of hysterical laughter from escaping.

'Um. Can you step backwards away from the gate and drag me with you?' suggested Robyn, her breath hot against Katie's neck. 'And I'll try and lift my other leg over.'

Katie nodded and did as instructed. She edged slowly backwards, staggering under the smaller woman's weight and Robyn's body bumped painfully over the gate.

Robyn winced. 'I'm regretting that last pancake now and that second mug of tea.'

'Now that's a Monday morning I can fully get on board with,' said Katie, holding on tight while Robyn set first one foot and then the other down on solid ground. On its way past the padlock, one of Robyn's boots knocked against it and it slithered to the floor, taking the chain with it.

'You're joking! It was open all along,' exclaimed Katie in dismay, gasping for breath.

'So it was,' said Robyn, examining a tear in the back of her leggings. 'But that was the best fun I've had in months.'

'Me too,' Katie admitted with a snigger. 'Gate one: Katie and Robyn nil.'

The two of them collapsed against each other in a fit of giggles before charging up the steps towards their next challenge. Just then Katie realised that for the last ten minutes, she hadn't given that photo a second thought – and that had to be a win.

Chapter Five

Grace didn't know whether to laugh or cry. Actually, correction, she couldn't do either at the moment. Any shuddering of her chest would be too uncomfortable. The best thing she could do was to take shallow breaths and say a prayer that her rescuers were fast, female and not too prudish.

She shifted her weight from her hands to her elbows and tried to ignore the pain running from her groin to her knee. She was such a fool. She'd only been here half an hour and already she'd unintentionally done the splits (not that she could remember ever attempting the splits deliberately), smashed a mug, done untold damage to the insides of her thighs and her *pièce de résistance*, which would be happening any second now, she'd be greeting two strangers by flashing her foof at them.

Grace risked a look down. Oh hell. Yes, definitely flashing. She was still wearing her towel, just about, but it was splayed open and there was a suspiciously cold breeze blowing up her backside.

She could almost hear Myles laughing at her from the great blue yonder. He'd always found it hilarious that she was so clumsy. 'Sack the juggler,' he'd always shout from the study when he heard her drop another glass in the sink. They'd had to replace all the champagne flutes they'd had as wedding presents before they'd even made it to their first anniversary. Still, at least it got her out of the washing up.

A coffee out on the terrace to admire the view. That had been the plan and now look at her. It had been the Byron family WhatsApp group's fault. Grace had opened it up to see if Liv and Austin had mentioned anything about the solicitor they'd appointed, only to find that they had both left the group! So now the only ones left were herself and Myles, whom she hadn't had the heart to remove. She'd been so hurt that she'd been too busy looking at the screen and not paying attention to where she put her feet.

Grace was not a woman who was ashamed of her body. At least, not anymore. Meeting Myles had changed all that. She'd spent her teenage years and her twenties hiding her curves under shapeless clothes that made her look like her gran, or dark colours to help her blend into the crowd. Myles had worshipped her. Every inch of her, every curve, dimple and wobbly bit. Because of his love, she'd learned to love herself. Words like chubby and plump had been replaced with Rubenesque and voluptuous. These days, she knew how to dress to suit her figure; the colours and silhouettes to flatter, the jewellery to add glamour to the simplest outfit.

But all of that notwithstanding, being found by complete strangers in this position was probably going to give her nightmares for a week. Mind you, it might possibly give them nightmares too.

After what felt like an eternity stuck in the most painful position on earth, Grace finally heard people coming up the stairs.

'Hello?' called a tentative voice.

'Praise be!' she cried. 'I'm over here, I've slipped behind the hot tub.'

A gurgle of laughter escaped from her involuntarily; Zoe would have a field day with this one. Was there a more middle-class accident than tripping up on the way to your own private hot tub? Slipping on an avocado skin, maybe, or crying over spilled almond milk . . .

It had seemed like a good idea to wander out onto the terrace, dressed only in a towel and flip-flops, to drink her coffee. That would teach her to pinch hotel flip-flops. The bit that anchored the toe-post to the base had always been dodgy. *Just a quick look to check out the hot tub*, she'd thought. But her left foot had skated forwards on the slippy patio and got lodged under the wooden steps to the hot tub. She'd flung her arms out trying to right herself and avoid pouring hot coffee down her cleavage. But all she'd succeeded in doing was to twist her ankle and smash the mug against a very expensive-looking terracotta pot. Now she couldn't move either leg and was leaning forward over her thigh supporting her weight on her hands.

'Good grief,' exclaimed a polite voice. 'How did you manage that?'

Grace tried to twist around to see who her rescuer was but couldn't manage it. 'Long story. One which I'd be happy to tell you when my two feet have been reunited.'

'Sure, sorry.' The owner of the voice appeared in front of her wearing a thick down coat. What Grace would give to be zipped into that right now. The woman was young and pretty, luminous skin, glossy brown hair piled on top of her head, olive-green eyes and the sort of cheekbones which wouldn't look out of place on the cover of *Vogue* magazine. 'I'm Katie.'

'And I'm Robyn,' said another woman, joining Katie.

Two females, thank goodness. This one looked a wee bit older, petite and pixie-like with fine features and enormous brown eyes.

'I'm not sure what I can do without causing you any more pain,' said Robyn, kneeling beside her. She had a professional-looking camera hanging around her neck. The lens cap was on, Grace was relieved to notice; she didn't need a photographic reminder of this particular moment; it was already destined to be engraved on her memory for eternity. Katie grabbed the back of Grace's towel and tucked it around her. 'There, at least you're decent again.'

'Can you try and take my flip-flops off?' Grace said. Her teeth were starting to chatter.

'Sure.'

While Katie wiggled Grace's feet free, Robyn took off her denim jacket and hung it over her shoulders. Grace smiled with thanks, secretly wishing she'd been given Katie's coat; she hadn't been Robyn's size since she hit puberty and the scrap of denim barely reached across her back.

'OK, they're off.' Katie held up the shredded flip-flops. 'Although I don't think you'll be wearing them again.'

'Too bloody right, I won't. They should come with a health warning: may split your difference and cause public humiliation,' said Grace. 'OK, time to get myself out of this knot.'

Leaning forward on trembling arms, she dragged her front leg towards her and brought her back knee in until she was on all fours. Every inch of her was in agony but at least the worst was over. She hung her head down and groaned with relief. 'Hallelujah.'

'Do you need a hand standing up?' said Robyn.

Grace nodded, biting her lip. Her ankle was throbbing really badly. Please God let it not be properly injured. Not now she'd moved to the arse end of nowhere, a good two miles from civilisation. *On her own.*

'What's your name, by the way?'

'Grace. Ironically. Grace by name and, as you have seen for your very own eyes, Grace by nature. Oh bollocks,' she groaned. 'This is going to be around the village before you can say lily-white ass.'

'Our lips are sealed,' said Robyn. 'We promise.'

'Lily-white ass with a tattoo,' Katie said with a cheeky grin.

'Ah yes.' Grace pulled a face; she saw her own bottom so rarely that sometimes she forgot it was there. 'That's a lesson that gambling is a bad thing.'

'You won that in a bet?' Robyn said, wide-eyed, hooking her hand under Grace's armpit.

Grace's eyes sparkled at the memory, despite the pain. 'I bet my husband that we'd never sell a house for a million pounds and that if we did, I'd get a house tattooed on my bum cheek.'

'Are you an estate agent?' Katie took her other arm.

Ah, the sweet relief of having some of her body weight supported by someone else. Grace shook her head, putting down first one foot and then the other. Her left foot, which had been trapped under the steps, hurt so much she thought she might pass out. 'Architect. We had a building company.'

Predictably Robyn's jacket slipped off her shoulders and the towel took a trip south too. Grace was beyond caring; getting two feet firmly back on the ground was all she was bothered about.

Robyn whipped the towel off the patio floor and handed it back to her.

'Thank you.' Grace's voice was shaking, her legs were trembling with pain and putting the towel back on meant letting go of Katie; she wasn't entirely convinced she wasn't going to collapse again.

'And sold a million-pound house? Wow.' Katie whistled.

'Sounds like a good bet to lose,' said Robyn.

'You know what . . . ' Grace's eyes softened.

She remembered the call from the sales director as if it was yesterday. They'd both asked Grace to join them. They'd both spoken to Alistair together to hear the good news. Their first million-pound sale. All the hard work, the risks they'd taken, and the knock-backs had paid off. It felt better than winning the lottery because they'd worked so hard for it.

Myles had picked her up and spun her round and then they'd held each other tightly, scarcely daring to believe their good fortune. Finally, Myles's hand had glided down low and he'd reminded her about the tattoo. It had been a proud moment and the tattoo was a symbol of all they'd achieved together. And although for obvious reasons, she couldn't see the detail easily herself, the tattoo artist had added a tiny heart with the initials M and G in the centre of the door because for Grace, wherever Myles was meant home.

The two women were staring at her and Grace realised she hadn't finished her own sentence.

'I'm glad I lost and I'm glad I got the tattoo,' she said wistfully.

She wiggled her legs to get some life back into them and then shook out her arms.

'It was a tiny little house when I first had it done. But as the years have rolled by, it seems to have grown. Heyho, that's life. Anyway, if you've both finished gawping at my derrière, perhaps you could help me back in the house; I've got nipples like coat pegs in this sea air.'

Robyn was screwing her face up tightly with the effort of not laughing and Katie had tucked her chin into her coat to hide her smile and suddenly Grace let out a snort of laughter. The other two joined in and with much merriment they helped Grace inside through enormous sliding glass doors and settled her on the sofa with her feet up. Katie slid the doors shut and Robyn went to locate the kettle in the sleek open-plan kitchen.

Grace shut her eyes for a moment, feeling wobbly and a bit teary. Sticking a brave face on was her *modus operandi* and humour was her default response to everything. But deep down, she was hurting. Not only was every muscle screaming but her heart was in agony too. She was missing Myles so much that her grief felt as if it was pressing her down, like one of those weighted blankets you could get to help you sleep. *Sleep, pah*, she hadn't had a single decent night's sleep since he'd gone.

'Here,' said a soft voice beside her. 'Drink this.'

She opened her eyes to see Robyn holding a mug out to her.

Grace swallowed and conjured up a smile. 'You star. You'll have one, won't you?'

Robyn nodded and retreated back to the kitchen to make more drinks and Katie appeared with a duvet.

She tucked it over Grace and perched on the end of the sofa. 'I hope you don't mind me snooping around, I've pinched this from one of the bedrooms, I was looking for a jumper or dressing gown or something, but this was all I could find.'

'I've only just moved in.' Grace revelled in the warmth of the duvet and clasped the hot mug tightly. It was a bit on the milky side, but the fact that it was hot, and she hadn't had to make it herself, made up for it. 'I haven't even done that properly, most of my stuff is still in the car.'

'I don't think you'll be doing any heavy lifting for a while,' said Robyn, handing Katie a cup of tea. 'That ankle looks a bit swollen.'

Grace smiled ruefully. 'It can wait.'

'We can help, can't we?' Robyn looked at Katie.

'Um.' Katie pulled her phone out her pocket and held it up.

Grace put a hand over her face. 'Oh Katie, don't take my picture, I must look a right state.'

Katie blinked. 'No, I wouldn't. I'd never do that, *never*. I just need to check in with work. My assistant will think I've dropped off the face of the earth.'

'Of course, go ahead,' said Grace, surprised by the strength of Katie's reaction.

'That's how Katie and I met,' said Robyn. She sat on the pale wool rug in the middle of the floor and crossed her legs. 'She thought I was taking her picture.'

Katie winced. 'Sorry about that, I'm a bit weird about having my photo taken.'

Robyn shrugged. 'Totally my fault. Anyway, it's just as well it happened, or we'd never have heard you scream.'

Grace raised an eyebrow. 'Do you mean you've only just met?'

The women nodded.

'Down on the beach by your gate,' Robyn confirmed.

'You seem like old friends,' she said, surprised.

Robyn and Katie explained that although they'd each known of the other, they'd never actually spoken until this morning. Katie told her about her underwear shop. Grace made a mental note to visit soon; some new lingerie would be a lovely way to cheer herself up. Robyn divulged virtually nothing about herself, other than that she was married to a fisherman, the last remaining fishing family in Merle Bay.

'I only popped out for a quick walk from work to clear my head and I've been gone far longer than planned.' Katie tucked her windblown hair behind her ears.

'Oh dear, do you have a headache?' Grace asked. 'I've got some tablets somewhere.'

'Tablets won't make this pain go away, unfortunately,' said Katie, not meeting her eye. 'But thank you.'

'No, thank *you*,' she replied. 'Both of you. I could have been stuck there for ages if you hadn't been around.'

'I'm really sorry you hurt yourself,' said Katie, 'but I must admit, I am a tiny bit glad that I've had a chance to see inside this house. I've always wanted to have a nose around.'

'Me too,' Robyn agreed. 'Sea Glass House is the coolest property in Merle Bay. It caused no end of controversy when the owner applied for planning permission.'

Grace remembered something about that. But Ned was an experienced builder, he was used to biding his time, reworking, resubmitting plans until he got the positive result he wanted.

'And how do the local people feel about it now?' she asked. Not that it was any skin off her nose, she was only a visitor, but it was handy to know how the land lay before she admitted to being a friend of Ned's.

'Mixed.' Robyn lifted a shoulder and cradled her tea. 'You know what people are like. Some hate modern design, some love it. There are those who automatically despise second-home owners and those who can see the benefit of tourism. This is the most gorgeous house I've ever been in. But I'm happy in my tiny little cottage with tiny rooms where I can leave my stuff out and shut the door on it, so we don't have to look at it.'

'I love it. I love the clean lines and the sparkle of the glass,' said Katie. 'I could sit and watch the sea all day.'

'That's a relief,' said Grace, letting out a breath. 'The owner is an old friend of mine and he's lent the house to me for a few months. It would have been a bit awkward if neither of you approved.'

'Wow, lucky you. My house is stuck in a time-warp and I haven't got around to changing anything because . . . ' Katie paused, and her face flushed.

Grace waited, not wanting to pry. She was a massive believer in fate. These two women, considerably younger than her, had come into her life for a reason, she was sure. Only time would tell what that was.

Katie cleared her throat. 'I suppose it still feels like my aunt's house and not mine to mess with. Although she passed away a year ago, so maybe I need to start putting my own stamp on it at some point.'

'Totally get that,' said Grace kindly.

'It takes time to adjust to losing someone you love,' Robyn added. 'You'll know when the time is right.'

'Thanks. Anyway,' said Katie, looking uncomfortable, 'something like this would be my dream home, although it's very big for one.'

Grace's heart squeezed. Katie was right. The house was incredible, but she had no one to share it with. No one to marvel over the gleaming kitchen surfaces, the shower with massage jets big enough for two. No one to sit in the hot tub, sipping Prosecco and soaking up the view across the bay. And on a practical level, she was alone in a massive house, in a remote location with at the very least a twisted ankle. If she couldn't drive, how would she manage, who could she call to come to her aid? Ned was based in Bristol these days, so he was no good and she couldn't rely on the kindness of these two strangers.

'I wish it wasn't for one,' she admitted. 'I'm used to being half of a couple and I was until recently. My husband died in November. Unexpectedly. One day he was there,

57

the next, he was gone. He was the love of my life, my soulmate. It sounds like a cliché but it's true. And I miss him so much that it hurts. The pain in my ankle doesn't even register by comparison. I'm not ready to be a widow, I assumed we'd have years together. He was only sixty-two. We were supposed to be exploring New Zealand this spring, our dream holiday. We spent ages planning it: Myles, me and a campervan, a trip filled with Hobbit houses, water-falls, wildlife and deserted beaches.' She caught the startled expressions on the other two women's faces and forced a smile. 'At least I managed the deserted beach part, eh?'

'You poor thing, I'm so sorry for your loss.' Katie got up to fetch some tissue from the bathroom; Grace hadn't even realised she was crying. 'He sounds like a wonderful man.'

'He was.' Grace took the tissue from Katie gratefully and blew her nose. 'And I'm lucky to have had him for seventeen blissful years, sixteen of them married to him.'

'I think you're amazing,' said Robyn. 'Not just for moving here by yourself but for talking about it. I'm rubbish at talking about things that matter.'

'I talk about everything. Wear my heart on my sleeve.' A ghost of a smile crossed Grace's lips and she looked at her bare skin. 'When I've got sleeves, that is. I suppose I should go and find some clothes.' She tested her foot on the floor and a sharp pain shot up her leg.

'Right, that does it,' said Robyn, getting to her feet and tapping a message out on her phone. 'I'm not leaving you on your own until we've unpacked your car and got you properly settled. I've texted my husband to let him know I'll be late for lunch.'

'Count me in too,' said Katie, 'as soon as I've made that call to let Nula know.' She pointed at the suitcases. 'Shall we start with those?'

'You're angels,' Grace said in a croaky voice, feeling a bit emotional.

Within half an hour, the car had been emptied, her food stored in the kitchen alongside the tantalising treats supplied by Ned, and Grace had directed the various boxes of her belongings to the appropriate room. She'd unpack all her clothes properly later, but for now she was dressed in one of her favourite jersey jumpsuits and had put on some mascara and a sweep of red lipstick and felt almost human again. After some prodding by Katie, who'd done a first-aid course, the three of them came to the conclusion that Grace's ankle was swollen but nothing more serious.

'How about a glass of Prosecco to celebrate me moving in,' said Grace, surprising herself as the words fell out of her mouth. Was it wrong, she thought belatedly, to raise a glass to a new episode in her life? Was it too soon to be celebrating anything?

Too late now, Katie was already finding glasses.

'I'm not normally a day drinker,' said Robyn, accepting a glass, nonetheless. 'But then this isn't a normal day.'

'To new friends!' Grace said, raising her glass.

'New friends,' the other two chimed in, chinking their glasses together.

Grace directed them to the dining table and the three of them sat, Grace facing out towards the sea, still captivated by the view.

'What made you want to move away from where you lived with Myles?' Katie asked.

'The last few months have been traumatic, but at least now the legal stuff is sorted out. Or I thought it was.' She hesitated, remembering the letter she'd just opened from her solicitor. If Austin and Olivia were contesting the will, the stress could be far from over. 'Because Myles and I lived and worked together, every aspect of my normal life just vanished overnight. Our house is full of echoes of the life I've lost. I thought some time alone in a neutral space without being surrounded by painful memories might help me find some peace.'

'I'll drink to that,' said Robyn, taking another sip.

Katie gave a heartfelt sigh. 'Gosh. Me too. To peace.'

There was a moment then when all three of them said nothing, seemingly lost in their thoughts, then Robyn reached into her pocket for something.

'I'll add these to the vase, if I may?' She held her hand out to show them pieces of green and blue glass, smooth like stones.

There was a cylindrical glass vase in the centre of the table half filled with stones just like it and Robyn placed hers gently on top of them.

'Is that sea glass?' Grace asked, thinking how beautiful all the colours were.

Robyn nodded. 'I picked these up this morning from the beach.'

'Let's see!' Grace leaned forward to reach the vase and ran her fingers through the stones; most of them were no bigger than her thumbnail, but the colours were glorious: some pink, white or orange, but most were blue or green and every shade in between.

'The beach is known for it locally,' said Katie. 'I've never collected it myself, but my aunt loved it, there are bags of it in my cottage.'

'It's very relaxing,' said Robyn, 'just wandering across the beach, picking up the sparkly bits. It's good for the soul, I think.'

Anything that was good for the soul had to be a winner as far as Grace was concerned.

'Why don't we do it together one day this week?' she suggested, topping up their glasses. 'Robyn could give us tips on how to find the best bits and I'll see if I can fill that vase before I leave.'

She was feeling quite impressed with herself; she'd only been here five minutes and already she'd met two lovely locals. She hoped they'd say yes, it would give her something to look forward to.

'Why not?' said Robyn, I don't have much else to do at the moment.'

Katie looked thoughtful for a moment but then nodded. 'Relaxing sounds good to me, but could we do it on Thursday? That's my day off.'

Once the arrangements were made, and the bottle was emptied, Katie and Robyn made their excuses and set off via the beach which, they told her, was a far quicker route into town than going by road.

Grace waved them off from the terrace and hobbled back inside to tidy up. It took her a few minutes to realise that she was humming. She'd have a bath, she decided, to ease her tender muscles and then she was going to ring Zoe to fill her in on her morning. About flashing her fandango al fresco, about her two new friends and most importantly, how for the first time since Myles died, she could feel a bit of her old self returning and it felt bloody marvellous.

Chapter Six

Robyn hurried back towards home and the harbour. What an unexpectedly lovely morning it had turned out to be after getting that bad news from *Our Eco Life* magazine. Grace and Katie: an architect and a shop owner. Robyn had really enjoyed meeting them; she felt inspired and uplifted and part of something new.

She could hardly wait until Thursday. She'd pick their brains about her job situation; they might have some good suggestions. He'd felt a bit guilty when she bumped into Katie that she'd never shopped in Auntie Small's. As a rule she was a firm believer in supporting local businesses, but she usually picked a multipack of knickers up from the supermarket when they did a big shop. And as for bras . . . she'd had a spell of not wearing anything at all, and at the moment was simply wearing soft crop tops or vests with hidden support. The window always looked lovely, if a bit above her budget. Claudia could obviously afford it though, she thought, and then chided herself for being uncharitable. Claudia had bought a feeding bra; it wasn't as if she'd splashed out on expensive lingerie.

As usual, her heart lifted when Admiral Cottage came into view. The entire house would probably fit into Grace's living room, but she wouldn't swap it for the world. It was hers and Finn's domain, their port in a storm, the perfect size for two. She went in by the kitchen door and the smell of baking greeted her.

Finn looked up and grinned. 'Just in time to witness my triumph.'

He was spreading frosting onto a carrot cake with a palette knife.

'Yum. I knew I married you for a reason.' Robyn sidled up to him, snuggling under his arm so that she could get close to him.

She pushed herself onto her tiptoes and kissed his cheek, smelling his delicious smell: fresh and clean with a faint hint of cinnamon. So different from his days on the boat, when he'd come home exhausted late in the afternoon, bringing the smell of the sea in with him. It used to be her favourite time of the day; she'd run him a hot bath and he'd relax while she massaged his shoulders and washed his hair and if he wasn't too tired, she'd strip off and join him. It had been their special time, just him and her and for as long as the water stayed hot enough, it was as if no one else in the world existed.

She still loved it when he came home and she still ran him a bath, but she'd stopped stripping off in front of him. Neither of them mentioned it. It was just an unspoken understanding. A self-consciousness that was permanently with her. But now part of her *did* want to speak about it, she wanted to know how he felt about her, *needed* to know if he still wanted her. The other part, of course, was frightened to death that she might not like the answer. Maybe she should simply do it; climb into the bath with him and see what happened? She bet that was what Grace would do. The thought made her smile.

She squeezed herself in between him and the kitchen worktop and forced him to put the knife down.

'I love you,' she whispered in his ear, touching her lips to the side of his neck. It was her secret weapon; he was

63

super-sensitive just there and usually a few seconds of her teasing him was all it took to get him interested.

But not today.

'Hey, you minx, I need to finish this.' He cupped her face to give her a bristly kiss on the lips. 'Tell me about your morning, your message was very cryptic: *on an exciting rescue mission, back soon*. Don't tell me another whale has been washed up on the beach?'

'No, it was a naked woman and a hot tub.' She laughed at his shocked expression. 'If I tell you the details, do I get cake?'

He pulled a face. 'Sorry, this one is for Claudia. She's permanently starving according to Callum and he's asked if we can pop over with food. I'm going there now with this and a stew. I think the euphoria of Betty's arrival is wearing off and the pair of them are knackered. There's some vegetable soup on the hob if you want some. Hey, kiss me again.'

Robyn obliged willingly, lust stirring inside her as she deepened the kiss. Maybe all was not lost. But again, he was the one to break their embrace and stroked her cheek with the back of his fingers.

'I thought I could smell alcohol; did the rescue mission include a drink by any chance?' he asked, bemused.

'Yep.' She bit back her disappointment at being brushed off. 'Prosecco with my new friends, Katie and Grace, to celebrate Grace moving into Sea Glass House.'

'Really? Very nice.' He looked impressed. 'Well, whoever these two are, I like them already for putting a smile on my girl's face.'

While Robyn helped herself to spicy carrot and pearl barley soup, and he decorated the top of the cake with chopped walnuts, she gave him the highlights of her morning.

'I feel more positive than I have in a long time. Just having someone to talk to.'

Finn looked hurt. 'You can talk to me.'

'I know,' she said, feeling guilty.

But there was so much she couldn't say. Not yet. About their relationship. About family. About how they were going to manage if she didn't pick up some work . . .

She stacked her empty bowl in the sink and fought to return to her happy mood. She dipped her finger in the bowl of frosting and licked it. 'Wow, this is really good.'

Finn washed his hands. 'I'm heading over to Callum's with this, do you want to come? Claudia might even share the cake with you.'

'I should probably send some emails, make some calls, put feelers out for freelance work, but that sounds like far more fun.'

'Hmm,' Finn frowned. 'At least you can keep Claudia chatting while I tell Callum the bad news about the loan repayments.'

A shiver of unease ran down Robyn's spine, but she managed a smile. 'Ready when you are.'

The walk to Claudia and Callum's house took no time at all. They lived at the far side of the harbour, their home was amid a row of traditional stone fishermen's cottages and overlooking the collection of shabby boatsheds. Most of them were disused these days, but the largest of them was the headquarters of McGill Enterprises: housing everything needed to run a small fishing business, from tangled ropes, weatherproof clothing and boots, plastic crates and an often ignored desk decorated in the obligatory red tape required to comply with the regulations of the day.

The brothers had taken over the fishing business from their father, Eddie McGill, some years ago. It had been hard for Eddie to accept that he wasn't the one at the helm anymore, and after few too many disagreements with his sons about how they should be running things, their mother Sheila took matters into her own hands and insisted she and Eddie move to the south coast where the warmer climate would be good for his arthritis. Their boys, she convinced him, could sail the ship without him. It had been the right move for the pair of them, but Robyn missed them both. She loved her in-laws dearly and had relished being fussed over, especially by Sheila who had filled the gap left by her own mother.

In theory, the brothers were equal partners, but as the eldest, Callum tended to have the casting vote on business decisions, and Finn, being easy-going, rarely rocked the boat.

Two best friends and two brothers: the two couples had been a foursome since she and Claudia were eighteen. Robyn, after fancying the pants off Finn for ages, had finally decided to do something about it when she spotted him in the pub with his friends celebrating passing his driving test. She'd done that thing of getting the barman to take him a drink over 'from an admirer' and had proceeded to catch his eye until he came over. Finn admitted later that he had had his eye on her too, but had wanted to pass his driving test first, so he could impress her by inviting her out for a drive in his dad's car. Their first date was driving twenty miles to find the nearest McDonalds drive-through. Then Callum plucked up the courage to ask Claudia out, so their second date was at an open-air cinema with Callum and Claudia in the back. Their lives had been intertwined ever since.

The house was quiet when Robyn and Finn arrived. It was usually so full of chaos and noise with nine-year old

William and seven-year old Hannah racing around shouting to one another, but they were still at school. Claudia was lying on the sofa in her dressing gown with three-week-old Betty asleep on her chest while Callum was napping in the armchair next to her. Finn's cooking was well received and after making hot drinks and serving up slices of cake to Claudia and Robyn, Finn retreated to the kitchen with Callum.

Robyn could hear the two brothers speaking in low, serious tones and her stomach lurched. The men couldn't really afford not to be out fishing this week, but Finn couldn't take the boat out alone. Callum and Finn had a strong work ethic and rarely had time off, but family came before profit. Claudia's mum had been here to help for the first few days after the baby arrived. Now that she'd gone, Claudia had wanted Callum on hand for another week before being left in charge of all three children by herself.

'I married the wrong brother,' said Claudia, stuffing a chunk of cake into her mouth and then picking up a fallen crumb from Betty's head. She was plump and pink-cheeked, her light brown hair scooped haphazardly into a topknot and despite the dark smudges under her eyes, she glowed with happiness. 'This is the best thing I've eaten since the last time you two came round.'

'You married the right brother,' said Robyn, settling herself into the armchair vacated by Callum and folding her legs underneath her. 'You get cake delivered fresh to your door without all the clearing up. Whereas I'll be scraping that frosting off the floor and ceiling for weeks.'

The two friends laughed. It was a longstanding joke between them about each other's husband being the best, but the truth was that they both knew they'd made the right choice and wouldn't swap their other halves for the world.

'I don't think business is great,' Robyn said quietly, jerking her head towards the kitchen.

Claudia wiped her mouth with the baby's muslin cloth. 'Neither do I. Callum was up in the early hours pacing the floor. So, something's bothering him. Of course, he managed to be fast asleep again by the time Betty woke up. Typical.'

The baby started to cry, tiny mewling sounds to begin with, gradually building up to a crescendo of yells.

'Here we go again.' Claudia tipped her plate up to catch the last few crumbs in her mouth and gulped her tea before pulling her dressing gown open and putting Betty to her breast. 'Afternoon tea is served, your ladyship.'

It took a moment for the baby to latch on and Claudia winced. Finally, the only noise in the room was the contented sound of Betty feeding.

'Good girl,' Claudia murmured.

The Madonna and child, Robyn mused. Take away the towelling dressing gown and Betty's white Babygro and the two of them together looked like a scene from a Renaissance painting.

Realising she was staring a little too hard at Claudia's massive boob, she looked out of the window to the boat-yard and the jetty where Hannah and William liked to go crabbing in summer. There was a man out there fishing and two seagulls were sneakily hopping sideways towards his bucket. She turned back to Claudia and opened her mouth to tell her about her adventure on Sea Glass Beach this morning, but Claudia's eyes were locked onto her baby and she was stroking her face, entirely wrapped up in the moment, so Robyn decided against it.

Around her were piles of laundry and toys pushed into stacks in the corners of the room, while socks hung from every radiator like multi-coloured bunting and abandoned mugs littered every surface . . . It was unsurprising in the circumstances; clutter came hand in hand with a growing family. Robyn loved Claudia and her tribe, but it also made her appreciate the quiet and tranquillity of her and Finn's home. Just the two of them.

Claudia, on the other hand, was completely unfazed by the state of the house. This was her natural habitat and she thrived in it. A true earth mother, Robyn thought, as Claudia sat Betty up and wiped her mouth on a muslin cloth before covering herself up. She'd taken to motherhood like a fish to water and she was so confident about her body, Robyn thought wistfully. Even if Finn were to walk in now while she was half naked, she wouldn't bat an eyelid. Grace had been the same; making jokes about her lily-white ass. Robyn would have been traumatised for days if that had happened to her. She didn't think she'd ever feel comfortable in a bikini again, let alone topless. The girl who'd dared her friends to go skinny-dipping on hot summer nights was gone.

Her face must have given her away because Claudia said in a soft voice. 'I'm in awe of you, you know. Dealing with all this.'

'Thank you.' Robyn chewed her lip. 'Although I don't think I have really.'

'Have you got used to the new girls yet?' Claudia nodded towards Robyn's chest.

Robyn hesitated before replying.

Claudia and Robyn had been friends since the start of secondary school and had been through everything together. It was an 'opposites attract' type of friendship. Robyn: wiry, sporty and petite, a daredevil who was always getting them into mischief and Claudia: curvy, good-natured and very girlie. She could never resist going along with Robyn's crazy schemes, even though she was terrified of getting into trouble. Unfortunately for Claudia, she was never fast enough to flee the scene, or quick-thinking enough to come up with an excuse, so she invariably got caught. Not that she ever minded.

Claudia was still Robyn's closest friend. But sometimes Robyn wished she had an ally outside of the family. Someone who was completely on her side no matter what. She'd learned a long time ago that when Claudia promised to keep something 'strictly *entre nous*' the *nous* included Callum. Robyn had made the mistake of confiding in Claudia about the cute snuffly noise Finn made when he was asleep and for the next six months, his big brother would only refer to him as Snuffle Bear.

And so now, although there were a million things she'd love to tell someone about her body, about her relationship with Finn, she daren't because she didn't want it getting back to him. So instead, all she said was, 'I'm getting there.'

Claudia nodded earnestly. 'I might get a boob job as well when I've finished feeding Betty. After three kids, they'll be swinging past my navel . . . Oh. Shit.' She clapped a hand over her forehead, looking stricken. 'Forget I said that. I didn't mean that you'd had a boob job, Robyn. I do know the difference, honestly.'

'I'm glad,' said Robyn through gritted teeth. 'Because given the choice between slightly saggy boobs and a bilateral mastectomy, I know what I'd choose.'

The elective surgery and reconstruction she'd had done early last year, followed by the removal of her ovaries, was to preserve her life, not for any aesthetic reasons. If her best friend, her sister-in-law, didn't get it, what chance did anyone else have? Robyn had read countless posts on online forums and knew that what she was going through wasn't unique. Even the most empathetic people struggled to comprehend how difficult the choices were that Robyn and women like her faced. She didn't hold it against Claudia, it just made her sad, that was all.

'Oh God, I've upset you, I'm such an idiot.' Claudia struggled to her feet, clutching the baby and crouched down in front of Robyn's chair, steadying herself on Robyn's thigh. 'I'm so sorry. Blame it on the baby brain.'

'It's fine.' Robyn avoided Claudia's eye, instead reaching a hand to Betty's head and stroking her soft hair.

'I've read up about it, you know,' Claudia continued. 'Things to do and say that might help. But then when you're here, all the things not to say just come tumbling out instead. I know I haven't been there for you as much as I should have been. I'm a rubbish friend.'

Robyn smiled; Claudia had a good heart.

'It's OK, you have been rather busy.' She nodded in Betty's direction. 'But honestly, you're a good friend and I love you.'

'Thank you. I love you too,' said Claudia meekly.

'If it hadn't been for you, I'd never have made it through my teens. Losing Mum, moving in with Dad and that woman . . . ' Robyn shuddered at the memories of that bleak period in her life. Her dad clearing out their junk room to make room for her, while his girlfriend stomped around muttering that this hadn't been part of the deal. Robyn had been made very aware that she was a burden to them both. Thank goodness Claudia and her family had made her welcome at their house at weekends. Robyn had a lot to be grateful for, which was why their friendship would withstand Claudia putting her foot in it occasionally.

The two friends smiled at each other and Claudia gave Robyn's leg another squeeze.

She glanced at Robyn's chest hidden under her jumper. 'I think your new boobs look good. What do they feel like from the inside?'

'My *foobs*? Weird,' said Robyn. 'Like not part of me. They're a second behind me whenever I try and move too fast.'

She'd never given her own boobs much thought until they were gone. Now, she realised how attached she'd been to them.

'You've still got a lovely figure,' Claudia continued. 'Not like my hormonally ravaged one. Do you still get hormones?'

Robyn gave her a warning look. 'Yes, Claude, I still get hormones.'

Just then Betty produced the cutest burp, opening her eyes wide with shock and then closing them again and they both laughed.

'Do you mind taking her?' Claudia deposited Betty in Robyn's arms. 'I feel like she's been glued to my bosom all day.'

Robyn cradled the little girl to her, letting her tiny head rest under her chin, and inhaled her sweet baby smell. The door from the kitchen opened and Finn came in. He sat on the arm of Robyn's chair and kissed the baby's head.

Claudia dashed out to the loo while she had a child-free moment and as soon as she'd gone, Robyn turned to Finn. 'Everything OK?'

He nodded without taking his eyes off Betty. 'Bills, bills and more bills. I think we're going to cut our week off short and get back to work a day early.'

'I'm sorry,' she said, leaning her head against him.

He wrapped his arm around her shoulders. 'Hey, what have you got to be sorry about?'

Everything. Scarcely working last year. Putting the financial burden on you. Pretending to want children because you said you did, then being relieved when it couldn't happen. Not being the woman you married anymore . . .

But she stayed silent. Betty made a cooing noise and Robyn turned her around and placed her in the crook of her arm so they could both see her face.

'Look at those tiny fingernails,' she said, changing the subject. 'They don't seem real. Isn't she just the most perfect thing?'

'Perfect,' Finn agreed. 'Can Betty have a cuddle with her Uncle Finn then?'

'Sure.' Robyn smelled the newness of her one more time before handing her to Finn.

'Well, hello, little one,' he whispered, holding her up to his face.

Betty opened her eyes and looked hazily at him, her lips twitching into a lopsided smile.

'She likes you,' Robyn laughed.

'Course she does. There's nothing to her, she's tiny,' said Finn, lifting her up and down as if he was weighing her.

'True,' said Callum, joining them in the living room. 'If she was a cod, you'd throw her back.'

Finn kissed Betty's downy head. 'Don't you listen, Bets, he doesn't mean it.'

Callum picked up his phone and knelt down in front of them. 'One for the family album, cheesy grins please.'

Robyn tilted her head close to Finn and the baby while Callum took a picture.

'Let's see,' said Finn, beckoning for his brother to hand the phone over. 'She's an absolute stunner. And the baby's not bad-looking either.'

Robyn and Finn smiled at each other.

'Aww, you two, that's so romantic,' said Claudia, arriving back and resuming her place on the sofa.

Callum plonked himself down next to his wife. 'You're a natural, Finn. Looks like we've got ourselves a babysitter.' He patted his wife's leg triumphantly and grinned. 'Won't be long before we can start going out again, Claude, have a few bevvies.'

Robyn smirked at Claudia, who was staring at her husband in disbelief. 'When you're both ready for that,' she said, 'we'll happily do it.'

'Definitely,' said Finn, kissing the top of the baby's head. 'Because I have to say, Betty McGill, you have stolen your uncle's heart. Spending time with you will be no hardship at all.'

The look on his face was a picture of pure adoration. Robyn's stomach fluttered with nerves as all of her insecurities rushed up to the surface. Was he wishing he had a baby of his own, a little son or daughter? Because Callum was right: Finn was great with Betty. But Robyn couldn't have a baby anymore, and if Finn really did want to be a father, where did that leave their marriage?

Chapter Seven

It was Wednesday afternoon and Katie was alone in the shop, unpacking some stock behind the counter, when the door opened and a man walked in. He hadn't been in before and she didn't think he was local. Mid-thirties, good-looking in a crumpled sort of way, he turned around in a circle and looked decidedly out of his comfort zone.

'Oh crikey,' he murmured.

It was hard not to jump to conclusions, but sometimes she did get male customers from out of town making a special trip to Auntie Small's because they didn't want to be spotted buying lingerie for women they perhaps weren't married to. Of course, he could want some underwear for himself; it was only a tiny part of the business, but Katie had added a small range of briefs and boxers to the shop since she'd been in charge. Or he could just have been passing, seen the shop and wanted to buy his lady a present; not all men were sleazeballs, she reminded herself.

'Can I help?' she asked, giving him her most welcoming smile.

'Yes please, if you don't mind. I don't know where to start.'

He scratched his head and laughed, a warm, friendly laugh, and she smiled back, genuinely this time. So far, not sleazy. For a split second he reminded her of her dad, and the funny face he used to pull when pegging her bralettes and thongs on the washing line at home, trying to work out which way up they went while also trying not to look at them.

'OK.' Katie pushed the sleeves of her jumper up and tucked her hands in her back pockets. 'What sort of thing did you have in mind?'

'I haven't bought women's underwear for a long time.' He approached the counter slowly, taking in the rails of lingerie to his left and right. 'Tried surprising my girlfriend for Valentine's Day. Never again.'

He winced at the memory.

'Don't tell me – red lace?' Katie grinned.

He held his hands up. 'I know, I know. I ticked all the cliché boxes in my youth. Luckily, she forgave me enough to marry me in spite of my dubious abilities at shopping for her. Hence getting some advice this time around.'

Katie liked him so far. She guessed he was probably buying for his wife. The one drawback of working in the lingerie business was that all the nice men she met were already spoken for.

'Very sensible,' she said. 'So, shall we steer away from lace altogether?'

'I think that would be wise.' His dark brows furrowed. 'Something plain and definitely comfy. She's big on comfort. And if you've got anything that somehow helps the planet at the same time, that will be a big plus.'

'I like a challenge.' Katie was intrigued; this was a first. He was definitely buying for someone he loved; it was written all over his face. 'We've got some really soft organic cotton and there's also a lovely bamboo collection. And are you looking for a set?'

'Possibly. What do you get in a set?' He laughed. 'Can you tell I haven't done this before?'

'Bra and briefs?'

'Um.' He thought about it again and Katie smiled to herself. Just as well there were no other customers in this afternoon, this one could take a while. Not that she was complaining; she often felt uncomfortable in the company of strange men, but she was enjoying helping this one.

'No, just the top half, she can get her own . . . ' he waved a hand vaguely. 'Bottoms.'

'Follow me and I'll show you what I've got.'

The back wall of the shop was where they kept the plainer collections and she led him in that direction.

'Blimey.' The man whistled softly. His eyes were out on stalks as they passed the foundation garments and support wear. 'A lot of these look . . . large. I'm looking for something smaller. *A lot* smaller.'

So far, he hadn't succumbed to any of the underwear-related jokes some of her male customers felt obliged to recount. *How's the underwear market then? Knickers down, bras still holding up?* This guy seemed to be taking the job seriously.

'I try my best to carry something for every woman,' she replied, hiding her smile. She led him to a rack containing one of the new spring collections in pastel shades with not a hint of red among them. 'This is the new season's colours. Sizes start at an A cup.'

The man picked up a plain T-shirt bra in the smallest size and frowned at it. He replaced it and picked up a larger one and then sighed.

Honestly, she thought, amused, it never ceased to amaze her that men thought they could waltz into a lingerie shop and expect to choose something to fit their partner without having a clue what size they were. Few women could do that themselves without trying things on.

'We do gift vouchers if you think that might be easier, that way the lady in question can choose something for herself and she'll still be thrilled with the gift.' More so, probably.

He scratched his chin. 'I guess I need to know her size to do this properly.'

'It would help.'

'The thing is, the lady in question is my fourteen-year-old daughter.' He looked down at the little cotton bra in his large hands. 'I know I'm out of my depth, but I've got to try. This will be her first bra and it's important that I get it right. Besides, if I bought her a voucher, I couldn't guarantee she wouldn't just stick it in a drawer and forget about it.'

Katie tried to hide her surprise. She'd sold countless girls their first bras over the last ten years; some of them had come in alone, some with mums or aunties or even a friend. Never a dad, and certainly never a dad without his daughter.

She took the underwired bra out of his hand and replaced it on the rail.

'Her breast tissue will still be growing, so we advise against wires for now. She won't necessarily need a lot of support unless she's bigger than you think. At that age it's about modesty as much as anything.'

He nodded, absorbing all her advice. 'Right. Good thinking. She's wearing these little crop tops at the moment. Her mum bought her them for her two years ago. I think Amber would quite happily carry on wearing them, she's very attached to anything Sophia bought, but . . . ' He scratched his head. 'This is really hard to describe without sounding weird.'

Katie took pity on him. 'But she has begun to develop?'

He smiled gratefully. 'Exactly. And I'm a single parent.'

'Understood.' She didn't pry. Instead, she offered him Auntie Jean's chair while she poured them both a coffee from the pot.

He refused sugar and milk and sniffed the coffee and grinned. 'I'd have come in here sooner if I'd known the coffee was this good.'

'All part of the service,' she said lightly, and raised her mug to her face to hide how pleased she was. 'Tell me about Amber.'

'OK. Where to start . . . she's a great kid.' His face flooded with pride. 'Sometimes she comes out with something so sensible that I wonder who the adult is between the two of us and then at other times she'll get excited about a basket of kittens. She's growing up, but she's not ready to leave childhood behind. Thank goodness. Because I'm certainly not ready.'

Something about this man made Katie want to wrap him up in her arms. The thought made her warm inside. She really hoped she wasn't blushing.

'You know, I probably shouldn't say this, but you might be better taking her to a big department store where there's more choice,' she suggested. 'You can let her wander around the rails and get a feel for what she likes.'

'Hmm.' He considered this and then shook his head. 'No, Sophia wouldn't have wanted that. Buying Amber's first bra was something she'd talked about. She looked forward to sharing these mum and daughter moments with her. She said getting your first bra is a rite of passage. And even though Amber has only got her old dad now that her—' He paused to clear his throat. 'Now that her mum has passed away, I don't want it to be any less special.'

'I'm so sorry for your loss.' Katie's heart twisted; poor girl losing her mum at such a tender age, and what a thoughtful dad she'd got.

He shook his head as if annoyed with himself. 'I don't know where that all came from. I'm not normally an oversharer.'

'I think that's a lovely way of thinking about it.' She tried to swallow the lump in her throat. 'When my Auntie Jean was alive and ran this shop and a teenager came in for a fitting, she used to treat her like a VIP and turn it into a real celebration. I can do that for Amber if you like?'

'That's kind of you to offer.' He smiled. 'How about this: I'll take home a few different styles for her to try on in the privacy of her own room. That will give me a way in to broach the subject. Then she can perhaps bring back any she doesn't like or that don't fit.'

'Perfect,' she replied. 'Sixty per cent of my clients are wearing the wrong size bra when they walk in here and they're grown women. I'd feel much happier sending her out into the world in something that she feels confident in and that fits her properly. There's actually quite a lot to bra fitting and it makes a massive difference if you get it right from the beginning.'

While he sipped his coffee, she gave him a quick demonstration of some of the main styles until he begged for mercy.

'Who knew there were so many names for bras.' His eyes crinkled with humour. 'Thanks so much. I've been dreading getting it wrong. Until Sophia died, I'd never even taken Amber to buy shoes. It's a very steep learning curve.'

'I'll make sure you don't get it wrong,' Katie promised.

'Shopping was Sophia's big thing. I'm more of a ninja when it comes to shops. I go in with a mission. I find it, pay for it and leave. I own four pairs of jeans all the same size and style in very slightly different colours. Why bother buying different jeans when I've already found the perfect ones? That's my motto. Sophia could never understand that.'

'I can't claim to have quite that many identical jeans,' Katie laughed, 'but I do have about twenty baggy jumpers, so I'm not one to talk.'

'I knew coming in here was a good move.' He grinned. 'Thank you, er . . . ?'

'Katie,' she supplied.

'Thanks, Katie, for helping me through something I'd been dreading. And who knew there was so much to learn about putting a bra on.'

She looked at him, waiting for the comment about him being more used to taking them off. But it didn't come. And she liked him a bit more.

'And thanks for making me feel at home in a new female world. I'm Barney, by the way.'

'You're very welcome.' Katie beamed at him. 'Shall I choose some for you to take home and give her, or would you rather make an appointment and bring her back with you?'

He scrunched up his face thoughtfully. 'The thing is, it's hard for a man to bring your daughter's chest up in conversation. We talk about everything under the sun normally, but this would be the first time the conversation turned intimate. She might not have even thought about bras yet.'

'She will have done, trust me,' Katie replied. 'Some girls can't wait to start wearing a bra, especially those who are body conscious. There'll be girls in her class who started developing at age nine.'

'Jesus,' Barney muttered. 'I think Amber was still running around on the beach topless at that age. I think I'll buy her a couple and just leave the bag on her bed with a note.'

'Sounds like a plan,' Katie looked across the racks of underwear. 'Is she sporty?'

He nodded. 'She was in the football team at her old school.'

'Then how about keeping it on a more practical level and getting her a sports bra, plus a couple of everyday ones?'

He nodded. 'I'll do that. Good idea.'

While Barney finished his coffee, Katie wrapped several different bras carefully in tissue paper to make them look extra special. She thought about how sad it was that Barney's wife didn't get chance to share this moment with her daughter and on impulse added a sample of perfume to the bag. Sophia married a decent man, she thought, sliding a sideways glance at him.

Barney handed over his credit card and once Katie had taken payment, she wrote her number down on a business card and dropped it into the bag.

'I've written my name and mobile number for you.'

Barney slotted it into his wallet. 'Oh, right.'

'I meant for Amber, not you,' Katie said, worried he'd misinterpreted her.

'I see.'

'So she can make an appointment to come back in and get measured properly. That's all.' She was gabbling. Once she started it was very difficult to stop. 'I wasn't trying to give you my number. Except I had to give it to you, to give it to her. I've made myself blush. I'm shutting up now.'

Barney grinned. 'You've been a star. I mean it, thank you.'

'You're welcome, I'm really glad you came in.'

'Me too.' He tucked his wallet back in his pocket and picked up the bag. 'Right, I'm going to go and google bralettes and balconies and all that other stuff you talked about and then I'm going to probably make a fool of myself in front of my teenage daughter. Wish me luck.'

She laughed. 'Good luck.'

Barney got as far as opening the door when Alice, the post lady, bustled through it, red-faced and out of breath and almost ran into him.

'Gosh, hello Barney!' she said, flustered. 'Didn't expect to see you in here.'

Katie smiled to herself. Trust Alice Jennings to know him; it wasn't that she was nosy, she just always seemed to be in the right place at the right time.

'You *didn't* see me,' he said, holding up his shopping bag and tapping his nose. 'OK?'

'Ooh, right,' she giggled much to Katie's amusement. Someone else who seemed to have fallen for Barney's charms. Not that she had, of course, well not beyond him shooting to the top of the list of favourite customers, anyway. 'Mum's the word.'

Katie cringed at her turn of phrase, but Barney didn't bat an eyelid. 'Thanks. Goodbye ladies!'

'You know him?' Katie asked, trying not to make it too obvious that she was following his progress up the high street.

'Of course.' Alice was rummaging around in her post bag. 'That's Barney Larkin. Moved into Mr Lewis's old cottage a couple of weeks ago with his daughter, Amber. Such a sad story, his wife was killed in a terrible car crash. Amber survived but with serious injuries. Although she seems OK now.'

'Oh my god. The poor man.' Katie pressed a hand to her mouth; when he'd said that his wife had passed away, he'd made it sound like a peaceful death. That must have been devastating to deal with for both of them.

'I know. Bless their hearts,' said Alice, pressing a hand to her chest. 'Still, well done to them for starting afresh in Merle Bay, I say. They're going to take one of Silky's kittens.'

Katie smiled, remembering Barney's comment about Amber and a basket of kittens. 'Fantastic.'

'There's one left. Would you like one?' Alice asked her this every other day.

'Still no thanks, but thanks.'

'I'm surprised you don't know who Barney is,' said Alice, pulling a crumpled envelope out of her bag. 'I thought you young people knew everything from reading it on Facebook.'

Katie shook her head. 'I hate Facebook with a passion. I'm an old-school newspaper girl.'

'Even more reason why you should know him then,' Alice chuckled. 'Barney is the new editor of the newspaper. The *North East Gazette*. Here you go.'

She handed Katie the envelope, which looked a bit worse for wear. 'Sorry it's so late, this one got mixed up in another mail bag and I didn't find it until I was on my way home. Must dash, our favourite vet programme is on at five o'clock and Graham doesn't like watching it by himself.'

Alice was in such a hurry to leave the shop that she didn't notice how pale Katie had gone, how her hands were trembling as she held onto the envelope. She stared at it, a cold fear creeping from her toes to her scalp; it was identical to the one she'd had on Monday, same manila paper, same handwriting. Feeling sick with nerves, she tore it open and pulled out the contents.

It contained another copy of that photograph but this time, there were also a couple of notes paperclipped to it.

The first was headed with the email address of the news desk of the *North East Gazette*.

Oh my God. Katie's heart banged ruthlessly against her chest. Had this been sent already? Would it have gone to Barney? Was that the reason behind his visit today, to see for himself?

Her hands shook as she picked up the final piece of paper.

Do you like the caption for your picture? You'll look great in the newspaper. We haven't sent it to the press. NOT YET. What happens next depends on you. We're going to give you the chance to buy the photos off us first. Keep watching the post. And DON'T do anything stupid, if we suspect you've gone to the police, we won't hesitate to send the email.

'Thank God.' Katie's knees went from under her and she collapsed into a chair, her head spinning.

Barney hadn't seen it. Nobody had so far.

As she'd suspected, this was blackmail. But why now? It was ancient history, or so she'd thought. She'd been eighteen. She'd made a mistake. Just one. Everyone made mistakes at that age, it was part of growing up. OK, hers had had particularly severe repercussions, but she had put it behind her as best she could. And she'd been doing well; she'd regained a lot of her confidence and hardly thought about the events of that summer anymore. She was aware she still had trust issues; it had affected her relationships, no doubt about it, and her friendships. She much preferred to be confided *in* than be a confider. If she talked to anyone, it was Auntie Jean, but now she was gone. Her parents were the only ones left who knew the whole story, but it hadn't been spoken about for years. Besides, she could hardly ring them up in Malta and tell them what was happening; it would ruin their holiday. Katie felt suddenly very alone and very young to be dealing with this on her own.

Robyn and Grace, perhaps? Her heartbeat quickened; she'd be seeing them tomorrow. They'd got on really well on Monday and although they were older than she was, she'd felt the beginnings of a bond.

Maybe it was time to open up and trust again. Maybe.

Chapter Eight

By Thursday morning, Grace's ankle was a lot less swollen. It was still tender, but certainly not bad enough to stop her from meeting the two girls on the beach later. For the last two days she'd been sensible and rested it as much as possible in between unpacking and attempting to make Sea Glass House feel homely. Ned's taste was impeccable, but the space had felt impersonal. Arranging a few of her own family photographs made her feel a little less homesick.

Ned had phoned her yesterday to check she was settling in all right and made her promise to let him know if there was anything he could do for her. She'd been touched by his kindness. She'd known Ned almost as long as she'd known Myles. He'd been single then. Since then, he'd been married and divorced and was now single again. She hoped he'd find someone one day, he deserved to be happy; he was a lovely man and he'd been a true friend to Grace. After the call ended she'd sat out on the terrace in the sunshine, listening to the waves, and felt calmer than she had for six months. Grace was perfectly capable of looking after herself, but she had to admit, it was comforting to know that someone cared.

Today so far, she hadn't spoken to a soul; she and Zoe had managed to miss each other's phone calls since she'd been in Merle Bay through one thing and another and she'd already left one voicemail message for her this morning. Now though, her sister had called her just as she was getting ready to go out.

'Sorry I haven't called you back,' said Zoe. 'I don't know who I've upset to get this rota, but my shifts have been horrendous. Is everything OK? Not too homesick?'

'No need to apologise, and I'm fine, everything is fine,' Grace laughed, deciding not to tell her about her slip-up on the patio on Monday; her sister would probably force her to wear one of those call buttons around her neck that they issue to the elderly. 'I miss you, that's all.'

'I miss you too. Don't be too proud to come home if you don't like it, will you?'

'I won't, promise.' Grace picked up a photograph of Zoe and the children and felt a rush of love for her family. 'Are the kids OK?'

'All good, thanks. Although I caught Daniel on his phone at eleven o'clock last night and then just as I finally got to bed, Ruby woke up. Ah well, sleep's overrated. Allegedly.'

A sudden wave of sadness hit Grace. She and Myles had always slept hand in hand, every night. Once their bedside lamps were out, they'd each reach across the sheet towards each other. She missed that: his warm hand covering hers. At home, getting into their big bed without him was something she'd ended up dreading. Here there was no indentation in the mattress made by his body, no hint of his aftershave lingering in the room. But oddly, she was sleeping better here than she had for months. She replaced the picture, retrieved her trainers from the bottom of the wardrobe and perched on the end of her bed to put them on.

'I don't know how you do it,' Grace said, full of admiration for her sister. She tucked the phone under her ear and wriggled her foot into the first one.

'I set two different alarms,' Zoe said with a giggle. 'What are you doing? You sound out of breath.'

'I am. And I'm only putting my trainers on,' Grace panted. 'I'm out of shape these days.'

'You and me both,' grumbled Zoe. 'I need to get back into an exercise regime.'

'Hmm,' said Grace, loosening the laces on her other shoe.

At one time she'd have agreed with her but when Myles died he'd never been fitter, which as far as Grace was concerned, was proof that when it was your time, it was your time. Whether you were ninety-four and inhaled your way through a packet of Marlborough Lights a day or were active and health-conscious like Myles.

Once he'd hit sixty, he'd decided to start looking after himself. He'd taken up cycling, joined a club and had begun going for long rides at weekends. Grace, inspired by his willpower, joined a gym with a swimming pool and had begun to swim regularly. When Myles died, she cancelled her membership. She already felt as if she was drowning, she didn't need to chuck herself into tepid communal water to do it. And besides, with Myles gone, she had no motivation to take care of herself.

'Anyway, it sounds like at least one of us is being healthy,' said Zoe. 'Where are you off to, anywhere nice?'

'Just meeting some friends on the beach,' Grace smiled, imagining her sister's eyebrows shooting heavenwards.

'Friends? That was quick!'

'Perhaps friends is a bit too strong,' Grace said, back-tracking. 'I only met them on Monday. But they seem nice.'

'You made friends on your first day? Go Gracie. Any of them male, single and devilishly good-looking?'

Grace ignored her; it was incomprehensible to think of

another man in her life. She hadn't got used to not having Myles in it yet.

'Sorry, sorry,' said her sister contritely. 'Too soon, I know. Anyway, what are they like, are they your neighbours?'

Grace looked out of the window across the headland and down to the beach. There were no other houses in view.

'I don't actually have any neighbours, but Katie and Robyn are local. We're going sea glass collecting.'

'Snap, I'm about to do a bit of collecting too!' said Zoe. 'Mr Warren in bed number seven has a stool sample for me.'

'I think I'll stick to sea glass,' Grace grimaced.

'Have you heard from Austin and Olivia this week?' Zoe asked.

'Not directly, but I've had a bit of bad news: they've appointed a solicitor.' She told Zoe about the letter from Roger Mathers that was waiting for her when she arrived on Monday and their plans to contest their father's will. 'If that's what they want to do, they can. I'm very disappointed in them and I know Myles would be appalled.'

'Bloody hell.' Zoe whistled under her breath.

'I don't want this to go to court,' Grace continued. 'But on the other hand, I don't want to go against Myles's wishes. He wanted half of his estate to be split between his children and that's what should happen.'

Zoe was silent on the other end of the line for so long that Grace thought she'd lost the signal.

'Zo? Do you agree?' she prompted.

'Sorry, I'm still here. I'm just thinking maybe you should give them what they want.'

Grace was startled. 'What?'

Zoe was a fighter. Had been since her premature birth at thirty weeks. Grace often attributed her own negotiation skills in business to a childhood spent arguing with her sister. It usually only took the mere mention of Austin and Olivia's names to make Zoe leap onto her high horse and ride to Grace's rescue.

'You moved to Merle Bay to get away from all this family drama,' Zoe reminded her. 'You've got enough money to do what they ask. Why don't you ask the solicitor what they'd be happy with and do a deal? Keep it out of court. That way everyone's happy.'

'Except me and probably Myles,' Grace pointed out. 'He loved his kids, but he always wanted them to have a strong work ethic. It's too tempting to be lazy if you get handed a fortune on a plate when you're young. Both of us came from working-class backgrounds, that's what made us hungry for success.'

'You know what I think: Austin and Olivia are greedy sods but whether they get twenty-five per cent or thirty-three per cent it is still a fortune. So, if I were you, I'd roll over one more time, agree to their demands and then cut them loose. Move on and forget all about it.'

Grace bit her lip, unconvinced. 'I don't know. I want to do the right thing, but sometimes knowing what that is isn't black and white.'

'I'm so proud of you, Grace,' Zoe said softly. 'You're such a loyal person, and so good, so honest. You don't deserve this to happen. You don't deserve anything bad to happen.'

'It doesn't matter about me, I'm tough enough to cope with anything. The sad thing is that Myles was such a good role model for them and then for them to act like this . . . ' Grace sighed. 'Listen, I'd better go, or I'll be late meeting the girls.'

'OK, off you go and remember I'm always here for you, you know. Whatever happens.'

Grace ended the call with a wry smile. Losing Myles was the worst thing that could have possibly happened to her. At least from now on the only way was up. She put on her lipstick, jacket and scarf and after locking up, she left the house and headed to the beach via her private path. She was calling her solicitor on the way. The sooner she let Roger Mathers know her position, the sooner she could put the whole will business behind her.

Chapter Nine

'I'm sure you've given yourself the lucky bucket, Robyn,' said Grace, giving Robyn a nudge. 'I haven't found a single piece yet.'

Robyn laughed, she was enjoying collecting sea glass with Katie and Grace much more than she'd imagined. Life had become so serious since her surgery; doing something frivolous made a very welcome change. Being with new people was refreshing too.

'Ah yes, fortune favours the blue, clearly,' she replied. 'Here, swap with me, I'll even throw in my sea glass.'

The three women had met at the bottom of Grace's private beach path. The first couple of minutes' conversation had been a bit stilted; after all, the women were still more or less strangers, but Grace had made a joke about deciding to put clothes on for their second meeting, which broke the ice, and after that they had soon fallen into a gentle banter.

'No thanks,' said Grace, 'I'll keep the yellow, seeing as it matches my bruises so well.'

She lifted up the hem of her maxi dress and showed them her ankle.

'Ouch,' said Katie. 'Does it hurt?'

'A bit,' she replied, 'but it's healed a lot faster than I expected, and the doctor said I could walk on it as long as I'm careful not to twist it.'

Robyn winced in sympathy and dropped a piece of bright blue glass into Grace's bucket. 'Here you go. To start you off.'

'Once you find one piece, it gets easier,' said Katie. 'You just need to get your eye in. Look at this beauty.'

She waved a chunk of turquoise glass in front of Grace's face before dropping it in her own pink bucket.

'Nobody likes a show-off,' Grace tutted, good-naturedly.

Finn had been so up for Robyn's beach date with Katie and Grace that he'd bought three buckets for her to take along. It was a thoughtful gesture, but initially Robyn wondered if she'd look as if she was taking their casual meet-up too seriously. The other two had seemed keen to collect sea glass but perhaps it was just a euphemism for a chance to chat? A bit like book clubs, the main purpose of which appeared to be drinking wine and never even getting around to talking about the book. Then she'd given herself a stern talking to; she had become so worried about doing or saying the wrong thing over the last couple of years. Once upon a time she'd have been the one to make outrageous suggestions, not giving two hoots about what others thought of her. So, with a flash of her old self she decided to take them anyway. It was the right decision; the buckets had gone down a treat. She had a rucksack containing refreshments with her too, also provided by Finn. But she'd keep quiet about that for the moment, save it as a surprise for when they needed a break.

The smell of the sea, the gentle rush of the waves, the crunch of shingle beneath her feet were helping her to relax. She felt weightless and free from the worries that had kept her awake since Monday.

'Nope, still nothing.' Grace shook her bucket a few minutes later. Her one donated piece of glass rattled about inside it. 'I think you two must be pouncing on it before I get there.'

'Like now,' Robyn laughed, bending down as a flash of yellow glass caught her eye. She rubbed it clean with her fingers and held it up to the light. It was smooth and shiny and as bright as a sliver of sunshine. She wondered where it had come from and how it had ended up on their beach, waiting to be found. She presented the glass to Grace.

'For you. More yellow to add to your collection.'

'I shall treasure it,' said Grace. 'Which is more than can be said for the bruises.'

'Let's try along the tide line.' Katie pointed down the shingle beach towards the sea. 'That might be a good place.'

Grace hurried ahead, hobbling slightly and shouting behind her that she was getting there first this time. The sky was white with cloud today and the breeze felt damp and cold against Robyn's face. She pulled the collar up on her jacket and tucked her chin into her scarf. Beside her, Katie folded her arms across her chest and shivered.

Suddenly Grace punched the air with. 'YES! Got one! Woohoo!'

The other two raced over to join her.

Robyn gasped. 'Bloody hell! You've got a red piece; that's really rare.'

Grace looked pleased with herself. 'Worth waiting for then. There might be more where that came from.' She squatted down again. 'OK, you two, go and find your own rare patch.'

They both laughed as Grace waved Katie and Robyn away.

Grace was dressed top to toe in dark shades today. She looked stylish and carefully put together; her hair gleamed with health and her red lipstick looked dramatic, but the inky denim jacket, long black jersey dress and pale grey angora scarf drained the colour from her face. Robyn wondered if she'd always worn black or whether bereavement had affected her choices. She could see Grace looking gorgeous in bright jewel colours: ruby, emerald, sapphire. Colours to match the strong personality which Robyn glimpsed between moments of sadness.

Katie, Robyn noticed, favoured neutral shades: caramel, oatmeal and camel, which toned beautifully with her chestnut hair, ivory complexion and sprinkle of freckles. She was tall with long slim legs and her jumper was voluminous. Robyn's wardrobe had consisted of much more body-hugging garments when she was in her twenties. A pang of sadness ran through her, sending a shiver down her spine; those days seemed like a lifetime ago.

'What makes this beach good for finding sea glass anyway?' Katie asked as they wandered further along the tide line together. 'I've always wondered.'

'There was a bottle factory just along the coast at one time,' Robyn told her, pleased to move away from her thoughts. 'Long gone now, but apparently at the end of the shift on a Friday, all the leftover bits of glass were thrown in the sea. Over time the edges get smoothed and years later it gets washed up by the tide, like little gemstones. You don't get it everywhere. That's why this beach is special.'

'What do people do with it? Besides filling tall glass vases in my house.' Grace came over, tilting her bucket to display her precious collection.

Robyn shrugged. 'All sorts: arts and crafts, pictures, lots of jewellery.'

'Or you can just do what my auntie did and leave bags of it in every nook and cranny of the house. She said it was too beautiful to get rid of,' said Katie.

'And what will you do with it?' Grace asked.

'Exactly the same,' Katie laughed, tucking wisps of hair behind her ears. 'I can't part with her collection either.'

Robyn dipped her hand into the sea glass in her bucket and let it slip through her fingers. It had become very popular over the last few years and she'd noticed an increase in visitors to Sea Glass Beach. In fact, there was a woman on the other side of the bay, near Grace's steps, who must be a collector. She seemed very intent on what she was doing and worked very fast, discarding almost as many stones as she kept as if she was only after a certain size or colour.

It was so pretty; there much be something creative she could do with it. But what? There were gift shops galore all along the coast selling sea glass items. She was pretty sure that given a bit of time, she could make things to sell too. Maybe sea glass art could supplement her income while she looked for more illustration work? The idea made her heart beat a little faster. She'd have to start off small because she didn't have a marketing budget to attract customers and although the sea glass itself might be free, all the other pieces of equipment and supplies wouldn't be. Still, it was a thought, and it was the best one she'd had, so she'd mull it over and see what came to mind. Pleased with her positive thinking, she spent the next few minutes racking her brains to come up with possible sea glass projects.

Katie sighed so deeply that it dragged Robyn out of her daydream.

'Penny for them?' she asked.

'Just thinking how therapeutic this is,' said Katie, without looking up. She seemed to have hit a good patch and was adding new sea glass to her bucket every few seconds. 'Mooching along with the gentle swoosh of the waves in the background. It makes you forget all your worries for a while. This is just what I needed.'

'Me too,' Robyn agreed, taking a deep breath.

'Me three.' Grace put her hands on both their shoulders and gazed out at the water.

'I look at the horizon and imagine the sea wrapping itself around the world, touching other beaches just like this,' Robyn said. 'And it puts the size of my problems into perspective.'

Grace looked at her sharply. 'And I thought I was the only one with worries. Seems like we're all in the same boat.'

'Gosh, I'm sorry, Grace,' Katie said, chastened. 'You're so upbeat and cheerful, I forget that you're still grieving.'

'I'll still be grieving for Myles when I'm old and grey,' said Grace with a hint of a smile. 'He was the love of my life. Nothing will replace him in my heart. But life has to carry on, so my goal for the immediate future is to try and be as happy as I can be and not let grief dictate the agenda.'

'Wise words. I wish I'd met you years ago,' said Robyn, feeling a rush of warmth for Grace. 'My mum died of breast cancer when I was fourteen and it took a long time to deal with the loss.'

'Oh, love,' Grace's face softened. 'That must have been tough.'

'It was. I'm thirty-four and I still miss her. Every day.' Robyn swallowed.

It was something she rarely talked about. Friends who hadn't experienced a major loss didn't get it. Even Finn couldn't really grasp what it had been like for her growing up without her mum. It had been horrendous. Even now, twenty years on, her stomach churned just thinking about it. The memory of her mother's face, contorted in pain, not only because of the cancer, which had been detected long after it had taken hold of her body, but because of the guilt that her daughter would soon be motherless and alone. Robyn had done her best to persuade her mum that she'd be just fine, that she was almost grown up and there was no need to worry, and that she'd be happy moving in with her dad and his girlfriend, but both of them had known it wasn't true. The last few conversations they'd had mostly consisted of her mum apologising; it had been heart-breaking. The bond between the two of them had been severed just when she'd needed her mum most. The impact on Robyn was so all-consuming that she vowed she'd never have children for fear of it happening again. She couldn't imagine saying goodbye to a child, not knowing what would happen to them after she'd gone. Even falling in love with Finn hadn't changed her mind.

'The only person I've lost who was close to me was Auntie Jean.' Katie set her bucket down and wrapped her arms around herself. 'We knew how ill she was, so in theory, I'd been able to prepare myself, but even so it was still a shock when she died. But your husband, Grace, and your mum, Robyn . . . that's much harder to cope with.'

Grace's eyes looked misty. 'I don't know if I am coping a lot of the time. I think I'm only just coming out of shock.'

'How did he die?' Robyn asked softly. 'If you don't mind me asking?'

'A massive heart attack.' Grace shook her head as if she still couldn't believe it. 'He hadn't had so much as a twinge in his chest before and then one day, his heart just stopped. He was out cycling at the time. The irony was that he was fitter then than he'd been for years.'

'Why does life have to be so unfair?' Katie said sadly.

'Heaven knows.' Grace lifted her shoulders. 'My only comfort is that it all happened so quickly that he wouldn't have known much about it. He'd been looking forward to retirement so much but then he only got a few weeks to enjoy it. Now I'm on my own again for the first time in seventeen years and I really want to ask his advice about something, but I can't. So, you're right, Katie, life is unfair.'

'Can we help?' Robyn fished a tissue from her pocket and handed it to Grace. 'A problem shared is a problem halved.'

'Or thirded in our case,' Katie added.

Our case. Being part of something made Robyn feel warm inside. Katie was right; this really was therapeutic.

'I'd like that.' Grace sniffed and wiped her eyes. 'But on one condition: if I'm baring my soul, you two are doing the same.'

'That's blackmail,' Robyn smiled, already calculating what she was and wasn't prepared to divulge to the other two. She wasn't great at sharing her problems but maybe here, with semi-strangers, she'd find the courage to be as brave as Grace. 'Katie? I'm in if you are?'

Katie had gone pale. 'Um.'

'Deal or no deal?' Grace looked at them both.

'Deal,' said Robyn and Katie together.

'OK, but this is a circle of trust,' said Grace. 'Nothing we say here gets repeated to anyone. Agreed?'

Grace put out her hand and the other two covered her hand with theirs.

'Agreed,' they chorused.

Robyn felt a bit like one of the three musketeers pledging allegiance to the other two and a fizz of anticipation bubbled up inside her; this was the start of something special, she could feel it in her bones.

Chapter Ten

The three women stared at each other, the sea air blowing around them. Katie held her breath, hoping they didn't ask her to go first. But Grace broke the silence. 'Shall I start?'

Katie nodded in relief. Her heart was thumping. She'd been on edge ever since receiving the second envelope yesterday. She'd been flip-flopping about confiding in Robyn and Grace and wondering whether, if the opportunity arose, she'd actually be brave enough to speak up. It wasn't just about the actual envelopes; it was the fact that she'd have to relive the whole hideous backstory which had been consigned to the past. Once she told Grace and Robyn what had happened, it would be part of her present, there'd be no going back.

But then the two brown envelopes were already part of her present, whether she liked it or not. Blackmail. She shuddered. How much money would her blackmailers ask for and how much time would they give her to pay? It was all so seedy.

Last night, she'd even gone to the police station with the letters, but once she parked the car, she panicked, worried that whoever was behind it would somehow know what she was doing. So she'd driven off quickly and gone home, hands shaking and stomach in knots.

'I'm probably going to sound like a wicked stepmother but here goes,' Grace began.

'A circle of trust,' Katie reminded her, hoping they all stuck to it. The thought of everyone in town knowing her sordid story made her feel faint. 'And absolutely no judgement.'

'Shall we walk?' Robyn suggested.

They headed along the tide line slowly, swinging their buckets, sea glass forgotten for the moment.

'Myles's grown-up children are contesting his will because they think they've been hard done by.' Grace pulled a face. 'It's really upset me. It's not the money that bothers me, it's the implication that I've cheated them out of what's theirs. Myles left them each a quarter of his estate, which is an awful lot of money for two people in their twenties.'

'Wow,' said Robyn, shaking her head. 'They sound nice.'

Grace smiled weakly. 'We always got on reasonably well, at least I thought we had. Now they've left our WhatsApp group chat and it feels like I'm losing even more of my old life.'

Katie's heart ached for Grace. She knew how that felt. It had started with her best friend Rose turning her back on her; pretty soon her other friends had dwindled away too.

Their shoes crunched along the shingle and pebbles as Grace filled them in on the background. About how exhausting the last few months had been, coming to terms with her sudden bereavement at the same time as wrapping up Myles's financial and legal affairs. How she'd hoped her time in Merle Bay would be a chance to mourn him and have a complete rest. She'd wanted to escape the demands from HMRC, the accountant, her solicitor and Myles's children. But the saga seemed to have followed her regardless.

'How upsetting for you,' Katie frowned and slipped an arm through Grace's. 'That's the last thing you need when you're feeling low.'

Fighting over money after someone had died seemed so grubby, thought Katie. After Auntie Jean had died, she'd been shocked to discover she was the sole beneficiary of Auntie Jean's estate, inheriting both the shop and the house. She'd felt guilty and unworthy. Her aunt didn't have any close family, but she and Katie's father did have distant cousins. She shuddered, imagining how awful it would have been if any of them had challenged her inheritance.

'You and Myles don't have children?' Robyn asked, one dark eyebrow raised.

Grace shook her head. 'Never wanted them. I was a swishy-haired, sharp-dressed businesswoman when I met him. A career woman all the way, certain that motherhood wasn't for me. Don't get me wrong, I do like kids, my sister's two are little darlings. Myles was divorced with two teenagers and happy not to go back to the baby days. He'd have probably agreed to more if I'd wanted to; he was a big softie and a great dad.' She smiled wistfully. 'It was one of the things which made our relationship so different to the ones I'd had before. You wouldn't believe how many men thought I was weird because I wasn't maternal.'

'Oh, I *would*,' said Robyn, with feeling. 'Actually, sometimes women are the worst for it. It's my body, my decision.' She paused and an expression Katie couldn't decipher crossed her face before she added quietly. 'And Finn's, of course.'

Grace chuckled under her breath. 'Very true.'

'I'm the opposite, I *would* like a family one day,' said Katie. 'But I can still sympathise; I get people making supposedly jokey comments about hurrying up and settling down before I miss the boat. As if I'm deliberately dragging my heels! I try and laugh it off, but it hurts because I worry it'll never happen for me.'

'Oh love, you're only a whippersnapper,' Grace exclaimed. 'Why do you think it won't happen?'

'Plus, you're stunning,' added Robyn sweetly.

Why? Because she always held back from giving a man one hundred per cent, because as soon as she felt herself getting close to someone she started to withdraw, because even when he promised she could trust him, that he was falling for her, deep down she doubted he was telling the truth.

'You're too kind.' Katie flushed. She tried to get the words out that seemed to be lodged in her throat. 'But I suppose I . . . actually, Grace, it's still your turn.'

Grace looked at her and Robyn for a second and then started to laugh. 'God, we're a right load of sad sacks, aren't we? We'll be breaking out the gin soon, to drown our sorrows.'

Katie blinked for a moment and let out a giggle and then Robyn joined in, and even though everyone seemed to have issues galore and Katie hadn't even told anyone what was bothering her, she already felt a little bit better.

Spending time on the beach in the fresh air with these two new friends was infinitely preferable to sitting at home worrying about what was going to arrive in the post next. Having fun like this, their laughter getting carried away on the wind, was exhilarating; it felt like a safe place where she might just be able to say what was on her mind.

'I haven't laughed like that since . . . actually since we were on your terrace on Monday,' Katie panted, pressing a hand to the stitch in her side. 'And I know what you mean about a drink. It's at moments like this I wish this beach had a little coffee kiosk.'

'Or a bar.' Grace quirked an eyebrow. 'We could all go to mine and have whatever we like.'

'No need to go anywhere.' Robyn scrambled to take off her rucksack. 'I can't do gin, but I can do coffee.'

'Perfect!' Grace rubbed her hands together. 'I've been wondering what you'd got in that big bag.'

Robyn pulled out a rug and handed it to Katie. 'If you wouldn't mind putting this down, refreshments will be served in a jiffy, courtesy of my husband.'

They chose a sheltered spot against the rocks and once Katie had spread out the rug, Grace flopped down on it, groaning about her ankle. Robyn set out a large flask of coffee, a smaller one of hot milk, three mugs and a container of freshly made cookies.

'This is much better than booze,' said Grace, hugging her mug to her. 'Thanks, Robyn.'

'Thanks to Finn really,' said Robyn proudly, tugging the lid off the cookies. 'Help yourselves.'

'Anyone watching us will think we're bonkers having a beach picnic in April,' said Katie with a giggle as the wind whipped her hair around her face.

'Nah,' said Grace with a grin, taking a mug from Robyn. 'All the best sea glass hunters do it. OK. So back to the *will* situation. On the way down to meet you, I quickly called my solicitor and told him to write back to them and say that I wasn't prepared to negotiate with Austin and Olivia and that if they wanted to pursue the matter in court, that was up to them. But I'm already having doubts and it doesn't help that my sister, Zoe, thinks I should just pay them off so that we can all move on.'

'I think you've done the right thing. Why should you be bullied by your stepchildren?' said Katie hotly. 'And why do people feel the need to money-grab? Is money so important that we'll ruin other people's lives for it?'

'Money is quite important when you don't have any,' Robyn said.

'Of course it is. Sorry, I got carried away there.' Katie sipped her coffee as an awful thought struck her: money could be an issue for her too. So far she'd been dealing with the shock of the photos turning up after ten years; she hadn't got as far as planning what she was going to do if, *or when*, she received a demand for money. She was lucky enough to own the shop and her house; Auntie Jean had paid off the mortgage years ago, but in terms of money in the bank, she didn't have much she could easily get her hands on. Perhaps she could secure a loan against her assets? Was that a thing? She'd never needed to borrow money before; it was all new territory.

Grace swallowed a mouthful of chocolate chip cookie. 'Don't apologise, I wanted an honest opinion and I got one. What do you think, Robyn?'

Robyn had tipped her sea glass onto the edge of the blanket and was sorting it into piles of different colours. 'I wonder whether sitting down face to face for a chat with the two of them might be better than communicating via solicitor?' she said. 'I don't know about you but anything in writing automatically puts me on edge and I always expect the worst.'

'Me too,' Katie muttered, thinking about those manila envelopes.

Grace looked thoughtful. 'I know what you mean, Robyn; my heart sinks at the sight of official letters, but in this instance, I don't think it would work. The other two have appointed a solicitor which makes me feel that we're beyond the talking stage.'

'When I'm not sure what to do, I ask myself what Mum's advice would be,' said Robyn. 'So, as this is Myles's estate, what do you think he would do?'

'That's a great idea,' said Katie, wondering whose advice she would use to help solve her own dilemma. Auntie Jean, probably. Although speaking to these two might be a bit more practical.

'He wouldn't want me to have to go through a court case, but on the other hand, he'd be furious with them for putting me in this position.' Grace's jaw was tense. 'And he'd probably try and retract every bloody penny they've received.'

'Then I think you have your answer,' said Katie.

Grace groaned. 'Bugger. Court case it is then. So much for a quiet life.'

'Myles sounds like a lovely man,' said Robyn, topping everyone's coffee up and handing round the cookies again. 'Shame on them for sullying his memory.'

'He was the best husband I could have asked for,' Grace said, her gaze softening. 'I was very lucky. I think we only had one real rough patch in our entire relationship.'

'My parents are the same,' Katie said fondly. Josie and Brian bickered constantly, but there was always a thread of humour running through it. The only time she remembered them arguing was about her. Her dad didn't want her to give up on her education and wanted her to go back to sixth form, but her mum had backed Katie one hundred per cent.

'What caused the rough patch?' Robyn asked, leaning towards Grace.

Grace sighed. 'Stupid really and I regret it now. It was over Christmas, the one before last, our final one together as it turned out. He'd gone to the doctor worried about a pain when he peed. The first lot of tests results weren't conclusive, and he had to go for more. He came back from the appointment convinced he'd got prostate cancer. So, what did he do? He googled it. Which made him worry even more. Whatever I said made it worse and, in the end, he refused to talk to me about it. I felt completely useless. At a time when we should have been close, I'd never felt further apart from him. Worst Christmas ever.'

Katie sympathised. 'Maybe he thought he was protecting you by not sharing what was on his mind? But that never works because the people who love you most will worry anyway.'

That was precisely what Katie had done. She'd bottled up her fears, letting them eat away inside her, convinced that no one knew what was going on inside her head. When in actual fact, her parents had been full of concern for her. She knew that now.

'That's what I thought,' said Grace. 'So, I suggested he went to see my sister. Zoe is a nurse on a men's hospital ward and there aren't many ailments she hasn't had to deal with. I knew she'd talk sense and calm him down. I think it worked because when he came back he apologised for shutting me out and was really affectionate again. A few weeks later, he got the results back and he didn't have cancer, thank heavens.'

'So, the threat of cancer was the root of the problem between you,' said Robyn, hanging on every word.

Grace nodded. 'In a way I'm glad it happened; it was a wake-up call for us both. We were workaholics up until then. Myles wasn't getting any younger, so we decided to sell our business and enjoy life to the full, do some travelling, see the world. Not that we got to do much of that in the end. Although we found a buyer quite quickly, the sale was only finalised at the end of summer. We got as far as planning our trip but then he died in November.'

Katie gripped Grace's hand and gave it a squeeze. 'I'm so sorry, Grace, life can be very unfair and cruel. But it was a good idea of yours to send Myles to see your sister. They obviously got on well.'

Grace nodded. 'They adored each other. He was the big brother she'd never had. Myles was an only child, so Zoe was the closest he'd had to a sibling. I was a bit jealous actually that he'd opened up to her and not me.'

'Sometimes it's easier to speak to someone who's not as emotionally involved,' said Robyn. 'I guess that's why talking to you both feels so much easier than talking to Finn.'

'In that case, lady,' Grace replied, 'it's probably time I shut up and let someone else get a word in. Who wants to spill their beans next?'

'Katie?' said Robyn hurriedly. 'Mine can wait.'

'Right.' Panic flooded Katie suddenly; this was her moment.

'You're among friends remember,' Grace said encouragingly, catching Katie just as she was checking her watch.

'Thanks,' said Katie, her throat dry with nerves. 'And this is definitely a circle of trust?'

The other two nodded solemnly. Katie's heart thundered against her ribs. Could she finally let someone in?

Chapter Eleven

'OK, here goes.' Katie's fingers fiddled with the edge of the blanket anxiously. 'When I was eighteen, I did such a stupid thing that even now, ten years later, it still makes me feel sick.'

'We all make mistakes.' Grace's voice was encouraging as she stretched her legs out in front of her to make herself more comfortable. 'It's what makes us human.'

'And whatever it is, we want to help, not judge,' Robyn said. 'Look.'

She had made a circle of sea glass on the shingle beside the rug in shades of blues and greens. She placed three larger pieces in the centre. 'Here's us in our circle of trust. When my best friend became my sister-in-law, I lost the person who could keep my secrets to herself. Whatever you tell me, I promise, it won't go any further.'

Katie summoned up a smile; they were so kind, so well-meaning and it sounded like Robyn was just as in need of someone to confide in as she was. Even so, it was very difficult to break the habit of a lifetime and open up.

'Same here.' Grace crossed one arm over her chest. 'Scouts honour.'

Katie couldn't help laughing; she was pretty sure that wasn't how scouts made their promises.

'It messed my life up in lots of ways, but I've done my best to move on. Then a few days ago, the whole thing reared its ugly head again.' She pulled the folded photographs and the notes out of her bag and spread them on the rug. 'I got sent this lot through the post. I think I've got a blackmailer.'

'What?' Both gasping in disbelief, Grace and Robyn picked up the photographs and read the notes.

Katie held her breath, watching the shock on their faces as they realised the naked girl in the pictures was none other than Katie Small, owner of a little underwear shop by the sea. Her stomach churned; how differently her life would have turned out without those pictures.

At school, she'd been brave and confident, not afraid to share her opinion, the girl on the debating team who never minded having to defend the juiciest, most controversial position.

You'd make a great barrister, her dad had muttered once, after tackling her on the state of her bedroom, only to find himself backing away, hands raised and full of apology after she'd lambasted him with her arguments. And Katie had liked that idea: a career spent building a convincing case to defend the innocent sounded just up her street. Her parents couldn't have been prouder.

'Our Catherine is head girl at the grammar school,' Mum and Dad would preen to their friends in the pub.

'Catherine's got a place at one of the top universities. To read law,' they'd tell colleagues in the textiles factory where they'd both worked since they were sixteen. Mum as a head machinist and Dad warehouse manager.

Josie and Brian Small had put their only child on a pedestal, which made her fall from grace that much further and more painful for all of them. She frowned at that; she was being unfair. Her parents' love and support had never faltered. It was Katie who had struggled to cope with the aftermath; all they'd wanted was for her to be happy. And she had been, mostly, right up until the first envelope had arrived.

'Bloody hell,' Robyn whistled under her breath. 'You've been dealing with this sort of crap all on your own?'

Katie nodded glumly. 'I'm so ashamed. I was duped into doing that shoot. I was very naïve back then, a complete swot at school. I'd never even had a serious boyfriend. I went from Miss Goody Two Shoes to Miss Glamour Model in the space of a couple of hours. Ever since then, the thought that I'd be labelled as something I'm not has haunted me.'

'You shouldn't feel ashamed, you were only a kid,' Grace said, all trace of humour drained from her face. 'Anyone can see you aren't complicit in these photos. The shame lies with the photographer. And whichever low-life scumbag sent you these notes.'

Robyn was holding the naked photograph. 'I never looked that beautiful, even before . . . I'm staring, I'm sorry, Katie, here.' Her voice cracked and she handed the picture back.

Katie hugged her knees up to her chest. Even though Robyn was looking at her photograph and not her actual body, she felt exposed. Ten years on and she still had flashbacks to that day.

'So, what happened?' Grace asked kindly. 'Can you tell us?'

Katie sipped her coffee. 'I think so. Because I'm going to need help dealing with what comes next.'

She cast her mind back to where it had all began and for the first time in her life told the whole story . . .

★

'Am I ugly?' Catherine Small peered at the tarnished mirror in the girls' changing rooms and inspected her nose for blackheads. She sort of hoped she'd got a decent one to squeeze, but she couldn't see anything.

'Are you for real?' Her best friend, Rose Dunbar, looked at her like she was a weirdo. She ticked off a list of attributes on her fingers. 'Symmetrical heart-shaped face, smouldering green eyes, cute nose *including* freckles. Those are the world's most popular facial features. Scientifically proven fact. And you got 'em baby. You're lucky I don't hate you.'

'You plonker.' Catherine grinned at Rose, who she thought was much prettier. Perfect height, unlike Catherine who had to bend one knee at parties, so she didn't tower over ninety per cent of the boys. Perfect-sized boobs, i.e. she could get away without wearing a bra if she wanted to. If Catherine tried that, it looked like she was smuggling boisterous puppies inside her top. Glossy auburn hair that she never even had to straighten, it just hung down. Catherine's was wayward and wavy. And then there was that other special something which Catherine lacked, and Rose oozed without even realising it: sex appeal. Rose was sexy and she was . . . she sighed at her reflection; she was girl-next-door wholesome. 'Why haven't I got a boyfriend then?'

'Ah, interesting question.' Rose pushed her to one side and applied her plump-it-up lip gloss with one swift stroke. 'But as you are head girl, teacher's pet, an effortless grade-A student, with legs longer than one of Mr Channing's lectures on using your phone in school, I think it's karma.'

Catherine groaned. 'I'm going to end up going to uni without even, um, you know . . . and that will be so embarrassing.'

'But you'll definitely be going to uni,' said Rose sagely. They both picked up their bags and headed back out to the corridor. 'Whereas I'll probably blow my chances wasting too much time doing, *um, you know . . .* '

Both girls were giggling as they left the changing rooms.

Later that week, Catherine stopped off in the city centre on her way home from sixth form. Rose's eighteenth birthday was coming up, and she had decided to get her a silver necklace with her star sign on it.

Weird to think she'd be leaving Nottingham in a few months, she thought as she headed towards the jewellery shop. If she got the grades she needed, she'd be living in Newcastle from September. Moving out of the house she'd grown up in. She'd be closer to her beloved Auntie Jean in Merle Bay than to Mum and Dad. Catherine's stomach fizzed; she was excited and nervous and worried all at once.

The University of Newcastle was posh. It didn't bother her so much, but when they'd gone up for a visit, she could tell her mum and dad were a bit overwhelmed. Mum wouldn't speak above a whisper and her dad kept pulling at his collar.

'This is where you'll all graduate,' said the student tour guide, as he took them into a magnificent wood-panelled hall. 'Not that you have to worry about that yet.'

Mum had squeezed her arm. 'Is that when you wear a cape and one of those flat hats?'

Catherine had giggled. 'A mortarboard and gown? Yes. But I've got my A levels to pass first, I might not even get to university.'

'Course you will. You'll pass without breaking a sweat.' Dad gave her a wink. 'The halls of residence are smart, aren't they? Perhaps we should all move in.'

'At that price per week?' Mum had pursed her lips. 'It's more than our mortgage.'

Dad had chuntered under his breath about tightening belts for the next three years and Catherine had vowed to get a job so that she wouldn't have to take a single penny more from them than she had to. A bar job, or a waitress maybe? Plus, she had five hundred pounds saved in the bank, she could use that in emergencies.

Now, heading to the jewellers, Catherine imagined how it would feel to be rich and be able to walk into any shop and buy anything she wanted. Maybe she could pretend, just for the day. Laughing at herself, she straightened her spine, put her shoulders back and with what she hoped was a mysterious smile, stalked down the pedestrianised street.

'Excuse me?' someone said, a hand on her arm stopping her in her tracks. It was a man around her dad's age, with glasses and a polite smile. He removed his hand and pulled an apologetic face. 'Sorry if I startled you.'

'No worries,' said Catherine, stepping back. 'Can I help you?'

'Actually, it might be the other way around.' He smiled, pushing his glasses higher up his nose. 'Have you ever done any modelling?'

'Me?' The question took her by surprise, and she laughed. 'No, never.'

His eyes flickered with interest. 'Really? I'm surprised you haven't been scouted by an agency already.'

'Er. No.' She looked at him dubiously, not sure whether he was serious or not.

'How old are you?'

She hesitated. She knew all about 'stranger danger' but had to admit she was flattered and in his neat shirt, jacket and jeans, he didn't look in the least bit threatening. Besides there was no harm in talking to him in a public place.

'Eighteen,' she replied.

'School, college, or are you working?' he asked, running his eyes from her head to the ground. As if he was assessing her height.

'Sixth form. I'm head girl. Going to uni in September if I get all As in my exams.' And then blushed for sounding like a show-off.

'Brains and beauty.' The man laughed and took out a business card from his wallet. 'Listen, I'm Howard. I'm setting up a new model agency and I'm looking for fresh faces. I can't promise fame and fortune, but if you fancy earning some extra cash this summer to keep you in Pot Noodles while you're a student, give me a call.'

A model? Her? Katie's heart started knocking against her chest. She skimmed the card, her eyes taking in the address: London. Had she really been scouted by an *actual* London modelling agency? Wait until she told Rose. Actually, she wouldn't tell her yet, just in case it was a hoax, she'd find out more first. Her mum always said that if something looked too good to be true, it probably was. And this was amazing.

'Yeah, thanks, I might,' she said, tapping the card against the palm of her hand nonchalantly.

'I think you'd be perfect for one of my clients.' His eyes narrowed thoughtfully. 'They're good payers so it would worth your while. We could do some test shots if you like, sound them out?'

'Really? Who is the client?' she said, instantly forgetting to be cool.

'Adidas. You've got more muscle tone than most of my girls.'

She didn't like the way he called the models 'my girls' but *Adidas* – wow – that was impressive. She was even wearing Adidas trainers now. 'I do do a lot of sport; I'm in the rowing team.'

'Good. Let's book you in. I'm very busy so don't waste my time.' He pulled a tatty diary out of his inside pocket and named a time and date. It was a school day but that didn't matter, she'd been forging her mum's signature on school forms for years, she could easily write a note and bunk off for the day. She'd tell her parents she was going to Rose's house for dinner straight from school. They wouldn't bat an eyelid.

'OK.' Catherine's heart raced with excitement. Nothing like this had ever happened to her before. She hadn't really planned on ringing him, but the chance to be in a photo-shoot for Adidas was too tempting. Plus having a major sports brand as a client meant Howard must be genuine.

'Oh, and no hangers-on.' He looked at her over his glasses. 'I want your full attention, you won't be able to do your best sexy, sultry poses if your mum or your boyfriend are there watching.'

'Got it.' She nodded.

Would Adidas want sexy and sultry? She frowned; she thought they were more into strong and athletic. Anyway, it was irrelevant; she had no intention of telling anyone else, let alone bringing them with her. Her mum probably wouldn't approve of doing something frivolous like this that might distract her from her schoolwork. And if she took Rose, there was a danger that Howard would prefer her instead. Rose did 'sexy and sultry' even when she was asking for custard on her Bakewell tart at lunchtime. No, this was going to be *her* adventure; a thrill ran down her spine. She was an adult now, opportunity didn't knock twice, she had to grab it while she had the chance.

The following week, she skived off school, used a scarily large amount of money to buy a ticket and boarded a train to London. She was terrified and couldn't quite believe how daring she was being. The most dangerous thing she'd done up until now was to get into bed without first turning off her electric blanket. She shivered with pleasure at the thought of telling Rose about it tomorrow; she'd be so gobsmacked. It might not come to anything, but imagine if it did! She might even earn enough money to pay for her university accommodation; her parents would be delighted.

The journey went without a hitch and she easily found the studios Howard had directed her to in Chalk Farm. She climbed the stairs to the top floor and emerged into a long, thin, windowless room. Howard was already there, thank goodness; so far, so good. He was facing the back of the room, fixing a camera to a tripod, dressed in baggy jeans and a fleece.

'Hello, Howard!' she said, in her most confident voice. 'I made it, I'm quite proud of myself. First time in London.'

'Hi.' He looked up and gave her a blank look. 'Name?'

'Catherine Small,' she replied, deflated. He hadn't even recognised her. Oh well, fair enough, he must meet hundreds of girls all the time, it was perfectly understandable that he didn't remember her face.

'Well, well, well, the head girl.'

'That's me!' she said, doing a jazz hands wave before realising how ridiculous she must look.

'Wasn't sure if you'd turn up.' He returned his attention to the camera. 'Go behind the screen, there's a form on the dressing table to put your details down on. Get yourself ready as quick as you can: hair, make-up, clothes off, gown on. I'm just waiting for Jay, my assistant, to come back with refreshments and we can get going.'

She vaguely registered the 'clothes off' instruction, but her stomach was making hollow rumbling noises and she was more interested in the word 'refreshments'. She hadn't eaten breakfast in case it made her stomach stick out in the photos and when she asked the price of a pot of fruit on the train she'd been horrified. Her mum's voice had popped up in her head saying *how much? I could buy a pound of apples for that!* So, she hadn't bothered.

She took a moment to study her surroundings. A wide roll of white paper hung on the back wall, spilling out onto the floor like a giant loo roll, big black metal lights either side like something you'd see on a film set. At the opposite end of the room was a small kitchenette and next to it a boxy little sofa and tucked into a corner was a fold-out screen, the sort you might get at the doctor's. It wasn't very glamorous, she thought, heading for the screen.

Once behind it, she sat down at the dressing table and took a few deep breaths, glad to be hidden from view for the time being. She found the form Howard had mentioned and filled it in, adding her bank details and home address before signing it. That was a good start, she reasoned, at least it looked as if she was going to get paid. Her reflection in the mirror was a bit of a shock; her hair had gone frizzy around her hairline and her skin was pink from the walk from the tube station. She put some make-up on, not really sure whether it was too much or not enough. She brushed her hair which made the frizz worse and she wondered whether she should put it in a ponytail. She poked her head back around the screen to ask Howard but before she could speak the door banged open and a second man walked in carrying a takeout tray of cups and a paper bag.

'Jay meet Catherine, Catherine meet Jay,' said Howard, pulling off his fleece and flinging it towards a holdall near the door.

'Hello,' she said, mustering up a smile.

She'd assumed Jay would be a young man but this one had receding hair, dirty jeans, a too-short T-shirt stretched over a flabby belly and a shirt over the top which had a rip in the elbow.

'Nice one, Howard,' Jay said without taking his eyes off her. He gave her a lazy smile and then put down the cups. 'Help yourself to coffee, Cath.'

'Thank you.' She opened her mouth to correct him: it was *Catherine*, she didn't like being called Cath, but thought better of it. He took out a Danish pastry from the bag and took an enormous bite, sending a cloud of icing sugar to the floor. He grinned at her and a ripple of unease ran through her; there was something wolf-like about him. This didn't seem like fun anymore. Howard wasn't too bad, but Jay gave her the creeps. It suddenly dawned on her that no one knew where she was. *She* didn't even know where she was, not really. She'd just followed directions.

Her heart began to thud. She was beginning to have serious doubts about this.

'Ready.' Howard nodded at Jay and then looked at Catherine, noticing she wasn't ready. 'Come on, love, chop-chop, clock is ticking. Behind the screen. Take everything off and stick the gown on.'

Her armpits prickled with perspiration. 'Everything? Why?'

Jay swore under his breath. 'We haven't got time for this. Do you want to be a model or not?'

Not, thought Catherine. Not if she had to take her clothes off. Her doubts were rapidly turning into certainty. She folded her arms across her chest and contemplated running for the door.

Howard must have sensed her reservations and came towards her smiling. 'Don't worry, princess, you don't have to do anything you're uncomfortable with.' He put a hand on her shoulders. 'I need to take some close-ups of your face and shoulders to send to Adidas, that's all. Bone structure is very important. We don't want any messy straps spoiling the pictures, that's all. And I've got some of their new sportswear to put you in afterwards and we don't want to see VPL, do we?'

She shook her head.

'Good girl.'

Catherine allowed herself to be led behind the screen by Howard. He disappeared discreetly while she stripped off. She couldn't believe she was doing this, taking her clothes off behind a flimsy screen with two strange men in the room. She could almost hear Rose's voice: *you did what? Are you for real?* She didn't dare contemplate what her parents would think.

The sooner this was over, the better. She'd never do this again; she felt a bit scared and vulnerable and lightheaded from not eating. It had better be worth it financially; she wondered when they'd talk about payment for today.

'Howard, there's no belt for this dressing gown,' she called, searching the floor in case it has slipped behind the dressing table.'

'It was there five minutes ago,' said Howard. 'Are you sure?'

'We pay for this studio by the hour,' Jay growled. 'The next girl will be here soon, so unless you want to miss your slot, I suggest you hold onto the bloody gown and get out here now.'

His tone frightened her, but she was determined not to show it. Everyone knew modelling was a tough profession, she reminded herself, you just had to get on with it.

'Coming.' With more confidence than she felt, she emerged from behind the screen, gripping the lapels of the cotton gown.

She stood on the spot indicated by Howard. As he adjusted the height of the tripod and tested the flash, Jay paced backwards and forwards impatiently, slurping at his coffee. Finally, Howard was ready. He told her to lower the gown so that her shoulders were bare and look directly into his lens, her eyes wide. She did as she was told and hoped the camera wouldn't pick up that her body was trembling with nerves. Howard began taking pictures, calling out instructions and murmuring words of encouragement. Jay stood out of the way near the door, lounging against the wall.

After a few minutes her breathing had slowed down a little; she wouldn't say she was relaxed, but this wasn't so bad after all. Her grip on her gown loosened. She couldn't wait to see the Adidas gear, she wondered if she'd get to keep any of it. That would be amazing, she thought, smiling to herself.

Howard released the camera from the tripod and stepped closer. 'You're doing really well. I knew I was right about you.'

'Really?' Her chest rose with pride.

He nodded. 'Now I want you to turn around, drop the robe right down and look back at me over your shoulder.'

'Right down?' She bit her lip, glancing at Jay who was looking right at her. 'Why would Adidas need to see me naked?'

Howard lifted the camera up to his face. 'They'll want to see your natural physique, lean shoulders and narrow waist.'

Out of the corner of her eye, she saw Jay moving closer to her.

'I'm not sure,' she began, nerves causing her skin to flush with goosebumps. She could feel her nipples through the thin fabric. 'I'm not comfortable with this.'

'It always feels a bit weird the first time, love, but try and relax; we're all professionals here,' said Howard. 'I've seen hundreds of naked bodies.'

'Yeah, nothing special about yours,' Jay sniggered.

Catherine steeled herself; she wished he'd just go away. 'Fine. Let's do it.'

She turned away from both men and gingerly lowered the gown until it reached the top of her bum. That should be enough to see her waist; it'd have to be, any further and she'd be naked.

'Jeez,' Jay hissed impatiently. 'Stop being so bloody coy, drop the damn thing.'

'I can't.' Her hands trembled as they gripped the edge of the gown.

'You can, Catherine,' Howard said reassuringly. 'There's nothing to it. Two minutes and I'll be done.'

'Oh God, oh God,' she whispered. She could feel Jay's eyes on her, and it made her feel sick. Tears pricked at her eyes – what had she got herself into? She'd been such an idiot to think she could be a model; she wasn't cut out for this sort of work. The best thing for it now was to do what they wanted and get out of here as fast as she could. Before she could change her mind, she dropped the gown to the floor.

'Good girl,' Howard murmured.

She'd had never been naked in front of a man before today and now here she was, baring all to two strangers.

She vowed never to tell another soul about this; she didn't even want the free gear anymore. All she could focus on was getting back in her clothes and getting out of here as fast as possible.

'Now twist to me and stare at the camera,' Howard demanded quietly. 'Big eyes.'

She turned and looked at him, conscious that her breast was on show, and her bum. She was so nervous that she couldn't peel her tongue from the roof of her mouth. Howard took shot after shot. Catherine remembered that he'd wanted sexy and sultry, but she was beyond that. She didn't feel in the least bit sexy. She felt stupid and cheap and completely humiliated.

'For Christ's sake, she looks terrified.' Jay whisked the gown from the floor. 'Let's have a bit of fun.'

'No!' Catherine shrieked in horror, trying desperately to cover herself with her arms. 'Give me that back.'

'Come and get it.' Jay dangled the gown just out of reach. She lunged for it and he stepped back laughing.

'That's not funny,' she cried. 'Howard, please?'

'That's more like it,' Howard started clicking the shutter again. 'Now there's fire in your eyes.'

'Stop taking pictures. Now! You're disgusting,' she cried. 'I'm not doing this anymore.'

'I'm not doing this anymore,' said Jay, mimicking her voice.

'Adidas won't want pictures like this.' She tried to grab the gown once more but missed. And still Howard kept snapping away.

'*Adidas*,' Jay sniggered, throwing the robe at her. 'Good one, Howard. Bloody Adidas.'

She saw a look pass between them as she caught it and she realised what Jay meant: Howard had lied to her. He wasn't working for Adidas at all. He must have said that to lure her in. Clutching the robe to her, she ran back behind the screen and pulled on her underwear, her heart racing and her entire body trembling with frustration. She didn't know what their game was, but it was obviously some sort of scam and she just wanted to get out of there. She could hear the two men talking in low voices. She didn't care what they said, or what they did, as long as they left her alone. What an idiot she'd been and what a dangerous thing she'd done. All for the promise of money.

Once she was dressed she grabbed her bag and sprinted across the studio.

'I'll send you a selection of prints for your portfolio,' Howard called as she reached the door.

'Don't bother,' she replied curtly, trying not to let the fear show in her voice. 'I never want to see you again. Or your photos.'

She slammed the door on their mocking laughter and flew down the stairs, her legs weak beneath her. The journey back to Nottingham was a blur of tears and recrimination; she was furious with herself for being sucked in but relieved to have got away without them laying a finger on her. She didn't know enough about the world of modelling to work out what Howard and Jay were up to; she was ready to put the whole episode behind her, just glad that the ordeal was over.

Except that it wasn't over.

She couldn't get it out of her head: the danger she'd put herself in, the shame of allowing herself to get involved in the first place, and her own stupidity for disappearing off to London without telling a soul. She'd escaped with her dignity in tatters, but at least she hadn't been physically harmed, that would have been impossible to keep to herself.

In the days that followed she couldn't sleep or eat. She couldn't face food and when she did eat, she couldn't keep it down. She was tired all the time because she couldn't sleep at night. She couldn't concentrate in lessons and her teachers were beginning to notice. She shut herself in her room when she was at home, claiming she had work to do. Her parents were worried, constantly asking if anything was wrong, was it something at school, had she fallen out with Rose?

After a couple of days of this, she was able to tell her mum that she and Rose had had a disagreement, because it was true. Her best friend had guessed immediately that Catherine was keeping secrets from her and when she tried to deny it, Rose had taken it as a personal snub and told her she was pathetic. Since then, she'd given Catherine the cold shoulder, either shooting her daggers across the sixth-form common room or ignoring her completely. Catherine regretted not confiding in her straightaway, but it was too late now; the longer it went on, the further the girls drifted away from each other.

Two weeks after the photoshoot, three hundred pounds disappeared from her savings account. Her heart nearly thumped out of her chest when she noticed. The description next to the transaction read 'portfolio photoshoot'. She came out in a cold sweat. All that money gone. The money she'd planned to use at university. Trembling with fear, she racked her brains, trying to remember if Howard had mentioned anything about charging her a fee. She was sure he hadn't; if he had, she'd never have agreed to it. He must have tricked her by getting her to fill in and sign that piece of paper, could it have been a direct debit form? How naïve she had been. She was furious with herself, and now instead of earning extra money to help with her studies, her emergency fund had dwindled to less than half.

All she could do now was pray that it was a one-off fee. She'd have to contact the bank without her parents finding out and make sure he couldn't access her account again. Then she remembered the photographs: if Howard was charging her for them, was there a possibility that he would post them to her? The thought of her parents seeing those pictures of her made her feel sick.

She plucked up courage to call the number on his business card and was relieved when it went to voicemail. Leaving as strident a message as she could, she made it clear that she didn't want any copies of the photographs under any circumstances and he was not to contact her again.

But it was too late.

A large envelope arrived the following day just as she was about to leave for school. The one saving grace was that she managed to intercept the post before either of her parents got to it. She shoved the envelope into her school bag and left the house.

She waited until she was locked into a cubicle in the girls' toilets at school before opening it. Dread made her stomach lurch as she pulled a stack of prints from the envelope. Howard had cherry-picked the sleaziest pictures of her. She could hardly bear to look at herself. The fear on her face was harder to stomach than the sight of her naked body. And to think that two strange men had been leering at her. Hot acid rose inside her throat. She staggered to her feet and lifted the toilet seat just in time to be sick. Afterwards, she sat back on her heels, feeling dizzy and weak. She wiped her mouth and stared at the photographs she'd dropped on the tiled floor; there must have been about ten of them. At that moment she hated her life and she hated herself. She wanted to die. Her vision began to cloud, and she couldn't breathe, then everything went black.

When she came round, the toilet door was open, and the cubicle was full of noisy people. Catherine felt groggy and weird as if she'd taken drugs. Everything sounded muffled. Eventually she recognised Rose; with her was her form teacher and the school nurse. Someone was calling her name, someone else wiped her face and then she felt hands under her arms pulling her up. The photographs were collected and slid back into the envelope.

'Bloody idiot,' Rose hissed, shoving one of the nude photos in her face. 'Why didn't you say something? We're supposed to be friends. I knew something was going on. And now I know. You shut me out and you lied to me. Thanks a lot.'

'Too ashamed,' Catherine mumbled. 'It was a mistake. Sorry.'

'Yeah,' Rose muttered. 'Whatever.'

Her parents arrived at school within the hour and drove her home in silence. Dad in the front and Mum in the back, holding her hand and stroking her hair off her face. Once she was home, she produced the envelope and told them the whole story. She thought Dad was going to have a coronary, his face had gone so purple. He snatched up the business card Howard had given her, and tried calling the phone number on it, but the number was unobtainable. For several days the ordeal continued. A search on the internet drew a blank so as soon as Dad could book a day off work, he retraced his daughter's steps to Chalk Farm. The studio Catherine had been in was being used for a photoshoot by a jewellery brand and the photographer, who'd never heard of a man called Howard, didn't appreciate Brian Small's attitude. Security was called and Dad was removed from the building. Her mum begged her to let them go to the police, but Catherine refused.

'I just want to put it behind me.'

Her parents, frantic and worried sick about their pale, lifeless daughter, hadn't dared to go against her wishes and so the matter had simply festered, making everyone miserable.

Catherine couldn't face going back to school. Rose didn't get in touch and that broke her heart. Josie offered to go and see Rose's mum about it, but Catherine refused to let her help. Tom from her English class called in one afternoon with a box of Maltesers and confirmed the worst: everyone knew what had happened to her. That was the final humiliation. She pulled out of her A-levels, even though it meant giving up on her university dream. Worried for her mental health, Josie took her daughter to the doctors where antidepressants were prescribed. It took weeks before Catherine began to take an interest in life outside of her own room, by which time school was over, and her so-called friends had moved on. Josie and Brian were at their wits' end until Auntie Jean phoned one weekend. She had a vacancy in her shop and wondered if Catherine would like a job for the summer.

It was the lifeline she needed. Katie grabbed it with both hands.

Chapter Twelve

Katie was nearly at the end of her story and the other two women had barely moved a muscle while she spoke, other than to nod their encouragement. She was surprised at the relief she felt at having confided in them.

'Within days, I had moved into Auntie Jean's cottage, started my new career as a lingerie sales assistant and shortened my name to Katie. I wanted everything about my life to change, including my name. What I'd been through dented my self-esteem and my confidence so much that there was no way I could even contemplate going away to university. The photoshoot was never mentioned again. Until now.'

'Bloody hell, chick.' Grace's face was full of sympathy. 'What a shit show.'

'I wonder why they've decided to dig it all up again now?' Robyn frowned.

'Heaven only knows,' Katie shrugged. 'But whoever has the photos knows where I am and wants me to pay up to make it all go away. It must be either Howard or Jay.'

'It's blackmail,' Robyn said grimly. 'And after all you went through at the time. It's not fair. You poor girl.'

'And for what it's worth, if someone had offered me the chance to be a model when I was your age, I'd have done the same as you,' said Grace. 'So sad that it had such repercussions for your studies. But good on you for making a go of it in Merle Bay. Running a business at your age is no mean feat, I think you should be proud of yourself.'

'Thanks.' Katie smiled but her heart wasn't in it. 'But I don't feel proud, I feel scared that they'll go to the *Gazette*. I've met the new editor, he's really nice. What if he prints the pictures and everyone in Merle Bay sees me naked? I'll be a laughing stock.'

'We'll have to make sure that doesn't happen,' Robyn said fiercely.

Grace leaned forward to squeeze Katie's hand. 'But if it did, no one would laugh. Everyone can see the fear on your face in those images, people will be on your side. And as for your body . . . ' She whistled. 'What a figure.'

Katie resisted the urge to cover her ears. She didn't want her body to be the subject of public opinion, good or bad. 'That's not how I want people to see me,' she said. 'I'm not the expert my aunt was yet, but I've worked hard to be professional in my career. I like to think that when women leave Auntie Small's they take some body confidence with them and feel a bit more able to face what life throws at them. My clients confide in me about everything, from breast cancer to the baby blues. I'm worried that once they've seen these pictures, they'll never be able to trust me again and my reputation as a businesswoman will be ruined.'

'It may have the opposite effect,' said Robyn. 'Maybe once they know the truth, they'll be inspired by how you made a success of your life?'

Katie shook her head slowly. 'The shop is doing well, but my private life is hardly a success story. I thought I'd make a name for myself in the British legal system. Instead, I've hidden myself away and kept a low profile. I'm so paranoid about my privacy that I don't use social media and when Auntie Jean suggested that after she passed away I might like to change the name of the shop, I couldn't even bring myself to do that. And then there's relationships. I look at my parents, happily married all these years, and you two both talk about your husbands with such love. I want that too, but don't seem able to trust anyone enough.'

'You trusted us enough to tell us that story,' said Grace. 'Give yourself some credit for that. It must have been hard.'

'I agree,' Robyn said earnestly. 'Whoever is behind this is malicious, and blackmail is a crime.'

Katie shuddered, then she felt arms around her holding her tight and Grace's hand rubbing her back.

'Group hug,' said Grace, pulling Robyn into the circle.

Relief washed over Katie. Maybe she wasn't so alone after all. Maybe sharing the problem *would* help to solve it.

'Thank you,' Katie mumbled into Grace's shoulder. 'Thank you for listening.'

'Any idea what you're going to do about it?' asked Robyn, the first to edge out of the hug.

'I know what I'd like to do,' said Grace, punching a fist into her other hand.

'Feel free,' Katie grinned. 'I'm glad you're on my side.'

'I know it says not to go to the police,' said Robyn, raising her eyebrows. 'But I think I would.'

Katie nodded. 'Every brain cell is screaming at me that that is precisely what I should do; it's just the risk of them finding out and sending the pictures to the press. Perhaps I should wait one more day and see what the post brings tomorrow.'

The suspense was awful; Katie half wished the sender would hurry up and get to the point. At least then she'd know what she was dealing with.

'If you get another envelope, how about waiting until you're with us to open it?' Robyn suggested. 'Then you wouldn't have to face it on your own.'

'That would be great.' Katie felt a surge of emotion and her eyes pricked with tears. 'I'd like that. I can't tell you how much better I feel just for saying the words out loud.'

It was true, she realised. Simply knowing that there were two others she could confide in eased the pressure in her head ever so slightly.

'I approve of that idea,' said Grace. 'Because it gives us an excuse to get together again. I was getting a bit lonely in that big house by myself.'

She circled her ankle round to get it moving again before brushing the crumbs from her lap and gingerly getting to her feet. Robyn began packing her things back into her rucksack. Katie shook the shingle from the rug and folded it up.

'Wait,' said Katie, 'We can't go yet. We haven't heard what's bothering Robyn.'

Robyn went pink and shook her head. 'It can wait. Honestly. And anyway, mine feels trivial compared to what you two are going through.'

'Nice try,' said Grace, picking up her bucket of sea glass. 'You can walk me back to the steps and talk on the way.'

Robyn said nothing but Katie didn't miss the nervous look on her face.

'You don't have to tell us if you don't want to,' she said, shaking the drips from her coffee mug and handing it to Robyn. 'But it has made me feel better, so hopefully it'll work for you too. By the way, please thank Finn for the coffee.'

'I will.' Robyn hoisted her rucksack onto her shoulders.

'And tell him he makes excellent cookies,' said Grace, producing a lipstick from her pocket and applying it perfectly. Katie was impressed – how did she do that without a mirror?

'My husband is an all-round good guy,' said Robyn, with a lopsided smile as they began their walk back along the beach towards Sea Glass House.

'That's nice to hear,' said Grace. 'So many of my mates are divorced and vow never to go down that road again. Sometimes I think that mine and Myles's marriage was the only one to work.'

'Well, ours has always worked, but lately—' Robyn paused, cocking her head to one side. 'Is that someone's mobile ringing?'

'Yes, mine!' said Grace, pulling it from her denim jacket. She frowned, reading the screen before answering it. 'Weird. It's Julia, Myles's ex-wife. Hello?'

'Shall we go and leave you to it?' Katie whispered but Grace shook her head.

'Julia, I'm confused,' Grace said curtly after listening to the other woman speak. 'I thought it was Austin and Olivia contesting the will, not you?'

Another pause while presumably Julia replied. Katie and Robyn exchanged awkward looks.

'I'm not being difficult.' Grace's voice was smooth, but she was clearly rattled. 'And to be honest, your attitude is very disrespectful. Just because your relationship with Myles ended in divorce, it doesn't mean he wasn't blissfully happy married to me.'

Julia said something else and Grace gasped.

'Unbelievable.' Grace covered the mouthpiece, her jaw set. 'She just said that I'm living in cloud cuckoo land if I think my marriage was perfect. I'm putting it on loudspeaker so you two can hear her too.'

Julia sounded awful, thought Katie. What sort of person would say that to someone who'd recently lost the man she loved?

'Calm down, Grace,' said a woman in a patronising drawl. 'I'm trying to do you a favour, give you a chance to do the right thing. Obviously the children don't want to go to court, but if you refuse to reallocate Myles's estate more fairly, then it will.'

'And how is that doing me a favour?' Grace demanded, her eyes flashing with annoyance.

Julia exhaled impatiently. 'Because if Austin and Olivia have to make a case against you, they'll be forced to admit what they know. About Myles. Everything will come out. And I mean everything.'

Grace frowned. Katie felt her face grow hot; this was beginning to sound like blackmail too. She exchanged looks with Robyn, who looked really uncomfortable to be listening in.

'Do you know what she means?' Robyn mouthed to Grace.

Grace shook her head. 'Julia, I've got nothing to hide.'

'*You* might not have; shame the same can't be said of Myles,' Julia said gleefully. 'Awful for you, I realise, to find out what a naughty boy your precious husband was. Especially now when you can't quiz him about it yourself.'

'Now that's enough. Don't you dare speak about Myles like that,' Grace said forcefully. 'You're a liar. I'm ending this call now.'

'You mean you really didn't know? Well, I'm sorry to be the bearer of bad news.' Julia's voice was snide and oily, and Katie had a sudden image of a snake slithering towards its prey. 'But Myles had an affair last year.'

Grace stabbed at the phone to cut the call. Katie froze and held her breath as she watched a thousand thoughts flicker across Grace's face. For a moment the only sounds were the tumble of waves onto the shore and the distant squeal of a seagull on the wing. None of them spoke.

'You OK?' Katie asked.

Grace exhaled. 'I don't believe that for a second. She's a bitter woman. She was jealous of me when we were married, but I didn't think even she would stoop this low now that he's gone.'

'Block her number from your phone,' said Robyn, 'then at least she can't bother you again.'

But Grace wasn't listening; she was staring into the distance, her face tormented with grief. 'Oh Myles,' she whispered, 'I miss you. So much.'

As her face crumpled and tears ran down her cheeks, Robyn and Katie stepped closer and held her while she wept.

'It's OK,' said Robyn. 'We've got you.'

'And you've got us,' said Katie firmly. 'We're in this together.'

Chapter Thirteen

The following Monday, Robyn was at her desk in her studio, her hand wrapped around a mug of tea. The room was sun-warmed and flooded with light, the fresh scent of the sea wafted in through the open Velux windows and the sound of the waves and the tinkle of masts from the boats moored in the harbour was soothing and comforting. Finn was out at work and she had the cottage to herself.

Despite finding it hard to focus, she was pleased with what she'd achieved. She'd updated her CV, shared a post about British illustrators on LinkedIn and she'd taken a couple of pictures of the sea glass she'd collected the other day and posted them on Instagram. But every now and then, her mind would return to that moment on the beach with Grace and Katie when she had been on the verge of confiding in them about her concerns over her marriage.

Ours has always worked, but lately . . .

Then poor Grace had received that phone call from her husband's ex and the opportunity had evaporated. If she was honest with herself, Robyn had been relieved at the interruption.

Because she was a coward.

She hadn't always been like this. But it had become a habit, ever since that conversation with Finn about starting a family. Two years had gone by since then and she still recalled the details of it as if it were yesterday. She sipped her tea and allowed her mind to travel back to the moment when everything had changed for her and Finn.

★

It had been a Friday evening in early spring, and Finn had come in tired and happy because although the sea had been rough, the catch had been fantastic that day.

She'd run him a bath, tipped a generous dollop of her birthday bubbles into it and lit some candles. The bathroom was steamy, warm and aromatic. She led him by the hand into the bathroom and kicked the door shut behind them.

'I'm glad you're home safe.' She wrapped her arms around his waist and rested her head on his chest, leaning into his strong body.

There were other more dangerous jobs than being a fisherman, she knew that, but she never underestimated the risks of working at sea. 'I've been in my studio listening to the waves pounding the harbour wall all day and I kept thinking of you in your little boat.'

He returned her embrace and grinned as she unbuttoned his shirt and tugged his T-shirt over his head. 'Not that little.'

'Little compared to the sea.'

'Aye, well, *I'm* glad the catch was good. We've turned a decent profit for a change. I'm doing grilled mackerel and wild samphire for dinner.' He waggled his eyebrows, pleased with himself.

'Ooh. Very fancy.' Robyn kissed him tenderly. 'You spoil me.'

'I figured if I'm going to keep feeding you catch of the day, I've got to up my game.' He unbuckled his jeans and let them drop to the floor.

'You're my catch of the day,' she replied, watching with a thrill as he stepped into the bath. 'And your game is just fine as it is.'

Leaving him to relax in the bubbles, she bundled up his clothes, went downstairs and stuck them straight in the washing machine and came back with a bottle of wine and two glasses.

She poured them both a drink, before peeling off her own clothes and then she climbed in the other end of the bath, making room for herself between his long legs.

'Cheers!' He tipped his glass to hers and laughed under his breath.

'What's funny?' she laughed with him, sipping her wine.

'Just comparing my Friday night with Callum's. Claudia will be waiting at the door for him, ready to go skipping merrily off to her mother's for the night, leaving him to do battle with Hannah about eating her vegetables and listening to William chew his ear off about getting a pet snake. He'll just about manage one beer once they've gone to bed before crashing out himself.'

He leaned forward and gave her a lingering kiss. She felt the heat of his hand on her face, the roughness of his stubble against her skin and the cold tingle of the wine on his tongue. She shivered with desire.

'Whereas I come home to a glass of wine and a candle-lit bath with a gorgeous naked woman.'

'I've got bad news for Callum,' Robyn giggled, resting her glass on her chest, just above her breasts. Finn's eyes followed her every move. 'Claudia wants at least one more baby.'

They laughed and chatted about their day: Robyn telling him about a new monthly column she'd been asked to illustrate for a magazine and Finn waxing lyrical about a new GPS system he and Callum wanted to invest in which, they reckoned, would pay for itself in less than eighteen months.

'Days like today give me hope for the future,' said Finn. He scooped up a handful of foam from the top of the water and blew it towards her. 'Bad days make me worry that there'll be no business to pass down to the family. The McGills have been fishing in Merle Bay for three generations. It would be criminal if Callum and I cocked that up for the next lot.'

'You won't cock it up,' she said softly.

Hannah and William were next in line. Callum's family. For Finn, it wasn't a case of *no business* to pass to his family, it would be *no family* to inherit the business. Was that what Finn was really worried about; that his genes would end with him? He and Robyn had always agreed that they didn't want children. It was one of the things which had cemented their relationship. But people changed, didn't they? Had Finn, she wondered.

'Hmm.' Finn looked into his glass, swirling the wine around. 'There were twenty-five families dependent on the sea when Dad took over from my granddad. Now there's just us. Callum and me. It probably sounds daft, but fishing in Merle Bay is part of our heritage. What if we do keep going and then none of Callum's kids want to take it on?'

Robyn's breath caught in her throat. The celebratory mood was beginning to disappear like the bubbles in their bath. She could feel what was coming; he *had* had a change of heart. She'd do anything for this man, anything to make him happy. But did that include having a child?

'It's important to you, isn't it?' She trailed her fingers through the water, aware of the speeding of her heart. 'The continuation of the family tradition?'

He smiled ruefully and sank down lower into the water. 'I guess it is. I must be more like my dad than I thought.'

A million things raced through her brain. She loved their life as it was. She liked lying in on Sunday morning, reading each other bits from their books or newspapers, only leaving their bed for tea and toast. She liked staying up late to watch a film or getting up when it was still dark to look at the sea shimmering silver under a bright moon. Doing what they wanted, whenever they wanted. It had been just the two of them for the last sixteen years. Having a baby would change all that.

But maybe change would be a good thing. Finn would be the best dad ever, she was sure of that. She might not have had the ideal start in life, but he was from a warm and loving family; she could learn from him. And she had enough room in her heart for Finn and a hundred children if needs be. Being a mother scared her but if it was what he wanted, well, that was what marriage was about wasn't it? Compromise.

She took a deep breath. 'I suppose we could do our bit to continue the McGill dynasty.'

He stared at her for a moment, his dark eyes wide. 'What do you mean?'

'We could—' She bought herself a moment by gulping her wine, her brain not quite believing her own words. 'If you wanted we could try for a baby. Start our own McGill family.'

He pushed himself up so fast that a mini tidal wave tipped over the edge of the bath. Water dripped onto the floor but neither of them commented on it. Their eyes were locked on each other.

'Us? You and me, you mean?' he stammered. 'Start a family?'

She nodded, her heart thumping.

A slow smile spread across his face. 'Is that what you want?'

Lying to your husband didn't count if it was for the right reasons, she decided. 'Yes. If you do?'

'Sure. Why not. Bloody hell. Me, a father! I think I need another drink.' He reached out for the wine bottle, topped up their glasses and took a swig of his wine. 'You were always so adamant you didn't want kids, what's changed?'

'I guess my main worry about being a mum was what would happen to my child if something happened to me,' she said, feeling her throat tighten with emotion.

'Like your own mum.' Finn groaned. 'Oh, love.'

Robyn nodded. 'But it wouldn't be just me, would it, because we'd be in it together.'

'Always,' Finn promised, taking her hand and kissing her fingers. 'And I'll look after you *and* our child. So, don't let that worry you anymore.'

'But what about you?' she asked. If this was going to happen, she had to be sure he really, really wanted it. 'When did you change your mind?'

He frowned, his thumb rubbing over her wedding ring. 'Me? Gosh, not sure. I think it's just crept up on me gradually. Being an uncle played a part; I'm surprised how much I love being with Callum's two. So, yeah, I'm up for being a dad.'

'OK, then . . . we're agreed,' she said, trying to ignore the fluttering of nerves in her stomach.

'Today just gets better and better,' said Finn with a cheeky grin.

She watched him get out of the bath and rub himself down with a towel. 'Before we get carried away, I think there's something I ought to do first.'

'Oh?' He held a towel out for her, and she stepped out, revelling in the soft warmth as he wrapped it around her.

It wasn't only her mum who'd been dealt a fatal hand by cancer, it was her gran too, who'd died before Robyn had been born. Too much of a coincidence to ignore. There was genetic testing which could be done now, her doctor had even brought the subject up in the past. There'd been loads of articles about it, which Robyn had made herself read. She knew the facts: women who tested positive were advised to consider risk-reducing surgery in their mid-thirties. Robyn had opted not to go down that path until now. Her life was just how she wanted it to be: she was happy, in love with a man who loved her and enjoying life. But deep down she'd known the clock was ticking. If she carried the BRCA gene, her chance of getting breast cancer and ovarian cancer was super high. It was time to pull her head out of the sand and take the test. Because it wasn't just about her anymore, it was about her children.

'I should get tested to make sure I don't carry the BRCA gene first. If there's a chance that I could pass it on to our baby, we need to find out.'

'Oh Robyn, thank God.' Finn exhaled and looked up to the ceiling. When his eyes met hers, there were tears in them. 'I'm so glad. I've always wanted you to take the test.'

'Have you?' She was shocked. 'I never knew you felt like that.'

'It wasn't my place to say.' He drew her into his arms and held her tightly. 'It had to be your decision. But I don't like taking risks; what we know about, we can deal with.'

'I know,' she murmured, snuggling into his chest.

But it was different for him; no one close to him had been affected. *Dealing with it* wasn't as straightforward as it sounded.

'I love you,' he continued. 'I want you to grow old with me. You're the most precious thing in my world and your babies will be beautiful.'

Babies. She felt a tremor of fear. She still wasn't entirely sure she wanted one, let alone more than one. This was the moment when she should have spoken up, expressed doubt, told him not to get carried away. But he looked so happy that she couldn't bring herself to spoil the moment.

So, she simply kissed him and said. '*Our* babies will be beautiful.'

And wished she'd never brought the subject up in the first place.

The baby plan moved quickly after that. If Robyn was honest with herself, she was swept along with the excitement, the newness of it all. Finn's happiness became her own. Finn researched how to increase the chance of conception, which involved him wearing loose boxer shorts and both of them cutting down on alcohol while Robyn booked herself into the doctors to get the ball rolling for the BRCA gene testing. She tried not to think too much about the tests; instead, she focused on their future.

Now in the bath, they'd sip tea and compile lists: of baby names (Amelie, Edie, Tilda for a girl and Billy, Atticus or Rex for a boy); equipment they'd need to buy, who would be godparents; places they wanted to take Baby McGill (Lapland to see Santa, the puffins on Coquet Island, London to see the Queen), new family traditions they'd form (birthday cakes, building snowmen, and sandcastle competitions . . .).

Six weeks later when Alice, the post lady, pushed a sheaf of mail through their letter box, Robyn had been on her own in the cottage. She sifted through the letters until she found the one she'd been dreading. Cream-coloured with one of those clear windows. She'd already come to know the hospital stationery well. Her fingers shook as she tore it open.

She scanned the page, holding her breath until she found it: *You have tested positive for the BRCA1 mutation.*

The words blurred into a smudge as her eyes welled with tears. She'd allowed herself to hope that the history of cancer in her family was nothing more than bad luck, that lightning couldn't possibly strike a third time, but the letter confirmed it. She knew the statistics off by heart: the risk of developing breast cancer was over seventy-three per cent and ovarian cancer sixty-three per cent.

She sank down onto the sofa and wrapped her arms around herself, taking it all in. Her mind already skipping ahead to what this would mean for her and Finn, remembering all the times her mother had tried to comfort her.

Just because I'm not there, doesn't mean I love you any less.

When I'm gone, I want you to be brave.

You're my mark on the world, being your mum is the best thing I could be.

I'll always be there to watch over you at night, just look up and find the twinkliest star and it will be me, blowing you a goodnight kiss.

Robyn had wanted to scream and yell that it wasn't enough.

A single sheet of paper. That was all. And yet its message had tipped her entire world on its head. There would be decisions to make, options to consider, appointments to attend . . . her priority would have to switch from creating a new life to preserving her own. She loosened her grip on the page, letting it twist to the floor, then curled up on the sofa and pulled a blanket up over her head to shut out the world for a while.

When Finn came home from work hours later, he found her still there in the dark. He switched on a lamp, discovered the letter and scanned through it. And then, scooping her up in his arms, they'd both cried for each other, for Robyn's mum who'd never been offered the BRCA testing which might have saved her life and even for the baby they both instinctively knew they would never have. There was no way.

The next few months were awash with appointments, consultations and counselling. Robyn was overwhelmed with decisions but was reassured at every turn by the team at the hospital. And beside her every step of the way, surrounding her in love, squeezing her hand and telling her how brave she was, was Finn.

She felt anything but brave. Those who had to deal with cancer were the brave ones, as far as she was concerned. All she was doing was keeping one step ahead of it. She opted to play it safe and scheduled in her surgeries: a double mastectomy and oophorectomy.

The last operation had been a year ago. Neither of them mentioned Lapland or puffins, birthday cakes or baby names. Gradually beer had crept its way back into the fridge and Finn took a bath on his own. From the outside, Robyn's body didn't look that different. Fully clothed, you couldn't tell at all; a little plumper because of the medication she'd been on, but that would settle in time. And nobody else would ever know she'd had an early menopause. Finn and the hospital staff were the only people who'd seen her reconstructed breasts, the scars, small plateaus where nipples used to be.

But she wasn't the same person, and neither was Finn.

They could have been parents by now. There might have been a little McGill in Admiral Cottage. A family of three. But it was still just the two of them, and Robyn – although she'd never admit it to another soul – was secretly quite glad about that.

★

Robyn's tea had gone cold and she set down her mug. Her eyes alighted on the sea glass that she'd arranged on the wooden floor in a spiral earlier and her mind drifted back to Grace and Katie.

They had a WhatsApp group now called *The Sea Glass Sisterhood*. Grace had set it up and had sent a message to apologise for her outburst on the beach after Myles's ex-wife had phoned her.

Poor Grace. Poor Katie, too.

Robyn had been a little envious of them both to begin with – not that being widowed was anything to be jealous of, but Robyn would hazard a guess that Grace didn't buy her knickers at Asda. And Katie, well Katie always looked so elegant and serene and sorted. Now she knew them a bit better she could see that their lives weren't perfect either. She scooped the sea glass up and put it in an empty mason jar on her bookshelf. People were a bit like the shingle beach, she thought; it looked perfectly ordinary on the surface, but take the time to dig a little deeper and you discovered the sea glass: unique in every way, with histories and stories you couldn't even begin to guess.

She checked the WhatsApp group again for any news. Nothing. They'd agreed to get together immediately if Katie received another letter. But what if Katie had had a change of heart and decided not to confide in them again and was dealing with it alone? And what if Grace was more upset about Julia's accusation than she'd let on?

She should find out, check up on them both, she decided. Starting right now.

Filled with purpose, she closed the windows in the studio, locked the cottage and set off for Auntie Small's.

Chapter Fourteen

Grace tied her dressing gown belt, dragged herself through to the kitchen in her slippers and flicked the kettle on. Her vision hadn't quite focused yet, which was good because she had a suspicion that the pristine glossy kitchen would look as if a bear had broken in and attempted to make itself a three-course dinner. Her head was banging, her tongue was furry, and her stomach was making noises like a blocked drain.

The LED clock on the cooker came into view and its red display burned into her eyes. She pressed a hand to her face to block the harsh light.

'No way,' she groaned. 'I can't have slept until noon. What have I turned into? Don't answer that, Grace.'

She had always been an early bird, instantly wide awake when the alarm went off, up with the larks and just as tuneful, humming to herself as she bustled around their house, throwing herself into the new day with gusto. Myles used to stay in bed a bit longer, coming to slowly with a double espresso in one hand, his phone in the other while scrolling through the news. What would he think of her now? She choked back a sob, tried to stop her hands from shaking as she made her tea and gradually cast her eyes around the open-plan space.

Two empty wine bottles sat on the work surface. Two! A red and a white. When Ned had told her to help herself to his wine cellar, she was sure he hadn't meant her to drink it dry. She dreaded to think how much she'd polished off in the last few days. She'd been managing her grief quite well recently. Myles was always there in her thoughts, but the pain had become less raw. But thanks to that phone call from Julia, it had all come flooding back.

This drinking was going to have to stop. Right now. She picked up the bottles and took them outside to the glass recycling box; only one fitted in, so she left the other next to it and wedged the lid back on. Then she stood and gulped in the fresh sea air and looked across the bay. The breeze danced in her hair, but she wasn't cold; the sun was overhead, and it was one of those April days that made you think that summer was just around the corner.

She turned and went back inside to drink her tea and make a plan for the day. No more prevaricating and pickling her liver. She didn't believe Julia for one minute; it didn't take a genius to work out that she was making it all up. Of course Myles hadn't had an affair. For starters, they'd scarcely spent a night apart in the whole time they'd been together. And he was an open book. She'd have noticed if he'd started behaving oddly or changing his routine. Not to mention the fact that she was very sure of his love for her; he'd never given her a moment's pause to doubt that.

It was obvious what Julia's game was. She'd do anything to get more of Myles's money for Austin and Olivia. Grace wouldn't be surprised if she'd got them to agree to a cut for her if she succeeded. And if Julia sullied Myles's reputation and broke Grace's heart during the process, she wouldn't care a jot. She was in mourning for the love of her life, how dare Julia not respect that? Julia, Grace decided hotly, could go boil her own head.

Today marked a fresh start. She was going to stop moping around and maltreating herself. She grabbed a pen and paper, pulled a bar stool out from the kitchen island and began to make a list of positive things she could do right away.

The first three items were easy enough: *buy fruit and vegetables, do some exercise, ring solicitor.* She was more determined than ever not to give in to Austin and Olivia's demands now, so she ought to call Roger Mathers and find out what the procedure would be for challenging a will. The thought of a court case made her feel sick. Austin and Olivia had been such sweet kids. When had they become so mercenary?

Before she could go any further with her list, there was a knock at the front door. She put down her pen and answered it.

The post lady was on her doorstep holding out a slim envelope that would definitely have fitted through the letter box. 'Morning, lovey. Ooh, someone's had a rough night!'

Understatement, thought Grace, tightening the belt on her dressing gown. 'Bit of a headache, that's all.'

'A walk in the fresh sea air, that's what you need. Here's your post. I'm Alice, by the way.'

Grace introduced herself and took the envelope from Alice; it looked like something from the bank, certainly nothing interesting.

'I think I will go for a walk,' she said, looking over Alice's shoulder at the clear sky. 'I'll go and do some shopping in town, maybe even treat myself to something from Auntie Small's.'

Alice beamed. 'You must! I swear by their thermals in winter. I was in there earlier. Brought young Katie a bit of good news by the look on her face. A letter from the

North East Gazette!' She clapped her hand over her mouth. 'Whoops. Probably shouldn't have said anything. I'm not normally one to gossip.'

'Of course you aren't.' Grace's heart thumped. Hadn't Katie's blackmailer threatened to go to the paper with those pictures. Had there been a development and Katie hadn't told them? 'But was it definitely good news?'

'Yes, I'm pretty sure.' The older woman's eyes narrowed with suspicion. 'Why?'

'Lovely to meet you, Alice.' Grace stepped back, preparing to close the door, 'I'd better get some clothes on. Bye!'

A flush of shame crept over her face as she got into the shower. Other than set up a WhatsApp group for the three of them, Grace had done nothing to support her two new friends. Robyn obviously had something she wanted to get off her chest and hadn't had the chance, thanks to bloody Julia. Poor Katie was in a terrible predicament and so far, all Grace had done was wallow in wine and self-pity. She'd get ready, give her solicitor a quick call and then set off.

An hour later, she looked more like the old Grace in Converse, a T-shirt and white capri trousers. Her hair shone, she'd added some colour to her cheeks and after a concerted effort with her electric toothbrush, all traces of last night's red wine had vanished. She'd even managed to cross something off her to-do list. But as she put a line through *ring solicitor* she half wished she hadn't bothered.

Roger was a darling. Sharp as a tack, eminently professional but still managed to be delightfully charming. Grace had always come away from a meeting or phone call feeling calmed because he had everything in hand. Today though, he hadn't soothed her at all. When she'd casually mentioned Julia's claim, he'd quizzed her for several minutes, pressing her for details which she couldn't supply. When and where had this confession to Julia supposedly taken place? How long ago was this alleged affair? Had Grace ever had cause to suspect anything . . . His probing, gentle though it had been, persisted until Grace, taken aback by the direction their conversation had taken, had cut it short by pretending that there was someone at the door.

She checked her reflection in the mirror one last time and massaged away the frown lines between her eyes, replacing her haunted expression with a cheerful one. Smile, and the world smiles with you, she told herself as she locked up and left Sea Glass House. She didn't know who said that first, but it seemed like sound advice, because maybe if she looked happy, the uneasiness Roger had stirred up would simply blow away on the North Sea breeze.

Chapter Fifteen

Robyn skirted the harbour, pausing to lean on the wall and watch a shoal of silver fish as they danced in perfect unison beneath the water, and then turned uphill onto Merle Bay high street. It had become somewhat gentrified over the last few years. Gone were the ancient shops: the old-fashioned hardware store, the fishing tackle shop, Mrs Cotton's fabric emporium where Robyn's mum used to buy scraps of material to make soft toys for her and the sweet shop that sold bonbons and lemon drops by the quarter in paper bags. Now there was an art gallery, bakery, bookshop and a café, along with several charity shops and of course Auntie Small's halfway up the hill overlooking the sea.

Robyn stopped outside Katie's shop and cast her eye over the window display. She approved; someone had a good eye for colour. She did notice that the shop's signage could do with being renewed. The moist salty air was lovely to breathe in, but it played havoc with paintwork. She painted the window frames at Admiral Cottage most summers because it cracked and peeled so often. Through the glass she could see Katie talking to someone, and another member of staff dealing with a customer at the cash desk. She pushed open the door and went inside.

Katie looked over and smiled, looking pleased to see her. 'Five minutes!' she mouthed.

Robyn gave her a thumbs-up and wandered over to the rails while she waited.

'See how you get on with that one, Mrs Craster,' the assistant was saying to her customer, an elderly lady wearing a thick coat and bobble hat despite the warmth of the spring day.

'I'm all fingers and thumbs, Nula,' Mrs Craster said. 'Albert has to do me up these days. Heaven knows what I'll do if he goes before me.'

'You've both got years left in you yet,' Nula laughed. 'And I'm sure he doesn't mind lending a hand.'

'No. How times have changed, eh, in our younger days, he used to boast he could undo it with one hand. Now he can't do me up quick enough.' The old lady hooted with laughter as Nula opened the door to help her out.

Robyn's heart twisted; growing old with someone you loved was such a privilege. She wondered if Finn would still want to get into her bra when she was as old as Mrs Craster. At the moment it didn't seem likely. He was more like Mrs Craster's Albert: happier to see her in her clothes than out. She knew she needed to do something about that, but she didn't know where to start.

A poster to one side of the door caught her eye and she went over to read it. It was an advertisement from a charity called Knitted Knockers. Knitted from cotton yarn, with or without nipples, and filled with soft wadding, the prostheses were available free of charge for post mastectomy or lumpectomy surgeries. Robyn smiled; they looked like knitted Belgian buns. There was even a different type especially for swimming called Aqua Knockers.

'Fun, aren't they?' said a voice beside her. 'Even though they serve a serious purpose. I'm wearing some now and I don't think you can even tell.'

Robyn looked around to see the sales assistant turning from side to side to display her bosom, realising that she must be a survivor of breast cancer herself. Then she had a sudden bolt of recognition. 'You were the dinner lady at my old school! Mrs Sullivan!'

Nula nodded. 'I was. And you haven't changed a bit.'

'Oh, I have,' Robyn said with feeling. Mum had been alive when she was at primary school and everything had changed since then. 'And no, you're right, Mrs Sullivan, you can't tell you're wearing them at all. They're great.'

'Call me Nula.' Nula looked at the poster and back at Robyn. 'Would you like some?'

'Me?' Robyn squirmed. 'Oh no, I only came in to talk to Katie. I was just thinking it was a shame they weren't around when my mum was alive.'

Her mum couldn't have a reconstruction after her mastectomy because of her ongoing treatment and then her time had run out.

'Katie won't be long; she's with a sales representative from a lingerie company.' Nula's face softened. 'I heard about your mother, I was so sad for you when she passed away.'

Robyn was taken aback; she hadn't known Mum knew Mrs Sullivan. But then it was a relatively small community and they'd have been around the same age.

Nula leaned forward and lowered her voice. 'She came to the school kitchens quite regularly to tell us about your latest food fads.'

'Oh no, I'm sorry, how embarrassing!' Robyn laughed, pressing her hands to her cheeks, but secretly she was also delighted. Her mum had no living relatives and Robyn's supply of anecdotes about her mother was limited. 'What sort of thing did she say?'

'Remember when we used to give you "swimming chicken" on a Friday?' Nula's eyes sparkled.

'Yes?' Robyn laughed; she'd forgotten all about that. 'I was always thrilled that I didn't have to have fish like everyone else.'

'I know.' Nula looked at her in bemusement.

'It *was* fish, wasn't it!' Robyn groaned when the penny finally dropped. 'How gullible was I! Well, you'll be pleased to know I adore it now. Good job because I married a fisherman.'

'Finn McGill,' Nula said, chuckling. 'I remember him well. Lovely-looking child. Always tried to make his brother eat his cabbage for him.'

'He's still lovely-looking,' said Robyn, feeling a tug at her heart. 'And he eats everything these days and cooks it, too.'

'Can you knit?' Nula asked, tapping the poster.

'Oh, er, me? No,' she replied.

'Shame. There are a few of us who volunteer locally and we're always on the lookout for new recruits, we send the knockers all over the country. We're not all good knitters, some of us are just enthusiastic, but we're nearly all cancer survivors. No one understands you better than someone who's been there, done that and got the T-shirt.'

'I can imagine,' said Robyn, thinking that it might be quite nice to talk to someone like herself. 'People who haven't been through it themselves want to help but often it's hard for them to say the right thing and more often than not, when they try, they end up putting their foot in it and making it worse.'

'Oh?' Nula was looking at her with her head on one side, like a little inquisitive bird. 'You sound as if you're speaking from experience.'

'I'm a previvor,' Robyn blurted out and then felt her face flood with colour. 'But I'm very private about it.'

'I understand.' Nula pinned her with her gaze, a gentle smile on her lips. 'Well, if you fancy learning to knit, we'd love to have you.'

Robyn thanked her and then Nula left her to browse while she waited for Katie. Everybody's cancer journey was different, and a *previvor*, like she was, had different issues to a *survivor*. She didn't want to join the Knitting Knockers group because she didn't know one end of a knitting needle from the other, but the idea of talking to others who understood the choices she'd made was beginning to appeal. Maybe there were other women in the area who had found it hard to come to terms with their new bodies too? She'd do an internet search later and see if she could find out.

Katie was seeing her visitor out and as she passed by Robyn she whispered, 'Thanks for waiting, so lovely to see you.' She smiled as she showed her visitor to the door. 'Great to meet you, Sasha.'

'Likewise,' said the visitor. 'And I'll talk to my marketing team about visual merchandising props if you put the new collection in the window.'

'Deal.' Katie shook her hand and then held up a lacy bra. 'And thanks for the sample. I'll get one of my models to trial it and come back to you.'

She closed the door, waved to Sasha as she walked away and turned back to Nula and Robyn. 'That went well.'

'Your *models*?' Nula said, raising an eyebrow. 'Would that be me and you?'

Katie grinned, 'Artistic licence. I was trying to compete with Sasha and her marketing team. It's a 34C.' She held the bra out to Robyn. 'Do me a favour and try it on, it's non-wired and I think it'll feel like a second skin.'

'How did you know what size I am?' Robyn began, folding her arms across her chest and wondering what else she could tell from a casual glance.

'It's my party trick. Oh no, that sales agent has just sent Grace flying!' Katie flung open the door again and went outside.

Robyn turned to see Sasha helping Grace up from the pavement, bags of shopping on the floor. She followed Katie outside to help.

'Hello girls!' Grace laughed. 'What a palaver! I buy all this healthy stuff and look what happens, fruit and veg scattered to the four winds.' She bent to pick up an aubergine. 'It's a sign. Me and Pringles were meant to be.'

'All my fault,' said Sasha, stuffing bread rolls back into a jute shopping bag. 'I was texting my boss to say our meeting went well. Oh dear!'

They all watched as two oranges rolled into the road and into the path of a car.

'Most of it is fine.' Katie picked up a courgette and blew on it. 'Five-second rule.'

'The oranges certainly aren't,' Sasha argued. 'Oh, I know, let me see if I have another sample that might fit you.'

Grace looked confused but Katie murmured something in Sasha's ear. Sasha rummaged in her bag and pulled out a black sheer lace bra with a large satin bow at the front.

'That's gorgeous! I was coming to Auntie Small's to treat myself to some new knickers.' Grace whooped with delight. 'Myles will think he's died and gone to . . . Oh.'

The smile fell from Grace's face at which point Robyn bundled her into the shop and Katie waved Sasha off again, before declaring it was high time for a coffee break.

Chapter Sixteen

Five minutes later, Nula had made them coffee while Katie did the introductions and Grace had brushed away her moment of grief by sharing the fresh plum loaf she'd bought from the bakery. Katie was touched that they'd both come to see her but hoped they were careful not to say anything about her secret in front of Nula.

'I'm so pleased Katie's making friends, finally,' said Nula, handing round milk and sugar. 'Seems a shame she keeps herself to herself. I've tried no end of times to get her to come along to line dancing with me. I can't understand it.'

Robyn met Katie's eye and they both smothered a giggle. It reminded Katie of when she'd started school and her mum had related embarrassing anecdotes to the other mums. 'I'm not *unfriendly*, I hope.'

'You've been a good friend to me already,' said Grace, giving her a meaningful look. 'Both you and Robyn have. Has Katie told you that I was a damsel in distress when they first met me?'

'She tells me nothing! Comes from being an only child,' Nula said in a stage whisper. 'My husband was the same. Well, up until he met me.'

'I'm the soul of discretion, that's all,' Katie retorted.

'So has anything happened since we last saw you, Katie?' Robyn asked, popping the last piece of cake into her mouth.

'Ooh, yes!' said Grace. 'The post lady said you'd had some news. Do tell!'

Robyn's eyes widened in alarm and she shot a look at Nula. Who from?

'Now there's a woman who couldn't keep a secret if her life depended on it,' Nula grumbled. 'Are you going to tell them, or is it *embargoed*?' She put imaginary quote marks around the last word.

Katie laughed. 'As long as it stays in this room, I think it's safe to divulge. We had a letter from the *Gazette* today informing us—'

Before she could continue, her mobile phone began to buzz. She picked it up and saw it was her mum phoning from Malta, or rather, FaceTiming her. She'd expected the call; she'd sent her parents a message as soon as the letter had arrived, knowing how pleased they'd be. She glanced at Grace and Robyn before accepting the call. 'Sorry, it's my mum. I won't be long, I promise.'

'No worries,' said Robyn. 'Mums should always take priority.'

A close-up picture of Josie's hair appeared on the screen.

'Darling!' her mum cried. 'We've just read your message. How exciting! Congratulations!'

'Thanks!' Katie laughed. 'Look at the screen, Mum, you'll be able to see me.'

'Silly me!' said her mum. Her face appeared on screen. She was outside in the sunshine, a bright blue sky behind her. 'Brian? Katie's here, look.'

Her dad came into the view, brushing a tear from his eye. 'I'm so proud of you, love. Well done.'

'What has she done?' Grace whispered to Nula.

'The *North East Gazette* hosts the regional business awards every year, and the shop has been nominated for the Independent Retailer of the Year Award,' Nula hissed.

Katie found the official letter from the *Gazette* and handed it to them to read. Grace clapped quietly and Robyn gave her the thumbs-up.

'And Auntie Jean would have been so proud of you too,' her mum was saying.

'I know she would.' And Katie was flattered. Being shortlisted was an honour. Especially as this wasn't something that businesses could nominate themselves for. It was up to readers of the newspaper to vote for shops and companies they felt deserved recognition. But she had mixed emotions about the nomination; of course, she was delighted, for Nula as much as herself. But the timing was awful. Right now, the last thing she wanted was to draw any attention to herself or the shop. But what could she do?

After a quick chat about how their holiday was going, she ended the FaceTime call with her parents, promising to keep them posted with more details about the evening event and turned back to face her friends.

'I hope you realise what a fantastic achievement this is,' Grace said, giving her a hug.

'And there's an awards night,' Robyn added, joining in with the hug. 'Imagine if you win!'

Katie gulped. 'Imagine.' As lovely as it would be to win, the thought of going on stage to collect a prize, all eyes upon her, made her head spin.

Nula sighed. 'I might even treat myself to a new frock.'

'Yes, well there's plenty of time to think about all that,' said Katie. That was another thing: she was far more comfortable hiding under baggy tops. Cocktail dresses were a lot more revealing. 'But for now, why don't you two go and try your bras on?'

Robyn needed a bit of persuading but eventually Katie managed to get them to the changing cubicles.

'Oh, that's a shame,' Grace called. 'I've just looked at the label and it's too small.'

'Just try it,' said Katie. 'Give me a shout when you're in and I'll come in and adjust it.'

Grace chuntered under her breath, but she did as she was told.

'Robyn?' Katie said, outside her cubicle. 'Are you getting on OK?'

'Don't come in!' Robyn squeaked.

'I won't, but how does it fit?'

There was a moment's silence before Robyn spoke. 'It's beautiful. I look . . . I actually look really good.'

Her voice sounded choked and Katie's heart filled with happiness. She suspected that Robyn didn't often treat herself to nice underwear and the difference that a properly fitting, well-made bra could make to a woman's self-esteem was immeasurable.

'Why don't you help Grace and I'll check the fit on Robyn's bra?' Nula suggested.

Katie agreed and after checking Grace was decent, entered the cubicle.

Grace was in jeans and bra, arms by her side, staring at herself. 'You were right, it *does* fit.'

Katie nodded. 'Boobs are often a good indicator of what's going on in a woman's life. My guess is that your appetite has decreased since Myles died and you've lost weight.'

Grace nodded but her eyes didn't move from her reflection. 'Although my calorie intake has gone through the roof these last few days; I've eaten so much rubbish and washed it down with too much wine.'

Katie stood behind her, adjusted the band and shortened the straps. Grace's chest rose another couple of inches. 'How does that feel?'

'It feels fine.' Grace's voice was flat.

Katie frowned. 'Only fine?'

'Sorry, I'm being ungrateful.' Grace gave herself a shake. 'It's the nicest bra I've ever had. Certainly, the smallest one I've had for a long time. It's just . . . ' She shrugged. 'I'm not at my best today. Head feels like it's full of cotton wool.'

'Because of that phone call from Myles's ex-wife?' Katie lowered her voice.

'It's not that I believe her,' Grace said with a sigh. 'It's just made me feel a bit down, that's all.'

'It seems to me that you're taking positive action: you've been shopping, and you've got a gorgeous new bra. Two reasons to celebrate.'

'Hmm.' Grace frowned.

Katie waited to see if Grace wanted to say any more but clearly whatever was on her mind, she wasn't in the mood to share it.

'I'll leave you to get changed in private,' Katie said.

She slid out of the cubicle to see Robyn fully dressed again holding the sample bra.

'How was it?' Katie asked.

Robyn beamed. 'Gorgeous. It fitted perfectly and I felt sexy!' She looked surprised at herself. 'First time I've thought that for a while.'

'Good for you, pet,' said Nula with a wink.

'But I'd better not buy it,' said Robyn, handing it back.

'It's not actually for sale,' said Katie, wrapping it in tissue and putting it into a bag. 'It's a sample. All yours, free of charge.'

'No way! Really?' The look of gratitude and astonishment on Robyn's face made Katie's day. 'I love it, thank you. I'll even write a review so you can send it to Sasha.'

After Grace's bra had been wrapped up too, both her friends left, and Katie sent a silent thank you to her Auntie Jean for showing her how to make other women feel good about themselves. Sometimes it didn't take a lot to put a smile on someone else's face.

Later that day, after Nula had gone home, Katie was vacuuming the floor before closing up when the door opened and a girl in school uniform came in. She was better at guessing chest sizes than ages, but Katie reckoned she was in her early teens. She had shiny auburn hair pulled back into a ponytail and big brown eyes which looked unsure as they flashed Katie the briefest of smiles. Katie smiled back. She'd leave her to have a little look around first. A thought struck her: was this perhaps Barney's daughter? The editor at the *North East Gazette*, the newspaper which was behind the North East Business Awards . . .

She stifled a groan, remembering the last message from her anonymous correspondent. *I've drafted an email to the editor . . .* She turned off the vacuum cleaner, feeling flustered. 'Hello, bear with me a second. I'll tidy up this cable before someone trips over it.'

'OK,' the girl mumbled. She hovered by the door uncertainly.

'Feel free to look around. My name's Katie Small by the way.'

'Thanks. I'm Amber Larkin.'

So, it was Barney's daughter. She was filled with a surge of dread. Her blackmailer – if that was what it was – could be sending naked photographs of Katie to this girl's father.

The girl who'd lost her mother. Poor kid. Putting her own concerns to one side for the moment, she gave Amber her full attention.

'So I think you met my dad.' Amber's face flushed. 'I can only imagine how cringeworthy that conversation was.'

'Not at all, he was charming and very sweet.' Now it was Katie's turn to feel embarrassed. She concentrated on gathering up the electric flex to hide her face and watched surreptitiously as Amber wandered around the shop, fingering the price tags.

'Bras are so expensive!' Amber whistled under her breath. She hefted her rucksack higher up on her shoulder and knocked half a dozen high-leg briefs off the rack behind her. 'Oops, sorry.'

'Don't worry.' Katie went to her aid and together they popped the knickers back on the rail. 'Happens all the time. And that bra is very special.'

Amber looked at the dove grey bra dubiously.

'Ok-ay,' she said. She didn't add 'if you say so' but it was evident from her tone.

Katie told her that the bra was made in an all-female factory in London from responsibly sourced materials and that the company had a zero-waste policy. Amber looked almost impressed before folding her arms across her school blazer.

'So unfair though. Women have to spend so much extra on their bodies compared to men. And all the fuss made over breasts, seriously? They are literally just glands, designed to feed babies. What's special about that?'

Katie smiled to herself; she remembered saying something similar at her age.

'Well, just glands or not, they are what make us mammals. And human mammary glands are different from every other species because ours are the only permanent ones. Other mammals' glands disappear when they've finished feeding their offspring. I think that's kind of special.'

Amber pulled a face. 'Never knew that.'

'I'm full of useless information when it comes to bras,' Katie said with a grin. 'For instance, did you know that the first-ever bra was made out of recycled handkerchiefs?'

'No way.' Amber sat down on Auntie Jean's velvet chair.

'Have you ever heard the expression "necessity is the mother of invention"?'

She wrinkled her nose. 'No, but it sounds like something my dad would say.'

Katie laughed. 'Well, there was a woman who was bigger than average up top. She was going to some big posh do and her corset kept popping up and ruining the look of her new dress. So, she got two old hankies and a piece of ribbon and cobbled together a bra.'

'That's really cool.' Amber played with her ponytail and looked thoughtful. 'I could probably make one.'

'You could, I suppose.' Katie could just imagine the confusion on her father's face when his handkerchiefs started disappearing and then reappearing in the laundry basket stitched to a ribbon. 'But bras have improved since then. Now they protect and support breast tissue, not just cover it up for modesty purposes. Especially while they're still developing.'

Amber gave her a lopsided smile. 'I hope I am still developing; the size of my boobs is currently tragic.'

'If I had a pound for everyone who wasn't happy with their size, I'd be a rich woman,' Katie admitted. 'So, were the ones your dad brought home for you any good?'

Amber pulled a crushed Auntie Small's bag out of her school rucksack.

'They're OK, but I'm not sure if they fit me properly.' Her shoulders sagged and she looked small and young all of a sudden. 'And I'm a bit worried about how much they cost. My mum was a bargain hunter. On Black Friday she used to get up really early and order a year's worth of underwear from Victoria's Secret. I don't know what she'd think about Dad blowing the budget on all this lot.'

Amber took the bras out of the bag and put them in her lap. Katie was disappointed; it looked as if she'd brought them all back.

'Buying in the sale is a very sensible strategy,' said Katie. 'I'm sure you could do that in the future when you're sure of your size. I did suggest to your dad that he take a trip to the supermarket if he wanted to spend less, but . . . ' she hesitated, but then found that she wanted Amber to know just how much thought Barney had put into this. 'Your dad said it was something your mum would have made into a fun shopping trip and so he wanted your first bras to be extra special.'

'True, she would.' Amber bowed her head.

Katie took the bras from her lap, unsure whether Amber was keeping her eyes downcast because she was remembering her mum, or she simply felt uncomfortable. She crossed to the door and flipped the sign to *closed*. 'Shall we check the fit of these?'

'Cool.' Amber stood up and headed to one of the changing cubicles.

'Can I get you a drink of anything?' Katie asked. 'Coffee or herbal tea?'

'Got any champagne?'

Katie laughed. 'Nice try. But I don't think you dad meant *that* special.'

'Worth a shot,' Amber said from behind the curtain.

Fifteen minutes later, they'd selected three plain bras: a white, a black and a pale pink. Katie wrapped them in tissue paper and put them in a new Auntie Small's bag.

'Those are much better for me than the ones Dad chose,' said Amber cheerfully. 'And cheaper.'

'I'm glad you like them. Although your dad did ask for anything sustainable or eco-friendly.'

Amber raised an eyebrow. 'So, he does listen. What a cutie.'

Yep. Katie remembered the tousled hair and lovely eyes, the dimple in his chin and his cheeky smile. 'I need to refund you the difference,' she said, aware her eyes had gone a bit swimmy. 'I don't suppose you have your dad's credit card on you?'

Amber shook her head. 'Sorry. I'll send him in.'

'Yes,' said Katie, unable to keep the smile from her face. 'That would be great.'

Some days she really loved her job.

Chapter Seventeen

On Saturday morning, Grace woke up and checked her phone. It was eight o clock! She'd managed to sleep for nine hours straight, longer than she'd slept for months. She'd swapped wine for water for the last few nights and felt much better for it. She headed to the kitchen, poured some orange juice and opened the sliding glass She breathed in the tangy sea air and listening to the waves rushing in and out on the shingle beach below the house. It was a gorgeous day, but her mind wasn't on the weather.

Nipping back to her bedroom, she pulled on a sweatshirt over her pyjamas, collected her phone and took her juice outside.

Her head might be clear after her new rule of no drinking alone, but her thoughts were anything but. Trying on that bra in Katie's shop had awakened emotions which she thought she'd banished years ago. She'd looked in the mirror and not liked what she'd seen. The bra was lovely, but Grace herself had felt flabby and frumpy.

She'd never been skinny. Zoe had inherited Dad's lean physique and indifference to food. Grace was more of an apple-shape, like her mum. Myles had loved her curves and since they'd been together, she'd rebranded herself as Rubenesque. But now, with Myles not there to love her anymore, she could feel negative thoughts beginning to crowd in.

Grace could just about handle crying into her pillow every night. She could cope with the occasional verbal slip-up like that one yesterday: *Myles will think he's died and gone to heaven.* She didn't mind replaying the DVD of their wedding and sobbing at the part when everyone was applauding their first dance. She and Myles had been totally absorbed in each other. She vividly remembered feeling lucky at the time at the thought of a Myles-and-Grace-filled future of loveliness.

Well, that wasn't strictly true, she *did* mind these things. Very much. But those feelings were all part of the grieving process, any article on bereavement could tell you that. No, what she minded was this new low-level anxiety which she couldn't shake.

Julia had planted a seed in Grace's brain and despite knowing how ludicrous it was, she couldn't ignore it. On one level, she instinctively knew that Myles hadn't had an affair. But she couldn't help torturing herself about it. Because if he *had* had an affair then he must have stopped being in love with her. Which meant that the memories she had of her perfect marriage were a lie. And without those happy memories to look back on, Grace would be lost.

She turned her phone over in her hands. The screen was full of notifications of text messages from Zoe. She felt a flicker of guilt; she'd avoided talking to her sister ever since that phone call from Julia because she didn't trust herself not to blurt it all out. Knowing Zoe, she'd jump in her car and drive straight over, completely incensed. She fired off a quick reply to fob her sister off for a while longer.

There was only one way she could think of to resolve this uncertainty: she was going to have to speak to Julia again. Because this was probably just Julia's way of getting even with Grace for not giving Austin and Olivia more of Myles's estate.

She drew in a breath. Time to take action; Myles had told her once that most of their male staff were a bit scared of her because she always cut to the chase, didn't take any crap. She'd been secretly quite proud of that. The construction industry wasn't known for its kick-ass women.

And Grace *was* one.

Without giving herself a chance to back out, she rang Julia on her mobile. The call was answered straight away.

'Well hello!' she drawled. 'I thought I might hear from you soon. You've decided to cooperate, I presume?'

Grace allowed a beat to pass before replying, refusing to let Julia bait her. Instead, she was going to stay strong and get straight to the point.

'About what you said the other day.' Her heart began to race; she could hardly believe she was even having this conversation. 'That Myles had an affair.'

'I'm *so* sorry that I had to be the bearer of bad news.' Grace gritted her teeth; the woman's saccharine sympathy made her want to scream. 'I expect you're devastated?'

'It seems so out of character for him,' Grace replied, ignoring the note of hope in Julia's question. 'I can't believe he'd cheat on me.'

'He wasn't unfaithful to me, but I suppose there's a first time for everything.'

'I just wonder if you could have misheard, or got the wrong end of the stick?' Grace's voice remained smooth, but her shoulders were hunched up by her ears.

'No, definitely not. Look, Grace,' Julia sighed as if the conversation bored her. 'We were both at the funeral of a friend from school. I don't know where you were.'

'Simon's? The one late last summer?' Grace sipped her orange juice, remembering. She hadn't accompanied him to the service because of an important meeting which would have been awkward to rearrange.

'That's the one. There was a crowd of us who went back to the pub after the service. Quite a nice do actually. A free bar which Myles particularly enjoyed.'

Grace had thought at the time how odd it was that he'd got drunk that day; he'd had to abandon his car and get a taxi. It had been most unlike Myles and she'd put it down to him losing a friend at a relatively young age. It had served as a stark reminder to him that life should be lived to the full because you never knew when your last day would come. It had been not long after that that he'd suggested they rewrote their wills.

'And he actually said the word "affair"?'

'His exact words were, "I've ballsed everything up, Ju." I knew then how drunk he was; he hasn't called me Ju since we were in our teens.'

Grace could hear the laugh in her voice and her stomach turned. The reminder that Myles and Julia were teenage sweethearts felt like a stab to the heart. She looked across the room and focused on the artwork: a giant piece of driftwood shaped like the hull of a boat with a billowing sail made from canvas. The angle of it made Grace think that the boat was on a stormy sea. Just like Julia and Myles's marriage had been, she thought uncharitably. Whereas hers and Myles's had been plain sailing.

'I assumed he was referring to a disaster at work,' Julia continued, 'that was what he usually talked about, used to bore me rigid. Still at least you had that in common with him.'

By the time of the funeral, the sale of Byron Homes had already been agreed. Myles was about to become a wealthy man; he certainly hadn't messed anything up.

'We did make a very successful team,' Grace couldn't resist saying. 'Very successful indeed.'

Julia made a noise that sounded like a blast of irritation. 'Anyway, I was wrong, because he followed it up with "I've broken my wedding vows. In the worst possible way." Then he blathered on about you for a bit until I told him that I wasn't interested.'

Grace stared and stared at the driftwood boat on the wall until it was nothing but a blur. Blood roared in her ears and she was half aware that Julia was still speaking but she couldn't tune into it. Listening to details made it much more difficult to ignore. And Myles had acted really oddly after that funeral. Even Ned had called up the next day to check up on him.

Could there be some truth in Julia's claims after all?

Cold liquid splashed over her hand. She looked down to see that her hand was trembling so much that she'd spilled her orange juice. Her whole body was shaking, and she could feel her teeth starting to chatter. Sweat pooled under her arms. She forced herself to tune back into Julia's joyful monologue.

'It did cross my mind that that piece of information could be quite valuable,' Julia tittered.

'Did he say anything more about . . .' Grace peeled her tongue from the roof of her mouth, wanting but not wanting to know who the woman was who'd just ripped her world in two.

'Did he name names?' Julia butted in. 'No, annoyingly. And then one of his friends came up and dragged him away and I didn't get another chance to ask.'

'I see.' Grace swallowed. Her throat was constricted, and her stomach felt full of acid.

'So.' Julia sounded triumphant. 'Now you know. And I think you'll agree that under the circumstances, it's clear that your marriage was on the rocks. Which means that it's entirely appropriate that Myles's children have a larger slice of his estate.'

'Goodbye, Julia.' Grace hung up. She couldn't bear to listen to another word.

It was her own fault; she'd been the one to call Julia. What had she expected? Actually, she knew the answer to that: she'd presumed that Julia would grudgingly admit that she'd been teasing Grace, and that of course Myles hadn't had an affair. Grace rubbed her tears away roughly as she contemplated her next move. She wasn't going to let Julia win. It was still only the word of one bitter woman. So, until – *unless* – Grace found proper evidence, as far as she was concerned, Myles was innocent.

Chapter Eighteen

After a weekend with not much to do, Robyn was having a productive Monday. One of her speculative emails had paid off and she had been working all morning on a commission for a book jacket. Only a small job, but hopefully if they were pleased with her, more work might follow. She'd sent off some pencil roughs this morning and had been thrilled when they'd come back a couple of hours later saying that the author loved the direction Robyn had taken and could she work up some colourways.

Buoyed by the positive feedback, Robyn had thrown herself into it immediately and it was mid-afternoon before she realised how hungry she was. She left her attic studio and went downstairs for a belated lunch.

Once her cheese on toast was under the grill and the kettle was on, she pulled out the neck of her jumper and peered down at her chest. She was wearing the new lacy bra and – she could hardly believe she was thinking this – her boobs looked quite good. Her stomach fizzed; it was happening, just like her nurse told her it would. She was accepting her new shape. She smiled: her boobs, her body, her choice, her life.

All the tests and operations and days spent in agony recuperating, all the drugs, the check-ups . . . all over. She had a beautiful healthy body and what was more, she'd given herself the greatest gift possible: the best chance of a long and cancer-free life. Her mum and her gran would be up there cheering her on. She felt a surge of optimism; she'd turned a corner and she was happy and without even having to prompt herself to think of her gratitudes, she knew she was grateful for all of it.

She was still gazing down at herself when there was a brisk knock at the front door. She dashed to open it and found Claudia with Betty in her pram on her doorstep.

'Hello, come in!' Robyn beamed, helping lift the cumbersome pram into her tiny cottage.

'You're in a good mood.' Claudia kissed her cheek and pushed Betty in her buggy into kitchen.

'I am,' Robyn said, relieved that her visitor had come to the front door and not gone straight around the back like she sometimes did and caught her peering at herself. 'Work's gone well today, and I've got a new bra. Want to see?'

Without waiting for an answer, Robyn gave her a flash.

'Wow, that's gorgeous.' Claudia looked impressed. 'You are such a fox. Lucky Finn, that's all I can say. Poor old Callum; never did the phrase *getting jiggy with it* ring so true, getting close to me is like climbing on a bouncy castle.'

'I'm sure that's not true, but thanks.' Robyn felt her cheeks infuse with heat and dropped her jumper down. It was ridiculous really; she'd known Claudia since before either of them had had breasts, or boyfriends. There'd been a time when as soon as anything significant happened, they'd race to tell the other to dissect the incident moment by moment. She felt a wave of nostalgia for those times and before she had time to think it through blurted out, 'Things haven't been great on that score; I don't think Finn does think he's lucky to be honest.'

She pulled the cheese on toast out from under the grill, cut it into quarters and indicated to Claudia to help herself.

'Course he does, what are you on about?' Claudia checked on Betty who was fast asleep and then picked up some toast and blew on it. 'Every time I see you together, you always look besotted.'

Robyn busied herself making them both tea.

'On the surface we might look the same, but deep down we've changed. We're . . . ' she swallowed, debating whether to say anything or not. Oh, why not; Claudia was her best friend after all. 'We're not close like we used to be.'

Sometimes she regretted never telling anyone that they'd been planning a family. At the time, she and Finn had decided against it in case they couldn't conceive. Instead, they'd hugged the plan to themselves, knowing how excited the rest of the family would be once a new baby was on the way, how wide their 'I told you so' smiles would stretch. They could never tell them now; Robyn found it hard enough dealing with the pity they tried to hide as it was; it would be a double whammy of disappointment if they ever found out about the baby that never was. But occasionally, like now, it would be nice to get everything out in the open and tell someone exactly how she felt.

'I'd never have guessed.' Claudia frowned. 'I watch you two saunter off from ours, hand in hand, unencumbered by child paraphernalia and picture you ripping each other's clothes off as soon as you get home.' She pulled a face. 'That came out wrong, don't worry, I don't *actually* picture that part, more the freedom to do what you want.'

Robyn laughed. 'That's just it, I want to, but Finn doesn't. Since my op, I'm not sure that Finn fancies me anymore.'

Annoyingly, tears pricked at her eyes and she tilted her head up, willing them to disappear.

Her best friend gave her a gentle hug. 'Oh, mate. I'm sure that's not true.'

Robyn nodded sadly. 'He pulls away when I try and get close and he's always the first to end a kiss.'

'Do you think he's scared of hurting you?' Claudia suggested.

'Possibly,' she replied, thinking that that scenario was certainly preferable to not desiring her. 'If that's the case, I'll have to convince him that he won't. I'm going all out tonight: candlelit bath, aromatherapy massage oil; just me and Finn, and the new undies of course.'

She swallowed down a pang of nerves; that would mean stripping off in front of him, which she usually avoided if she could.

Claudia closed her eyes and sighed. 'An uninterrupted bath. Door locked. Bliss.'

How different they were these days, Robyn mused, finishing her toast. Claudia craved solitude, but Robyn wanted intimacy.

'Has he said anything to Callum about me?' Robyn asked, adding hurriedly, 'Please don't tell him I asked.'

'Callum tells me bits and pieces that Finn has said. But I don't remember hearing anything about your sex life. And I would have remembered that. I'm living vicariously at the moment.'

That had to be a good sign. She knew Finn wasn't great at opening up either, but if something serious was bothering him, she was sure he'd tell his brother.

'More tea, more cheese on toast?' Robyn offered. She lifted the lid off the cake tin. 'Or we've got cherry and almond muffins.'

'I'll take a muffin for later.' Claudia took a last sip of her tea and put the cup down in the sink. 'Lovely that, thanks. Now, the reason why I came round: we're having the kids christened, all three, a job lot. Callum and I would like

179

to ask you if you'd be their godmother. Callum is asking Finn today to be godfather.'

'I'd be honoured!' Robyn was delighted and threw her arms around her friend, hugging her close. 'And thank you for listening.'

'Anytime. I know I'm a bit preoccupied with Betty at the moment, but I mean it. And good luck tonight.' Claudia winked and nudged Robyn in the ribs. 'I'd better go, I'm hoping Mel can fit me in for a quick trim before the kids finish school.'

'You can leave Betty with me if you like,' Robyn said. She could take her out for a walk, maybe down to the beach. She'd been in all day; it would be good to get some fresh air.

Claudia shook her head. 'Thanks for the offer, but she'll wake up soon and want feeding and you haven't got the equipment . . . ' She froze and then she groaned. 'Bugger. I've done it again. Robyn, I'm sorry.'

'Hello girls. Sorry for what?' Finn appeared at the kitchen doorway, having let himself noiselessly into the cottage. His eyes scanned her face for clues.

Robyn's heart flickered. He was her everything, what would she do if his love for her had changed? 'Nothing, because there's no need to apologise,' she managed a laugh. 'Claudia was just saying that I couldn't look after Betty because I can't breastfeed her. But neither could anyone else in the family.'

'That's true, thank you,' Claudia said meekly. 'Anyway, I'll leave you two lovebirds to it. Finn, you're on a promise tonight; Robyn's wearing her sexy undies.'

She kissed them both goodbye and Finn stood aside to let her manoeuvre the pram back to the front door.

Thanks, Claudia. Robyn sighed inwardly; so much for her plans for a slow and gentle seduction.

Finn gazed at her, his eyebrows raised. Robyn tried to read his expression; was it shock or fear? The lack of accompanying smile wasn't encouraging. Maybe Claudia was right, perhaps he was worried about hurting her. If so, it was up to her to convince him otherwise.

'Hello handsome,' she murmured as she stepped towards him; she could feel the thud of her heart speeding up with every beat.

'Hello beautiful,' he replied. 'What's Claudia talking about?'

'About us. About how jealous she is that we can have a relaxing candlelit bath together without anyone interrupting us.' She slipped her arms around his neck, pressing herself against the full length of his taut, lean body. She reached up to his ear and whispered. 'Want to see what's under my jumper?'

He laughed and leaned back. 'Bloody hell, Robyn, it's a bit early, isn't it?'

She felt her courage beginning to wane, but held tight, pressing her lips fiercely to his. 'Nope. It's the perfect time.'

He kissed her forehead and groaned. 'I'd love to. But I only popped in to tell you that I'll be working late at the yard and then Callum's asked the lads to meet for a drink to wet the baby's head. Is that OK?'

'Sure, but you don't have to rush off, do you?' She gave him a smile which she hoped was seductive, took one of his hands and pressed it to her breast. 'You won't hurt me.'

Robyn held her breath, hoping that this would be the moment which reconnected them. For a second or two neither of them moved or spoke; her pulse was loud in her ears and her stomach fluttered with nerves as she willed Finn to relax. But he was stiff with tension.

'I want to, but . . . ' he stuttered, dropping his hand. 'I can't. I'm sorry.'

Robyn was devastated. 'Finn, what's wrong?'

'Nothing, honestly!' He gave her a smile which didn't meet his eyes and kissed her roughly. 'I need to get back to work, that's all.'

She watched him leave, her heart in tatters as he strode away. She couldn't help feeling that she was losing him. Or maybe she'd lost him already.

Chapter Nineteen

Katie had kept an eye out for Barney passing by to give him his refund, but then, over a week after Amber's visit, in he walked.

'Hello, ladies.' Barney hesitated at the door as everyone turned to stare.

Katie's heart surprised her by giving a little leap at the sight of him. It was probably because of his story, she thought: losing his wife, bringing up his daughter by himself and the adorable way he'd wanted Amber's first bra experience to be special.

'Hello again,' she said, willing her face not to betray how nice it was to see him.

She and Nula were both with customers. Nula's customer was a holidaymaker in her fifties, trying on swimwear, while Katie was helping Mel, the hairdresser. Much to Katie's delight, Mel had dashed in between clients looking for something to boost her confidence. She'd started internet dating and was meeting someone in real life for the first time later.

'I'll be right with you,' said Nula, practically tripping over her own tongue.

'Actually,' he said, rubbing the back of his neck, 'it's Katie I've come to see.'

'Oh.' Nula gave her a look which said that she'd kept *that one* quiet.

'I'll be right with you,' said Katie.

'No rush.' He shoved his hands in his pockets and looked around, whistling softly under his breath before noticing Mel. 'Oh, hey.'

'Hi,' Mel simpered, shoving the lacy thong she was inspecting back on the rail, and whispered to Katie. 'That's my hot new neighbour. How do you know him?'

Katie felt her face heat up. 'I don't. Well, other than as a customer. His daughter, I mean,' she added, at Mel's raised eyebrow.

'Men are so lucky,' Mel said with a sigh, with a side-eyed glance at Barney. She held up a pair of control briefs, testing the strength of the tummy panel. 'They simply pull on their old boxers and go. While we women have to shoehorn ourselves into all sorts of things to look good.'

'Not on my watch, you don't,' said Katie, taking the big knickers out of her hands and replacing them with a pair of Brazilian knickers which were far more appropriate. 'You'll leave here with underwear as soft and comfortable as a second skin.'

'These?' Mel huffed. 'With my mum-tum?'

Barney smiled. 'I feel like I might be wading into treacherous waters by joining in, but I'll just say you look wonderful to me.'

'Oh.' Mel practically melted on the spot and Nula let out a dreamy sigh.

Just then the changing–cubicle curtain was whipped aside.

'What do you think?' The visiting tourist did a half-twirl to show Nula her swimsuit and placed a hand over her decolletage. 'I'm not sure it's long enough in the body. It feels a bit low at the front.'

That was an understatement. She'd had balls to come out like that, Katie thought. Although, to be honest, if she did have balls, they'd be currently on display; the one-piece was high where it needed to be low, and low where it should have been high, and consequently left very little to the imagination.

Katie coughed loudly and grabbed Barney's arm to pull him out of her eyeline while Nula bundled the woman back inside the cubicle, trying to shield the woman's dimply bottom from view.

'You've got it on back to front,' Nula muttered. 'And we do ask customers to keep their underwear on.'

'That's me put off thongs for a while,' Mel said in a whisper. She took out her credit card. 'I'll take your advice and go for these Brazilians.'

'Good choice.' Katie quickly wrapped them in tissue paper. 'And good luck with the man.'

'Likewise,' Mel murmured, her lips twitching as she cast a furtive glance to where Barney was waiting.

Katie tried to think of a witty response but failed. Anyway, the more she said, the more likely she was to blush. She couldn't help it; good-looking single men were in short supply in Merle Bay and there was just something so lovely about Barney. 'See you soon,' she said simply, handing Mel the bag.

Mel waved at Barney before leaving just as Nula and her lady approached the cash desk to pay for the swimsuit.

'So.' Katie fought to keep her smile under control. 'Hello again.'

'Apparently a miracle has happened,' Barney said, feigning amazement. 'And you owe me money.'

'That's true. One sec.' Katie rummaged under the counter to find the note she'd made of the amount.

The swimsuit lady paid cash and left hurriedly, giving Nula the opportunity to loiter and gaze unashamedly at Barney.

'Four pounds ninety pence to go back on your credit card,' said Katie.

'Thank you.' Barney delved into the pocket of his jeans and brought out his wallet. 'And thanks for helping her out. . . ' He glanced awkwardly in Nula's direction.

'You're welcome. Nula, would you mind putting the kettle on?' Katie asked her. 'I'm parched.'

Nula had propped her elbow on the counter, chin in hand. 'There's coffee in the pot.'

'I'd like herbal tea please,' said Katie, keen to have Barney to herself.

Nula reluctantly offered Barney a drink, but he declined, and she gave Katie a sulky look before trudging off to the kettle.

'We had a good chat, Amber and I,' Barney continued, with a shy smile. 'I told her about the time I'd bought Sophia underwear for Valentine's Day and messed it up and she said her goal is one day to order a massive amount of posh underwear just like her mum used to do.'

'On Black Friday,' Katie said, nodding. 'She told me that too.'

'Did she?' His face lit up and then faded. 'Bless her.'

Her heart twisted, watching the emotions flash across his face; love for other women in his life, his past, his present.

'Herbal tea.' Nula thumped the mug down on the counter and resumed her position admiring Barney.

'Oh, I probably shouldn't say anything, but I guess you've received the letter?'

Katie's heart pounded. 'Letter?'

He nodded. 'Congratulations! Nominated for Independent Retailer of the Year! You must be chuffed.'

She let out a breath and chided herself; what did she think he meant? There was no way he'd know about the other letters. She suppressed a shiver; she hadn't heard anything else from the mystery sender. Was it too much to hope that whoever was behind them had decided not to pursue her?

'Oh that, yes, thanks.' She smiled shakily. 'Lovely news.'

'*Oh that.*' Nula mimicked and rolled her eyes.

'Barney is the editor of the *Gazette*,' Katie told Nula.

'You've done well to get this far,' said Barney with a grin. 'That's what I always tell myself anyway when I've been nominated for a journalism award and don't win. Which, by the way, is every time so far. And it's great publicity for you.'

'Yes, I know,' said Katie flatly.

'That's what I keep saying,' Nula exclaimed. 'It's your time to shine, pet.'

'Hmm.' Publicity was exactly what she didn't want right now. The idea of sticking her head above the parapet made her want to run for the Cheviot Hills.

'I'll be doing some features on the nominees,' said Barney. 'And I know advertising won't miss the opportunity to get in touch.'

'Ooh!' Nula's eyes sparkled. 'Imagine that, Katie. Us in the paper!'

Yeah, imagine. Katie's stomach flipped; that was all she needed. 'Glad to hear that you do do some work.' Katie ignored Nula and arched an eyebrow playfully. 'You never seem to be in the office.'

Barney laughed. 'It's a small team, which means that sometimes I get to go out and about and do my own reporting.'

'Well, I'm happy to give you an interview.' Nula folded her arms and leaned forward on the counter. 'When Jean Small died, Katie thought sales would drop off. The shop being called Auntie Small's, you know. But no, have they 'eck – sales are up! Katie has brought all sorts of new products into the shop, swimwear, hosiery, even men's undies. I've had to increase my hours.' She stopped to peer at Barney. 'Don't you want to get any of this down?'

Barney scratched his nose and gallantly hid a smile. 'Sorry, I was planning on sitting down to do the feature.' He hesitated and looked at Katie. 'I was wondering if I could meet you for coffee, to do an interview?'

Katie's insides fizzed with excitement. It was just business, she knew that. He'd be talking to all the nominees. But all the same, the thought of spending some time alone, away from the shop, in his company made her heart swoop.

'Yes,' she found herself saying, despite her aversion to publicity. 'That would be lovely.'

Nula elbowed her way in front of Katie again. 'You probably wouldn't guess it but I'm sixty-eight, you know. I'd have retired by now, but—' She paused to pat her hair. 'I'm an indispensable part of this shop. Anyway, working keeps you young and fit. Look at this.' Nula kicked her leg up high in the air and rested the heel of her court shoe on the counter like a geriatric ballerina. 'I'm very flexible.'

A bubble of laughter escaped as Katie met Barney's eye and she sent up a silent prayer of thanks that at least Nula was in her slacks today.

'Impressive,' said Barney, deadpan.

The bell above the door jangled as the door opened. Nula yelped and grabbed hold of her leg to lower it. The three of them turned to see Amber hovering in the doorway. Her school skirt looked a bit short and Katie wondered if she'd started rolling up the waistband like she and Rose used to do at her age.

'Hello, trouble,' Barney grinned and held his arm out to her.

'Dad!' Amber said, startled, her face flushing bright pink, but she dutifully tucked herself into his side and let him hug her.

Nula had gone a funny colour too – ash grey in her case. Katie led her over to a chair.

'Serves you right, Darcey Bussell,' she whispered to her. 'What were you thinking, flinging yourself about like that?'

'I wasn't thinking at all,' Nula muttered, rubbing her the back of her thigh. 'I'm a silly old fool. A handsome man walks in and my hormones go wild.'

'You get off home,' said Katie, shaking her head fondly. 'A hot bath with some Radox in it.'

Nula nodded and with Katie's help got to her feet and limped into the storeroom at the back to collect her handbag.

'Were you looking for me?' Barney said to his daughter.

'No, I . . . ' She flashed Katie a look of panic. 'I wondered if Katie wanted to come and see the kittens with me?'

'Alice's kittens, by any chance?' Katie smiled.

Amber nodded. 'We're getting a black boy one. Dad wants to call him Elvis.'

'Ah-huh-huh,' said Barney, doing an Elvis impression.

'Kill me now.' Amber closed her eyes in embarrassment.

Katie giggled. 'I'd love to come and see the kittens. The shop closes at five, can we go then?'

'Great.' Amber's face softened with relief, which made Katie suspect that she'd come in to see her for something else entirely. 'Come on Dad, you can buy me an ice cream at the beach. See you later, Katie.'

'Lucky me.' Barney shook his head in amusement.

'After that Elvis impersonation?' His daughter gave him a stern look. 'Believe me, you're lucky I'm still talking to you.'

'I'll give you a call then, shall I?' Barney said. 'To set up that coffee?'

Katie felt her face pinken and managed a half-hearted nod.

'What coffee?' Amber's head shot up like a meerkat. She looked from her father to Katie suspiciously.

'I'll tell you on the way,' said Barney, ruffling her hair.

The two of them left and Katie gazed after them, hardly aware of the dreamy smile on her face.

Nula reappeared at her side ready for home. 'What a dish. If only I were twenty years younger,' she sighed.

'You'd still be a decade too old for him,' Katie teased her.

'Rude,' Nula huffed. 'Ooh look, parcel delivery.'

A courier's van had pulled up on the narrow pavement outside the shop. Katie's heart sank. Not a stock delivery at this time of the day? She made it a rule to always unpack new stock as soon as it arrived; it was easier to report any missing items that way. Normally it wouldn't bother her, but she wanted to be free for Amber at five o'clock.

'You go home,' said Katie, 'I'll deal with it.'

Nula limped to the door, muttering under her breath about being too old for this lark and held it open for the courier before slipping out into the afternoon sunshine.

'Just this.' The delivery driver placed an envelope on the counter and held out a clipboard. 'Sign here, please.'

A spike of adrenaline pulsed through her. It was a manila envelope, identical to the previous two. Her name, Catherine Small, handwritten in capitals just as before. Her hand was shaking so much that her signature was illegible.

The door closed behind the man as he left and Katie stared at the envelope, terrified at what the message might be this time. As her fingers felt for the edge of the flap, she remembered Robyn's suggestion and exhaled with relief.

Katie's mouth was dry as she picked up her phone and took a photograph of the envelope. She sent the picture to the Sea Glass Sisterhood WhatsApp group along with a message.

Katie: Anyone free to meet on the beach tonight at 7? I think I've had another letter X

Robyn: Yes of course, try not to panic, we're in it together xx

Grace: Definitely. Chin up, see you later x

Chapter Twenty

At five o'clock, Katie shoved the letter in her bag, shut the shop and walked the couple of steps to her own cottage. She was turning the key in the lock when someone yelled her name. She gasped and clutched her chest; she'd been on edge ever since the courier had delivered the letter. Her head had been so preoccupied running through all the 'what if' scenarios that she'd totally forgotten about meeting Amber.

'Hi, perfect timing. Come on in.' She painted on a big smile as the girl charged towards her, hair flying.

'Cool,' said Amber, sliding in ahead of her.

'Make yourself at home,' said Katie, amused, as Amber dumped her school bag and tugged her school blazer off. 'Do you want a drink of anything, or shall we go and look at those kittens straight away?'

Amber looked sheepish and twirled a lock of her hair round her fingers. 'Actually, can we forget the kittens? I came to ask you something but seeing Dad in the shop freaked me out, so I said the first thing that came into my head.'

'I did wonder.' Katie was intrigued and also touched that Amber would think of asking her anything.

The teenager walked around the living room, inspecting it. 'Your house isn't what I expected.'

'Oh?' Katie took her shoes off and sat down on the sofa, amused.

'It's a bit old ladyish.' Amber wrinkled her nose. 'And you're not *that* old.'

'Thanks.' Katie gave a bark of laughter. She hadn't considered twenty-eight as old at all.

'Sorry, that's really rude.' Amber winced. 'It's probably retro and really trendy? I can't tell. Mum did all our interior stuff and she liked quite modernish. Not weird modern. Just IKEA modern.'

'I like modern, but I like cosy cottage too.' She paused, realising that she hadn't really ever thought about what styles she liked; she'd either lived with her parents or her aunt and neither place had been hers to decorate.

'Yeah?' Amber looked around her doubtfully, her eyes settling on Auntie Jean's collection of miniature cottages which took up three whole shelves in the built-in bookcase one side of the fireplace. The other two were sun-faded cookery books mostly by Delia Smith and Mary Berry.

'My aunt used to collect those pottery cottages,' Katie explained, in case Amber thought that was *her* idea of cosy cottage. 'Lots of people did when I was little. I inherited this house from her, so what you see is her taste.'

'That explains a lot,' Amber grinned, peering into one of Auntie Jean's bags for life. 'Why do you have this big bag of stones in here?'

'It's sea glass. My aunt collected it. There are more bags in other rooms.'

'Right?' Amber looked at her, waiting for the rest of the answer.

'And, well, I haven't got around to moving many of her things since she died.'

'I get that.' Amber flopped down at the other end of the sofa. 'Me and Dad were the same about our house when

Mum died. Even buying a new cushion felt like we were cheating on her.'

'Is that why you moved up north?'

She shrugged. 'It's one reason. He got headhunted by the newspaper and he said it felt like the right time for a change. His old job used to be really long hours and he wanted to be around more for me. I think Dad came here when he was little, and he remembered it as being the best holiday ever.'

'You must miss your friends.'

'Not really.' Amber wrinkled her nose. 'I've made some new friends here, which is good. Most of the girls from my old school ghosted me after the accident. Nobody knew what to say so they decided to say nothing. And I was off school for ages because of my injuries. By the time I went back, my group had shut me out.'

Poor kid, Katie's heart squeezed for her.

'You say most of the girls,' Katie prompted, hoping that at least one of them had stood by her.

'My best friend Ellie kept in touch. Still does. Except now she's going out with this boy and all the messages I get from her are about how gorgeous he is.' She rolled her eyes.

How resilient and courageous she was. Katie was reminded of her own situation, how Rose had been as close as a sister and then, like Amber's friends, had ghosted her.

Weirdly, Katie's mum had run into Rose's mother last year after joining a choir. At her first session she'd stood next to a dark-haired woman and after introducing herself, found out that it was none other than Valerie Dunbar. Her mum hadn't really known Valerie when Katie was at school; parents didn't meet at the secondary school gates like they did in primary, but Katie had always been a bit scared of her. Over the course of the last year, although not friends exactly, Josie and Valerie swapped information about their daughters and what they were up to with their lives. Rose still had a difficult relationship with her mother apparently but was doing quite well at work; she was an accountant, already divorced, no kids. There'd been no suggestion of putting the young women in touch. Fine with Katie; she had no wish to be reminded of being eighteen again.

Life didn't seem very even-handed when it doled out its challenges, thought Katie watching Amber flick through a pile of Auntie Jean's old puzzle books; some people definitely got more than their fair share. She checked the time on her phone. She had an hour and a half before she needed to meet Grace and Robyn; hopefully, that would be plenty of time to get to the bottom of whatever was troubling Amber today.

Amber caught her gesture. 'You're probably busy so I'll get straight to the point. I need some help with something.'

'I've got plenty of time, I promise, and I'm honoured that you're asking me,' said Katie.

'Don't be too honoured, I don't know many other women.' Amber gave her a lopsided smile and Katie couldn't help laughing. There was no chance of an inflated ego with this girl around.

'OK. Fire away,' said Katie.

Amber tucked her hair behind her ears. 'It's about periods.'

'Have you started?' Katie wanted to wrap her arms around her and hug her tightly, the precious thing.

There was a slight flush to her cheeks and Amber shook her head. 'No. But I was in the loos in school and there was a girl washing her hands and crying. I don't know her, I think she's in the year above, but I asked what was wrong.

And she said she had her period and didn't have any pads and asked if I had any spare. I didn't. I said maybe her friends could give her one. But she said she couldn't ask because she asked them too many times before. So I said maybe the nurse had them. But she started crying harder and said that she'd been to the nurse before and got told off for never bringing them to school and being prepared. Then she went back in the cubicle and I could hear her crying. So, I went to the nurse's room myself and pretended it was for me and I went back and slid it under the door.'

'You were very kind,' said Katie, when Amber paused for breath. 'I'm sure that girl was really grateful.'

'She didn't open the door,' Amber continued, 'but she told me that her mum can't afford food *and* pads and she usually uses loo paper but that she keeps leaking. Her name is Ciara and she said she sometimes misses school because her period is too heavy.'

'That's awful. I bet she was so grateful that a kind girl like you came along.' Katie's heart brimmed with sadness; that girls in this country had to face this sort of poverty was appalling.

'And there's something else.' Amber nibbled her bottom lip. 'She wasn't wearing a bra and, well, she should have been. She isn't as big as . . . ' She glanced quickly at Katie. 'As some people.'

Katie folded her arms self-consciously.

'But big for a schoolgirl,' Amber continued. 'I think maybe her mum can't afford a bra for her either.'

'Right, well we can do something about that.'

Her eyes widened. '*We?*'

Katie nodded. 'You and me.'

'Thank you.' Amber's shoulders sagged with relief. She kicked off her shoes and folded her legs under her. 'I was going to do it by myself, I just wanted your advice, but it would be amazing if you could help.'

'What were you going to do?'

'Put a box of emergency stuff in the girls' toilets so people can help themselves for free.'

'It's a brilliant idea!' said Katie.'

'Do you think so?' The girl's eyes shone with pride.

Katie nodded. 'How can I help?'

Amber bit her lip. 'I've got some money and I'm sure school would let me if I asked them. But I'm not sure what to actually buy. I looked in the shop but there are so many different ones. If Mum was here she'd probably storm into school, demand to see the nurse and give her a right earful for not being kinder to Ciara. But she's not, so . . . ' She paused, shrugging.

Katie was in awe of her, not just for helping the girl out in her hour of need, or for her willingness to spend her own money to help others, but for her unquestioning belief that this was a problem that she, Amber Larkin, aged fourteen could solve. She got to her feet and picked up her handbag. 'Come on, we can sort this out between us. Let's go and raid the shelves in the little supermarket.'

Amber scrambled to her feet. 'And what about bras?'

Katie frowned. 'That's a bit more tricky. I don't think we can put a box of bras in the toilets, can we?'

'No.' She looked thoughtful. 'And I can't afford to buy bras from your shop; not on my budget. The only place we've got for clothes is the lost property box.'

'Would second-hand bras work, do you think?' Katie had read of a charity which sent donations of bras to Third World countries. A bra was a status symbol in some cultures, a sign that someone was looking after a woman, which sent a signal to would-be predators to leave her alone. Maybe

Katie could set up something similar to help British girls and women too? She certainly had the contacts and the bra knowledge.

Amber shrugged. 'As long as they're not too scabby.'

Katie grinned. 'Noted. No scabby bras.'

'Weird, isn't it,' said Amber, leaning on the wall as Katie pulled the cottage door closed behind them, 'how small things can make a massive difference?'

Katie nodded. 'Small things matter.'

Amber peeled herself away from the wall. 'Don't take this the wrong way, but I think you should maybe make your house a bit more, you know. You.'

'I'm going to take that as a compliment,' Katie said, hiding a smile.

'Oh totally,' said Amber innocently. 'You're quite cool.'

'For an old person?' Katie added.

'You're not *that* old.'

Such a wise and confident head on young shoulders, thought Katie as they made their way to the Merle Bay supermarket. She wondered what Amber would make of her naked photos and the mystery sender's plan to discredit her. She'd be furious at the injustice of it, no doubt. Not that Katie would dream of discussing it with a child; no, this was a matter for the Sea Glass Sisterhood.

Chapter Twenty-One

The atmosphere crackled with anticipation as Grace, Robyn and Katie stared at the newly delivered envelope on the table in front of them. They'd met on the beach as planned but Grace had persuaded them both up to her terrace to sit in comfort and out of the cool sea breeze with a gin and tonic and a bowl of pistachio nuts. She did feel for Katie; it was obvious the poor girl was terrified about what fresh hell the latest envelope might contain.

Katie's hands were shaking. 'I feel sick; I don't think I can open it.'

'You do look pale.' Grace glanced around for a suitable receptacle, just in case. The bucket Robyn had given her for collecting sea glass was at the top of the steps. If needs be, Grace could tip out the glass and hand it to her in a flash. 'Take your time,' she said, 'and remember you're not in this by yourself.'

'Deep breaths,' said Robyn, reaching a hand across the table to squeeze Katie's arm. She looked almost as pale as Katie, Grace noticed. There were dark smudges under her eyes and her face had a pinched look.

Katie inhaled and exhaled a couple of times and picked up the envelope. 'OK, here goes.'

She peeled back the flap carefully and took out two sheets of paper. 'A letter and then some sort of map.'

'What does it say?' Robyn leaned forward.

Katie cleared her throat and read the short note out loud and then put it down so the other two could read it themselves.

This is what we want you to do. Five thousand pounds cash to be put in a holdall and left in a waste bin near the bandstand in Jubilee Park (see page two for directions) and you'll never hear from us again. Don't waste your time going to the police, the minute we suspect that you're not playing ball, the pictures will be sent to the press. Do as you're told, and this will soon be over.

The second page showed a map of Jubilee Park with a spot circled in red marker pen beside the bandstand. Scribbled at the edge of the page, also in red pen, was the time and date for the drop-off. It was two weeks from today.

'Five thousand pounds!' Robyn gasped.

'Who's doing this?' Katie said, picking absently at a discarded pistachio shell. 'Who'd want to blackmail me?'

'Whoever it is has had access to the pictures of you,' Grace said. 'Apart from the photographer and the assistant, can you think of anyone else?'

Katie shook her head. 'I can't think of anyone. Dad picked me up from school that day and took me home. Mum made me show her, but I begged her not to let Dad see them. We kept them in the envelope for a while. Dad was adamant that we should keep them as evidence. But one day when they were out, I burned them.'

'What if the photographer passed away and whoever has gone through his stuff found all his old photos and has decided to exploit the models again?' said Robyn.

Katie's eyes widened. 'You mean it might not just be me who's being targeted? I never thought of that. But why now? Ten years on?'

'Maybe exactly for that reason,' said Grace. 'Ten years on, lives will have changed. The models will be women now whose reputations could be ruined by these pictures coming out now.'

'Like me,' Katie said in a small voice. 'It's like something out of a bad film.'

The three of them went quiet, sipping at their gin.

Grace helped herself to a handful of pistachios and read the note again. Katie was right; it was exactly like the plot of a bad film. She could give Katie five thousand pounds right now; it would scarcely make a dent in her bank balance. It would be worth it to see the anxiety disappear from the poor girl's face. But in films the blackmailer usually got greedy and came back for more. She thought about Julia and Austin and Olivia. All three of them clamouring for a bigger slice of pie. They made her sick. And Julia . . . she was the worst. Threatening her with exposing Myles's affair – *alleged* affair, she corrected herself – purely for monetary gain, regardless of the emotional cost to his widow. Julia's behaviour was as bad as that of Katie's blackmailer.

'It's the greed I don't understand,' Grace said bitterly. 'Screwing innocent, hardworking people for money they don't deserve. It's beyond me how people can be so callous for their own wicked ends.'

She had found absolutely nothing to suggest that Julia was telling the truth. She'd spent the entire day going back meticulously through his computerised diary looking for unusual entries, through his online banking for unusual spending. She'd discovered nothing except disgust at her own treacherous mind. The only thing she couldn't do was go through his clothes to see if he had incriminating receipts in his pockets, or stray lipstick marks on his shirts or the smell of perfume lingering on his jumpers. All his clothes still hung in their wardrobe at home. She could go back and look, but there was no point; if there'd been anything to find, she'd have found it by now. There was just one last thing to do before consigning this whole unsavoury episode to the bin and that was to speak to Ned. Grace knew he'd been at that funeral; all she needed was for him to say Myles had never mentioned anything about an affair to him and then as far as she was concerned, the subject was closed. She'd phoned him that afternoon, but he hadn't picked up, so she'd called his office to be told that he was travelling long haul. She'd left a message but had been told it might take a while for him to get back to her. So, until then, all she could do was wait.

'Grace?' Robyn waved a hand in front of her face. 'Are you still with us?'

She shifted in her seat and blinked. 'Sorry, what did you say?'

Katie wrapped her arms around herself protectively. 'What would you do now, if this was you?'

Grace blew out a long breath. She thought back to before she and Myles had sold the company. To when she'd been a director of Byron Homes and staff looked up to her. She imagined the shock or the smirks on their faces, the laughing behind her back. However confident she was about her body, people would feel differently about her and she knew she wouldn't like it. As Robyn had said, it was the threat to her reputation which would hurt her the most.

'I'd hate it,' she said strongly. 'And I'd move heaven and earth to make sure the pictures never saw the light of day.'

'That's how I feel.' Katie's eyes filled with tears and Grace took her hand; she was so glad that Katie had reached out to them and agreed to share her troubles. It seemed a shame that such a lovely girl had no one in her life she felt she could turn to. She understood not wanting to upset her parents, but where were her old friends?

'Whatever you do,' Grace promised, 'you've got us on your side. Right, Robyn?'

'Absolutely,' Robyn agreed, her dark eyes full of concern for her friend. 'If I'd been in your shoes at eighteen, I'd have gone to London and done the shoot too, so I'm totally with you there. I was an "act first, think it through later" sort of girl at that age. You were a young woman who was misled. You have nothing to be ashamed of. And what would I do now if this was happening to me?' Robyn's jaw was set firmly. 'I'd fight back. Tooth and bloody nail. So much of our lives is outside of our control. But our bodies are an intrinsic part of what makes us *us*. Your body is yours and yours alone; it should be your decision who gets to see it. Not some photographer cretin in it for the cheap thrills.'

'Hear, hear.' Grace raised her glass. 'So. Action plan. The way I see it, there are three options. We pay up, we go to the police, or we ignore it and call their bluff.'

'And like Grace says, it's definitely a "we",' said Robyn.

'Thanks, girls,' Katie smiled weakly. 'I'm really grateful. But there's something else to factor into the equation: the regional business awards.'

'Oh yes!' said Robyn. She chinked her glass against Katie's. 'We should definitely toast that.'

'And, looking on the bright side, you'll have something nice to look forward to: a fancy night out. I love getting dressed up.' Grace swallowed the lump in her throat remembering the last such event she and Myles had been to. Byron Homes had been nominated for the 'Sustainability' category at the National Housebuilder Awards. They'd taken all the managers and their partners, booked three tables and bought champagne for everyone, no expense spared. It had been such a celebration. They didn't win but Myles had toasted Grace and told her that he didn't care about an engraved lump of crystal because he was going home with the ultimate prize – her.

'Yes, but the timing couldn't be any worse,' Katie pointed out. 'The event is on Thursday, just over two weeks from now, the day after I'm supposed to be dropping five grand at Jubilee Park. The list of nominees is going to be printed in the paper this week. Don't you think this is going to provoke the blackmailer even more? It might even put the price up if they think I've got more to lose by having these pictures exposed. And look at who's organising it – the *Gazette*. The very place my pictures are going to end up if I don't play ball! On top of that I've agreed that Barney can interview me.'

'Barney?' Robyn and Grace asked together.

'Barney Larkin, the editor.' Katie blushed prettily. 'He came into buy his daughter's first bra. That's how we met.'

'What is your heart telling you to do?' Grace asked her.

Katie sighed. 'Pay up, ask them to delete the pictures and hope it all goes away?'

'But if you pay up once, what's to stop them asking again?' said Grace.

'And you'll never know if they actually did delete them. They could do this forever,' Robyn pointed out.

They batted the options backwards and forwards between them and came to the conclusion that they weren't going to do anything hasty. Katie was going to keep trying to find the whereabouts of Howard the photographer and his 'assistant', Jay. Grace offered to speak to her solicitor to see if he had any advice, and Robyn was going to research similar cases of blackmail to work out what the most successful course of action might be.

A sharp gust of wind made it over the glass balustrade and swirled around them, liberating the discarded pistachio shells from their bowl. Robyn pulled her jumper more tightly around her while Grace scooped up the shells.

'It's gone chilly. I know what we need.' Grace jumped to her feet. 'A dip in the hot tub. I've been waiting for an excuse to use it.'

'I haven't brought a swimsuit,' Robyn protested.

'Nor me,' Katie said. 'Nice idea, but maybe next time.'

'Just leave your undies on,' said Grace with a grin. 'You're amongst friends. And just think how nice and warm it will be in the water. I'll fetch us some towels.'

'It's a lovely thought.' Katie crossed her arms over chest. 'But I'd rather not.'

Grace noted the set of Katie's jaw and cursed the photographer who was behind Katie's lack of confidence; if she ever got her hands on him, he'd be sorry. 'You're a beautiful woman,' she said softly. 'Don't be afraid to show off your assets.'

'*Assets*? As in boobs?' Robyn's reaction was so violent that Grace was taken aback. 'And if you haven't got your boobs anymore, does that make you asset-less? Without value? *Not* a beautiful woman?'

'Of course not!' Grace gave a bewildered laugh but fell silent when she saw Robyn's hurt expression. 'That wasn't what I meant. Sorry love, I don't understand.'

Robyn blinked rapidly. 'Nobody does. Unless you've walked in my shoes, you couldn't possibly.'

'What's wrong?' Katie asked. 'Talk to us.'

'I've had a bilateral mastectomy and had my ovaries removed.' Robyn blurted out in a rush. 'I find it hard to

205

talk about it. Hardly surprising when my friends and family seem intent on reminding me how much less of a woman I am at every opportunity. I should go.'

Robyn pushed her chair back so rapidly that the legs scraped harshly on the patio and strode to the gate leading down to the beach, disappearing through it before either of them could react.

'Shit.' Katie stared at Grace, horrified. 'I should have guessed when she was in the shop; she spent ages reading a poster in the shop aimed at ladies who've had mastectomies.'

'And she lost her mum to breast cancer, too.' Grace groaned. 'Poor chick. We can't let her leave like this.' She ran after her; Robyn was almost down at the beach.

'Robyn, I'm sorry. Please come and talk to us,' she shouted at the top of her voice. 'We made a deal, remember? To bare our souls.'

Robyn stopped in her tracks and turned back to look at her. She'd got her attention. Good.

'The Sea Glass Sisterhood,' she pressed on. 'We're in this together. Friends. So, let us be a friend to you.'

Robyn rubbed her face, hesitating, and then nodded. Grace breathed a sigh of relief as she met Robyn halfway up the steps.

'I'm sorry,' said Grace, pulling her into a hug. 'You are an amazing, brave and fabulous woman, with more assets than I can shake a stick at. I'm so sorry if I made you feel any differently.'

'Apology accepted.' Robyn managed a smile. 'Providing you pour me another gin.'

Grace swept an arm in front of her, leading the way back to where Katie was waiting at the table.

'Coming right up.'

Chapter Twenty-Two

'I'm so sorry.' Katie stood up as Robyn reappeared on the patio and held her arms out to hug her. 'Who said you can't keep a secret in this village, eh? I had no idea. And I'm supposed to be an expert.'

'Not your fault,' Robyn said gruffly. 'With my clothes on I look the same as anyone else.'

Secretly Robyn was pleased to have had an excuse to come back. She'd regretted her actions as soon as she'd stood up, aware she was behaving like a sulky teen, but her ego wouldn't let her easily turn back.

Grace pressed a hand to her forehead. 'And there was me, telling you to strip off to go in the hot tub. If I'd known . . . '

Robyn shrugged. 'But you *weren't* to know, and I apologise for overreacting. I kept it secret because I didn't want anyone's pity, and because people never know how to react when I tell them. And because . . . ' she swallowed, desperately trying to keep control of her emotions. 'Because I feel guilty.'

Katie frowned. 'What can you possibly have to feel guilty about?'

The sky had darkened, and the air had a chill to it. Robyn shivered. She'd been out for hours and hadn't taken her mobile with her. Finn would be worried. *Or would he?* she thought with a pang. Maybe he'd be relieved.

'Oh Katie,' she sighed. 'Where to start.'

'Let's go inside.' Grace put an arm around her waist. 'And if you want to talk about it, we're listening, OK?'

Once inside, the women decided that more gin might make them maudlin and that hot chocolate would be much more soothing. While Grace heated milk and Katie made herself comfy on the sofa, Robyn paced the large open-plan space, trying to put her thoughts in order. The sun had sunk out of view, but the sky still held its amber glow, and the room was drenched in gentle, golden light. Grace's presence was evident now: there was a new rug on the floor; a vase of pink lilies; fat creamy candles, their scent adding a sweet warmth to the room and photographs everywhere. Of Myles, and of Grace and Myles, and some of a woman with a baby in her arms. The little touches had knocked the stark edges off the room, made it feel more like a home than the showhouse it had been the first time she'd seen it. Robyn felt safe here, and she knew she was among friends. Each time she met them, her affection for these two women deepened. She knew she had to confide in them. Firstly, because that was what friends did and secondly because she was running out of options; if she didn't find a way to reach Finn soon, she risked losing him altogether.

'Here we go.' Grace set a table with three mugs of hot chocolate and a box of truffles on the table. 'Dig in, girls.'

Robyn picked up a mug, chose a chocolate from the box and walked across to the long sweep of glass which separated them from the outdoors. She bit into a dark chocolate truffle and wiped the cocoa powder from her mouth, preparing herself to speak.

You can do this, she told herself. She turned back to Grace and Katie, sitting side by side on the sofa: Grace, smiling encouragement; Katie, face taut with worry.

'Finn and I were about to start trying for a family when I found out I was at a high risk of developing breast or ovarian cancer,' Robyn began. 'I had to make a choice between having the baby that Finn wanted, or having elective surgery to beat the odds of developing cancer. I chose to save myself.'

'That *Finn* wanted?' Grace asked astutely. 'Not you?'

Robyn nodded. Heat infused her face; it was the first time she'd ever admitted the truth to another soul.

Katie shook her head. 'What you've been through . . . it puts my problems into perspective. I feel embarrassed for making a fuss. Your situation is life and death stuff. If those pictures come to light, I'll be humiliated, but I'll live.'

'There's no need to think like that. It's not a competition.' Robyn smiled at her friend. 'Crap stuff can happen to both of us. Unfortunately. Let me tell you the whole story.'

And with the sea behind her perpetually in motion, and her two friends as still as statues, she finally opened up. From the girl-meets-boy joyful beginning, the simple DIY wedding, through to the decision to start a family which she'd found herself mistakenly swept along with. Then she told them of the discovery of her faulty gene, the surgery, the reconstruction, the drugs, pain, scars, the conversation she and Finn should have had but didn't about their abandoned plans to have a baby, and all of the million and one tiny, unscheduled things which had unbalanced the equilibrium of their marriage.

Her breath hitched as she reached the end and realised that she was crying. Grace and Katie's eyes were shiny with tears too.

Katie jumped to her feet, offered Robyn a tissue and hugged her. 'You are so brave. Thank you for telling us.'

'I'm sorry I didn't tell you straight away.' Robyn returned Katie's hug. 'But it was refreshing to meet two new people who didn't know my history. And quite liberating not to have taboo subjects. My sister-in-law, Claudia, either tiptoes around me trying not to mention breast cancer, or else drops breasts unintentionally into the conversation every five minutes. It's hard to pull the right face when someone says the wrong thing and then spends the next hour trying to apologise.'

'Katie's right, you are brave. And even more so because of what happened to your mum and your gran,' said Grace, patting the cushion beside her.

Robyn sat down. 'I don't feel brave. I feel guilty. Once I knew I had the gene I wanted the surgery right away, even though that meant us not having the baby that Finn had so wanted. I'd even been offered IVF to avoid passing on the BRCA genes, but I didn't want anything holding up the process. Maybe if I had, Finn and I would still have a strong relationship. As it is, there's a space between us, a no-man's land and neither of us is brave enough to step into it.'

'He loves you. It's natural that what you've been through has affected him,' Katie said, lowering herself into the space on the other side of Grace.

'Yeah, I know, and I feel guilty about that too,' Robyn sighed. 'But it feels like he's fallen out of love with me. He cares for me, but I could be his sister. I wore the bra you gave me and I felt sexy and womanly for the first time in months. I all but threw myself at him and he couldn't get away from me quick enough. He apologised, said he couldn't, and then left the house as quick as he could.' Her biggest worry was that her new body repulsed him, but she couldn't bring herself to voice the words. Not yet.

'And since then?' Grace prompted.

'I haven't dared mention it and neither has he. Since then, we've slept back to back, pretending everything is fine when it clearly isn't.' She gulped back tears, shaking her head in disbelief about how bad things had become. 'I've spent most of the day walking the coastal path today. When Katie sent that message, I came and waited on the beach until seven o'clock.'

'Oh love.' Grace squeezed her hand. 'You should have come in; I've been here all day.'

'I'd have been rubbish company. I'm too sad,' said Robyn, 'or maybe I'm angry.'

'You're entitled to be both,' said Katie darkly. 'I know I am.'

'And either way, you'd still be welcome, both of you,' Grace reassured them.

Robyn pressed both hands over her face and groaned. 'I'm losing him. I'm losing my best friend and my husband. He's been my family, my world since I was eighteen and without him . . . I don't even know who I am anymore. Or what I am. Finn's business is struggling, and I haven't been well enough to work so I can't even pay my share of the bills, I can't be a mother and I'm not sure I'm the wife he wants anymore either. I feel redundant on every score. I'm a failure.'

'That's not who I see when I look at you,' said Grace. 'I see a woman who's been dealt a tricky set of cards and who's handled it brilliantly and is still here to tell the tale. Maybe you don't feel like that now, but I think you'll look back and be proud of how you coped. Your mum and grandmother would certainly be proud.'

'Really?' said Robyn, her voice catching in her throat.

'Absolutely!' Grace declared.

'I know talking is difficult,' Katie began. 'But I'm sure you won't be alone in this. Have you thought of trying to find a local group? Maybe you need the reassurance of others in the same boat. Women like you – previvors – will probably have had the same thoughts, body issues and relationship setbacks as you are dealing with.'

Robyn pulled a face. 'The idea of attending a session to discuss my feelings gives me the heebie jeebies; actual nails-down-the-blackboard goosebumps. But you're right. I won't be the first person who's gone through this. Maybe group therapy will help me find a way to work this out.'

Grace sipped her hot chocolate. 'I came to Merle Bay for solitude, but I'd been here less than an hour when I realised that solitude wasn't all it's cracked up to be. Thank goodness I met you two. Just knowing you'd come to my aid if I asked you makes me want to weep with gratitude. It goes without saying that I'm here for you whenever, but on this occasion, Robyn, I agree with Katie: talking to women who've been through this themselves is bound to help you.'

'I will,' Robyn promised. 'I have to do something.'

Outside the sky had faded from candyfloss pink to chalky grey and the light in the living room had dimmed along with it. Grace stood up and switched on some lamps, then picked up her iPad from the dining table.

'Oh damn, Ned has tried to FaceTime me three times, and I've missed him,' she muttered, frowning. 'Now he'll be worried about me.'

'Ned, the man who owns this house?' Katie asked.

Grace nodded. 'I called him earlier because he was at the funeral where Myles allegedly admitted to Julia he'd had an affair. I just wondered if he'd heard Myles say anything.'

'I thought you'd dismissed that as evil gossip?' Robyn said, helping herself to another truffle.

'I have.' Grace flushed. 'But hearing it from Ned would finally mean I can forget all about it.'

'Shall we go?' Katie asked, shuffling to the edge of her seat. 'So you can call him back?'

'No, please don't,' Grace said quickly. 'I don't want to be on my own. Just in case.'

She squeezed back onto the sofa and propped the iPad on the coffee table in front of them. The three of them waited as the iPad made its connection and then a man appeared on screen.

'Hi Ned,' said Grace over-brightly.

'Grace! I got your message. How are you, my darling girl?' Ned had the sort of smile which lit up his whole face and probably everyone else's within his orbit. Even Robyn found herself beaming back at him.

'Great!' she replied with a shake to her voice. 'Meet my new Merle Bay friends, Katie and Robyn.'

'Hello ladies, that sofa looks a lot more interesting than I remember it,' Ned laughed, his eyes hinting at mischief. 'So, what's up, everything all right with the house?'

'The house is perfect,' said Grace.

'Ha! I knew you'd like it!' Ned grinned. 'You can stay as long as you like, remember.'

'Thanks.' Grace cleared her throat. 'Ned, there's something I need to ask you. Remember the funeral you went to with Myles last summer?'

He looked startled at the change of direction. 'Yes, what about it?'

Grace swallowed so loud that Robyn heard the gulp. 'Did Myles seem out of character to you?'

Ned gave a harsh laugh. 'He got blind drunk, Gracie, so yes, that was pretty out of character.'

'Yes, I know, but did he tell you anything odd?' she pressed him further.

'Um.' He looked at his hands. 'Can't say I remember.'

Ned was a terrible liar, thought Robyn, casting a sideways glance at Katie, who raised an eyebrow knowingly.

'Are you sure?' Grace asked. 'Because Julia called me to say that at that funeral, he confessed to her that he'd had an affair. She said that other people heard too. She's probably just trying to cause trouble.' Grace gave a humourless laugh. 'So, I'm hoping you'll be able to tell me she's lying.'

Robyn stared at the iPad, willing Ned to put her out of her misery. Yes or no. Preferably no.

'Ned?' Grace pushed him to reply.

He lifted his head and stared at her for a few seconds. 'Oh Grace. Don't do this to me.'

Robyn's heart broke for Grace as she felt the hope escape from her in one shuddering breath.

'Oh no.' Grace pressed a hand to her mouth.

'I'm so sorry.' Ned raked a hand through his hair. 'Bloody Julia. She's always been a troublemaker.'

'So it's true?' she said, her voice barely audible.

Ned held his hands out in a gesture of helplessness. 'He wasn't making a lot of sense at the time, but I got the impression it was just a one-off, not a full-blown affair.'

'Once is enough.' Grace's whole body heaved with a sob.

'He hated himself for it, Gracie,' Ned insisted. The easy smile had gone now, and Robyn felt quite sorry for him. 'That was why he got so drunk that day.'

'Who?' she croaked. 'Who was it?'

He shook his head, looking increasingly uncomfortable. 'He didn't say. I promise, I don't know, I'm sorry.'

Grace wiped her eyes and the two old friends stared at each other for a long moment. 'Thanks for being honest,' she said, mustering up a wobbly smile. 'Goodnight.'

'Wait!' Ned put up a hand as Grace leaned towards the iPad to end the call. 'I'm due in Merle Bay over the next week or so, can I come and visit?'

'Sure.' She shrugged, defeated. Right then, Robyn thought Grace would have agreed to anything, it was as if she'd given up caring.

He let out a breath and nodded. 'Good, hang on in there, lovely girl. I'll be thinking of you.'

Grace ended the call and Ned's anxious face disappeared.

'That's it,' she said, tears running silently down her cheeks. 'Rock bottom has officially been reached. So much for thinking I had a perfect marriage. Myles was unfaithful. Maybe he didn't even love me, maybe our whole relationship was a sham. How could he? How bloody could he? Who is she? And he's not even here for me to get angry with. The bastard.'

Katie stared down at the letter from her blackmailer. 'That is exactly how I feel too, like I've hit rock bottom. Angry with someone I don't know and out of control.'

Robyn's heart began to pound. She couldn't let this happen. Only a couple of weeks ago, she marched away from Sea Glass House after meeting these two, full of inspiration and energy, determined to get her life back on track. Now she, like them, had hit an all-time low. She'd ignored all the little signs Finn had given, the lack of intimacy even when she encouraged him, the way he fussed around her treating her like an invalid instead of his lover and then, the killer blow, turning her down when she'd offered him her body.

'Yep,' she said bitterly. 'Rock bottom just about covers it for me, too. But you know what? The future is in our hands. It's up to us to make a change. I've been in denial, but now I accept I need help, specialist help. I need to speak to other women who've been through what I've been through and learn from them. Maybe Finn has fallen out of love with me, maybe he's decided that a life without being a father isn't enough for him anymore. But I can't keep turning a blind eye to it. I need to face it and do something positive. Maybe we all needed to hit rock bottom before we could find a way back up.'

Grace looked unconvinced.

'Katie, the letter that came today?' Robyn stood up and paced the room again, filled with a surge of energy. 'Yes, the situation is horrible, but getting this letter is a good thing. You've been paralysed by fear since the first letter arrived. But now you know what you're dealing with and we can make a plan. You needn't let fear hold you back anymore.'

'I suppose so,' Katie replied cautiously. 'I don't like where I am, but at least the next move is ours.'

'And Grace. Same with you,' said Robyn. 'That phone call from Ned is a good thing too. Because now we know the truth.'

Grace's jaw was rigid with anger and hurt and disappointment. 'Ever since that phone call from Julia I've had an internal battle going on: on one hand, not wanting to believe that Myles could do that to me, and on the other, this tiny chink of doubt worming into my brain tormenting me with images of all the women we knew. Who might he have slept with? My heart is broken all over again. I don't see how knowing the truth can be a good thing.'

Katie put her arm around Grace's shoulders and the two of them leaned their heads together.

'Because knowledge is power,' said Robyn.

She pulled herself up tall and gazed out at the bay. Dusk had settled over calm waters. The sky and the sea blurred into one on the horizon and it was impossible to see where one ended and the other began. Grace, Katie and her, three women, three stories and three fights on their hands. They might be at rock bottom today, but as of tomorrow, the only way was up.

'The three of us are going to fight back. We're not going to cower away, afraid of what others think of us. We're going to show the world what we're made of.' Words weren't enough, Robyn realised, looking at Grace and Katie's uncertain faces. They needed a gesture, something with impact to show them she meant what she said. Straightaway she knew what to do and before she had a chance to talk herself out of it, she pulled her jumper off over her head.

Katie and Grace gasped in surprise.

'So, on that note,' Robyn said, challenging them with a grin. 'Who's going to join me in the hot tub?'

Chapter Twenty-Three

Katie glanced at her shopping list as she powered her way uphill to the Merle Bay supermarket: juice, crisps, something healthy for dinner and maybe, as it was a Friday, a bottle of rosé.

Since the other night at Grace's, she'd been propelled by an invisible force, teeth permanently gritted and full of a new determination not to beaten by this blackmail stuff. Unable to sleep last night, she'd fired up her laptop and googled 'how to respond to blackmail'. The search had yielded pages and pages of results and the overriding evidence was that if you gave them what they wanted, blackmailers never went away. It was about 3 a.m. when she'd finally made her decision: she wasn't going to pay up. She hadn't quite worked out how she was going to play it, but one thing was for certain, she didn't intend to sit by and let someone try and ruin her life. And in the meantime, she was turning her attention to more important things: her business, her home, her friends.

Katie wasn't short of ideas. It was time to make the cottage hers, starting with giving it a name. Lots of the cottages had names, but hers was simply 27 High Street. She wanted a name plaque up on the front door so eye-catching that tourists would want to take pictures of it. The interior would take longer to sort out. She was contemplating knocking through all the downstairs rooms into one large light and bright space. She'd consult Grace the next time she saw her; her architect's eye would probably be able to visualise a new layout instantly. Everything needed updating: décor, furniture, soft furnishings, and when funds allowed it, a new bathroom was definitely on the list.

She'd also had some thoughts about the shop, the price range in particular. The story Amber had told her about the girl who couldn't afford underwear had really struck a chord with her and she'd been wondering if she could help in some small way. And Robyn, poor gorgeous Robyn, having to go through what she had and having to readjust to her new body. Nula was brilliant with ladies looking for post-mastectomy bras, but now Katie wondered if there was more she could do to help in this area too.

That evening, they'd all climbed into the hot tub wearing only their underwear, even Grace, who could easily have put on her swimsuit. Katie had been far too self-conscious about her own semi-nakedness to be aware of how the other two were feeling. She never wore a bikini these days, she was strictly a one-piece girl. Baring her all, albeit in bra and knickers, had sent her anxiety level through the roof. But she'd done it, and once they were all submerged in the warm bubbly water, she'd found it quite liberating.

She paused on her upward march to catch her breath beside the charity shop window. It was closed for the day and the lights were off inside, but she could make out rails of clothing and a rack of shoes. No bras though, she knew that because she'd sent customers there in the past to hand over their old ones which no longer fitted. Hygiene reasons, apparently. She understood that, but it was a shame; most of them were still perfectly serviceable and had lots more wear in them.

One of the mannequins in the window wore a T-shirt which caught Katie's eye. It was by Paul Smith, a designer she'd always had a soft spot for because he'd come from Nottingham like her. It looked like it would fit her and at less than five pounds was an absolute steal. She sighed and turned away, continuing upwards. The T-shirt was no good for her, bargain or not, she'd never wear anything fitted like that. She'd found her style long ago: loose, comfortable, androgynous. It suited her figure, it was easy to work in and most importantly, nothing she wore would ever catch anyone's eye for the wrong reason. *So much for feeling liberated in the hot tub*, she thought wryly. *Old habits die hard.*

She turned at the top of the hill, entered the supermarket and picked up a basket. A few minutes later, she'd picked up most of the things on her list: juice, crisps, a punnet of strawberries she'd been unable to resist, some salad, a pomegranate and bunches of fresh mint and coriander. She fancied something different for a change, something really tasty. She aimed for the spice section for inspiration and there, arguing in front of the packets of rice were Amber and Barney, a small shopping trolley in front of them.

'It'll be delicious,' Barney laughed at the grimace on Amber's face. 'Trust me.'

'That's what you said last time,' she said, hand on hip.

Before Katie knew it her feet had carried her towards them.

'Yay!' Amber yelled, noticing Katie approaching. 'Tell him, please. He's trying to give me curried aubergine for dinner.'

'Hey, again.' Barney's eyes lit up as if he was genuinely pleased to see her. He slotted the sachet of microwave rice back onto the shelf. 'Please be on my side in this.

Everything tastes good in curry; you can't go wrong. Am I right or am I right?'

Katie tried to ignore the fizz of pleasure caused by seeing him again.

'You're probably right,' she replied, aware that she was staring at him and not even sure what she was agreeing to.

'Katie!' Amber gasped, pretending to be insulted. 'So much for the sisterhood.'

Katie put her arm around Amber's shoulders. 'Sorry, but I like curry.'

'Yes!' Barney did a double thumbs-up and laughed, a glorious triumphant laugh which made Katie smile.

Amber pretended to give him a withering look. 'You wouldn't say that if you lived in our house. We had curried fishfingers yesterday.'

'Euww,' Katie pulled a face. 'In that, case I take it back. Sorry, Barney, but that sounds gross.'

'I was going for a Katsu curry vibe,' Barney said haughtily. 'Rice, steamed greens, curry sauce and—'

'Fish fingers!' Katie and Amber hooted with laughter.

'Please, Dad,' Amber added, giving her father a side-eye look, 'people over thirty shouldn't say vibe. It's wrong.' She studied Katie briefly. 'You can still get away with it. How old are you?'

Barney grabbed his daughter playfully and hugged her to him, clapping a hand over her mouth. 'Apologies for my child; she has no filter whatsoever.'

Katie laughed. 'It's fine. I'm twenty-eight.'

'A mere babe.' Barney released his daughter and kissed the top of her head.

'Watch out, Katie,' Amber giggled, 'he just called you a babe, next thing you know, he'll be inviting you round for a curried fish finger.'

'Amber,' Barney said in a low voice. 'Careful.'

His daughter flushed and muttered an apology under her breath and Katie felt a pang of pity for her.

Barney rubbed a hand through his curls. 'I just meant you're still young enough to say vibe, I wasn't trying to say you're a babe. Although, obviously, you are, I mean— I should shut up, I'm digging myself a bigger hole.'

'I'll take it as a compliment,' Katie smiled, secretly delighted and turned away to find the couscous among the bags of grains on the shelf.

'Your food looks far nicer than ours.' Amber peered into her basket. 'Dad, can't we have what she's having?'

'No, because we've got to use our delivery,' he reminded her.

She rolled her eyes at Katie. 'We get an organic veg box delivery once a week.'

'That's right,' Barney said proudly. 'We're challenging ourselves to try new recipes and use things in the box and supplement it from our local shop.'

'It's awful,' Amber said heavily. 'And today we got an *aubergine*. What are we going to do with that?'

'Other than curry it,' Barney added.

'Baba ganoush?' Katie suggested.

Amber opened her mouth and closed it again and Barney roared with laughter. 'Someone has actually rendered my daughter speechless. It's a miracle.'

'Baba what?' Amber asked, giving her dad a playful push.

'It's an aubergine dip. Do you like hummous?' Katie asked Amber, who nodded. 'Then you'll love it.'

'Deal.' Amber linked arms with Katie. 'If you come around to ours, we can have it tonight. What else do we need to make it?'

Katie looked at Barney, who sighed with amusement.

'Katie,' he said formally, giving her a little bow. 'Would you care to join us for dinner?'

A million fireflies lit up inside her as she looked at Amber's hopeful face and Barney's handsome smile. 'I'd love to.'

'You know you're cooking it, right?' said Amber, tugging Katie to the checkout.

'What?' she feigned outrage and looked over her shoulder at Barney.

He grinned. 'It's either that or a curried fish finger.'

A little over an hour later, Katie surveyed the kitchen table on which lay a Middle-Eastern feast she'd concocted with Barney and Amber: couscous studded with pomegranate, toasted pitta bread with garlicky baba ganoush, a crisp salad and baby baked potatoes. Amber was outside transferring lamb kebabs and thick slices of halloumi from the barbeque to a plate.

Cooking with, *and for,* these two had made such a nice change to making dinner for one, and it was a treat to witness their father–daughter relationship. Amber had lost her mum and that was terrible, but she was fortunate to have a wonderful dad; anyone could see that the bond that they had was special. Barney was patient with his girl, he talked to her like a grown-up, but let her know where the boundaries were too. But as happy and cheerful as the pair of them were, Katie sensed that Sophia was very much missed. It was in the way they casually referred to 'Mum's special bowl', and the flowers in the vase by the front door (peonies, Amber pointed out, were Mum's favourites), the photographs on surfaces, cataloguing her place in the family.

Barney ushered her into a chair and took the seat opposite her.

'Thank you for inviting me for dinner,' said Katie, smiling her thanks at Barney as he poured her a glass of red wine. She took a sip and let the flavours roll over her tongue.

'Thank *you* for taking my aubergine in hand,' said Barney.

Did he really just say that? Now she couldn't look at him. All she could think of was an aubergine emoji. She gulped at the wine and it hit the back of her throat, making her cough. By the time her eyes had stopped streaming, Amber had arrived with a plateful of fragrant food and set it down on the table, and thankfully the moment was glossed over.

'That looks amazing, Amber!' she said.

'Yes,' said Barney, his glass obscuring most of his face. 'Well done, darling, let's get stuck in!'

Amber held her glass out hopefully and he filled it with water from a jug on the table.

'In France, children are given wine at the dinner table,' she huffed. 'It teaches them to be mature around alcohol.'

'*Chacun à son goût*,' said Barney.

Amber looked at him blankly. 'What?'

'They also speak French at the dinner table,' said Barney. 'Do you want to do that as well?'

'*Non*,' she replied darkly. She swirled some pitta bread into the aubergine dip and made a show of how much more delicious it was than curry.

Touché. Katie risked smiling at him and he smiled back.

'How are you both enjoying life in Merle Bay?' she asked.

'Well . . . ' Amber thought about it. 'I miss the shops and I miss being able to get a bus or the tube whenever I need to be somewhere. But I love being by the sea and we're getting a kitten so it's cool.'

'I love the quaint cottages and the harbour.' Barney offered her the plate of halloumi and she took a piece. 'I love the lack of traffic and the proximity to the sea.'

Katie nodded. 'It's peaceful here, isn't it?'

'Except for the seagulls!' Barney shook his head in disbelief. 'What a racket.'

'We don't need a morning alarm, that's for sure,' said Amber. 'If they're not squawking, they're scrabbling on the roof fighting.'

'You'll get used to them,' Katie laughed. 'I don't think I even hear them anymore. Alice says you're renting this house?'

Barney grinned. 'I honestly think I should recruit our post lady as a news reporter – she misses nothing. Yes, we're renting, which is a shame because I'd love to rip the bathroom out, swap the green suite for a new white one and put in a big power shower.'

A fleeting image of Barney entered her mind: naked behind a steamy glass shower screen, head thrown back and eyes closed, rivulets of hot water running down his body.

'I told Dad about the girl at school. In the toilets.' Amber helped herself to more baba ganoush.

'I'm pleased,' Katie said. 'You did a good thing there.'

'You're a star, darling.' Barney watched his daughter with quiet pride. 'Tell Katie what happened the next day.'

'Well, I took all the stuff you and I bought into school and asked to see the head teacher, Mrs Hallam.' A faint blush coloured Amber's cheeks.

'Good for you!' said Katie.

'I told her that I thought it was really bad that some girls missed school because of their periods,' she continued. 'And she said she totally agreed. I told her what had happened in the toilets without naming names; she listened to me and said that she'd make sure that all the girls would be told about how to access free products if they needed them. She said it was a good thing that her pupils had a strong sense of social justice.'

Amber went on to explain that she'd done some googling and that 'period poverty' was a real problem and that there were already organisations out there that could help schools. So, she'd gone back to Mrs Hallam and now they were expecting a visit from the Red Box charity and Amber was going to be part of it.

'She's only been there a month,' Barney marvelled, shaking his head. 'She'll be head girl before the end of term.'

'Dad!' Amber groaned. 'So embarrassing.'

'I was head girl once,' said Katie.

'Wow? Were you really clever?' Amber looked impressed.

'Not half as clever as you,' she replied.

'You must let me reimburse you for all the stuff you bought for school,' said Barney. 'Amber said you insisted on paying.'

Katie shook her head and indicated the glass of wine which Barney had kept topped up. 'Being wined and dined is payment enough. It gets boring cooking for one. And actually, thanks to Amber, I've been thinking about starting some sort of charitable venture myself.'

Amber's eyes widened. 'To do with second-hand bras?'

'Exactly,' Katie grinned. 'I'm going to ask my clients to donate any gently worn bras and distribute them to people in poorer areas. What I haven't worked out is how I can get them to those in need.'

'I can spread the word at school,' Amber put in. 'Some girls might even want to donate. I can ask Mrs Hallam if we can have a special collection day.'

'Thanks, Amber,' Katie said, touched by her enthusiasm. 'I'm going to start small for now and see how I get on. I thought I'd call it Small Things Matter.'

'I'm going to go and tell Imogen at school,' said Amber, scrambling to her feet. 'Her family is absolutely loaded – I bet her mum's got plenty to get rid of.'

Katie and Barney watched her leave the kitchen and then heard her thump upstairs to her room.

'She's adorable,' said Katie, slightly on edge now the two of them were on their own. She should probably leave soon anyway, give the man some peace.

'It's certainly never dull around here,' he nodded, leaning back in his chair. His fingers twirled the stem of his wine glass. 'Not that I'd ever change her for the world. When I think about how close I came to losing her too . . . ' He shook his head. 'Did you notice her shins?'

She nodded. Amber had changed into shorts and T-shirt when they got in and Katie had caught a glimpse of long scars down the front of both of her legs.

'The scars are from the accident,' Barney told her. 'She had to be cut out of the front of the car, her legs were trapped in the footwell. She was off school for a long time. I didn't know what to do for the best: send her back where she'd be faced with kids who didn't know what to say to her or send her somewhere new where she could start all over again.' He gave her a rueful smile. 'In the end, I realised we both had the same dilemma. I didn't have physical scars, but everyone who knew me knew what had happened. I felt as if I was having to make light of my grief, to make things easier for others.'

'My friend Grace lost her husband suddenly,' she said. 'That's partly why she moved to Merle Bay too, to get away from the pitying looks.'

'Grace Byron?' His eyes flickered with interest.

'You know her!' Katie smiled. 'Small world!'

'No, I've never met her,' said Barney, 'but Alice said she's moved into the big glass house overlooking the bay. I googled her, she's an amazing architect,' he looked impressed. 'She was definitely the brains behind Byron

Homes. Terrible shame that her husband died, just after they'd sold their company for several million.'

Several million! Katie tried to hide her surprise. She knew Grace had money, she made no secret of that, but she'd had no idea she was as wealthy as that.

'I don't think she cares about the money without Myles here to spend it. I suspect she'd give it all away for a chance of more time with him,' she said. Although would Grace still feel the same after discovering he'd been unfaithful? She wasn't so sure.

Barney nodded sympathetically. 'Grief changes your perspective on lots of things that seemed important before. My priority is Amber, not my career. I couldn't have done my old job and been a hands-on dad.'

'What did you do previously?'

'I worked on big national, and international, news stories. I was away a lot. Sophia made that possible because she worked from home, she was always there when Amber needed her to show up for school stuff. Now that's my job.' His tone was light and his smile constant, but Katie was good at reading people and she didn't miss the sadness in his eyes.

'But Merle Bay is a long way from London. That's quite a change?'

His eyes crinkled at the corners when he smiled. 'It's a million miles from London. And right now, it's exactly what I need.'

Right now. So, he'd head back to London eventually, thought Katie, disappointed. Still, he was here now, she thought, holding her glass up as he offered her more wine. She'd just have to enjoy his company while it lasted.

'Why the north east?'

He nodded. 'Journalism is quite a tight community and print journalism even more so. Word had got around the industry about me losing Sophia and coming close to losing Amber. It was obvious I wouldn't be able to carry on where I was; I was approached by the boss at the *Gazette* asking me if I'd come for a chat. The rest is history.'

Amber reappeared in the kitchen, cleared the table and fetched the bowl of strawberries Katie had washed and hulled.

'The girls loved the Smalls Things Matter idea,' she said, dropping back onto her chair. 'I told them I was helping with it and they've promised to bring in any old ones.'

'That's good,' Katie smiled indulgently.

'Watch out,' said Barney. 'Madam will be in charge before you know it.'

They all laughed, and Barney handed round bowls and found some ice cream in the freezer.

'I'm so glad you came for dinner.' Amber picked up a strawberry and bit into it, sending juice running down her chin. 'It's good for Dad to make friends with people his own age. It takes the pressure off me to entertain him.'

Katie and Barney looked at each other and hid their smiles.

How would Amber feel when her dad started dating again, Katie wondered. Friends was one thing, but a woman coming into their home, encroaching on her relationship with Barney, would be something entirely different.

Barney tutted with mock indignation. 'You make it sound like you're my carer!'

'Just saying. I won't be around to look after you forever, you know,' she said breezily. 'I've got my own friends.'

'You've met some nice people here then?' Katie asked, helping herself to ice cream.

'Yeah. Some.' Pink spots stained Amber's cheeks and she grabbed a napkin and scrubbed it over her mouth.

Katie guessed from her reticence that there was a special person amongst that 'some'. Good for her; having someone special made school days much calmer waters to navigate. It had been the same with her and Rose. It was the two of them against the world, until suddenly it wasn't.

'I've got friends too,' said Barney. 'Old friends from school and uni and work. We don't have to see each other every day to be there for each other.'

Katie felt a touch of envy at how easy he made it sound. 'I'm impressed. I lost touch with all my school friends, I didn't go to uni and the only colleagues I've had are Nula and my aunt, who sadly passed away.'

'But what about social media?' Amber looked appalled. 'I thought all old . . . I mean *adults*, use Facebook.'

'Not me,' she said, a shiver feathering its way down her spine. 'I don't like the idea that anyone can dig into the past of a stranger.'

'Whoops.' Amber pressed her lips together and flashed her father a mischievous look. 'Did you hear that, Dad?'

Barney winced and put his hands up. 'Guilty as charged. As I mentioned when I came into the shop, I'm planning an interview with all the businesses, I was just getting some background information. It's amazing what you can find if you know where to look. The skeletons in some people's closets would turn your hair white.'

Katie held her breath. 'Did you find anything on me?'

'Nothing. Amazingly.' Barney hitched his shoulders up. 'There's not even a Facebook page for the shop.'

Tension uncoiled in her stomach. 'Thank goodness.'

'Hey, don't worry,' he said, as if sensing her unease. 'I'm not trying to catch anyone out.'

Katie forced herself to smile. 'Sorry, I'm naturally suspicious.'

Barney placed a hand on her arm reassuringly. 'All I want to do is draw attention to the awards and to generate positive publicity for the shop.'

Katie nodded slowly, absorbing what he was saying. She wanted to make changes to the business, expand their customer base and maybe offer a wider range of underwear. A feature about Auntie Small's would help enormously with that.

'You'd be able to launch Small Things Matter in the article,' Amber chimed in.

'Good idea,' Katie smiled, thinking back to herself at that age. She'd been quite feisty at fourteen; not afraid to stand up for what she believed in. She'd loved nothing more than a good debate on any topic. *And now look at me*, she thought in frustration: so worried about what people thought of her that she'd been careful not to leave a digital footprint.

Was it time for a rethink? Maybe, she thought, her heart fluttering. And Barney was handing her the perfect opportunity to do it.

'Thank you, Barney,' Katie said, giving him a determined smile. 'That would be great.'

Chapter Twenty-Four

Thirty miles from Merle Bay in a community health centre on the outskirts of Morpeth, the group leader, whose name Robyn had already forgotten, handed her a marker pen and asked her to write her name on a sticker and put it on her chest.

'And then help yourself to coffee and tea, Robyn,' said the woman. She wore a long sheath dress and Doc Marten boots and had friendly green eyes which twinkled beneath a blunt fringe and hands which circled constantly as if she was conducting an invisible orchestra. 'And do try a shortbread finger, I made them myself.'

Robyn quickly scribbled her name and stuck the label onto her top, keen to get away and disappear into the crowd. She'd been given a leaflet for this Previvors Support Group last year. At the time she'd been adamant that group support wasn't for her. But since meeting Katie and Grace, she'd found herself opening up a bit more. So, she'd emailed the organiser and allowed herself to be talked into coming along to the next session. And here she was.

To Robyn's relief, the group leader spotted another newcomer at the door and fluttered away to deal with her, giving Robyn a quiet moment to get acclimatised to her surroundings.

She'd imagined somewhere with squeaky floors and smelling of disinfectant but had been pleasantly surprised.

This room was kitted out as a library: bookshelves lined one wall while an assortment of armchairs and low tables with piles of magazines and reading lamps gave the room a homely feel. The only heart-sinking thing was that the chairs for this afternoon's meeting were arranged in a large semi-circle at one end of the room. No chance of squirrelling herself away at the back as she'd hoped.

'You look like you wish the ground would swallow you up.' Robyn turned and found herself looking into another woman's eyes. 'In her defence, Sadie is probably the most nervous person here. I'm Tess, by the way.'

Sadie – *that* was the group leader's name. Robyn smiled and introduced herself.

'I'm back at work now, but I try and come every month,' said Tess, steering her to a couple of vacant chairs. 'Between work, hospital appointments, kids, life . . . you know how it is.' She rolled her eyes and Robyn nodded in sympathy.

'And what do you actually do here?' Robyn asked. She had visions of an Alcoholics Anonymous-style meeting and everyone being invited to share their story with the group. *My name's Robyn and I'm a previvor.*

'Sadie starts off with an introduction, welcomes any new members and tells us what's coming up.'

Robyn panicked. 'Do we all have to say something?'

Tess laughed. 'No, although some people can't help themselves.'

She let out a breath. 'Thank goodness.'

'Don't worry, I was nervous too, my first time.'

'I'm not great at talking about my feelings and group therapy is my worst nightmare.' Robyn's throat thickened; saying the words aloud to a stranger made it so much more real. To her dismay, she felt her eyes fill with tears. 'But I know I need help.'

'Then you're in the right place.' Tess smiled kindly as if to say well done and handed her a tissue. 'After the intros we usually have a speaker of some sort. Today's talk is about self-care.'

Sadie clapped her hands and brought the room to attention.

'Welcome, everyone, to our monthly Previvors group! I hope you've had chance to get tea, coffee and one of my shortbread biscuits? Before we get going . . . ' Sadie began, hopping from foot to foot, hands swooping and circling as she spoke, reminding Robyn of a bird. Not a seagull, Sadie wasn't nearly as cocky as a gull; she was a little tern, timid and dainty.

Sadie reminded people to turn their mobile phones to silent and then proceeded to point out the exit doors and told everyone where to assemble in the event of a fire alarm.

There were twenty women, Robyn noted, glancing round. Quite a few young ones, with glossy hair, smooth faces and flat stomachs. So early in life to have been thrown such a curveball. Others were her age and upwards, and even a mum and daughter pair, if the identical smile they each had was anything to go by.

She had worn her mum's necklace today for comfort: a little silver kingfisher on a fine chain. Her fingers crept up to it and she held it tight, wishing she and her mum had had the chance to still be here, surviving together. She couldn't change the past, Robyn thought determinedly, but she could make the most of her future. Medicine had moved on in the two decades since her mum had died. Robyn had been given choices; she'd chosen life and now it was up to her to grab every bit of it. All the women here had made the same choices. She was part of something and for the first time since she'd started this journey, she felt proud of herself; what she had put her body through over the last two years had been traumatic, but she'd pulled through. It was time to rewrite her inner dialogue: she *was* brave, all these women were. She sat up straighter, smiled at Tess and bit into her shortbread finger. Delicious.

'I'm delighted to welcome Pam from the Belief Foundation who's going to talk to us about self-care.' Sadie started off the applause and everyone joined in while the woman next to her raised her hand in a wave and flashed her white teeth as she smiled.

'OK,' said Pam, slapping her hands on her thighs. 'How many people here have felt guilt since their BRCA test results? Raise your hand.'

Robyn's gut twisted. She looked around the circle as slowly every single person raised their hand like little surrender flags. Slowly she put up her hand to join them. The women's eyes slid sideways, and they smiled at each other, recognising one another's discomfort.

'Thank you, ladies,' Pam said softly, nodding. 'You don't need me to tell you how common that is, I think you've seen it for yourselves, am I right?'

Soft laughter tinged with sadness echoed around the circle. Beside her, Tess sniffed back tears.

'Guilt that you're a previvor, when maybe a friend or family member might not have survived. Guilt that you've been less available for your family while you've been recovering. Guilt that you haven't been able to contribute to the household bills. Guilt that you may have passed your faulty genes on to your kids. Guilt that you aren't living the amazing purpose-filled life that you feel you should.' Pam fell silent. Sadie got up and passed tissues along to those who needed one.

Pam held Robyn's gaze. Robyn squirmed in her seat, sure Pam could see what was written in her heart. Her own guilt was multi-faceted; Finn had been denied the baby he wanted because of her; she'd put her own life before the chance to have a baby and she felt relieved that the opportunity to be a mother had been taken out of her hands and then she felt guilty about all the women who'd give their right arm to have a baby and couldn't. Robyn squeezed her eyes tight shut for a second and when she opened them Pam was looking elsewhere.

'You are not alone,' said Pam. 'It's a perfectly normal reaction to what you've been through, and more than that, it shows that you have compassion. So, let's break out into smaller groups and share what makes us feel guilty with each other.'

Robyn's heart sank. Now it would be impossible to hide. There was a bit of muted chatting while people started to shuffle chairs around.

Tess looked at Robyn and jerked her head towards the table where the coffee was still out. 'Fancy another brew and a group of two?' she hissed.

'Yes,' Robyn sighed with relief.

'I feel a bit guilty bunking off work to come here.' There was an inch of cold coffee in Tess's cup, so she put it on the end of the table and picked up a fresh one. 'My boss has been great but we're overstretched. It does me good though, talking about it. It's been three years since I found I had dodgy genes and I get the impression my colleagues have had enough of me talking about it.'

Robyn helped herself to more coffee. 'You find it easy to talk about it?'

'Try shutting me up,' Tess replied. 'I'm practically evangelical about it. If my constant jabber makes even one person who suspects they might be at risk get tested for the BRCA gene, it'll be worth it. Besides, Sadie is a great baker.' She picked up another shortbread finger and bit into it. 'Bliss. What brings you here?'

'To be honest, my marriage is going through a rough patch,' Robyn admitted. 'I was hoping I might get some tips from people who've had the same problems.'

'I'm probably not the best person to ask,' Tess gave her a resigned smile. 'My partner headed for the hills as soon as I tested positive. Said he didn't have the bedside manner for it. It was pretty shit. It made me think he only loved me for my boobs. I suppose I should be grateful he was honest and left straight away instead of pretending he was fine about it and playing away behind my back.'

Tess looked at the wedding ring on Robyn's finger. 'At least your fella stuck by you.'

'Yeah.' Robyn twisted the ring round and nodded. 'He's been really great. Looked after me so well. He tells me I'm gorgeous, he cooks nutritious meals for me, encourages me to spend time with my friends. Treats me like a china doll.'

'Yeah, he sounds dreadful, dump him immediately and give me his number.' Tess cackled wickedly and reached for another piece of shortbread, but she noticed the stricken look on Robyn's face and her hand stopped mid-air and she touched her arm. 'Sorry, I shouldn't joke. What do you think is the source of the rough patch?'

'When this first all happened, it felt like we were a team. I was scared to death, but he kept me cheerful. He was so tender and loving towards me. We even gave my boobs a little send-off celebration, just him and me and an early night.' Robyn's voice wavered; back then she hadn't appreciated how special their closeness made her feel. She missed him pulling her close in the night and making love to her while they were both half asleep. 'He's still incred-ibly kind, but he doesn't fancy me anymore and there's nothing I can do about it.'

'I find that hard to believe,' Tess wrinkled her brow. 'You are super cute!'

Robyn grinned and told her about the humiliating new bra incident.

Tess nodded wisely. 'I don't know about you, but it took me a long time to adjust to my new shape. Perhaps he's still adjusting. My advice is to give him time. Your body has changed but you're still the same person.'

'But I'm not,' Robyn insisted. 'The old me had agreed to start a family with him, I can't do that anymore. I love him to bits, but I think I'm losing him.'

'Oh, bless you.' Tess's face crumpled with sadness and she laid a hand on Robyn's arm. 'That's rough.'

Robyn took a deep breath, preparing herself to admit that she'd never wanted children in the first place when Tess started speaking again.

'My advice is to tell him you love him and keep telling him,' she said kindly. 'I work in advertising and we work on the principle that a consumer has to hear or see a message twenty times before they act on it. And he's a man so, you know, make it forty.' She finished with a wink.

They were both laughing when Pam clapped her hands again and asked them to reform the circle.

'Judging by the noise levels, it sounds like there's a lot of guilt in the room,' said Pam, crossing her legs. 'But what I also heard was lots of reassurance, we told each other that we shouldn't feel guilty about x, y and z . . . Funny how we can extend kindness to others but find it so hard to go easy on ourselves. So, let's talk about self-care next. What can we do for ourselves to combat the guilty feelings when they arise? What strategies, what coping mechanisms can we use? It could be a gratitude journal, or exercise class. Anything. Would anyone like to share what they do?'

'I hope *drink gin* is on the list,' Tess muttered to Robyn behind her hand, 'or I'm buggered.'

Hands went up.

'I lost my sister to cancer and I feel guilty that I'm still here, so I volunteer in my local cancer charity shop,' one of the older ladies called Madge said. 'It's my way of giving back.'

'Good on you,' Pam said, giving her a thumbs-up.

'My work colleagues had a collection and bought me and Martin, my husband, a spa break,' said Anita. 'It was magical: two days floating around in our dressing gowns and flip-flops. We can't afford to do that regularly, but we've managed it a couple of times since. Just being out of the house on neutral ground makes it easier for us to talk about our feelings.'

'That's a good one,' Pam agreed. 'And I like the idea of neutral ground.'

'I try and meditate,' said a jolly-looking young woman with plaits and freckles called Freya. 'Especially when I'm feeling low. I remember my surgeon telling me that my scars will be someone else's sign of hope. That keeps me going.'

'Wise words, and a lovely way of looking at it,' said Pam, nodding. 'Anyone else, anyone not said anything yet?' Her gaze rested on Robyn before she had chance to look at her empty mug.

'I . . . ' Robyn's voice dried up as all eyes turned in her direction. She took a deep breath and remembered how the old Robyn was never afraid to jump into a conversation. And what if her suggestion helped someone else? That was the point of sharing their stories.

'It's OK,' Pam rushed to reassure her. 'No need to speak at all if you'd rather not.'

'Thanks, but I'd like to.' She cleared her throat and felt the comforting pressure of Tess's leg against hers. 'OK. There's a shingle beach near where I live. It's quiet and natural and at first it doesn't look anything special but if you scoop away the top level of shingle you can find hidden treasure.'

'No way!' Freya gasped.

Robyn smiled. 'Not actual *valuable* treasure, but sea glass.'

'Mermaid's tears!' said Madge. 'That's what I've always called it.'

Robyn smiled at her. 'Exactly. The glass is beautiful and all colours and shapes. My friends and I collect it. We walk along the tideline hunting for sea glass, and share our news and, well, it's like open-air therapy I suppose.' She paused, feeling a bit silly, but every single person was listening intently.

'Go on,' Pam nodded encouragement.

'The air is sea-salt fresh and the sound of the waves rushing in and out is so powerful and grounding, if that doesn't sound a weird way to describe water!' she continued, allowing her gaze to drift. 'There's something about being on the edge of land and looking out across miles and miles of sea and sky and it reminds me how small we are. But at the same time, we're just as precious as the little jewels of glass, we are part of something vital and we're alive.' Robyn stopped. 'That's it, really.'

For a second the room was in complete silence and then suddenly everyone was clapping.

'That was beautiful,' said Pam, blinking hard.

Sadie jumped to her feet and handed out tissue after tissue.

'Wow,' Tess breathed beside her. 'You ought to work for tourist information; I'm sold.'

'What do you do with the sea glass, once you've collected it?' Freya asked. She inched to the edge of her seat. Others did the same.

Robyn smiled. 'Sometimes nothing, but there's a christening coming up in the family, so I'm making all the children one of these.' She pulled her phone out of her bag, scrolled through her pictures until she came to the one of the mosaics she'd started for Betty. She'd taken a piece of flat driftwood and spelled the baby's name out in green sea glass. It wasn't finished yet, but the rest of the wood would be covered in mix of white and blue glass with a few shells dotted about.

The group cooed over Robyn's phone as it was passed around the circle and she answered their questions and basked in their praise.

'I'd love to do that!'

'You're so creative.'

'Which beach is it?'

'Fancy a trip to Merle Bay, Mum?'

Finally, Robyn got her phone back and took her seat again.

'Thank you for sharing, Robyn,' Pam beamed. 'That sounds like the perfect self-care. Now, anyone else . . . '

Robyn's heart was racing while the discussion continued around her. That had been so much fun, and the others seemed to be really interested in what she had to say. She was so glad she'd come, she felt invigorated and . . . a bit more like the old Robyn.

At the end of the session, Sadie approached her.

'No pressure,' she said, leading her away from a group who were asking for directions to Merle Bay. 'But how would you feel about leading a sea glass walk, like you mentioned, and possibly running a workshop to make a mosaic?'

Robyn hesitated, wondering whether she really wanted to share the beach with everyone; one of the things which made it so special was how deserted it was.

'We'd pay, of course,' said Sadie, possibly noticing her reticence and named a generous sum.

Robyn thought back to the measly balance of her bank account. There were a lot worse ways of earning money than spending a few hours on the beach with women whom she could relate to.

'I'd like that very much,' Robyn grinned, taking Sadie's number.

She left the session feeling far more confident than when she'd arrived: she'd had some advice about Finn, made some new friends and generated a potential source of income. And with a sea glass walk organised for Saturday, the Sea Glass Sisterhood might well have just swelled its membership by a considerable number.

Chapter Twenty-Five

Grace had cabin fever today and needed to get out. Sea Glass House was gorgeous, but she was rattling around it like the last strawberry cream in the tin of Christmas chocolates. Grey pillowy clouds were scudding across the sky, and she wouldn't be surprised if there was a storm brewing, but frankly she was willing to risk it. After ten whole days of letting herself wallow after talking to Ned, it was time to pick herself up, straighten her crown and set forth.

She was in the process of hunting down her umbrella when her phone rang.

A glance at the screen told her it was Zoe. Grace steeled herself. She should really take this call and get it over with. She'd been avoiding talking to her sister for days because she knew she'd end up telling her about what Ned had confirmed; she wouldn't be able to keep it out of her voice. It was one thing Robyn and Katie knowing the truth about Myles, but they were part of her new life and they'd never known him. Telling Zoe was going to make Myles's affair or one-night stand, whatever it was, seem far more real. Plus, Zoe was going to be devastated on Grace's behalf and furious with Myles. It was all about to get messy.

'Zoe! Just caught me.' Grace tucked the phone under her chin as she continued rummaging through her various bags in the bedroom.

'Caught you what – *in flagranté* I hope?' Zoe teased.

'Yes,' Grace replied deadpan.

Zoe gasped. 'OH MY GOD! What? Really?'

Grace spotted her brolly, wedged inside one of her boots. She pulled it out and stuck it in her pocket.

'Kidding,' said Grace. 'I'm off out for a walk.'

She opened the front door and a gust of wind almost tore it out of her hand.

'Shame,' Zoe said, deflated. 'What's that noise?'

'A bracing sea breeze,' Grace shouted into the phone, holding onto her hood. 'How are things with you?'

She headed towards Merle Bay, keeping to the edge of the lane to face oncoming traffic, not that there was much likelihood of that. Below her was the beach and the waves kept up a constant roar in her ears. She had a vague idea of exploring the harbour and taking a peek at Robyn's husband's boatyard.

'Fine, except I have a nocturnal daughter,' Zoe said, 'and a son who likes his sleep so much he practically sleepwalks to school, extremely slowly.'

'Oh Zoe, I do miss you all.' Grace's voice wobbled. She'd always been close to Daniel and she and Myles had always had a soft spot for baby Ruby. They were godparents to her, and Myles had set up a savings account for both children when they'd sold the business last year. Her throat burned suddenly with longing to be with her sister.

'OK, what's up?' Zoe said immediately. 'Come on, out with it.'

'It's bad news.' Grace's eyes were watering and only partly because of the wind. 'I've found something out.'

'Let me guess – you're homesick?' Her sister sounded slightly smug. 'I knew it. Come home, Gracie. You've been there for long enough; we miss you and—'

244

'It's not that.' Grace stopped for a moment, pulled up her hood and turned away from the wind so Zoe would hear her clearly. 'It's Myles.'

'Myles?' Zoe exclaimed. 'What about him?'

OK, this was it; Grace blew out a breath. 'I found out from Julia that Myles had an affair.'

There was silence for such a long time that Grace wondered if the line had gone dead.

'Zoe, are you still there?'

'Yes, I just . . . ' Zoe's voice cracked. 'It's such a shock, that's all. But Julia might be trying to cause trouble – how do you know she isn't lying?'

Grace's heart went out to her sister; maybe she shouldn't have delivered the news over the phone after all. 'I didn't believe it at first, but Ned then confirmed it, although he suggested it was a one-off rather than an affair. So, it looks like it's true, Zoe – Myles was unfaithful to me.'

'Oh God,' Zoe said hoarsely. 'You don't deserve this. I'm so, so sorry, Grace.'

'So am I.' Grace wiped away her tears with the back of her free hand. 'And I'm sorry to have told you over the phone but I couldn't keep it to myself anymore.'

'Of course not,' Zoe said kindly. 'You poor thing. Do you know . . . I mean, did Ned say who she was, or when this was supposed to have happened?'

'No, he doesn't know. But Julia says if we go to court over Myles's will, she'll make sure it all comes out then.'

Zoe gasped. 'That's dreadful. You'd hate that all being dragged up publicly.'

'True, but I'm not letting her blackmail me either,' she said, anger swirling inside her.

'Don't do anything rash, please,' Zoe begged.

'I won't.' Grace sighed. She stared out to sea, vaguely

aware that the crash and tumble of the waves mirrored her emotions right now. 'I feel like an idiot. I never suspected a thing. Never. I wish you were here to give me a hug.'

'Well . . . ' Zoe hesitated. 'I could come up to see you, if you like? And we can talk this through together.'

'Really?' A sob formed in Grace's throat. 'I'd love that.'

'Me too.'

Zoe sifted through her diary and they settled on the weekend after next. Daniel was camping with the Scouts so it would just be Zoe and Ruby. After they'd said their goodbyes, Grace felt her spirits lift a fraction; she had something to look forward to in a week that had otherwise been bleak.

Within ten minutes, the clouds had thickened to a solid grey blanket and the air was heavy with damp. Grace contemplated turning back, but she remembered her dad once saying that there was no such thing as bad weather, only bad clothing, and as she was in boots, a rainproof coat and had her umbrella tucked in her pocket, she decided to soldier on.

Walking had always been her thing. Getting outdoors had been a way to untangle knots in her brain, inhaling fresh oxygen-rich air and exhaling all the adrenaline and cortisol which built up in her bloodstream during the week. She'd had some of her best ideas for work while tramping across the Lickey Hills near her Birmingham home with only disinterested sheep for company. Nature, she'd discovered, when she looked hard enough, had the most ingenious ways of doing things and it had regularly inspired her own designs.

She stopped to pick up a chipped clam shell at the side of the road and turned it over in her hand, her thumb rubbing first across the rough ribbed outer and then the smooth, iridescent inside. There was a building in Abu Dhabi modelled on a clam shell. She remembered reading about it and telling Myles she'd like to go one day. They never made it, but he did take her to the Gherkin in London for dinner instead. That iconic building had been modelled on a sea anemone, he'd told her, and there were clams on the menu. He'd kissed her hand and said it was the best he could do for now.

She smiled at the memory. That was one of the things she'd loved about him the most: she never had to drop hints at Christmas or her birthday. If she as much as mentioned that she liked something, he'd always remember. Her gifts from him were always exactly what she'd wanted, always perfect. Her smile faded as quickly as it had begun; well, maybe not always. It seemed that his final gift from beyond the grave was the knowledge that he hadn't been perfect at all.

She put the shell in her pocket and trudged onwards towards the harbour, letting the breeze blow the cobwebs away and with it her gloomy thoughts. It was time to start looking forwards rather than dwelling on the past. One of her reasons for coming to stay in Merle Bay had been about planning for her future as a single woman and that hadn't changed. She needed to think what she wanted to do with the rest of her life. She had money in the bank, she had family, people who loved her and she had friends. What she didn't have much of at the moment, was purpose.

Grace had always been busy, always had a schedule packed full of meetings, appointments and presentations. She'd been a member of organisations too; everything from architecture, businesswomen, the Women's Institute, right down to the residents' committee which planned street parties and family fundays in their little cul-de-sac at home.

What she needed, she thought, was a project, a distraction. A property perhaps, or a worthwhile cause?

She felt rain droplets first on her eyelashes and then on her face. Water splashed onto her jacket and a drip found the gap between her collar and her cleavage and made her flinch. She put up her umbrella and picked up her pace. Before long, the curve of the harbour came into view up ahead on her left, and to her right, a row of sturdy cottages built from chunky stone with small windows, designed to withstand anything that the North Sea could throw their way. Despite the God-awful weather, Merle Bay was exceptionally pretty. She could see why Ned had been attracted to it. The place was just on the right side of quaint. The only thing that Merle Bay lacked as far as she was concerned was her nearest and dearest and, she thought with a rush of warmth, Robyn and Katie were already beginning to feel as if they could fill that gap.

As she got closer, her professional eye roamed the architecture of the cottages: the squat chimney pots, capped to ward off seagulls, an array of colourful paintwork, pots stuffed with grasses on doorsteps. The effect was practical and pretty. If Ned was here, she thought, he'd probably reimagine the entire row into one large luxury guest house; he loved nothing better than gentrifying coastal properties. But not Grace; she got a kick out of seeing families turn the houses she'd designed into homes. Properties which blended in with their environment, or even enhanced it: that was what made her heart glow. No, she thought, turning her gaze from the cottages to the harbour, those homes were perfect just as they were.

The harbour wall was built in a long, smooth curve. The ends formed the mouth of the harbour within, close together, to shield the boats from the worst of the waves.

A wooden boardwalk jutted out into the water at the centre of the curve. Small boats, their masts tinkling in the breeze, clustered around it, with names painted jauntily on their hulls like *Misty* and *Sea Shanty*. At the furthest point, two men, head to toe in yellow waterproofs, were unloading an orange and white fishing boat. Plastic crates dripping with water and packed with crushed ice were being lifted ashore and loaded onto pallets. Above them, seagulls wheeled and circled excitedly, swooping down occasionally for treasure and hopping onto the end of the pier, their beady eyes fixed on the prize. She was sure Robyn had said that Finn's family had the last remaining fishing boat in Merle Bay. In which case, one of those two men might be Finn himself.

She watched a while longer. A van appeared and reversed down the pier to where the pallets were waiting. The driver and a passenger jumped out, lowered the tailgate at the back and between them the crates were loaded up. Within minutes the van doors were slammed, and the driver pulled off, back up to the harbour road and drove away. One of the fishermen began walking away from the boat, leaving the other one hosing down the deck.

At that moment the heavens opened, and the rain began in earnest. Sheets of water fell from the sky and courtesy of the wind blowing in from the sea, it came at Grace like icy darts. She pulled the umbrella down sideways to protect her face, but the wind tore it inside out.

'Bloody hell!' she yelled, trying to refold it the right way.

She started to run towards the harbour to look for shelter. Her hood blew back and within seconds her hair was plastered to her head. Ahead of her, the fisherman had his head down and looked well protected from the torrent. He jogged off along the road purposefully and, with a lack of bright ideas of her own, she splashed through the puddles after him.

Grace was already out of breath and sweating inside her plastic coat; she hoped his destination was close by. He unlocked a set of double doors set into a long stone building. It looked like a row of deserted garages, but as she got closer she realised it was a run of boatsheds. Faded signs above each door confirmed it. Grace stopped outside the one which the fisherman had gone through and read the sign: McGill and Sons.

Grace pushed the door open, intending to just poke her head inside, but the weather had other ideas and the wind and rain blew her in. 'Whoops! Hello.'

'Hello.' The fisherman was taking off his yellow coat and gave her a bemused smile. 'Come on in.'

'Sorry.' She leaned against the door to shut it, panting with exertion. 'I was going to ask if I could come in out of the rain, but I already have.'

'Um. Sure.' He stepped out of his waterproof trousers and hung them up next to his jacket. His dark hair stuck to his forehead in damp clumps.

'Are you Finn, by any chance?' She stood there dripping, taking in the alien world of the boatshed with its heaps of crates, lobster pots and nets, engine parts, oil drums, coils of ropes, shelves of storage boxes.

'I am,' he said, surprised.

'I'm Grace, a friend of your wife.'

His face split into a broad smile and reached out to shake her hand. 'Great to meet you.'

'I've heard all about you.' They both spoke together and smiled.

'All good, I hope?' Again, they said it in unison and this time they laughed.

'The best,' Grace reassured him swiftly. It was a little white lie but there was no way on this earth that she could let on that she knew Robyn had tried to tempt him to bed and he'd refused her. He'd probably chuck her back out in the rain.

'Tea?' Finn inclined his head to a tiny kitchenette on the far side of the boatshed.

Grace shivered. 'Yes please.'

'I should thank you,' said Finn, over his shoulder at her while he washed his hands and then filled the kettle. 'Meeting you and Katie has come just at the right time for her. She's had it rough the last couple of years.'

'You both have.' Grace caught sight of herself in a tarnished mirror which hung from the wall and almost passed out with shock. Finn's encounter with the elements had left him looking windswept and handsomely damp; she looked like the crazy scientist in *Back to the Future*. She quickly ran her hands through her hair, but her fingers snagged on so many knots that she gave up.

'Yep.' He frowned and pressed his lips together as if the subject was closed.

Poor guy. She wondered if he found it as difficult to open up as Robyn did? She said nothing for a few moments while the kettle boiled and Finn poured water into mugs, sniffed at the milk and poured a dribble into his.

'Oh, I've just remembered something.' He rummaged under the sink and brought out an old biscuit tin. He pulled the lid off and offered her the tin. 'Would you like a coconut flapjack?'

'Yes please.' Her mouth was already watering. She took a bite. It was sweet and chewy with the added crunch of the coconut. 'Delicious.'

He grinned. 'Thanks. It's my own recipe.'

'I used to bake,' said Grace wistfully, 'but there's not much point making a fuss for one.'

Finn sucked in a breath. 'I should have said something, pet, I'm so sorry for your loss. Robyn told me all about it. Well, anytime you want feeding and you can't be bothered, come round ours, you'll always be welcome.'

'That's very kind,' she nodded gratefully, aware that her eyes were probably glittering with tears as she nodded. 'Thank you very much.'

'So, this sea glass club,' he handed her a mug of tea. 'Robyn's now completely obsessed with collecting the stuff. It's taking over our house.'

'It is addictive,' she admitted. 'Plus, we enjoy each other's company while we're doing it. And the sea glass itself is gorgeous.'

'Not when you find a piece on the stairs carpet when you come down barefoot in the morning, it isn't.' He winced and then held his hands up. 'Not that I'm complaining, anything that puts a smile on my girl's face is fine with me.'

The warmth in his voice, and on his face, touched her heart. He obviously loved his wife.

'Has she shown you the mosaics she's making for our godchildren's christening? They're amazing. She's so artistic.' His eyes shone with pride. 'They're really good. I've told her she could be on to something. This could be a new little earner for her.'

'I haven't see the mosaics yet,' said Grace carefully. 'But she has talked about your new niece quite a bit.'

'Betty?' Finn's head whipped round to look at her. 'What did she say, *exactly*?'

Grace puffed her cheeks out, trying to remember and trying to say the right thing without breaching Robyn's confidence. 'I can't remember specifics,' she said carefully, 'she just said that you both adored her.'

Finn swallowed. 'She wanted a baby . . . well, we both did, obviously. It made sense to have the gene testing done before we went any further. It broke my heart when the test came back positive. The thought that she'd suffer like her mum did—' He stopped abruptly, his dark eyes almost black with anger. 'Bloody cancer.'

She laid a hand on his arm. 'And you've suffered, too.'

He cast his eyes down and shook his head. 'It was always about her, not me. I don't care for myself, but I feel terrible for her and guilty that . . . ' His face flushed red. 'Forget I said that. Don't say anything to Robyn. Please. Things are difficult enough as it is.'

'Of course not.' She wondered what it was that Finn had to feel guilty about and wished they'd both find time to open up to each other. 'She loves you very much, you know.'

He rubbed his face wearily. 'Yeah, I know.'

'So,' she said, deciding that it was time for a change of subject. 'Do you and your brother own the whole run of these boatsheds?'

'We don't own any of them,' he said. 'We rent this one and the others are either deserted or used for storage by other businesses. The McGill brothers make up the entire fishing fleet of Merle Bay.'

For the next few minutes, Finn showed Grace around the premises, even digging out old black and white photographs from sixty years ago showing his grandfather with his arms around other fishermen, a bustling boatyard in the background. Grace was enthralled. She loved the passion and pride in his voice and she really enjoyed getting to know the man she'd heard so much about from his wife.

'I can make you another brew if you like?' he offered.

'I'd better be getting back,' she smiled. 'And I bet Robyn will be wondering where you are.'

He picked up their two mugs and stacked them in the sink. 'She's gone to some support thing this afternoon. Won't be back for ages.'

'Good for her.' Grace eyed him thoughtfully. 'You can't beat talking about it when there's something on your mind.'

'Oh, look. I spy a tiny patch of blue.' He pointed out of the window.

He'd changed the topic of conversation, but she let it go.

'Enough to make a sailor a pair of trousers?' she said, remembering an old saying of her granddad's.

He laughed. 'Not even enough to make him a pair of Speedos. Which is probably a good thing. But at least the rain has stopped.'

'Then I'll be on my way.' She gave him a warm smile and slipped her arms into her coat. 'It was lovely to meet you.'

'Likewise.' He opened the door for her and handed her her umbrella. 'I can't wait to tell Robyn I met you.'

'Goodbye.' She stepped outside and tucked her hair into her hood against the wind. She'd only gone a few paces when she heard footsteps behind her splashing through the rain.

'Wait!' he called. He held out a small parcel wrapped in kitchen paper. 'A piece of flapjack for when you get home.'

She laughed. 'You're too kind.'

He grinned sheepishly. 'Robyn says I'm a feeder. I can't help it.'

Thoughts of Robyn and her lovely husband occupied Grace's head all the way home. Something didn't add up. Robyn had said that she felt guilty and explained why. Now Finn was saying the same thing. What would he have to feel guilty about? There was no doubt in her mind about one thing: Finn was deeply in love with his wife. But then again, hadn't she thought exactly the same about Myles?

Chapter Twenty-Six

It was early, but the sun was already warm, and yesterday's bad weather felt like a distant memory. Katie only had an hour before she needed to open the shop, but Robyn had asked them if they'd mind collecting sea glass with her that morning. She hadn't seen either of them since the evening when she'd opened the blackmail note and she was looking forward to a catch-up. She hurried down the path to the beach. Robyn was already down there, and she could see Grace striding towards her.

'It feels like ages since I've seen you. I've missed you both. Come here.' Grace held her arms out and they all hugged.

'Same here,' said Robyn. 'I feel guilty for not being in touch until now when I need help. Thanks girls, I appreciate this. I know you've got enough to do already.'

'Anything for the sisterhood.' Katie rolled her shoulders back and inhaled the sea air. 'When you're tired of collecting sea glass, you're tired of life.'

'Agreed.' Grace produced a tube of sunscreen and dotted it onto her face. 'Sea glass collection should be recommended by doctors for stress relief.'

Robyn's message on the WhatsApp group asking for help had come just at the right time for Katie. So much had been going on recently she hadn't felt the sun on her skin for days. The weather was incredible for May: a deep cobalt-blue sky hovered cloudlessly over a calm sea.

'Show us the mosaic again,' said Grace. 'I need to fix the colours in my head.'

Robyn got out her phone. 'I'm making one each for Hannah, William and Betty. I've got plenty of the white and the pale blues and greens; it's bright blue bits I need, to make the names pop. And interesting-looking shells.'

'On it,' said Grace. 'Like a seagull on a chip.'

Robyn handed out buckets and they began scouring the shore for blue treasure and Robyn told them about her group therapy session, and how interested the other women were to come and collect sea glass for themselves and the invitation to run her own workshop.

'I've suggested a date, but I wanted to run it by you two first.' She bit her lip. 'Check that you don't mind other people gatecrashing our beach.'

'Of course not,' Grace protested. 'I think it's a great idea.'

'Me too! You can have all my auntie's sea glass if you like,' Katie offered. 'Then you'll have enough sea glass for ten workshops just in case people don't collect enough.'

'That would be great!' Robyn said. 'I'll definitely use it. I'm hoping to make sea glass workshops a regular thing if the first one is successful.'

'It will be,' said Grace. 'I'd definitely come on one.'

'So would lots of my customers,' Katie agreed. 'Sea glass is really popular; if you offer to teach people how to make mosaics or jewellery or art with it, they'll snap your hand off.'

'I hope so,' said Robyn. 'Once I've made these name signs for the christening, I'm going to make a few more and set up an online shop to help promote the workshops. There's loads to sort out yet but I'm excited to get stuck in. If I could make this pay, I'd be so happy.'

She already looked more content than Katie had seen her. Maybe things with Finn had improved too.

'I'll help,' said Grace. 'I've been thinking that I need a project to divert my energy and stop me being so angry about Myles and his one-night stand. It's been driving me mad trying to work out when it could have happened and who with. I've been looking for clues, but there are no unexplained hotel bills, no restaurant receipts and I can't find anything suspicious in his diary. The only people he seemed to have spent money on was me, his two children and my sister and her kids.'

Katie frowned. 'Your sister?'

'Zoe has struggled for money sometimes,' Grace explained. 'After we sold the business last year, Myles began helping her out a lot more, making sure she had what she needed for when the new baby came along.' Grace sighed. 'He was generous and kind. That's what makes his infidelity so hard to stomach. I told Zoe about his affair on the phone and she was devastated; he was like a big brother to her. She's coming up for a visit with the baby next weekend. It'll be so lovely to see her. Hopefully you'll both get to meet her too.'

Katie squeezed her arm. 'I'd like that. I've always wanted to have a sister to confide in; at least now I've got you two.'

'Same,' said Robyn, smiling. She dropped a handful of sea glass into her bucket. 'I suppose if the woman he had a fling with was someone close to him, there wouldn't necessarily be a financial paper trail. Maybe someone at work?'

'Hmm.' Grace thought for a moment and then shuddered. 'Now I'm thinking about our lovely staff and trying to imagine who went behind my back. I can't do this, it's too awful. Let's change the subject. Katie, what's new with you?'

Katie's heart lurched; getting to know Barney and Amber a bit more had made her see that people could get past traumatic events. Barney's life had been totally derailed by his wife's accident, but instead of treading water and dwelling on it, he'd pushed ahead and changed direction. It was an example that she was determined to learn from.

'Since I last saw you, I've realised that I need to stop blaming that dodgy photoshoot for everything,' she told them. 'Because actually, setting aside for a moment that some shitbag is trying to blackmail me, the truth is, I'm doing OK. And I know I've been fortunate in inheriting a shop and a home, but the shop has thrived without Auntie Jean and I've made that happen. Our customers have nominated us for retailer of the year while I've been in charge. I think it's time I owned that success and accept that although I didn't go to uni and get a degree, and though I might not be fighting for justice with a career in law, I can make the world a better place one bra at a time.'

Robyn and Grace both put their buckets down on the pebbles and gave her a round of applause.

'Go you!' Robyn beamed.

'That's a great attitude. I'm so proud of you.' Grace pulled her into a bosomy hug. 'Have you decided what you're going to do about the blackmail?'

'I'm not handing over any money.' She jutted out her chin defiantly. 'I'd rather spend my money on my cottage, which I'm renaming Mermaid Cottage by the way.'

'Cute,' said Grace. 'And that's a wise move. Don't feed the trolls, I say.'

'Are you going to the police?' Robyn asked.

Katie swallowed, recalling the threat in the letter to expose her to the press if she dared go to the police. She nodded. 'I have to. It's a crime and whoever's behind it needs to be stopped in case they do it to someone else.'

'And if the blackmailer carries out their threat of sending the pictures to the newspaper?' Grace raised an eyebrow.

Dread trickled through Katie like icy water; it was quite literally her worst fear. She imagined Barney opening the envelope and taking out naked pictures of her. He might cut off all contact with her. Her voice trembled as she answered. 'I'll have to take that risk.'

'I think you're amazing,' Robyn marvelled.

'Me?' Katie shook her head. 'All I've done is run away, scared of what other people might think of me. When I got the first letter, I was so shocked, I thought my head might explode. That's when the three of us met for the first time, remember?'

'Remember?' Grace spluttered. 'I was doing the splits on my patio. As first impressions go, that one will take some beating.'

Katie gave a snort of laughter. 'I love your body confidence. It's something I need to work on. Partly because I'll never manage to hold down a relationship if I don't, but also for work. We have lots of ladies come into the shop for post-surgery bras. I know what they need in the way of comfort and support. But I've never stopped to think about the ripples that losing such an intimate part of your body can cause on the rest of your life. Robyn, you've opened my eyes to that. I've got a healthy body, which I've hidden away under baggy clothes for a decade because of that one day in a photographic studio. How can I ensure women leave Auntie Small's feeling proud of their bodies if I'm doing the exact opposite myself? And Grace,' she continued, not giving Robyn a chance to argue, 'you face up to whatever life throws at you. I'm taking resilience lessons from you.'

'That's incredibly sweet,' said Grace wistfully. 'But I'm not feeling resilient at all. And my body confidence has taken a tumble this last week. I keep imagining a gorgeous tall, skinny woman with cascading dark hair.'

'Why?' Katie and Robyn asked together.

'Because that's the polar opposite of me.' Grace gave a half smile.

'But *you're* gorgeous!' Katie argued.

'And vivacious and clever. . . ' Robyn protested. 'He can't have been right in the head.'

'Thanks.' Grace rubbed the pad of her thumb over her wedding ring. 'Myles was the first man who I genuinely believed loved every inch of me, and after a while I started to love every inch of me too. Now when I look in the mirror all I see is faults. I imagine him studying me and finding me lacking in some way compared to mystery woman.'

Katie was cross on Grace's behalf; how dare Myles make this wonderful woman doubt herself? And now her memories of him would be tarnished forever.

'It doesn't matter what shape we are, does it?' said Robyn darkly. 'Crises about our bodies can strike anyone at any time.'

'How are things with you and Finn?' Katie asked.

'Such a nice guy,' Grace said. 'I got a coconut flapjack and a potted history of fishing in Merle Bay when I met him.'

'You've met Finn?' Katie asked.

Grace told Katie how she'd taken shelter from the rain in the boatshed and been treated to his hospitality.

Robyn smiled proudly. 'He liked you too. Things are still not great between us, to be honest.' She pounced on a shell and placed it carefully in her bucket. 'We cuddled up together last night in bed and it felt just like it used to, so I thought I'd slide a leg over his and see what came up.'

'And?' Grace asked.

'Absolutely nothing,' Robyn said with a sigh. 'He just wanted to go to sleep. Claudia asked him to make three christening cakes and he started them when he got in last night after a long day fishing. He was probably stressed.'

'I have nothing useful to add to this discussion,' Katie said. 'My sex life would make a giant panda look like a nymphomaniac. That's another thing I have to take in hand.' A sudden image of Barney and his aubergine popped into her head and her face flooded with heat.

'Same,' said Robyn, thankfully not noticing Katie's blushing cheeks. 'And I know I need a proper conversation with him. I'm going to wait until after the christenings and talk about how I feel and get him to do the same.'

'Ooh, a blue bit!' Katie cried, bending down, only to retrieve a piece of plastic from the beach. She dropped it into her bucket to dispose of later. 'By the way, I've made another decision. I'm setting up a charity to send bras to women who can't afford them.'

'Love it!' said Grace. 'My sister went through about five different sizes when she was pregnant with Ruby, and then there are feeding bras and sleep bras. It cost her a fortune.'

Robyn nodded. 'And some young girls struggle, too. After Mum died and I went to live with Dad, I ended up with Claudia's cast-offs.'

'It was a teenage girl who gave me the idea,' Katie told them. 'We even came up with the name together: Small Things Matter.'

Robyn and Grace made suitably impressed noises and Katie told them all about Barney and Amber. How Amber had asked for help buying period supplies for the less well-off in her school and how over the dinner they'd come up with the name for the charity.

'Dinner?' Grace teased. 'I mean great news about the charity, but I want to know more about Barney.'

'It wasn't that sort of dinner,' said Katie, keen to shut down that topic. In truth, there'd been moments when'd she thought there might be a connection between them. Still, no point letting her mind wander in that direction. Not right now. 'It was Amber who invited me. And Amber who persuaded me to be interviewed for the newspaper.'

It would be the first thing she'd ever done to actively raise her profile. She felt a surge of nerves every time she thought about it. But it would be worth it to promote her new charity venture.

The more she'd researched it, the greater she realised the need was; bras didn't just have health benefits, women could feel empowered by wearing a good bra, they could feel safe even. This charity could actually accomplish something important. She felt more passionate about this than she'd felt about anything for a long time.

She glanced at her watch and Robyn took the hint. 'I think we've got enough sea glass for what I need,' she said, collecting their buckets and tipping the glass into one.

The three of them walked back along the beach.

'I've got loads of bras to donate,' said Grace. 'When I go back to Birmingham to fetch more of my stuff, I'll bring some.'

Katie looked at Grace hopefully. 'Does that mean you're planning on staying in Merle Bay a bit longer?'

'If Ned lets me,' she said. 'The house Myles and I shared was supposed to be our forever home. But forever didn't work out, and now I know he was unfaithful to me, the memories don't hold the same place in my heart. So as soon as the will is sorted out, I'm selling our house. You might be stuck with me permanently. And I meant it when I said I needed a project. I'll help both of you if you want?'

'I'd like that.' Katie hugged her. 'They don't teach you this in school, do they? That life isn't smooth sailing for anyone. There are a million and one things that can throw you off course.'

She felt Robyn's arm around her waist. 'Finn's dad had a saying: *you can't direct the wind, but you can adjust the sails.*'

'Very true. But as my dad would say,' Grace took in a deep breath and effected a deep northern accent, 'Gracie, you're up shit creek without a paddle.'

The three of them laughed so hard that Grace had to rush off before she wet herself and Katie was still giggling when she made it back to the shop. A handwritten note had been pushed through the letter box and lay on the doormat. Her heart thumped as she opened it, expecting the worst. But her face broke into a smile when she realised who'd sent it.

'Yes,' she said aloud into the empty shop, 'yes, I will.'

Chapter Twenty-Seven

'One with salt and vinegar?' Marco, who'd been running the Merle Bay Fish Bar ever since Katie could remember, handed the first parcel to Barney, who had his hand up. 'And the one with salt, vinegar, curry sauce *and* gravy, has to be for Katie.'

'It is. Thanks,' she said, laughing at the horror on Barney's face. She took the proffered receipt from Marco and handed it to him. 'Don't knock it till you've tried it.'

'You're a cheap date, I'll give you that. The *Gazette* would have sprung for a three-course dinner at the Anchor. We could have the best table in the house, proper cutlery, the works,' said Barney, folding the slip of paper into his wallet. His pockets clinked with the cans he'd brought along at her request. 'I think this is a first for me: conducting an interview over a bag of takeaway chips and a gin in a tin.'

'You're at the seaside now,' said Katie, as they stepped outside past the long queue which stretched along the pavement. 'Friday night, chips straight from the paper with a wooden fork – you're living the dream. And we will have the best seat in the house – follow me.'

She led him down a narrow, cobbled lane, away from the busy main street.

'This is nice,' he said, looking around.

The lane was lined both sides with chunky cottages, their slate roofs topped with fat chimney pots. Each had deep-set windows beneath stone lintels, tiny attic rooms up in the eaves and had names like Seagulls Nest and Harbour View and Puffin Cottage. Bright pops of colour from pots of pink geraniums adorned every doorstep. An energetic lady in her seventies called Marjorie was the organiser of the street's uniform floral display. Nula had recently convinced her to go up from a 38DD to a 40C, Katie remembered, making a mental note to tell her about her new charity.

'If I could live anywhere in Merle Bay, it would be this pretty street,' she said, pleased he liked it. 'Come on, it's down there.'

She pointed to a small alleyway and he followed her along it for a couple of minutes. They juggled their bags of hot chips from hand to hand, mourning the demise of the old newspaper wrappers they remembered from their childhood. Despite her reluctance to be interviewed, she'd replied to the note he'd delivered straight away, saying she'd be happy to meet him tonight. He was so easy to be around and, she admitted, sneaking a glance every now and again, easy on the eye, too. He had such a warmth about him. He was clearly comfortable in his own skin, just the right side of confident and permanently wore a genuinely interested expression that Katie imagined made him very good at his job. But her favourite feature of his was his eyes. She'd never thought people could truly have smiley eyes before meeting him. Yet that was exactly what his did – they smiled. She hadn't been exaggerating when she'd said this was her dream Friday night.

They crossed an expanse of hillocky ground, sandy underfoot with clumps of wispy grass and pretty drifts of sea rocket fringing the path. To the uninitiated, it appeared they were heading into no-man's land and Barney kept shooting her quizzical looks.

'This is a magical mystery tour,' he said at one point. 'It'll be worth it, I promise.'

They stopped at an oak bench, silvered with age, which had been perfectly positioned to make the most of the views. In front of them, the land fell gently away. Down below, frothy waves broke continuously over the rocks and the thinnest ribbon of sand separated land from sea. Dusk was almost upon them, the sky was soft with orange light from the setting sun and the sea, reflecting the light, glittered so brightly she almost couldn't look.

'Wow.' Barney seemed mesmerised.

'Ta dah!' She grinned, waving at the bench. 'You like?'

'I love,' said Barney, gesturing for her to sit first. 'And I agree – best seat in town.'

She'd taken him to the main beach at Merle Bay, the tourist beach as the locals called it. But holidaymakers rarely made it to the wild end, and they had the place to themselves.

'I used to come here and eat my chips with my parents when we visited my aunt every summer,' said Katie, unwrapping her parcel. Somewhere under all the chips and the sauce was a fish. It smelled delicious and her tummy gave an ecstatic rumble. 'Dad called it our sunset supper.'

Barney unwrapped his battered sausage and chips and popped a chip in his mouth, blowing on it first.

'So, you're not local?' He offered her a can from his pocket. 'I did wonder why your accent isn't very strong.'

'Thanks.' She opened the tin at arm's length to avoid the fizz. 'Not originally. I've been here ten years. Another fifteen and I'll probably stop being referred to as the new girl.'

He laughed. 'Tell me about it. My team at the *Gazette* like to do really bad London accents when I walk into a room.'

'All right, guv?' said Katie, in her best Cockney. 'That sort of thing?'

'Exactly,' he confirmed. 'I don't think I even sound like a Southerner.'

Katie spluttered on her gin and tonic. 'You so do.'

'Fair enough,' he laughed. He took out his phone. 'So. I'm going to record this then I won't have to make notes. I hope that's OK?'

Ah, of course, he was working; for a few delicious minutes, she'd forgotten that. It had felt like a date. She attempted to keep the disappointment from her face.

'Sure. Makes sense.' She cleared her throat and told herself to concentrate.

'Now you look worried.' Barney pulled a face. 'Sorry. I hope I haven't ruined the mood?'

'Not at all,' she assured him. 'I want to do the interview. Really.'

It was true. The announcement about the shortlisted businesses would appear in the newspaper tomorrow and interviews with the nominees would follow all week, up until the awards were announced next Friday at the Clifftop Hotel.

At first, she told herself that she was doing this for Nula, who was excited about the prospect of winning, and for her mum who, now she was back from Malta, had bought a new outfit for the event, and her dad who would be dusting off his best suit. But deep down, she couldn't deny it – the excitement was contagious. She had won over the hearts and minds of the people of Merle Bay and whether she picked up the award or not, she was overwhelmed by the vote of support they'd shown her by getting her this far.

'So,' she began, taking a slurp of her gin. 'I moved here when I was eighteen. I had a bit of bother at school and ended up dropping out of education. I started working for my aunt at Auntie Small's. It was only ever meant to be a temporary move, but,' she spread her hands, 'here I am, ten years later. I took over when she died and now I can't imagine living or working anywhere else.'

Barney's gaze softened. 'I'm so sorry to hear that.'

'It's fine.' She shrugged.

Then she told him about her place at university, her teenage dream of making the world a fairer place by working in the legal system.

'I pictured myself as a modern-day Joan of Arc, leading a crusade against injustice and I ended up in a bra shop.' She laughed mischievously. 'Perhaps I should call myself the patron saint of perky boobs instead.'

'Just as valuable a public service, I say,' Barney said, and they shared a laugh. 'What caused the breakdown, if you don't mind me asking?'

'Um.' She hesitated. Would she tell him if he were an ordinary man instead of a newspaper editor? Probably. She hadn't felt this comfortable with anyone for years and she was enjoying herself. But she was too cautious to fall into any traps.

'Sorry, sorry, I shouldn't have pried,' Barney said, rushing over his words. 'You don't have to answer and it's beyond the remit of this interview anyway. I'll delete that question.'

'Thank you,' she said. His heartfelt apology was so sweet. 'Maybe it's for another time, when our conversation isn't being recorded.'

She'd said *another time* as if they'd be doing this again. She opened her mouth to backtrack but then realised he'd be listening to this interview and anything she said now would probably make it worse. Besides, why should she backtrack? Maybe letting people know how she felt wasn't so bad. Because she did want to meet up again. Very much.

Barney's shoulders seemed to drop a little, almost in relief. 'I'd like that.'

'I said I dropped out of education,' she said, directing the conversation to safer waters. 'But I should have said formal education, because we never stop learning, do we?' She twirled a chip around on her fork and bit it in half. 'We're basically giant sponges, soaking up facts: history and geography and politics. We learn from each other, like me learning about period poverty from your daughter, and you learning the art of a curry sauce/gravy mix on chips and of course, we're always learning about ourselves.'

'Art?' He looked doubtful and took a pull from his own drink. 'And what have you learned about yourself recently?'

'That you don't have to be a barrister to make a difference in the world. That anyone can make life better for another human being. At Auntie Small's we might not be able to rescue someone from a desperate situation, or secure justice for a person who's been badly treated. But we can do our bit: we can be a friend; we can listen and keep their secrets. Pull them up by their bra straps and send them on their way with a bounce in their step and a smile on their face.'

'Sounds like a noble cause to me,' Barney grinned. 'How did you feel when you found out Auntie Small's had been shortlisted for independent retailer of the year?'

'Honestly?'

Barney nodded.

'Terrified.' A memory flashed up: Nula handing her the envelope, Katie opening it, her chest feeling like someone had fixed a tight band around it as she read the congratulations from the *Gazette*. What if they found out about the photos? Would they still be congratulating her then? 'But also deeply flattered; my Auntie Jean would have been very proud.' Katie took a bite of her fish.

'You talk a lot about Auntie Small's, but what about Katie Small? Tell me about her.'

She swallowed hard; talking about herself was so far out of her comfort zone she might as well be on another planet. She thought about the Sea Glass Sisterhood. About how Grace and Robyn were facing their fears head on. If she was really determined not to let her past cloud her life anymore, it was about time she followed suit.

She returned his gaze, her stomach fizzing with resolve. 'I was a teenager when I arrived in Merle Bay, but I'm an adult now, a businesswoman. The shop was Auntie Jean's legacy, but the future of the business is in my hands and I've got big plans, so watch this space.'

'Brilliant.' Barney picked up his phone and halted the recording. 'That's a great place to end the interview.'

'Thanks.' She shovelled in a few chips in quick succession. 'And just in time; my dinner was going cold.'

Barney eyed her. 'You're very driven. It's quite inspiring to listen to you.'

'I don't know about that.' She waved a hand dismissively; inside she was beaming with pride. 'I think I was on auto-pilot for a long time. It feels good to be in the driving seat.'

'I sympathise with that,' he said heavily. 'And auto-pilot feels like a hell of a safer way to travel at times.'

'What drives you?' she asked.

He raised an eyebrow. 'The old *turn the tables on the interviewer* trick? I see you.'

She laughed. 'Busted. But you've finished interrogating me, so now it's my turn.'

He grinned. 'Fair enough. For me it's the sniff of an untold story. The chance to get in there, uncover the truth and give readers a story which informs, educates and entertains.'

'Regardless of who the investigation hurts in the process?' she asked with a flash of concern.

She still hadn't been to the police. It was on her list of jobs for tomorrow after the sea glass walk with Robyn's previvor ladies. Robyn had asked her and Grace to lend her some moral support and afterwards, she was hoping to take Grace aside and ask her to go with her. But what if it all went pear-shaped? What if Barney got hold of the pictures? Would he print them, she wondered, knowing how mortified she'd be?

'I operate to a strict ethical code,' he said, with a frown. 'Not all journalists are morally corrupt. But even though I'm sympathetic, inevitably some stories find their way into the public arena which are going to hurt some people.'

A shiver of fear ran down her spine and before she could stop it, she gave a high-pitched nervous laugh.

Barney didn't appear to notice. He stretched his legs out in front of him and stared out at the water. 'There's something hypnotic about watching the sea, I could listen to the waves all day. What's that?' He sat forward and pointed at a black blob in the water.

'A seal,' Katie said. 'Another reason why I like this spot. If you keep looking, you'll spot more.'

'No way!' His face lit up like a little boy's. 'I've never seen a seal in the wild.'

For the next few minutes, they kept their eyes trained on the water, counting a total of five seals playing together, disappearing one moment and popping up again the next.

'That was amazing. Will they all be one family?' he asked.

She shrugged. 'They'll be a pod. Otherwise known as a herd or harem.'

'A harem?' he questioned. 'Does that mean there's one lucky guy?'

She nodded. 'Sometimes.'

'And what about you, is there one lucky guy in your life?' His eyes stayed glued to the water ahead of him. 'Although I guess I should have checked that before I asked you to dinner.'

She regarded him out of the corner of her eye, not sure how to respond. This was work, wasn't it? The chip supper was simply a vehicle for them to conduct the interview. She hardly dared speak in case she said something wrong. All of a sudden, she realised how much she wanted it to be dinner. Just dinner. Not work.

'I'm single.' Her voice came out sounding like a strangled cat. 'But aren't you interviewing all the shortlisted businesses over dinner?'

A guilty smile crept over his face. 'More like coffee. In some instances. In others, I just did it over the phone.'

'Oh.' She'd had special treatment. A bubble of happiness burst inside her chest. She'd been drawn to him from the first moment she met him. Did this mean he liked her too?

She looked at him, taking in the gentle humour in his eyes, the slightly sheepish smile. He was lovely. They were sitting side by side on the bench. Suddenly she was aware of his aftershave, of the gentle pressure of his leg against hers, the sound of his breath and found herself letting out a tiny happy sigh.

'So, if I did have a man in my life, you wouldn't have interviewed me?' she teased him.

His face reddened, making her heart swoop with joy; he was adorable.

'I would! Definitely. Especially as you've been such a good friend to Amber. And to me.'

'But over coffee, not chips?'

'No. Yes, I just meant . . . ' He scratched his head. 'I don't know what I meant. But I'm glad we're both here.'

'Me too,' she laughed, storing up the happiness she felt to examine it later, replay the conversation and check it out from every angle. 'So, how's the vegetable box challenge doing?'

He rolled his eyes. 'Me and my worthy principles. This week we got given kohlrabi. We had to google them. I think I must have ticked the box which said please bring us weird, knobbly vegetables.'

'Let me guess – you made curry?' she said.

He grinned sheepishly. 'They haven't made it out of the fridge. I'm beginning to wish I'd stuck to frozen peas and sweetcorn. We need you to come back and have dinner with us.'

Her heart fluttered. 'Or you come to mine?'

'I'd like that. I could bring my knobbly vegetables.' He looked down at his lap while he wrapped up his uneaten chips. Which was probably a good thing because she was holding in a giggle and berating the fact that she seemed to have the sense of humour of a thirteen-year-old boy.

'Date,' she said, swallowing her mirth. 'Shall we make it after the awards?'

'Great!'

By unspoken agreement, they both stood and walked towards the bin to dispose of their rubbish.

'So, are you looking forward to the awards dinner?' he asked.

She groaned. 'I haven't done anything about it. No dress, no speech . . . my parents are coming, Nula and her husband and Grace and Robyn, but I've been allocated a table of eight. I meant to ask you—'

'Believe me,' he cut in, touching her arm, 'I'd love to sit with you. But as the sponsor, it might look a bit dodgy if I'm at your table. And actually, I've been given the job of entertaining our compere. But rest assured, I'll be cheering you on when you win.'

'Actually, Barney, I wasn't inviting you,' she said, her eyes twinkling at him as he clamped a hand over his forehead in embarrassment. 'But thank you for your faith in us. No, I wanted to invite Amber. She's the inspiration behind my new venture and if she's there and we do win, I can thank her in person. And even if we don't win, it's a chance to dress up for the night.'

'Amber?' he said, his voice light with laughter. 'She'd . . . I mean . . . that would be—' He swallowed. 'She'd love it. It's exceptionally kind of you.'

'My friends will adore her. I'll look after her, make sure she doesn't nick the free wine.'

Barney grinned. 'All I'll hear about for the next week is what she should wear. There'll be online deliveries of outfits night and day.'

'That's the best part of going out,' said Katie, thinking that she ought to give her own outfit some consideration. 'Tell her if she wants a second opinion, bring her clothes round and give me a fashion show.'

Without warning, she found herself pressed to his chest in a hug.

'Thank you,' he murmured into her hair.

Her breath caught at the delicious shock of his touch and she had to fight the urge to bury herself in his embrace. Instead, she made the most of his closeness, the roughness of his cheek against hers, his smell, his breath, warm in her hair. Her heart thundered as loud as the sea and she wondered if he could feel it. 'I'm so glad she has a strong woman in her life again.'

He kissed her cheek, rough and tender all at the same time. Her eyes felt hot with the burn of happy tears. She blinked them back.

'Not sure about that, but thanks.' And then she shut up because his arms were still around her and she didn't want to waste the moment with words.

They smiled at each other, and the smile turned into a gentle laugh, and the sound, Katie felt, held the promise of more laughter to come.

'You're buzzing.' Barney released her.

'It's all the excitement,' she laughed. 'Oh.'

Her voice trailed away as she felt her phone vibrating in the back pocket of her jeans. That sort of buzzing. Barney pressed his lips together, a muffled laugh escaping as she answered the call.

'Mum! Hi! Everyone OK?'

'It's your dad,' Mum's voice wavered. 'He's in hospital.'

'Oh no,' Katie gasped. 'What's happened to him?'

Barney reached out to take her hand and squeezed it while she tried to catch her mum's words: pneumonia, struggling to breathe, lungs too weak, an intravenous drip.

Her poor, lovely dad. They'd only been back from their holiday for a couple of weeks; he'd been in the best of health then, or so she'd thought.

'Mum, listen.' She forced herself to sound calm. 'I'll come as soon as I can. I love you.'

Chapter Twenty-Eight

A nurse opened the door to the ward for her and Katie stepped inside, her eyes scanning the corridor for any sign of her parents.

'Brian Small?' she asked. 'I'm his daughter.'

'Your dad's over there by the window.'

The nurse gestured to the end bed. Katie smiled her thanks and strode towards him. Brian was lying back on a heap of pillows wearing the pyjamas she'd bought him for Christmas. Her breath hitched at the sight of him hooked up to monitors. Josie sat beside him, gripping his hand as if he might leave her at any second.

Looking up, she spotted Katie and leapt from her chair. 'Katie's here!'

'Hello, Mum.' Katie held her tight, feeling her mum's tears against her cheek.

'Do I get a look in?' said Brian, his voice breathy and weak.

'Oh Dad!' She leaned over and kissed his cheek. 'I've been so worried!'

After leaving Barney at the beach last night, she'd rushed home to get some things together. She rarely regretted not having taken driving lessons, but this had been one occasion when she could really have used a car because she didn't have enough time to catch the last train to Nottingham. Instead, she'd had to begin her journey at the crack of dawn this morning. Mum had called first thing to say Dad had had a comfortable night and was showing signs of recovery. But Katie had still wanted to check on him for herself.

'Here, sit down.' Josie patted the spare chair. 'You must be exhausted. Have you eaten?'

'I'm fine. You sit down.' Katie studied her mother's face. Mascara was smudged under her eyes and her demeanour had none of its usual bounce. She was most likely the exhausted one who hadn't bothered to eat.

'Rushing all that way,' her dad grumbled. 'I'm nothing but a nuisance. It's great to see you, but there was no need.'

Katie forced herself to smile. He looked small and old, his skin almost grey. Not the big bear of a man from her childhood she still saw in her mind's eye. She took his hand carefully. There was a canula fitted to the back of it, held in place with a large gauzy plaster. His fingers felt cold and clammy despite the warmth of the ward. She'd never seen him ill, not like this.

'There was every need,' she said firmly. 'And I wasn't doing anything today.'

In truth, she'd promised to help Robyn with her support group meeting later today. They were collecting sea glass which they'd then use to make their mosaic at the workshop Robyn was running for them in a week or so. Grace would be there, and her sister Zoe, whom she was looking forward to meeting. But there'd be other times; her place was here with her parents.

'Listen to him,' Josie huffed. 'Gives us all the fright of our lives, coughing his guts up, wheezing like a strangled mule, drenched in sweat and now, sits there like a contented Buddha when he could have *died*. Died, for pity's sake!'

'Is it being so cheerful that keeps you going?' said Brian, winking at Katie.

Katie laughed, letting out the tension which had built and built since her mum's phone call.

'I'm the one needing oxygen,' Josie retorted. 'I've half a mind to make him budge over and give me a go in bed.'

'Now there's a challenge,' said Brian. He laughed, which turned into a coughing fit and Katie poured him some water from a jug by his bed.

'Oh, you,' Josie chuckled.

Katie smiled, used to their banter. The two of them had been inseparable since they were fourteen. Brian used to skive off school to go and visit her in their dinner break, sharing a kiss and a cheese sandwich through the school-yard fence.

'Now you're here to watch him, I'll go and fetch us a cup of tea,' said Josie, standing up and pulling at Brian's blankets for no other reason than to feel useful. 'And notice I didn't say a *nice* cup of tea. But needs must. Three teas, no sugar?'

Katie and her dad nodded and watched Josie leave the ward before grinning at each other.

'Ahhh, peace at last.' Her dad closed her eyes.

'She loves you,' said Katie with a pang, thinking how lucky he was. Her mind slipped to Grace, who'd loved Myles and believed he'd loved her, and Robyn, who was starting to doubt Finn's love for her. Thank goodness for Mum and Dad and their enduring love for one another. There were happy endings in the world; her parents were proof of that. She leaned in to whisper to him. 'Are you really all right, Dad? You're not just saying it for Mum's benefit?'

'I'm a lot better for seeing you.' Brian squeezed her hand, his breath shallow. 'But I don't think I'll be strong enough to see you get your award next week. I'm gutted about it.'

He absolutely wouldn't make it. She and Mum had even discussed it on the phone last night. And Mum wouldn't come without him, not while he was ill. Katie nodded, sad that her parents wouldn't be there to cheer her on, but relieved he was being sensible about it. 'I'll take lots of pictures,' she promised.

His eyes shone with tears. 'Oh, kiddo. I don't know where you get your brains, but I'm happy to take the credit.'

She smiled at him. He hadn't called her kiddo for years. Suddenly she was a teenager again and she remembered all the other times he'd said those exact words. Both her parents had been so proud of her achievements: every glowing school report, every sporting medal, any certificate she brought home, Josie and Brian had celebrated them all. At the time she'd been mildly embarrassed by their constant praise. Now she realised how lucky she was.

'Thanks, Dad, but in this case Auntie Jean should probably take the credit; she taught me all I know about the business.'

From nowhere, her throat tightened. She missed her aunt. Grief was always with her but sometimes, like now, it was sharp and cutting, like a stone in her shoe.

A quick glance at her dad told her that he felt the same. A tear was trickling down his cheek and she looked away, not wanting to embarrass him. Instead, she opened her bag and began taking out the treats she'd brought: Turkish delight, Dad's favourite; a carton of fruit smoothie, because he didn't eat fruit, but would just about countenance fruity drinks; a puzzle book for them to bicker over; and a copy of a posh magazine for Mum who liked looking at the jobs in the back, marvelling at the sort of money people must have if they could afford a full time, live-in dog walker.

She tore open the Turkish delight and handed him a small piece.

'Have you written a speech?' he asked, touching the end of his tongue to the powdered sugar.

She shook her head. 'Not yet. I've tried but it felt like showing off, as if I'm assuming I'm going to win.'

'Look at it like this. You're already a winner because you've made it onto the shortlist but if your name gets called out on the night, you'll want to make the most of your moment in the spotlight. Write what you want to say and practise in the mirror. If you don't need the speech, at least you'll have had the experience of writing one for next time. And whether you win or not, you've made your old dad very proud.'

He curled his hand around hers and she nodded, swallowing down the ball of emotion in her throat.

'I'm glad I've made you proud eventually,' she said gruffly. 'When I dropped out of uni, I let you down. You and Mum were so looking forward to me going away to study. I remember how you used to boast to all your friends.'

'Oh, love,' Dad said softly. 'You didn't let anyone down. It was a tough time for me when you were applying for university, I admit; I wanted to keep you at home, safe under my roof where I could keep an eye on you. And I was worried I'd lose you; you'd have been living in a world much grander than the one you'd grown up in, mixing with clever people who use big words that I can't even spell.'

'I'd have been the same person inside, Dad, and I'd love you just the same,' she said, stroking his hand. 'Besides, sometimes the people with the most letters after their names are the ones who do the most stupid things.'

'Don't get me started on the politicians.' He gave a wheezy laugh and gestured to his water.

She held the glass up for him and he took a sip.

'Well anyway,' he continued, 'it turned out that I hadn't kept you safe at all. When all that photoshoot business happened, I felt like I'd let you down. I hadn't protected my little girl. When Jean suggested having you to stay in Merle Bay, part of me was relieved that you didn't go away to university. Your mum felt the same.'

Katie shook her head, amazed; all these years she'd felt guilty for not living up to their expectations. 'I can't believe how naïve I was,' she said. 'Thinking I could make enough money to see me through uni.'

'You were a just a kid. I'm not a violent man but if I'd ever got hold of that photographer, I'd have cheerfully punched his lights out.'

'Listen to him. He thinks he's Lennox Lewis. Who are you having a go at now?' Mum was back, carrying a cardboard tray with three plastic cups wedged into it.

'Katie thinks she's let us down by not going to university. If anyone let anyone down it was that gobshite photographer.' Dad tried to hoist himself upwards to drink his tea but gave up. He looked very tired.

'Pervert,' Josie sniffed.

Katie was glad she hadn't mentioned the reappearance of the photographs, not when their feelings were clearly still raw. And now with Dad ill, there was no question of it. Mum had enough to deal with, having her beloved Brian in hospital. Katie vowed she would handle it herself and hope that they never found out.

'All we ever wanted was for you to be happy, Katie.' Her mum sipped her tea and winced. 'I'm glad you didn't end up as a hotshot lawyer. I watch all the law programmes on telly. They're all stressed to high heaven and look as miserable as sin. Do you think if me and your dad had double the amount of money we'd be twice as happy as we are now?'

The look on Dad's face suggested that he'd like the chance to find out, but wisely he said nothing.

'I know that money doesn't buy happiness,' said Katie. 'That was never my motivation. School pushed us to fulfil our academic potential. Anyone who wasn't university material got overlooked. It's only now looking back I see what a narrow-minded view that is. Every student should be encouraged and nurtured regardless of ability. And running a lingerie shop might not have been part of my plan, but I am happy.'

She pushed the blackmail letters to the back of her mind.

'As long as you're not lonely.' Josie gave her a long stare. 'Especially with Jean gone.'

'Watch out, Katie,' Dad murmured. He'd closed his eyes and wasn't far away from drifting off to sleep. 'She'll be angling for another invite to stay with you in a minute.'

'And she'd be welcome, you both are, any time. I do miss Auntie Jean,' Katie said. 'But being single doesn't mean I'm lonely.'

Josie pinched her lips together in disbelief. 'I'm glad to hear it. Although I'd love it if you had somebody special in your life.'

A memory of Barney's lips brushing against her cheek yesterday popped into her head and before she knew it her face was warm.

Josie registered Katie's blush, and squeezed her daughter's hand. 'I'll say no more about it.'

'Tell her about Valerie Dunbar,' said Brian.

Katie frowned. 'Rose's mum?'

Josie gasped. 'Oh yes! Valerie! With all the fuss about your father, I forgot. I had a message from one of the ladies in the choir, day before yesterday. Apparently she died of a massive stroke, poor thing. Must have been just before we went to Malta. The worst thing was that nobody found her for two weeks.'

'Can you imagine.' Brian closed his eyes. 'Bad business.'

'Fancy not being missed for two whole weeks.' Katie shuddered; she'd only met Rose's mum a couple of times, and that had been at parents' evenings at school.

'I know Valerie and her daughter had their differences,' said Josie. 'But I'd like to think you'd be worried about me if you didn't hear anything for a fortnight.'

'I'd know something's wrong if you're quiet for more than fifteen minutes,' said Brian, his lips twitching.

Josie tutted. 'It was a neighbour in the end, who noticed the post hadn't moved from the letter box. Apparently, Rose has moved into her mother's old house for the foreseeable, to sort out her affairs and what-not.'

'Is it still the same house?' Katie asked as an idea occurred to her.

Josie nodded. 'As far as I know.'

Brian's breathing had slowed, and he was wheezing softly, eyes closed, hovering between being asleep and awake.

Josie reached for Katie's hand across the bed. 'It's meant the world to him, seeing you. He's already brighter. Are you going to stay the night with us?'

'Yes please. I think I'm going to see Rose while I'm here. Maybe it's time to patch things up. And even if we can't be friends, at least I'll have offered an olive branch.'

When Katie had first moved to Merle Bay, she'd thought about Rose a lot. She missed her best friend, but at the same time knew that the way Rose had treated her was not how a good friend should behave. She'd waited for an apology, but it never came. As time went by, her school life lost its colour until it was nothing more than a misty memory.

'You're a good girl,' said Josie. 'And you're right: kindness costs nothing.'

Katie checked the time. Her dad was sleeping, there was nothing to stop her going now. It was the right thing to do and she had to admit, she was interested to see what Rose looked like these days. They weren't kids any more, it was time to let go of the past. The Sea Glass Sisterhood had come along just when Katie had needed a shoulder to cry on, so perhaps now she could pay it forward and be there for her old friend.

Chapter Twenty-Nine

Rose's family home was on the other of the city, eight miles from Brian and Josie's house. Katie's school had been a Catholic secondary, which meant that the catchment area was much bigger than usual, taking children from primary feeder schools from all four corners of the city. Long bus journeys into school, and to visit each other, had been the norm. Katie took the bus, just as she had when she was a teenager. It was bizarre being back; so much had changed. Huge modern buildings had sprung up and lots of the old ones demolished to make room for new trams and roads. As the bus trundled across Nottingham, she was flooded with memories, mostly good. She and Rose had had great fun together. Right up until suddenly they hadn't. One studious, one scraping through school by the seat of her pants . . . Katie had been the wholesome sunshine to Rose's seductive darkness. Katie had felt humiliated and alone when Rose cut her out of her life; she'd been caught in a downward spiral which eventually led to depression. If it had been the other way around, Katie would have been there for Rose. It broke her heart that Rose didn't do that for her.

She found Rose's Victorian mid-terraced house easily; it was just as she remembered it: stained-glass panel in the door, racing-green paintwork and small square of gravelled front garden with a sundial in the centre.

Her whole body tingled with nerves as she pushed open the gate; she wasn't sure what to expect. Would Rose be pleased to see her? Unlikely, thought Katie. But the fact that she'd come to pay her respects would soften Rose's reaction. Before she could give herself time to change her mind, her finger rang the doorbell.

At first, there was silence. She rang again and this time, she could make out a thumping noise. There was someone in there and they were heading her way. Instinctively, Katie took a step back as muffled footsteps grew louder, and a dark shape came into view through the patterned glass.

A woman with flushed cheeks and a sheen of sweat on her forehead opened the door and glared at her. 'Yes?'

Her black hair was tied up in a messy bun, a T-shirt hung off one shoulder and there were dusty streaks on her leggings and her face had lost the softness of youth, but Katie would recognise her anywhere. 'Rose?' Katie's voice came out as a croak and she curled her fingers tightly into fists to stop her hands from shaking. 'It's me, Katie Small. Catherine.'

'What the hell . . . ?' Rose's body tensed, she looked over Katie's shoulder towards the street and then shrank back behind the door. Behind her, boxes and bags lined both sides of the tiled hallway all the way to the kitchen. Even the staircase was cluttered with objects. It looked like she was in the middle of clearing the house.

Katie forced herself to remember that Rose was grieving for her mum, and she'd turned up unannounced, it was perfectly understandable that she wasn't being very welcoming.

'It's been a long time, but I wanted to come to—' Katie began.

'I know why you've come.' Rose gave a harsh laugh. Her fingers gripped the edge of the door, eyes narrowed.

'How did you know? Oh, of course, you were always the smart one, always the golden girl, doing the right thing.' Her voice dripped with sarcasm.

'I don't understand,' Katie tried again, bewildered at Rose's reaction.

Rose stepped back inside and began to shut the door in her face. But her foot got caught on a plastic bag and she slipped sideways. Arms flailing, she lost her balance and fell against the wall, screaming as she pitched backwards. The crack of her skull on the tiled floor turned Katie's stomach.

'Oh my God!' Katie cried. The door was only half open and Rose's legs were blocking her path, but she managed to push her way inside and dropped to her knees beside Rose's prone body. 'Rose! Rose!'

She shook her shoulders gently, but there was no response. It looked as if she was out cold. Katie was trembling properly now, her hands clammy. Panic gushed through her as she tried to remember what you were supposed to do when someone was unconscious. *Check for breathing, put in them in the recovery position, call for help.* Instructions from her school first-aid training came flooding back. She bent over Rose's face. She didn't appear to be breathing at all.

'HELP!' she shouted through the open door towards the street, hoping to attract the attention of a neighbour. 'Somebody please HELP ME!'

But the street was deserted.

'I'm putting you in the recovery position,' Katie said loudly, hoping to bring her round with the sound of her voice.

There was hardly any room to manoeuvre in the narrow hallway and the line of black bags wasn't helping, but she grabbed hold of Rose's T-shirt and the leg furthest away from her and tugged with all her strength. It was when she knelt back on her heels, panting from exertion that she noticed the blood in Rose's hair. There was a cut on the back of her head, and it was bleeding fast.

Oh God. She felt her stomach lurch; she'd never been very good with blood. Three closed doors led from the hallway. Katie vaguely remembered the layout, a living room at the front, dining room in the middle and a long thin kitchen at the far end leading straight out into the back yard. She scrambled to her feet and ran into the kitchen. The sink was just inside the door. She scooped up a towel lying on the draining board and ran straight back to Rose, pulling her phone from the back pocket of her jeans and dialling 999.

'Wake up, Rose, wake up,' Katie pleaded, pressing the towel to the wound as she waited for the line to connect.

'Which emergency service do you require?'

Her throat was so dry she could barely speak. 'Ambulance please.'

The minutes ticked slowly by. At the point when her arms and her legs had gone numb from being cramped in the same position over Rose's prone body, Katie heard an approaching siren. Tears of relief pricked at her eyes.

'The ambulance is coming,' she said. 'It's going to be OK.'

Rose's arm twitched and she gave a low moan.

Thank heavens. Katie let out a shaky sob; she must be coming round at last. Blood was still oozing from the wound and she refolded the towel and tucked it under Rose's head. The sound of the ambulance was really loud now. Katie clambered to her feet and dashed outside to flag it down. Her head spun from getting up too quickly and she had to lean against the gate to steady herself.

She raised a hand as the ambulance pulled up, blue lights flashing, siren wailing.

Two paramedics, a man and a woman, jumped out from the ambulance, one carrying a big green medical bag.

'Over here!' Katie called weakly.

'I'm Jess. This is my colleague, Mike. Did you make the call?' said the female paramedic, pushing open the gate.

Katie nodded. She stuttered over her own name and tried to tell Jess what had happened as she led them inside. Her head felt thick and her legs had gone rubbery. Rose hadn't moved but her eyes were flickering. The paramedics got to work straight away, picking over the clutter in the hall, talking clearly and calmly to Rose. Katie stood back out of their way by the entrance to the kitchen.

'She hit her head as she fell,' said Katie in a wobbly voice.

Mike nodded. 'And caught herself on that nail by the look of it.'

Katie followed his gaze to a rectangular patch of wall lighter than the rest where a picture or a mirror must have hung at some point. A nail protruded from the wall and there was a smear of blood below it. Rose's head must have gone straight into it. The thought made Katie feel sick. In the next instant her knees sagged from under her.

'Whoah.' Jess jumped up and hooked her arm through Katie's. 'Let's get you sitting down.'

Katie was trembling as the paramedic led her into the kitchen, past the sink and the cooker and to a small wooden table at the end of the room. She sat on a chair and leaned her head back against the wall.

Jess washed a glass under the tap, refilled it with cold water and handed it to her. Katie took it and murmured her thanks; her throat was aching with thirst and she took a big gulp.

'OK?' Jess studied her carefully. 'Will you be all right here if I go back to Rose?'

Katie nodded.

'What relationship are you to Rose? Sister?'

'Friend. Old school friend,' Katie rasped.

Jess smiled. 'Ah, that's nice that you've kept in touch.'

Katie stayed quiet; if only Jess knew that the reason Rose had fallen over was because she'd tried to slam the door in her face. Jess picked up a blanket which had been left folded over the chair next to her and draped it around Katie's shoulders. 'You've done brilliantly, Katie. Give us five minutes and I'll be back to check on you.'

'OK.' Katie closed her eyes and took a deep breath.

What a day: a crack of dawn start to see Dad and now this. It had been one adrenaline rush after another, no wonder she felt shaky. She definitely shouldn't have come, that was for certain. She hadn't known what Rose's reaction would be, but she certainly hadn't expected such venom.

'We're going to try and get you on your feet now,' said Mike loudly to Rose. 'Can you manage that?'

Katie couldn't catch Rose's reply, but she sounded agitated.

'Yes, we're getting you out now.' The paramedics were talking to her clearly as if she was a child.

'Her!' Rose said. 'Her.'

'Steady now. Mind your head,' said Mike firmly.

'No! Out!' Rose shouted.

Katie held her breath. It was obvious who Rose was referring to. She half expected Jess or Mike to appear and ask her to leave, but they were clearly having enough trouble getting Rose to her feet.

'Come on now, Rose,' Jess coaxed, adding in a lower voice. 'Very likely concussion.'

'Yes,' Mike agreed. 'And she's going to need stitches.'

Katie stood up to go and see what was going on. As she did so, her eye was drawn to a neat brown folder on the table with the initials CS on it. Her initials. It was probably nothing but a coincidence, but Katie couldn't resist opening it. Her heart almost stopped beating. Inside was a handful of documents and the uppermost one was a black and white photograph of Katie naked. *The* photograph. The same one which had been sent in manila envelopes to the shop.

Shock pulsed through her veins like ice.

'Oh my god. No.' Katie pressed a hand to her mouth, swallowing as nausea rose up her throat.

Every hair on her body stood up, her flesh prickled in goosebumps. There were other pictures, too. An image of Auntie Small's printed from Google Maps. An old class photograph, the last one they'd had taken in sixth form. Katie's face picked out with a red marker pen. What did this mean? Why would Rose have these in a folder? How did she get that photograph?

Katie's heart suddenly felt too big for her chest; it pounded against her ribcage and no matter how hard she tried, she could barely breathe as the reality of this evidence hit home.

'It's Rose,' she gasped.

The person sending her threatening letters, blackmailing her, was her old school friend Rose Dunbar.

'That's it, slowly does it,' Mike was saying to Rose.

In slow motion, Katie turned to looked down the thin hallway. The three of them were in a line: Mike nearest to the door, supporting Rose who was in the middle and Jess bringing up the rear, holding a dressing to Rose's head.

'Why?' Katie called. Her mouth so dry she could barely form the words. 'Rose, why?'

Rose twisted away from the paramedics and stared straight at Katie, she looked like she was in pain, but there was contempt there too. 'I hate you.'

Jess glanced from Rose to Katie uncertainly. 'How are you feeling, chick? You still look very pale.'

'I'm fine,' Katie lied, her eyes trained on Rose. 'You were supposed to be my best friend. Have you any idea what you've been putting me though? Why would you do this to me?'

Mike was pushing bags of stuff out of the way with his boot, clearing a path to the door. He pinned it right back with his foot and daylight flooded into the dim hallway. 'OK, mind the step.'

Mike led them outside over the threshold and onto the path and Katie followed. Jess darted past them to the ambulance.

Rose's face was ashen and sweaty. Katie looked at her, her heart heavy with sadness. She couldn't help but wonder what had gone wrong for her friend. Where had that bubbly extrovert with the flashing eyes and flirty smile gone? She'd spent the last weeks terrified of her invisible tormentor. And now here she was face to face with her. Her head was spinning with emotions: anger and hurt and relief.

'Rose, I don't understand?' she said quietly.

'Get off me.' Rose tried to free herself from the paramedic's support and staggered backwards.

'Let's calm down, shall we?' Jess ran back up the path pushing a wheelchair. Between them, she and Mike manoeuvred Rose into it.

Rose began to cry.

'Can we get your things for you?' Mike asked. 'Keys? Handbag?'

She shook her head. 'Don't want to go. I want you all to leave me alone.'

'I know,' Jess soothed, 'but we need to get that head X-rayed.'

'I'll check the back door's locked and fetch her handbag,' Katie offered.

Back in the kitchen she took the photograph from the folder. The memory of the day that the envelope had arrived through the post came flooding back. She remembered her panic, how she'd shut herself into the toilets at school to open it. How the shock had made her pass out, her horror at coming round to find two teachers and Rose standing over her, the contents of the envelope spilled onto the floor. Rose must have stolen the photograph then. It would have been easy for her and Katie would never have missed it; she hadn't counted the exact number of prints she'd been sent. Now, she put it in her own bag, locked the back door and collected a grey leather handbag from the hall.

Jess waited with the wheelchair while Mike pulled out a ramp from the back of the ambulance. Katie worked through the keys until she found one which fitted the front door and double-locked it.

'Is this the right one?' Katie held the bag up to Rose. Rose turned her face away but gave the briefest of nods. The wheelchair was rolled up into the ambulance. Jess jumped out again.

'Two ticks and we'll be off,' said Mike.

He and Jess stood to one side out of earshot and conducted a low volume conversation leaving Katie to stare into the ambulance at Rose.

'Are you going to the police?' Rose asked sullenly.

'Depends on you,' Katie said. She pulled the edge of the photograph out of her bag. 'Is this the only one?'

She nodded.

'And you haven't got copies?'

'The only copies I had I already sent you,' Rose scowled. 'So, what now?'

'Now you tell me what's behind all this,' Katie said, more fiercely than she felt. She could feel her heart thumping against her ribs. But she was in the driving seat now. Rose knew she had to cooperate or face criminal charges. 'What have I ever done to you?'

'Little Miss Perfect,' Rose turned away, her face taut with disgust. 'Even when you dropped out of school you rose to the top like cream: a nice job and a nice house. Mum hasn't stopped going on about you since your mum joined that choir. Telling me how well you were doing, how good you are to your parents, how hard you work. I was never good enough at anything as far as she was concerned. *Why can't you be more like her, Rose*, she used to say. Drove me insane.'

Katie was confused. 'But I thought you had a good job? An accountant I heard?'

Rose curled her lip. 'I work in an accounts' office; I never qualified, but Mum liked to pretend otherwise. The last time I saw her alive we had a row. All I wanted was to borrow a bit of money, just for a couple of months. But she wouldn't let me have it and I lost my temper. *I bet Catherine Small doesn't speak to her mother like that*, she said in her you're-such-a-disappointment voice. I stormed out. I didn't call her again after that. I decided to let her stew for a couple of weeks, and I didn't return her calls. She might have been calling to tell me she felt ill. But now I'll never know. All because of you.'

'I'm sorry about your mum.' Katie was flabbergasted. 'But surely you can't blame me?'

'It's your fault we rowed. Your fault I left her alone.' Rose looked away, her face contorted with anger. 'I'd forgotten about that photo until I came back to clear the house. You didn't notice me take it in the girls' loos.' A faint smirk crossed her features. 'After you left school I made a fortune showing it to all the boys. Then we all left, and I shoved the photo in a drawer. When I found it again a few weeks ago it seemed like a good way make you pay.'

It was displaced guilt, thought Katie, a defence mechanism. In Rose's grief, she'd sought out someone to pin the blame on. Katie had been the unlucky target.

'There's a prison sentence for blackmail, you know.' Katie lowered her voice as Jess bounded up into the back of the ambulance.

Rose's eyes, red-rimmed from crying, looked pleadingly at her.

Katie sighed. 'I lost my aunt last year; I know how devastating it is to lose someone you love. But, Rose, what you're doing. . . it's never going to bring you happiness. However hard it might seem, you need to start living your own life, moving on. According to my mum, Valerie always spoke lovingly about you, she was proud of you.' That hadn't been strictly true, but Katie decided that she could be forgiven using a little bit of artistic licence under the circumstances. 'She wouldn't want you to be living like this, would she?'

Rose shook her head and tears coursed down her cheeks.

'Ready to go?' Jess asked.

'I don't need to go to hospital,' Rose muttered.

'I'm sure you're fine, but we have to check,' she replied. 'Are you coming with us, Katie?'

'No!' Rose said sharply.

'I wasn't planning to,' said Katie. 'Actually, I've just come from the hospital and I'm due back there later. My dad's got pneumonia.' She addressed this last comment to Jess.

'Oh dear,' Jess winced. 'Not been your lucky day, has it?'

'It's certainly had its ups and downs,' Katie replied. 'But now I think the worst is behind us, wouldn't you agree, Rose?'

Rose closed her eyes and turned away.

'Thanks for your help, Jess.' Katie blinked back tears of relief. She had no intention of crying in front of Rose. She waved one final time as Jess shut the doors. 'Goodbye.'

As she watched the ambulance pull away from the kerb, she let out a long breath.

It was over.

The photograph was in her possession, there'd be no more blackmail letters; crisis averted. Right now, she felt hollow and sick to her stomach, but as she'd said to Rose, the worst was definitely behind her. Rose had acted wrongly – criminally, Katie reminded herself – but a part of her couldn't help feeling sorry for her. Maybe today's encounter would serve as a wake-up call, provide Rose with the catalyst for a fresh start. Katie hoped so. Now she wanted to get home, back to the shop and her cottage and back to the Sea Glass Sisterhood. The awards dinner was less than a week away and now she could look forward to the future without looking back over her shoulder. As far as she was concerned, she could hold her head up high, this episode of her life was history.

Chapter Thirty

Robyn paused from rearranging the deckchairs she and Finn had ferried down to the beach from home, begging and borrowing from neighbours. She wiped perspiration from her forehead and took a deep breath.

Today was the day. The idea she'd had of sharing her beach with her fellow previvors was actually happening and the sea glass walk was due to begin in ten minutes. It was a perfect afternoon. Despite only being early May, Merle Bay was in the grip of a mini heatwave and the beach was looking its sparkliest, glitteriest best. The sea was an oasis of turquoise calm and above them an azure blue sky had but a sprinkling of cotton wool clouds.

She was thrilled with the turnout: thirty women and around twelve kids so far. Seeing them all here on the beach . . . all these smiling faces made her heart sing. There were at least ten women she recognised from the previvors group including Sadie, the leader and Tess. The rest had heard through word of mouth.

To make it feel like a proper event, they'd set deckchairs and two fold-up tables around the edge of three picnic blankets at Grace's end of the beach. There were a couple of parasols to shield people from the sun. Grace had offered the use of her loo, which could be accessed from a little utility room and which was a godsend. She'd also been the one to suggest selling some refreshments, which Finn had thrown himself into organising.

'Well done, pet.' Finn put his arm around her and kissed the side of her head. 'This is a great idea.'

'It is, isn't it?' She leaned against him, feeling his taut muscles under his T-shirt. She felt giddy with success and they hadn't even started collecting sea glass yet. 'And thanks for coming with me to help.'

He squeezed her to him. 'Of course. Wouldn't have missed it for the world. But I still think you should have charged everyone to take part. Not just for the refreshments.'

She shook her head.

'These are women who've had a crap time and probably a financially hard time, too. Besides, it's all part of the master plan.' She waggled her eyebrows. 'Once they've collected the sea glass, I'm hoping I'll persuade them to book onto a creative workshop to make things with it.'

Finn grinned. 'Good thinking, Batman.'

'I want to make a go of this, Finn.' She turned to face him. 'I really hope I can make a business out of sea glass: workshops, making things and selling them online. I feel so bad that I haven't been able to contribute financially.'

'Hey, you've been investing in your health.' He cupped a hand to her cheek. 'And that's more precious to me than anything.'

Her heart swelled with love for him. She was so grateful to have him by her side, but at the same time, she felt as restless as a caged bird. She wasn't a patient anymore; she didn't want handling with kid gloves. She wanted him to not simply love her but to desire her.

She untangled herself from him gently. 'I am back on my feet, Finn. I just want life to go back to how it was before my surgery.' She trailed her fingertips down the front of his T-shirt and held his gaze. 'You and me.'

The smile faded from his eyes and discomfort appeared in its place. 'Yeah, me too.'

And just like that, the happy mood between them vanished; Robyn could have kicked herself. Instead of looking ahead, Finn was probably now thinking back to the time of choosing baby names and reading up on ovulation and conception.

'How much are the brown paper bags, please?' a voice interrupted them. A girl smiled at them; she wore a vest top and denim shorts and had a pink paisley scarf wrapped tightly around her head. 'I never thought to bring a bucket.'

'No charge. Help yourself!' Robyn glanced apologetically at Finn and darted to the table where all their things were laid out: bags to put the sea glass in; cool boxes full of ice lollies and cold drinks; some giant thermos jugs for hot water, and several tins containing a variety of Finn's cakes.

'Thanks.' The girl beamed. 'And thanks for doing this. I heard about it through an online forum I'm a member of. I've been looking for something creative to do.'

'If you leave your email address,' Robyn said, pointing to a sheet of paper attached to a clipboard, 'I'll let you know what else we've got coming up.'

'Cool.' She filled in her details and wandered back to join her friend.

People were milling around, chatting and looking at their watches. Robyn felt a spike of nerves; Katie had left a message on the WhatsApp group telling them about her dad, poor thing, so she knew she wouldn't make it. She hoped Grace wouldn't have to bail out too; there was no sign of her so far.

'Hi everyone!' Robyn raised her voice. 'Would you all like to find a space in the circle? We'll be starting in a second.'

The kids bounced onto the picnic blankets, buckets in hand, followed by their mothers. The chairs filled up quickly; some people choosing the shade of the parasols, others unfurling in the sun and tilting their faces to the sky.

Sadie touched her arm as she passed by. 'This is beyond exciting! I've already told the regional director about this initiative; it ticks all the boxes. You've done wonders for the profile of the north-east group. Anything I can help with, you must let me know.'

'There is something,' Robyn said. 'You could introduce me, like you introduced Pam, at the meeting.'

Sadie's hands fluttered. 'Of course! Now?'

Above her on the path, Robyn heard laughter and voices. She looked up to see Grace and her sister on their way down. 'In two minutes?'

Sadie gave a thumbs-up and went to hover near the tables where Finn was selling ice lollies to Tess and her children.

'For a small human she certainly has a lot of kit,' Grace sounded out of breath. 'And I'm sure this pushchair weighs the same as a small car.'

'I know,' said another voice, 'sorry about that. I'd have brought her in the papoose but I'm hoping she'll have a sleep.'

'I'll go and help.' Finn opened the gate at the bottom of Grace's beach steps and ran up the hill.

Several of the women turned and watched him, admiring glances on their faces. Robyn smiled to herself. *Hands off*, she thought.

'Help yourself to bags,' she announced, 'if you need somewhere to put your sea glass.'

Seconds later, there were several gasps as Finn reappeared holding a ginormous pushchair over his head. He trotted down the last few steps and plonked it roughly on the shingle.

'Don't worry!' Grace cried, following behind him, 'there's no baby on board.'

Behind Grace was her sister, Zoe, holding a baby.

'Robyn, Finn, meet Zoe and Ruby.' Grace dumped the bags on the picnic rug. 'Sorry we're late. We had to pack enough kit for a month away from the house.'

'Welcome to my life, sis,' said Zoe, laughing. She tucked the baby into the pram, handed her a toy to play with and then turned to Robyn and gave her a hug. 'Lovely to meet you. I've heard a lot about you. Thanks for looking after my sister.'

A plastic toy came flying out of the pram. Finn retrieved it and handed it back to the baby.

'It's more like the other way round really,' Robyn replied, watching Finn interact with Ruby out of the corner of her eye. 'Thanks for joining in today. I'm glad of the support, especially now that Katie had to dash to Nottingham.'

'What a nightmare for her,' Grace tutted. 'Any news? I haven't had a chance to check WhatsApp.'

Robyn shook her head. 'Nothing yet.'

Finn was making Ruby laugh by playing peekaboo with a small teddy bear. Her heart sank. He'd never be able to do that with a child of his own. Not if he stayed with her, anyway.

'Hello gorgeous,' Finn laughed as the baby grabbed at his finger.

'Ooh, she likes *you*,' said Zoe, crouching down right beside him and steadying herself with a hand on his shoulder.

'She likes everyone,' said Grace. 'She's going to be the life and soul of parties when she's older, I can tell. Should we . . . ?' She caught Robyn's eye and nodded towards the assembled group.

'Definitely.' Robyn tore her eyes away from Zoe and Finn and signalled to Sadie, who immediately stepped into the circle and clapped her hands to get everyone's attention.

'Good afternoon everyone,' Sadie began, smiling round at the group. 'Well, this is a first! And thanks to Robyn for organising this event. Being here today embodies everything that our Previvors Group stands for: nurturing, encouraging, exploring new things. I really hope events like these event will develop a community not only united by the journey to health we're on, but by sharing our own talents and passions. Which leads me neatly to hand over to the woman whose passion brought us to Merle Bay. Over to you, Robyn.'

Robyn joined Sadie and cleared her throat.

'Today is about sharing something with you that makes me and my friends happy: spending time on the beach in the sunshine, breathing in the fresh sea air, doing something different and active. This is something to take our minds off what we've been through or what we're still going through. For an hour or so we can just chat away to each other or stay quiet and enjoy being surrounded by nature. This is a chance to leave our real lives with all their worries behind, just for a little while. A good tip for you: the best bits are often found on the tide line. OK, that's it,' she gave a little self-conscious shrug. 'Enjoy yourselves and happy hunting!'

Grace started them off in a round of applause while Robyn gave a wobbly sigh of relief. She hadn't addressed a big group of people like that for years, but she'd done it, she thought proudly. And then everyone was on their feet, laughing and talking and making a beeline for the water.

Grace dabbed her eyes and beamed. 'That was ace. I'm proud of you. Anything you need a hand with, just shout, otherwise I'm going to introduce my sister and my niece to the magical world of sea glass.' She picked up a bag for her and Zoe.

'Robyn?' She turned to find Finn behind her looking at her oddly. 'Is that really why you come to the beach? To get away from your life. Is it that bad?'

'No, that's not what I meant.' Robyn was horrified. She reached for him, putting her arms around his waist. 'My life has everything in it that I want, I promise.'

But has yours?

The words were on the tip of her tongue. She knew she should ask him, but did she really want to hear the answer?

He gave her a searching look as if he didn't quite believe her.

'When I'm here with Grace and Katie and we're collecting sea glass, I find it easier to talk about how I'm feeling. We all need someone to talk to, don't we?' she said. 'Even though we love our partners with all our hearts, sometimes they're the people we find it hardest to open up to.'

'I understand that.' Finn drew her close and his heart beat against hers, connecting them. If only she could read his mind as well has his body. 'But whatever is bothering you, I want you to tell me. I can take it; however bad it is, it won't change how I feel about you. Promise?'

Her mouth was dry. As far as she was concerned, he'd already changed the way he felt. Was he paving the way to finally admit it?

'Promise,' she agreed. 'But you've got to promise too. It has to work both ways, Finn.'

A look of nerves flashed across his face and his lovely eyes held her gaze. Finally, he nodded.

'OK. That's fair.' He gave her a lopsided smile. 'It looks like the beach really is a good place to talk. I think—'

He stopped, distracted by something over her shoulder. Robyn froze. 'What? What do you think?'

'Tell you another time. You're needed,' he said, kissing her cheek and releasing her as Tess came crunching across the shingle, a child holding onto each of her hands.

'Is there a loo around here? Both these two urchins are desperate.'

'Sure. Follow me.' Robyn stepped away from her husband and led Tess and the children up the steps to Grace's house.

By the time Robyn returned a few minutes later, the beach had filled up even more. Freya, one of the girls she'd met at the previvors group, held a white oval in the palm of her hand. 'Robyn, is this sea glass?'

Robyn peered at it and shook her head. 'It's a stone, washed smooth by the sea.'

Freya's face fell. 'Oh, I thought I'd found treasure.'

'In that case, you have. Beauty is in the eye of the beholder and you're the beholder. Which means that if you think something is beautiful, it is.' Robyn tapped the stone. 'Keep the stone, treasure it, because this is your beautiful.'

Freya grinned. 'Wow, that's really inspiring. I love that. Thanks.'

Robyn felt a wave of pride as she watched Freya trudge back to her friend. Her eye roamed the beach and took in the little huddles of women talking and laughing, their kids running in and out of the waves. She'd made this happen, she thought. Somehow, without planning it, she appeared to have hit on something special. With a bit of organisation, she could potentially make a small business using sea glass to bring people together. She needed a venue to run workshops, she needed a website to sell what she made and to publicise her events . . . There was lots to do, but that was OK; she didn't mind hard work. It was creative, it was fun and best of all, none of this would have happened if she hadn't tested positive with the BRCA gene. The morning of the day she'd met Katie and Grace for the first time, she'd challenged herself to be positive, proactive and perky. She didn't manage it every day, and things weren't perfect between her and Finn, but she was getting there, one step at a time.

Her gaze alighted on Finn who was at the refreshment table talking to another man. What had he been about to say when Tess had interrupted them? She had a feeling it was important. Somehow she had to make an opportunity to recreate that moment and get him to open up. For better or worse, he'd promised to talk to her.

She went to join him.

'And when I'm not at sea, I'm with this wonderful woman. My wife, the brains behind today,' Finn said, holding a hand out to her. 'Robyn, this is Barney Larkin from the *North East Gazette* and his daughter, Amber.'

'Great event. I love the sentiment behind it.' Barney shook Robyn's hand. 'It would make a nice story for the paper.'

Robyn blinked. 'Would it?'

Amber pulled a lollipop out of her mouth to speak. 'Katie told us about today. I think what you're doing is brilliant. Women supporting women. That's cool.' She nodded and put her lollipop back in.

Robyn grinned. 'Thanks. I've heard about your campaigns, too. Katie is always singing your praises.'

'Seriously?' For a split second, Amber's face lit up before apparently remembering she was a teenager and therefore supposed to look bored by everything. 'Yeah, Katie's cool, too.'

'I hope you don't mind us gatecrashing?' Barney said. 'We were going to meet Katie here, but we decided to come even though she had to cancel.'

Robyn was trying to remember everything Katie had told her about Barney. She hadn't said much, and she definitely hadn't mentioned how good-looking he was.

'Of course not,' she smiled. 'The more the merrier. Poor Katie; I hope her dad is OK.'

'He's improved already,' Barney told her. 'Out of danger apparently.'

'You've heard from her?' Robyn said, surprised. 'Grace and I haven't.'

'She sent me a very brief text, that's all.' A hint of colour rose to Barney's cheeks. 'Is it OK if I take a picture of you with the sea in the background?'

'In these old dungarees?' Robyn yelped.

'You look great, love,' said Finn.

'Aww.' Amber sighed dreamily. 'I hope I'm in love when I'm old.'

The three adults laughed.

'What's funny?' Amber demanded and looked at Robyn. 'The dungarees are perfect. You look arty and bohemian. Just fold your arms and tilt your chin up and boom.'

Robyn felt completely self-conscious but did as she was told and followed Amber's various directions while Barney took some photos.

'Have you always been a fisherman?' Barney said to Finn when he'd finished. Amber took his phone off him and started selecting the best photos.

Finn nodded. 'Man and boy. We're a dying breed. The McGills are the last fishing family in Merle Bay.'

'Please take Dad out on your boat,' Amber begged, clasping her hands together. 'He's been going on about

307

fishing since we arrived. The sea is earth's greatest ecosystem.' This last phrase was said in a deep voice obviously mimicking Barney's.

'The sea is also the best place on earth,' Finn grinned. 'I'd be glad to take you. My brother and I can always use an extra pair of hands, even if they're soft southern ones.'

Barney laughed and showed his palms to Finn. 'They don't come softer than mine. I'm a pen pusher through and through.'

'But he doesn't get seasick,' Amber put in loyally. 'We once went on the ferry to France and everyone was sick except Dad. I had to get completely changed into clean clothes. The basins in the toilets were literally full of sick. The deck of the boat, total vomitsville. They had to close the cafeteria because someone puked in the chips.'

'Euww.' Robyn blocked her ears.

'We get it.' Barney clapped a hand over his daughter's mouth. 'Thanks.'

'Get what?' Grace asked, leaving Zoe.

'It starts with "v" and ends in "omit",' Amber giggled, twisting out of her dad's grasp and running off to towards the sea.

'Sorry about my revolting child,' Finn laughed.

'Grace, meet Barney Larkin from the *Gazette*,' said Robyn. 'Barney, Grace is staying in Sea Glass House.'

'Grace Byron!' Barney pumped her hand. 'Great to meet you. I'd love to talk to you about architecture in Merle Bay some time and get your views on regeneration.'

Grace's face lit up. 'That's very sweet of you. But I'm only here for a short while. I can't imagine your readers will be interested in what I think.'

Robyn raised an eyebrow. 'I am.'

'Me too,' said Barney. 'Finn was just saying there's a rumour that the boatsheds could be put up for sale. I wondered what you thought about it.'

Grace looked blank. 'The boatsheds in Merle Bay? Where Finn's family's boatshed is?'

Robyn's blood ran cold; he hadn't mentioned that to her. She stared at Finn who avoided her gaze and suddenly decided to check the lids of the two cool boxes were properly closed.

'Finn?' she said, her mouth dry. 'Is this true?'

'Just a rumour, nothing concrete,' he muttered. 'I was going to tell you.'

Barney winced. 'Oh shoot, I've put my foot in it.'

Robyn gave him a weak smile. 'It's fine. We've both been busy, that's all.'

'DAD! Come and look at this!' Amber was by the edge of the water waving her arms above her head.

'I'd better go and see what she wants,' said Barney, relief written all over his face.

He jogged off towards her and for a moment or two an awkward silence hung between them.

'Rumours abound in the property industry,' Grace reassured them. 'Might never happen and if it does it could take years. Keep your pecker up, Finn.'

'It's just one thing after another,' Finn said, shooting a sideways glance at Robyn. 'Sorry I haven't mentioned it.'

Robyn's cheeks burned. If the McGills lost the boatshed, it would be impossible to carry on with the business. There'd been a time when they'd shared every single detail of their respective days. How could he have not told her this? There was a chasm opening up in this relationship, she thought with a shudder. She had no idea what was going on in his head anymore. She couldn't live on a knife edge like this much longer, it was exhausting.

'Did someone say there's refreshments?' Grace said brightly, bringing the awkward moment to an end.

'Tea, coffee, cold drink?' Finn jumped to attention. 'And I've got three types of cake.'

'Tea please,' said Grace, reaching into her pocket for money. 'And some of your delicious cake.'

'Me too,' said Zoe, joining them. 'but I shouldn't really. *Food pickers wear bigger knickers*, as the saying goes.'

Grace's face fell. 'That is very true. Although in your case, you're rushing around after two kids. I think you deserve cake. I should probably just have a cup of tea.'

Bloody Myles, thought Robyn crossly. Grace had been so confident in her own skin when Robyn met her. It was only since she'd discovered that he'd cheated on her that she'd become body-conscious.

'Absolutely nothing wrong with big knickers,' Robyn said, cutting a slice of carrot cake for her friend. 'And this cake is so full of carrots it's practically health food.'

Finn poured her some tea and waved away Grace's attempt to pay. 'On the house. You're a friend.'

'Oh, Finn what a lovely thing to say,' Grace looked genuinely touched. 'Thank you.'

'Is that flapjack?' Zoe asked. 'I adore flapjack. That's healthy too, right?

Finn put a piece of flapjack on a plate for Zoe. She took a delicate bite and closed her eyes in rapture. 'That is seriously good.'

'Thanks,' he grinned. 'I added maple syrup for a change.'

'Lucky Robyn, having a handsome man who knows how to handle himself in the kitchen.' She smiled at Finn.

'Hands off, he's mine,' Robyn said, forcing a laugh. She wrapped an arm around her husband's waist.

'Ignore my sister,' said Grace. 'Besides, she has terrible taste in men. Finn is far too nice to be her type.'

Zoe choked on a crumb of flapjack and Grace had to

thump her back.

'I think that's a compliment,' Finn looked embarrassed.

There was a sudden wail from Ruby's pram and Zoe groaned. 'Typical. I'm sure my daughter has a sensor which picks up a signal as soon as I get a cup of tea.'

'I'll get her, you finish your tea,' said Finn, striding towards the wailing baby.

Robyn watched as he scooped Ruby up into his arms. Immediately she stopped crying. She patted his face and tried to chew his chin.

'Look at that!' said Zoe, cramming another piece of flapjack into her mouth. 'I hereby appoint you the baby whisperer.'

Finn laughed and pressed his mouth to Ruby's ear. The baby squealed with delight. Grace wolfed down the rest of her cake and took her niece out of Finn's arms.

'My turn,' she said, plonking a kiss on Ruby's cheek.

'Bye Ruby.' Finn waved his fingers and returned to the refreshments table, smiling at Zoe. 'She's adorable,' he said to her.

Robyn's stomach dropped like a stone. His desire for a baby was still there, as strong as ever. She'd seen it when he held his baby niece, but that was different. Betty was family, he was bound to love her. But seeing his face light up when he'd had a stranger's baby in his arms confirmed it. He wanted what Robyn couldn't give him and she didn't know how they'd ever get past this. Not as a couple anyway.

'Excuse me,' she mumbled. She strode off across the beach, head low and let the tears flow.

'Wait for me!' said Grace.

She waited, blinking away the tears.

Grace handed her a tissue. 'Come and help me find some sea glass.'

'OK.' Robyn wiped her eyes and watched while Grace kicked through the shingle looking for glass.

'So, what's up?' asked Grace.

'Finn,' she sighed. 'He flirts with Zoe and treats me like an elderly aunt.'

'Did he flirt?' Grace raised an eyebrow. 'I thought he was just being charming.'

Robyn swallowed. 'Whatever, he still doesn't fancy me.'

'Nor me,' said Grace, deadpan. 'Bastard.'

Robyn let out a little laugh in spite of herself. 'You are lovely.'

Grace bent down and picked up a piece of bright blue glass. 'Look at that! Do you want it for your mosaic?'

Robyn squatted down and poked through the shingle next to her. 'No thanks, they're finished now. All ready for the christening tomorrow. I'm dreading that,' Robyn shuddered. 'Distant family members never know what to say to me. And then Finn mooning over little Betty . . . I used to love family get-togethers; now I can't wait for them to be over.'

'It'll get easier.' Grace stopped and slapped herself on the forehead. 'Oh, bloody hell, listen to me dishing out the platitudes, I'm as bad as the well-meaning lunatics who tell me time is a great healer.'

Robyn gave her a wry smile. 'So, it won't get easier? Thanks.'

'Nope,' said Grace. 'You'll have to avoid family gatherings forever and I'm going to be stuck in a loop mourning my husband one minute and wanting to chop his willy off the next.'

'I might as well chop Finn's off. He doesn't want it to use it anymore. At least not with me.'

'I'm sure he does. Not to put too fine a point on it, but men rarely go off sex without good reason. Do you think he might be stressed?' Grace asked.

'He's never said anything,' Robyn replied. 'Having said that, it wouldn't surprise me. There's my two years of treatment, bills galore at work and now, with the prospect of the boatsheds being sold, his stress levels are bound to rise.'

'Hmm.' Grace straightened up and looked at her thoughtfully. 'Remember I said that Myles had only ever had one health scare before he died?'

Robyn frowned. 'Vaguely. Prostate cancer, I think you said. Why?'

'Surgery to cure prostate cancer may cause impotence. It was the thing Myles was most bothered about.' She chuckled. 'Honestly, boys and their appendages. Anyway, the more he stressed about it, the more problems he had in the bedroom department, if you catch my drift. In the end he couldn't do it at all. Once he'd had the all-clear he was fine again. Men are very sensitive when it comes to their performance. Anything can throw them off kilter: stress, illness, tiredness, guilt.'

'Poor Finn, he's had all of that to deal with.' Robyn chewed her lip. 'Do you think that might be why he's not interested in me anymore?'

Grace smiled fondly at her. 'He is interested in you, love. His eyes never leave your face. But if his flag is flying at half-mast, he might not want you near his flagpole.'

'I never thought about that from his point of view.' A wave of guilt rushed over her. 'I feel really selfish now. I've had counselling and therapy, and more recently, you and Katie to talk to about my feelings. Meanwhile he's had nothing but the odd chat with his brother. So, what do I do?'

'Talk to him, like you've talked to me. Be honest with him and hopefully he'll be honest with you. If you can find out what's holding him back, you'll be halfway to solving the problem.'

Robyn hugged her friend. 'Thanks. You give the best advice.'

Suddenly both of their mobiles beeped simultaneously.

'Katie!' they said together.

Grace was the first to retrieve her phone and read out the message to Robyn.

'All good in Nottingham. Dad doing well and coming out of hospital tonight. And you won't believe this . . . I've found who was behind the blackmail AND I've shut it down. Can't wait to tell you all about it. Get your party outfits ready for Thursday, girls, because we are going to PART-AYYY Love K xxx'

Robyn was stunned. 'She *found* the blackmailer?'

Grace stared back at her in shock. 'Yep. And she certainly sounds like she's on a high.'

'That's fantastic!' Robyn gave Grace another hug. 'What a relief for her!'

'Hooray for the Sea Glass Sisterhood!' Grace laughed. 'Finally, that's one problem sorted.'

Robyn's stomach fluttered; and if Grace was right about Finn, by tonight, another of their problems could be sorted too . . .

Chapter Thirty-One

Grace pulled the cork out of a bottle of Sauvignon Blanc. Since Zoe and Ruby had arrived this morning, she'd been so caught up with the practicalities of the day that other than a tearful hug when they'd arrived, by mutual consent neither of them had spoken about Grace's latest bombshell. But soon Ruby would be tucked up in her travel cot and they'd be able to have a proper heart-to-heart.

'Wine, madam?' she asked, holding up the bottle.

'God yes,' Zoe said heavily. 'This feels like being in a hotel.'

She was sitting cross-legged on the sofa with Ruby lying in the crook of her elbow, having her last feed of the day.

'Good. It's about time I looked after you for a change.' Grace poured them both wine and put a glass on the coffee table next to Zoe.

Ruby lay totally relaxed in her mother's arms, one hand on her bottle, fat little fingers splayed, the other wound into Zoe's hair. Grace's heart had contracted a thousand times over today with little bolts of love for her niece. It had only been a few weeks since she last saw her but already the little person was beginning to emerge from her baby features.

'Adorable,' she said, touching Ruby's downy red hair. 'Her hair's getting even more vibrant as she gets older. She's going to be a stunner. I'm glad you came; it's made me realise how much I miss seeing her grow.'

It wasn't just Ruby she'd missed. Making friends with Robyn and Katie had made a massive difference to her life in Merle Bay, but the bond between her and her sister was special.

'Well, obviously I'm biased, so I think she's perfect.' Zoe leaned against her sister's hand and smiled. 'And I'm glad I came, too.'

The three of them had had fun on the beach earlier but now Ruby was worn out and she was rosy-cheeked with sunshine and drowsy with sleep. Grace had already prepared dinner: steaks with herb butter, a watercress salad and baby roast potatoes. She'd finish it off while Zoe was settling the baby down to sleep.

The glass doors were open to the evening and the air was warm and heavy with the sharp smell of the sea, softened by the scent of lavender growing in pots on the terrace.

Ruby finished her milk and pushed the bottle away.

'OK, missy, I hear you.' Zoe lifted her onto her chest and stood up, rocking from foot to foot while patting the baby's back. She moved to the open doors and stared out at the distant sea. 'Is it like being on holiday, living here?'

Grace gave a wry laugh. 'The setting might be, but life has been anything but.'

Zoe cringed. 'I know. I haven't mentioned, you know . . . what you told me, because I didn't want to spoil a lovely day. But I have been thinking about it a lot.'

Grace smiled at her sister. 'Me too. Half of me wants details and the other half just wants to block out the whole sordid affair.'

Ruby joined in the conversation with a delicate burp and both women laughed.

'Well said, Ruby.' Zoe kissed her daughter. 'Right, shall we see about getting you to bed?'

Just as Zoe passed the kitchen worktop, Grace's phone buzzed. 'Roger Mathers,' she said, handing the phone to her.

'On a Saturday night?' Grace frowned. 'Hello?'

'I'm so sorry to bother you at the weekend.' Roger sounded agitated and not quite like his normal unflappable self. 'I'm going away with my wife on Monday and can't bear to leave any loose ends, and something has been niggling at me.'

She pressed the phone to her ear and took a sip of wine. 'Oh?'

'Everything all right?' Zoe mouthed.

Grace shrugged.

'It's Myles's will,' Roger continued. 'Ever since you told me that you believe that there may have been an indiscretion, I've been pondering some of the wording.'

Grace's stomach dropped like a stone. Now what? This will was the gift that kept on giving.

'Go on.' She gripped the phone tightly. Zoe was hovering nearby, her face pinched with concern.

'In his previous will, Myles was very specific: the estate to be split between yourself, Austin Byron and Olivia Byron. But when the two of you rewrote your wills last year, Myles was insistent that their names were removed and replaced with a general reference to children.'

'I see,' said Grace, although she didn't really see at all. It didn't make sense. Myles had been a man of sixty and she had had no desire to have children.

A thought struck her. Maybe this wasn't about her at all, maybe this had something to do with the other woman. She shivered as goose pimples covered her skin. 'Roger, do you think . . . maybe he was planning a future with whoever he was having an affair with?'

'What's he saying?' Zoe whispered, coming closer, her brow creased with concern. Ruby had dropped off to sleep in her mother's arms, her thumb tucked into her mouth.

'You put Ruby to bed, I'll tell you in a minute,' Grace mouthed.

But Zoe didn't move. Roger was still speaking, so she forced herself to focus on what he was saying. 'That's a possibility. There could be a number of reasons,' he said gently. 'He could already have another child.'

'You mean as well as Olivia and Austin?' Grace's heart was racing. 'I don't think so. He was going out with Julia when he was still at school. He'd only have been a boy himself before then.'

Roger cleared his throat. 'What I'm trying to say is, that if Myles's recent affair had resulted in a pregnancy—'

'Oh my god!' Grace grabbed the worktop for support and stared at Zoe.

'Grace?' Zoe demanded. 'What is it? What is he saying?'

She shook her head; she couldn't answer right now, it was difficult enough to follow one conversation, let alone start another.

'*If* it had,' Roger continued, 'then it would be natural for Myles to want to make provision for another child in his will.'

'But . . . but . . . ' Grace's head was spinning, trying to connect the dots. 'He didn't say anything.'

'Grace?' Zoe's voice sounded distant and echoey. Grace put her other hand to her ear, trying to block out her sister.

'In a minute,' Grace said absently and twisted away so she couldn't see her.

'No,' Roger confirmed. 'He didn't. And we might never know. Myles's death was completely unexpected, he assumed he'd be around for decades to come. It's only a theory, but if there was. . . *is* . . . a child, he may have thought that he'd have the chance to tell you about it at some point in the future. But that chance never came.'

'So, let me get this straight.' Her head was all over the place; she had no chance of getting anything straight, but she had to try. 'You think the wording in Myles's will was left deliberately vague to allow for other children to claim a share from his estate.'

Zoe gasped loudly but Grace couldn't meet her eye; she needed to process it herself first without having to manage Zoe's reaction, too.

'Um. Yes,' Roger confirmed. 'I counselled Myles against the particular phrasing, but he was adamant.'

'So now what?' Grace felt for her wine and took a gulp. It had gone straight to her head and she was grateful for the buzz, glad of the slight remove from reality.

'No one has come forward with a claim on his estate except of course Austin and Olivia. Speaking frankly, without proof that any other children exist, there's not a lot else we can do, but I felt I should make you aware of the facts. As it stands now, each of Myles's offspring has an equal claim on his estate.'

Grace pressed a hand to her mouth. Roger made it sound as if her husband had left a whole tribe of descendants behind him. But even if it was only one extra child, it was too horrific for words.

'Each of Myles's offspring has an equal claim on his estate,' Grace repeated slowly, swallowing the lump in her throat.

Her underarms prickled with perspiration and the phone felt slippery in her hand. Heat radiated from her body in waves and she wondered vaguely if she was going to faint. She blinked and looked around for Zoe, suddenly needing the touch of another human. But Zoe was out of reach, laying a sleeping Ruby down on her playmat on the floor.

'I don't know what to do,' she murmured.

She heard him sigh softly down the phone. 'You don't *have* to do anything, but if you felt up to it, you could go back through his bank statements and diaries once more, see if anything looks amiss.'

Amiss. What a feeble word to describe the hell Grace now found herself in. A child. Myles and his mistress may have had a child.

It was difficult enough to imagine the man she'd been married to ever being unfaithful to her. But what Roger was suggesting presented her with an entirely different picture. What if he'd been in love with this woman? What if he'd been planning to leave Grace and set up home with her and this child? Had she been at his funeral? Her mind whirred, desperately trying to recall who'd been there. The service had passed by in a blur. She'd sat at the front of the chapel, her parents on one side, Zoe on the other. She had sobbed as 'It Must Be Love' by Madness, Myles's favourite song, played while the curtains closed for one final time in front of his coffin. If his lover had been there, she probably wouldn't have even noticed, she was too wrapped up in her own grief to absorb anyone else's.

'I thought he wanted to change the wills because we'd sold the business, but maybe that was just an excuse,' Grace mused aloud. 'Which means he knew something last summer that I didn't. Myles was a good father; whatever else he'd done, whoever else he'd let down, he would want to do right by his children. However many there are.'

Grace walked over to the sofa and sank down, still with the phone pressed to her ear; she was exhausted with all this.

'As I said, there's no need for you to do anything if you don't wish, but . . . ' Roger drifted off, sounding uncomfortable.

'You OK?' Zoe sat beside her, her own eyes brimming with tears.

Grace shook her head. How could she be?

In her head, she'd imagined a one-night stand. Although even that had been a stretch; the two of them had rarely spent the night apart. But a proper relationship, a *family* even – it was inconceivable. Had Myles been living a double life? Had he been secretly plotting to leave her? He had been her world. Now she felt as if she was mourning a marriage that hadn't even been real. She missed him so much, but her love for him was confused and tainted. Life kept dealing her blow after blow; she wasn't sure she could take much more of this. Right now, she wanted to pack a bag, jump in the car and keep driving, and forget about Myles and Austin and Olivia and any other as yet undiscovered offspring.

'Grace?' Roger prompted after a lengthy silence.

'Yes, sorry. Thank you, Roger.' Grace was suddenly desperate to terminate this conversation. 'I appreciate you getting in touch. Enjoy your holiday, I'll give this some thought while you're away. Goodbye.'

She ended the call and dropped her head into her hands. 'My husband made provision for other children in his will. I feel as if I'm going to wake up in a minute and find out all this was a dream.'

Zoe rubbed her sister's back. 'Oh Grace, I'm so sorry you're going through this.'

'When he died, I was in shock. It didn't seem real. Then reality hit and I realised I wasn't going to see him again. Some days I wished I was dead, too, so that I could escape from the grief.' She looked up at Zoe. 'Then I started to have better days when I felt like my old self. Now I don't know what to feel or think.'

Tears ran in tracks down Zoe's face. 'I can't bear this. I hate to see you angry and confused and hurt. Myles loved you with all his heart. He despised himself for what happened.'

Grace's breath caught in her throat and she stared at her sister. 'What did you say? What do you mean?'

Fear and guilt flashed across Zoe's face, but she said nothing.

'Oh my god. You knew, didn't you?' Grace said with sudden realisation. 'You knew he'd had an affair and you didn't say.'

Zoe tucked her hands into her lap and nodded miserably, not meeting Grace's eye.

'And was there a baby? Come on,' Grace grabbed her by the shoulders, 'Zoe, tell me, I need to know.'

'Yes.' Zoe's voice was almost inaudible. 'I'm sorry. There is a baby.'

Grace gasped for air; her lungs felt as if someone had crushed them in a vice. All this time, Zoe had kept this a secret from her. Myles had fathered a child and Zoe didn't tell her. It was unbearable.

'I feel terrible.' Zoe's pallor had turned from pink to yellow and her lips were trembling. 'I'm a terrible person, Grace. It's all my fault and I don't blame you if you hate me. I hate myself.'

'What are you talking about?' Grace frowned. 'What was your fault?'

Zoe looked at first at Ruby lying like a little starfish in the centre of her mat and then back at Grace.

Grace scanned Zoe's face, praying that she had got the wrong end of the stick. But Zoe started to sob.

'Oh no.' Grace pressed a hand to her mouth as bile rose in her throat. 'Are you saying what I think you're saying?'

'I'm so, so sorry,' Zoe wailed. 'It was never meant to happen, it just . . .'

Whatever she said next, Grace didn't catch. She sprang to her feet and flew to the bathroom and threw up. When she'd finished, she reached for a towel and wiped her mouth. She felt drained of every ounce of energy.

After Myles died so suddenly, her pain was all-consuming. At the time she'd been sure that it would be impossible to hurt any more than she did. She'd been wrong. Today was infinitely worse; today felt as if glass shards were being pressed into her heart. She'd been betrayed by the two people she trusted most in the world.

She forced herself back to the sofa in the living room. Zoe was hunched over, making herself as small as possible. Grace's body flooded with adrenaline and anger; her fingers curled in tight fists.

'Look at me,' she demanded, staring coldly at her sister. Zoe looked up from under her lashes. 'That story you told me about the sperm bank?'

'I lied,' said Zoe.

Grace's heart was pumping as she twisted in her seat and folded her arms. 'I think it's time you told me the truth. Don't you?'

Chapter Thirty-Two

'I need to hear you say it,' said Grace in a low voice. 'Who is Ruby's father?'

'Grace, I—'

'Just say it.'

'It's Myles.'

Zoe wet her lips and cast her eyes sideways to meet Grace's. They bulged with tears, but Grace didn't feel sorry for her; it was all she could do not to grab her by the throat and shake her.

She stared at her sister, her heart splintering into pieces. 'How could you do that to me, both of you?'

'Please hear me out,' Zoe began, her voice cracked with the effort of not crying. 'What we did was wrong. I don't deserve anything from you, but if you could just let me tell you what happened, I promise I'll tell you the truth. After that, I'll accept whatever you say, if you never want to see me again, fair enough.'

'I'm listening.'

Grace's heart was pounding, and she touched her hand to her chest to still it. If someone had told her she'd be able to feel such anger towards her sister, she wouldn't have believed it.

Zoe pulled a tissue from a box on the coffee table and blew her nose. She was an attractive, bubbly woman who'd never been short of male attention. How could she have gone after the only man in the world who'd been strictly off-limits to her?

And Myles's behaviour was sickening. Why Zoe? If he had to stray, surely he didn't have to stray quite so close to home? It was cruel. Both of them were cruel.

As far as Grace had been aware, the two of them had always got on well; Myles was the big brother Zoe had never had. And in the absence of any other reliable man in her life, she'd idolised him. Myles for his part was fond of her in a brotherly way and had got on well with her son, Daniel. She had never, ever, had any cause to doubt that their relationship was anything other than it should be. Which just went to prove what an idiot she was. Oh, how they must have laughed at her behind her back . . .

Grace gritted her teeth. 'I'm waiting.'

Zoe dabbed her eyes and exhaled. 'Firstly, in all the years that you were with Myles, did he ever, *ever* give you cause to think that he didn't love you? Did you ever catch him looking at another woman?'

Grace's mind flittered backwards and forwards through years of memories. Almost all of them happy. He had been vocal about his love for her. His goddess, he'd called her. She'd never had reason to doubt him. She stopped her train of thought and gave an exasperated sigh. 'Stick to the facts, OK? Just get on with it.'

'You didn't, did you?' Zoe continued. 'Because the only woman he ever wanted was you.'

How had he coped, how had he managed to carry on as normal and not say a word? All those times he and Grace had been to visit Zoe and the baby, *his* baby, and he'd not given anything away. She'd had no clue that anything had been, as Roger would call it, *amiss*.

'So, can you please explain why my husband and my sister had an affair behind my back?' Steel bands tightened around Grace's chest; she was so close to giving in to her tears, but she strengthened her resolve not to break down.

'I promised the truth. Ruby *is* his daughter. But we didn't have an affair, we didn't love each other, we got together once, completely unplanned, and hated ourselves for it immediately.' Zoe's eyes were pleading for understanding, Grace averted her gaze. 'Myles barely spoke to me again after that, not for months.'

'Until you found out you were pregnant, I suppose,' she said flatly.

Zoe nodded. 'I didn't know what to do. I considered a termination, but then I kept thinking of the baby growing inside me. And I thought that I'm forty, I'd always wanted a second child and I might not get another chance so—'

'So, you and Myles became parents.'

'Technically. Although I told Myles I wasn't expecting any input from him.' Zoe's voice faltered when she caught the look of contempt on her sister's face. Myles had gone above and beyond his uncle duties with Ruby and Daniel. Now it was obvious why. 'The guilt has been burning away at me ever since,' Zoe added.

'You managed to hide it well,' she said bitterly. Her throat felt like sandpaper. She needed water desperately but there was no way she could get up to fetch some; she didn't trust her limbs to hold her up.

Zoe had told them she'd had an appointment with the sperm bank over the Christmas period. Ruby came along in September. Realisation bubbled up inside her like a hot spring.

'This *one time* was at Christmas, wasn't it?' Grace narrowed her eyes. 'I asked you to help him deal with his anxiety over those prostrate tests. You were supposed to help him, Zoe, not have sex with him.'

'I did help him,' she insisted.

Grace shuddered, remembering what a difficult time it had been. The only time in their entire relationship when she and Myles had found it difficult to communicate. He'd been so scared of being ill. He'd read everything he could find on Google and frightened himself. He'd even joined a few online support forums for men with prostate problems. He automatically thought that every worst-case scenario would happen to him. 'You helped him *how*, exactly?'

'He came round, like you suggested, and I got him to talk. Everything came out, all the things which had been preying on his mind. He worried that he'd spent too many years of his life working and not enough living. He worried that he was so much older than you and that you'd end up being his carer and resenting him for it.'

Grace's throat burned with sadness; she would never have minded looking after him. It would have been her pleasure. Why couldn't he have said this to her, his wife? If only he had, none of this might have happened.

'But the thing he was worried most about was . . . making love, or rather, not being able to.' Zoe flicked a glance at Grace and bit her lip nervously. 'He'd read that treatment could make him impotent. He was already mortified at the thought and worried that he'd disappoint you, let you down. I tried telling him that it was a really common condition and that millions of men experience it at some stage or other of their lives. I asked if he'd talked to you about it and he said he couldn't and made me promise that I wouldn't breathe a word. And I didn't.' Zoe dashed the tears from her face with the heel of her hand.

Grace got all of this. She nodded impatiently, waiting for Zoe to get on with the story. 'Then what?'

'And then he started to cry,' she continued. 'I think he'd kept all his worries pent up inside him and they all came tumbling out. So, I put my arms around him and gave him a cuddle.' She looked up at Grace, her eyes pleading. 'It started out innocently, I promise.'

Grace held up her hands. 'Whatever comes next, I don't want to hear it. Do you understand? Every word of this sick confession of yours chips away at my marriage. I'm not even sure what's left of it now.'

Zoe flushed. 'I understand. But I will say that he never felt anything for me, it meant nothing to either of us. He left immediately afterwards. I waited until I was sixteen weeks pregnant before letting anyone know. You were the first person I told.'

'Is that supposed to make me feel better? You were carrying your brother-in-law's baby, for heaven's sake.' Grace was scathing.

'I hate what I've done to you.' Zoe dropped her head into her hands. 'You've got to believe that.'

Grace was too numb to know what she believed or even how she felt. She wanted Zoe out of her house, but that wasn't a possibility, not at this time of day when she'd been drinking and had Ruby to look after.

Ruby. Her niece. And also, her stepdaughter.

This was all too much to absorb; she had a sudden desire to be on her own.

'I'm going to bed,' she announced. 'And I'd like very much if you'd be gone when I get up in the morning.'

Zoe nodded. 'Of course. Grace, I never meant for any of this to happen. I would never have asked Myles for anything; you have to believe me. It was enough for me to have a man like Myles in Ruby's life, I'd never have told her he was her father. And I don't expect your forgiveness.'

'Good! Because you're not getting it.' Grace gaped at her sister. Could she not see what she'd done? She *and* Myles. Between them they had rewritten the story of her happy marriage. 'None of this is Ruby's fault, so I'm going to make sure she is looked after as Myles would wish. She's entitled to a share of his estate. You'll be hearing from my solicitor.'

'Thank you,' Zoe whispered under her breath. 'That's very generous.'

'No,' said Grace firmly. 'It's my legal obligation, that's all.'

She looked at Ruby. Her little cheeks, peachy soft, her hands and arms stretched out in slumber. Her love for this little one had been unconditional and pure, now it would be forever tainted in betrayal and anger. Ruby was the fallout from this fiasco and Grace's heart ached for her. She could never forgive Zoe for this. Never.

Chapter Thirty-Three

The Sea Glass Sisterhood WhatsApp Group

KATIE
Hi ladies. Grace, I hope you're having fun with your sister and the baby? Robyn, I know it's the christening today, hope it goes well and you have a lovely time with the family. I'll be back from Nottingham later this afternoon. Anyone free for a catch-up on the beach? So much has happened and if I don't tell someone soon, I'm going to BURST! xx

ROBYN
I'm free! Sort of dreading the christening because everyone will be doing their how-are-you-feeling pity faces. It should finish around five-ish, shall we say six?

GRACE
Girls, to be honest, am not doing great at the moment and didn't sleep a wink last night. Thanks for the invitation but I'm not good company right now. Love G xxx

KATIE
So so sorry to hear this. Please don't hide away, I miss you. Plus, we had a deal: a problem shared is a problem thirded, right? So, whatever is going on, we want to help. The Sea Glass Sisterhood rules. Be kind to yourself xxx

ROBYN
Katie's right, please don't shut us out, let us be there for you.
Don't be sad on your own. I'll be there on the beach at six, I
hope to see you both there. Sending love xoxox

Chapter Thirty-Four

As soon as the organist played the first few bars of the final hymn, the congregation stood and gathered bags and belongings, anxious to escape the stale air of Merle Bay's sixteenth-century church. The temperature had risen again today, and everyone was itching to be outside in the sunshine. The children among them recognised the hymn and began competing with each other for who could shout 'He's got the whole world in his hands' loudest without getting told off by their parents. Robyn and Finn were in the front pew with Claudia, Callum and the children.

'If I'd known it was going to be this hot,' Claudia muttered to Robyn, trying to peel Betty's hot cheek from her chest, 'I'd have postponed the christening.'

'I'm glad you didn't.' Robyn smiled in sympathy and fanned herself with the order of service. 'It was such good fun.'

Finn leaned across. 'Speak for yourself. I'm soaked.'

Claudia and Robyn stifled their giggles. Hannah had taken exception to having water poured on her forehead by the vicar and had scooped her own hand in the font and tried to splash him back, only for the vicar to dodge aside and Finn to get the full force of her revenge.

'Three at once!' Callum rolled his eyes. 'What possessed us?'

'But only one christening party,' Robyn reminded him. 'Good planning.'

'Dad!' William was jiggling on the spot at the end of their row, clutching the front of his shorts. 'I need to go. Now.'

'Duty calls,' Callum sighed and ducked out of the row, leading William by the hand.

The hymn ended, and after thanking the vicar, who admitted he'd never done a job lot like that before, they filed out of the little church and into the heat of the day. Robyn slid her sunglasses down over her eyes and checked her handbag for suncream. She had chosen the coolest outfit she could find: a sleeveless sundress cut on the bias which barely touched her skin, and flat leather sandals. Claudia had poured herself into a tight fitted dress and her feet looked hot and swollen in smart court shoes. To make matters worse, Betty was clinging to her like a limpet.

'Colic,' Claudia explained, stroking Betty's vivid red face. 'Poor tot must be in agony. Do you think people will be bothered if we don't let the party go on for hours? I just want to get the kids' paddling pool out and wallow in it with an ice-cold beer.'

'That sounds like heaven,' Robyn said, secretly relieved. 'No one will mind.'

Least of all her; she had a serious talk with Finn planned as soon as they were home. She had to know what was behind his lack of interest in her physically. If he was stressed or worried or anxious, she needed to know, and she wanted to help. If he wouldn't open up to her, she didn't know what she'd do next. Couples' counselling sessions, maybe? The thought made her squirm. Finn would absolutely hate that, and she wasn't too keen herself.

'Can we have the godparents and the children please?' the photographer called, mopping his pink bald head with a handkerchief. 'Over here in the shade.'

Finn touched Robyn's arm. 'Ready for your close-up?'

'Not really,' she grinned, taking his hand in hers. 'I could do with powdering my nose. It's all right for you. You're the most photogenic person I know. You and your film-star good looks, you never look bad in pictures.'

'Me?' He shot her a look of surprise. 'A scrawny fisherman with a stubbly chin?'

'Oh, but you're *my* scrawny fisherman with a stubbly chin.' She laughed and pulled him towards her, standing on her toes to brush her lips against his.

'Oi,' said Callum, delivering William to them and squeezing him between them. 'We'll have godly behaviour from the godparents please.'

Robyn and Finn laughed and then groaned in disgust as William slid his wet hands into theirs.

'Who's having Betty?' Claudia asked, holding the red-faced baby out to them at arm's length.

'Finn,' said Robyn, knowing how much Finn would probably be itching for a cuddle with his niece.

Finn said simultaneously, 'Robyn.'

'Charming!' Claudia said with a huff and shoved her towards Robyn.

'Hey, angel.' Robyn took Betty and bounced her gently, whispering softly, 'Don't cry. Sshh-sshh-sshh.'

The photographer swigged from a water bottle and then picked up his camera. 'Ready?'

'We're missing Hannah,' said Robyn, scouring the crowd.

'HANNAH, you silly bumhead!' William yelled, causing a rippled of laughter.

Hannah slouched over, looking grumpy but adorable in a dress and sandals. 'I wanted to wear shorts too. It's not fair.'

'I'll give you a pound if you stand still and smile at the man,' said Finn under his breath to both of them.

'Two,' said William immediately.

'Deal.' Finn looked at Robyn as if to say, what the hell. Robyn's cheeks ached with the effort of not laughing.

'OK, look at me!' The photographer pressed the shutter and then stood up. 'Has anyone got a tissue? The baby has been sick.'

Claudia stepped forward with a muslin cloth, wiped Betty's face and Robyn's arm.

'Sorry,' Robyn whispered to Claudia. 'I didn't notice.'

'Too busy flirting with your own husband,' Claudia replied, arching a bemused eyebrow. 'I remember those days. There we go, poppet.' She kissed Betty's head and stood back.

Hannah was staring at the end of her finger. 'Where does snot come from?'

'That's not snot,' William said scornfully. 'That's part of your brain. Your brain is falling out.'

'Kids, eh?' Finn murmured to Robyn with a grin.

As if on command, Betty chose that moment to arch her back and let out a stream of vomit all over Finn's shirt.

'Oh.' Finn stared in horror at his shirt. 'That is gross.'

'Maybe I could do some candid shots next?' the poor photographer said.

But no one was paying any attention. Claudia was handing Hannah a tissue and making her wipe her nose, Callum was having stern words with William, and Robyn was holding Betty at arm's length wondering if it would be really awful if she passed her to someone else. She loved her nieces and nephew dearly. But this wasn't for her. Did it make her a bad person because she wasn't maternal? She hoped not. It was just the way she was.

'Jeez. We've dodged a bullet here,' Finn muttered under his breath, peeling his wet shirt away from his chest. 'Every cloud and all that.'

Robyn blinked rapidly. He'd echoed her thoughts completely. Everything she had been through health-wise had been traumatic and painful and life-changing, but it had given her a legitimate excuse not to have a baby. She'd felt as if she'd dodged a bullet. Was that what Finn was referring to or was he talking about something else entirely? Finn caught her expression and his eyes rounded guiltily. 'Shit. Sorry. I shouldn't have said that.'

'It's OK.' She pressed a hand to his arm, feeling the heat of his skin. 'If that's how you feel, you should say it.'

William gasped with glee. 'Dad, Uncle Finn just swore!'

Callum mumbled something that Robyn didn't catch. All she cared about was her and Finn. This was important.

'No, it was insensitive.' He kissed her temple, taking care not to brush against her dress with his soiled shirt. 'Forget I said it. Please.'

Her stomach felt jittery. Had she got it all wrong all this time? Did he feel the same as her? Or was this a throwaway comment, a reaction to the circumstances? She felt an urgent need to find out now, because this could change everything.

Chapter Thirty-Five

Around her, everyone continued to laugh and chat as the photographer did his best to corral people into position. But Robyn's attention was solely fixed on Finn, her heart thumping.

'But you meant it?' she whispered. 'Finn? Is that how you feel? I need to know. Please tell me the truth.'

He rubbed a hand over his eyes and sighed with resignation. 'I suppose . . . yes, it is.' He scuffed the toe of his shoe in the ground. 'I'm sorry.'

'Don't apologise.' Robyn felt a bubble of hope rise up inside her. 'My thoughts exactly.'

Finn's brow furrowed. 'Really? But I thought—'

'Really,' she repeated. 'I feel the same.'

His dark eyes held hers and her heart pounded with the weight of her words.

'Oh petal! Come to Granny.' Claudia's mum held her arms out for Betty and Robyn relinquished her willingly.

Robyn smiled at him, her heart so full of love and relief that it was all she could do not to leap into his arms. 'Can we talk later? I mean properly?'

He looked down at his shirt. 'How about now?'

'But we can't leave the christening,' she said, only half meaning it. Her breath caught in her throat as Finn's lips twitched.

'We can,' he said. He took her hand and glanced over

his shoulder to make sure no one was watching. 'There's no way I can stay here with this amount of puke on me, let's go home.'

He started to walk across the churchyard, picking up his pace so that she had to run to keep up with his long legs. They ran out through the gate and into the lane where the car was parked.

Ten minutes later they were standing facing each other in the kitchen. Robyn unbuttoned Finn's shirt with shaking hands. For days she'd been wondering how to get Finn to open up to her and now she had the perfect opportunity. She was so anxious to get it right that her insides were fluttering, and her mouth was dry.

He shrugged off his shirt and dropped it in the sink. 'Beer?'
She nodded.

He took two bottles from the fridge, flipped off the lids and handed one to her. Together they went into the tiny garden at the back of the house and sat beside each other on the bench.

Finn took her hand. 'Just to make sure. What I said about dodging a bullet, that honestly didn't upset you?'

'No.' She sipped her beer and allowed the cold liquid to run down her throat. 'It worked out OK for us, didn't it?'

Finn gave her a quizzical look. 'All those operations you've had. Everything you've been through? I don't think I can quite say it worked out.'

She turned to face him. 'Those operations mean that I've decreased my chance of getting cancer. I've got a much healthier future now and I've got you. And that's all I ever wanted.'

He took a long draught of his beer.

'But you wanted a baby,' Finn said, confused. 'I remember the conversation vividly. We were in the bath and you asked me about starting a family.'

'Yes, I remember it, too. I thought *you* wanted to start a family. You were worried about continuing the McGill tradition of fishing in Merle Bay if Callum's kids didn't want to take over the business. And then when I suggested it, you leapt on it.'

'Because of *you*. It's always been about you.' He stroked her cheek. 'I'd do literally anything to make you happy. Even have a baby.'

'Same here.'

He held his bottle out and she chinked hers against it and they both laughed softly.

'When I came home that day and you'd had your test results, my heart broke for you,' he said, his voice husky with emotion. 'I knew how scared you were, worrying that cancer would do to you what it had done to your mum. My biggest fear was that you'd stick two fingers up to the risk of cancer and carry on just as before. I kept thinking that if we had a child and then you developed cancer because of the delay that I might resent the baby. But it wasn't my call, I had to let you make your own mind up. It was you who had the most at stake. But then you surprised me again: you opted for surgery even though that put an end to the baby plans.'

She set her bottle down on the ground. 'I knew I had to go ahead. For my mum and for my gran. I felt I owed it to them for having a choice when they weren't given one. But I felt like such a coward for putting my own health over giving you a family.'

'No one could ever accuse you of being cowardly,' said Finn. He slid an arm around her, pulling her close. 'You are the bravest human I know. You've never shied away from risk.'

She leaned into him, feeling his body against hers and relishing the closeness. 'I felt like I'd stolen your chance to be a father. I've been wracked with guilt ever since.'

'Oh Robyn, love,' he said sadly. 'Me too. But my guilt was because I was *glad* we weren't going to be parents when I thought that you wanted us to be.'

'I wish I'd never brought up the subject of kids in the first place,' she mused. 'It ruined a perfectly lovely bath, I seem to remember.'

'I'm glad you did.' He leaned in for a kiss. His lips were cold and tasted of beer and a shiver of longing went through her. 'If we'd never had that conversation, you might not have taken the BRCA test. Now at least we know you've done everything possible to protect yourself.'

She shook her head, remembering the details of that time of their lives. 'All the baby names we thought of, the Christmas traditions we said we were going to make, and you reading ovulation charts! I thought you were really into it!'

His gaze softened. 'It was all for you. I'm making myself sound really soppy but making you happy is my job.'

'Thank you for sticking by me, through everything, particularly the reconstruction,' she said. 'Some of the women I met in the support group haven't been so lucky.'

'Why wouldn't I stick by you?' He looked baffled. 'I love you, Robyn. Your body is incredible. You're incredible.'

She felt her heart rate gather pace.

'If you think that, why don't you want to touch me anymore? I know my body has changed but I'm still the same person on the inside. Sometimes it feels as if you treat me like an elderly aunt.'

Her stomach dropped as he pulled away from her and leaned forwards, swinging his empty bottle. The seconds ticked by and he remained silent. She sensed he was struggling to find the right words.

'Finn, do you still want me?' she asked, unable to keep the tremor of fear from her voice.

He nodded.

'Talk to me,' she whispered, reaching for his hand.

He rubbed his other hand over his face and gave a half laugh. 'This is awkward.'

'Yep. Totally with you on that,' she agreed. 'Meeting Grace and Katie made me realise how important it is to have people we can confide in. You and I have been dancing around each other not saying the things that really matter. We have to get better at being open and honest.'

'OK, here goes.' He puffed out his cheeks and then sat up straight to face her. 'Every time we get close, all I can think about is how we would have been trying for a baby. And that you were probably thinking the same. Except in my case, I was glad we weren't, which made me feel like the worst human on the planet. And then I couldn't do it. I couldn't make love to my own wife. I've felt like a failure.'

'Oh Finn.' She reached up and stroked his curls, her heart aching for him. 'I'd have been thinking about you and how much I love you. And how much I want us to go back to how we were.'

'Me too,' he said softly. 'But the longer it has gone on, the worse it's become, so now I've just avoided it.' He took her face in his hands. 'But it's not because I don't love you, or want you anymore, I promise. The stronger you've become since your surgery, the more pathetic I feel.'

'You've carried everything on your shoulders,' she protested. 'Worrying about me, supporting us both when I haven't been working, stress about the business . . . You're not pathetic, Finn. You're just human.'

She kissed him, sliding her arms around his neck, and as the kiss deepened, he pulled her closer to him.

'Why are we only talking about this now?' He murmured when the kiss ended. 'All this wasted time.'

'Because I was scared that if I asked you to tell the truth, I'd lose you,' she admitted. 'You looked so besotted with Betty that I thought you might swap me for a wife who can give you a family.'

He shook his head. 'I'd never do that. Betty is amazing. All three kids are great. But honestly? The noise and the mess do my head in. Being at home in our cottage, just you and me, is my idea of heaven.'

'Mine too.' Her breath caught in her throat. 'Especially our bedroom.'

His eyes flickered with a look she hadn't seen for a long time. 'You look lovely in that dress.'

'Thank you.' She smiled. 'What about out of it?'

He pressed his mouth to her ear, making her shiver. 'Perhaps we should find out. Right now.'

He stood up slowly and reached out to pull her up. Hand in hand they made their way upstairs. She kicked the bedroom door shut behind them, feeling heady with desire.

'I love you, Finn,' she gasped, as he slowly pulled down the zip of her dress.

His eyes burned fiercely into hers. 'I love you too, more than ever.'

'Show me,' Robyn demanded, stepping out of her dress.

He drew her to him, pressing her against the solid length of him. She curled her arms around his neck, wanting to be close, then closer still. Her mouth dissolved against his and the rest of the world fell away. They kissed with an intensity that shocked her, as if they'd been apart for a hundred years. She had him back and she would never let him go again. Every cell in her body wanted to rejoice with joy. She ran her hands down his chest, then lower still and gasped.

'Hello, sailor.'

Chapter Thirty-Six

Katie was the first to arrive on the beach at six o'clock on the dot. As soon as she stepped onto the shingle, she could almost feel her breathing begin to slow. The sun was still warm on her skin and she felt sticky and restless after the train journey. She kicked off her Birkenstocks and walked into the sea, gasping as the cold water took her breath away. She closed her eyes for a moment and stretched her arms out, grounding herself as the coarse sand shifted beneath her feet.

'You look like a poster girl for mindfulness,' a voice teased behind her.

Katie opened her eyes to see Robyn unbuckling her sandals.

'Someone looks happy!' she said, wrapping Robyn up in a hug.

Robyn smiled shyly. 'I am happy. It's been a lovely day. But tell me about your weekend,' she insisted. 'Mine'll be boring in comparison.'

Judging by the bloom in her cheeks, Katie reckoned Robyn's weekend had been anything but boring, but before she had chance to argue, another set of footsteps crunched across the beach towards them.

'Room for a little one in that group hug?' came a familiar voice.

'Grace!' Katie and Robyn yelled together.

'I'm so glad you came,' Katie pressed a kiss to her cheek after they'd finished hugging.

'I almost didn't,' said Grace, kicking off her trainers and not meeting her eye. 'But FOMOG got me in the end.'

'Do you mean FOMO?' Robyn said. 'Fear of missing out?'

'No,' said Grace. 'I mean FOMOG. Fear of missing out on—'

'Gin?' Katie cried with glee, pulling some slim cans from her bag.

Grace gave a faint smile and tugged the ring pull to open the can. 'I meant gossip. But gin works for me.'

'What's happened?' Katie asked.

Grace was normally so animated, her hands drawing pictures in the air as she spoke, her face, her shoulders . . . every part of her usually told a story. It was obvious that something major had upset her. But Grace downed some of her gin and shook her head.

'I want to hear from you first. You said you'd discovered who's been blackmailing you . . . '

Fifteen minutes later, the three women had paddled to the far end of the beach and were on their way back. Katie had filled them in on what had happened when she went round to give her condolences to her old school friend and got a lot more than she'd bargained for.

'It mystifies me that anyone would do such a malicious thing like that,' Robyn frowned.

Katie shrugged. 'It doesn't really make sense, but grief can make people act irrationally, I suppose. The last time she spoke to her mum they rowed. I think Rose felt guilty about that and because my name had come up in the conversation, she laid the blame at my feet. Then when she went back to her mother's house and found that old photo of me, she became fixated with making me pay.'

Grace shuddered. 'That's given me the creeps. But at least you've got the original back.'

'And it's far better that it had nothing to do with the original photographer because now it means that Katie's case was a one-off and not part of a bigger scam,' Robyn added.

Katie nodded and sipped from her can. She felt like a weight had been lifted from her shoulders.

'Hopefully, I'll never hear another word from her. She knows that I could report her to the police, and I suppose I could. I took the photo of me from her folder. And if she's got copies, then . . . ' Katie's voice trailed off. Then what? She thought for a moment. 'Then I don't really care.'

Joy and relief surged inside her. It was true. She really didn't care. She laughed in surprise.

'Those photos only had power over me because I let them. I've been ashamed of something which I had no reason to be. It's had a huge impact on my life, and I've wasted a lot of time hiding myself away. But you know what? I refuse to be defined by one snapshot of time. Those naked photos aren't me. I'm me: I'm a strong independent woman who works hard and does her best. From now on I'm going to be braver; things can only affect my life if I let them.'

'Cheers to that!' Robyn tapped her can against Katie's.

'Good for you,' said Grace, joining in.

Katie smiled. 'So, all in all it's been a good weekend. Not to mention Dad being a lot better. Apparently, he'd had been feeling ill on holiday but hadn't wanted to worry Mum. Now he's feeling bad because the two of them are missing Thursday's event on his account. Anyway, I've promised to send them lots of photos. And talking of events, how was your sea glass walk?'

'Great!' Robyn was aglow with her success. 'The women loved it; everyone left with their own little sea glass collection. And I've got a full house for my first workshop, so that's good, too. That journalist, Barney, turned up with his daughter. He took my picture, said it might make the paper.'

'That's brilliant, and Amber came?' Katie was thrilled. 'She is such a cool kid.'

'Nice guy,' said Grace. 'He wants to talk to me to get an architect's view on redeveloping Merle Bay. Goodness knows what I can possibly add to the debate. He'd be better off talking to Finn and his brother, people who have strong ties to the place.'

'That's interesting,' said Katie distractedly. 'What else did Barney say?'

Robyn and Grace exchanged amused looks.

'About you, you mean?' Robyn prompted.

'No! Well, yes,' Katie blustered. She felt her face go hot. 'So? Anything?'

'He told us that you'd sent him a message when you reached the hospital, which was quite interesting, seeing as you hadn't given us an update at all after dashing off,' said Grace, raising an eyebrow.

Katie's face couldn't be any hotter if it tried. 'Sorry, it's just I was with him on Friday night when I got the call from my mum and had to rush off. I felt I owed him an apology.'

Grace shook her head. 'I'm teasing; you had enough on your plate.'

'He's such a lovely man,' Katie sighed dreamily.

'I thought so, too.' Robyn grinned. 'And I get the feeling it's mutual.'

'Hmm, I'm not sure about that,' Katie sighed. 'It's obvious he really loved his wife and then there's Amber to consider as well. How will I ever know when it's appropriate to make my interest known? God, listen to me; I sound like something out of a Jane Austen novel.'

'I suppose you've got to be prepared for the fact that he might compare you to his wife,' said Robyn gently. 'That could be tough, trying to live up to someone like that, especially if they'd had a good relationship.'

'Sorry for being blunt, but at least she can't come back into his life,' Grace added. 'So you have nothing to worry about on that score. Not like in my case. Julia was the mother of Myles's children, so consequently she was always rearing her bloody head. It took me a good five years to fully accept that she was in his past and there was no going back for him.'

'Good advice, thank you,' said Katie, taking it all in. 'I think I'll let him take the lead and if he shows any sign of interest, I'll encourage him to act. What?'

Robyn and Grace were trying not to laugh.

'Sorry,' said Grace. 'It's just that you're making it sound like the mating ritual of a penguin. Just try and relax and be yourself.'

Katie pulled a face. 'That's the thing. My old self would have kept him at arm's length and ruined it all by pushing him away if he tried to get too close. But if I'm ever going to have a serious relationship, I've got to get over that and be more confident. I like Barney a lot; this time I really want to make it work.'

'Then I wish you luck,' said Grace warmly. 'And maybe, if you're feeling confident, you might want to think about wearing something on Thursday to show off that fabulous figure of yours instead of hiding it away.'

Katie's heart thumped. She knew Grace was right, but the thought of having her body on show . . .

'And now enough about me,' she insisted, putting her hands on their shoulders as they ambled along the edge of the water. 'We've all had busy weekends. I'll shut up and let someone else do the talking.'

Grace shook her empty can. 'I might need another before I spill any beans.'

Katie obliged and produced another one for her.

'OK, well I'll go next then,' Robyn let out a dreamy sigh. 'Suffice to say, Finn and I are back on track.'

Grace lifted an eyebrow. 'And in the sack?'

'Still got the knack,' Robyn winked.

'What are you on about?' Katie demanded to know as the other two hooted with laughter.

Robyn crushed her can in her hand and Katie swapped it for a new one.

'We talked,' she said simply. 'Properly talked. Neither of us have dared to tell each other the truth for so long that we'd got out of the habit. Turns out we both wanted the same thing all along.'

Robyn told them about the mix-up about wanting a baby and the feelings of guilt they'd both had but hadn't felt able to voice. And about how they'd made love for the first time in months.

'And afterwards we talked and talked. Now it feels like a fresh start for us both. We've promised not to keep secrets anymore. Finn wasn't just worried about me; he's been worried about the rumour that the boatsheds might be for sale. If he and Callum lose theirs, it'll be the end of the family's fishing business. And then Finn admitted that he wasn't sure he wanted to be a fisherman for the rest of his life; he'd love to do something with food.' She widened her eyes. 'And I had no idea! Tomorrow is my first sea glass workshop at the cancer support centre and Finn is taking the day off to help me. And then we're going to make some plans for the future.' Her eyes sparkled with tears. 'I'm just glad we've *got* a future.'

'Me too, lovey,' Grace said in a wobbly voice. 'You make a lovely couple. I'm glad you've found your way back to each other. Life's too short to be anything but happy. Like Myles and me, we were so happy once. And now that's all gone.'

Tears began to run down her face.

'What is it?' Robyn asked. 'You seemed to be having a nice time with Zoe and the baby yesterday.'

Grace nodded. 'I was. Until I found out that Zoe was the woman who Myles had the affair with.'

'No!' Katie clapped a hand over her mouth.

Grace met her eye. 'And it gets worse.'

Robyn and Katie hugged her while she told them what her sister and her husband had done and how her world, and her family, would never be the same again.

'I feel numb. It's so much to take in.' Tears trickled down Grace's face. 'A few weeks ago, I thought that losing Myles was the worst thing that could ever happen to me. But now I feel even worse than I did then. I can't believe that he and Zoe would do that behind my back. And then to have his baby.' She shook her head. 'How can life be so cruel?'

'And why does shit have to happen to good people?' Katie felt physically sick on Grace's behalf.

Robyn handed her a tissue. 'I hope you kicked her out?'

Grace dabbed her eyes. 'She left at the crack of dawn this morning. Poor Ruby must have wondered what was going on. I'm so angry with Myles for being weak. He must have been beside himself when Zoe announced she was pregnant. I even wondered . . . ' she lowered her head and tears dripped from her chin. Robyn swapped her wet tissue for a dry one. 'I mean, heart attacks can be brought on by stress, can't they?'

Katie put an arm around her. 'I don't suppose you're ever going to find out the effect that it had on Myles's health. But I imagine from what Zoe told you that he bitterly regretted what had happened. I'm sure he never stopped loving you.'

'Maybe,' she replied, 'but he's not the man I thought he was. I came to Merle Bay with grand plans of getting my act together and planning for the future. I was grieving, but I was secure in that grief. The life we had together anchored me. Now I feel cast adrift again. I have nothing, and right now it feels like I have no one.'

'You have us,' Robyn announced. 'And we're not going anywhere.'

'Correct,' Katie agreed. 'And who's to say that you won't fall in love again? You're only forty-six. If I can advance on the mating techniques of a penguin, I'm sure you can.'

'True. Thank you.' Grace laughed softly, gripping their hands.

'It's all very raw now,' said Robyn, 'but maybe as time passes and you're less angry, you might feel open to forgiving them both, let your happy memories take over from the bad ones.'

Grace gave a half smile. 'You're probably right. But for now, I'm going to put some space between us. And Ruby . . . ' she swallowed. 'Ruby is Myles's daughter whether I like it or not. He'd want me to have some sort of relationship with her. And when I'm feeling brave, I will.'

'To feeling brave!' Katie said, raising her drink.

'To feeling brave!' the other two chorused just as a big wave sent them rushing back up the beach squealing at the cold water.

'BARKLY! BARKLY!'

The three women whirled round to find the source of the voice and a small wet dog launched itself at their legs, yapping and bouncing happily. In the distance a man was running towards them swinging a dog lead from his hand.

'Oh, hello, puppy.' Robyn bent to stroke the tiny blond ball of fluff.

'It's a Cocker Spaniel, I think. Very cute,' said Katie, laughing as the puppy shook itself and gave her legs an impromptu shower.

'And that looks like . . . it is!' Grace gasped and then shouted. 'NED!'

The man waved. 'Grace! Grab that naughty pup for me!'

Robyn scooped up the dog and Grace ran to meet its owner.

'Isn't Ned the owner of Sea Glass House?' said Katie as they watched the man hug Grace tightly and kiss her cheek. The dog wriggled out of Robyn's hands and raced back to them.

'Yep. And he looks rather handsome,' said Robyn. 'Grace certainly seems to think so.'

Grace had linked his arm and was dragging him back to meet them and the dog was running in excited circles around their feet.

'Listen, I meant to say,' said Katie. 'I've got two spare tickets to the awards night now that my parents can't come. Would you like to bring Finn?'

'I'd love to,' Robyn beamed. 'Thank you. We haven't had a night out for months.'

'Which just leaves one spare ticket . . . ' Katie waggled her eyebrows suggestively. 'Shall I?'

Robyn sucked in air. 'Maybe give it to Grace and let her decide.'

'Ned,' Grace said breathlessly. 'I'd like you to meet the Sea Glass Sisterhood: Robyn and Katie.'

'Lovely to meet you.' Ned kissed them both. 'So, you're the ladies responsible for putting the smile back on Grace's face.'

'Actually, no,' Katie grinned. 'That, it seems, would be you.'

Chapter Thirty-Seven

'Forty-eight, forty-nine,' Amber counted. 'And this little lacy bralette that I'd quite like to keep. But I won't obviously because their need is greater.'

She relinquished this last one and added it to the pile.

'Well done pet.' Nula ruffled Amber's hair.

'Fifty bras for our first shipment,' Katie whistled. 'I think that's something to celebrate.'

'With champagne?' Amber suggested, ever hopeful.

'With tea and biscuits,' said Nula. 'Chocolate ones.'

Katie laughed to herself as Amber stomped over to flick the kettle on.

It was Monday afternoon and Amber had joined them at Auntie Small's to help sort through the donations to Small Things Matter. It had been so simple to put a collection box in the shop and spread the word. And in a matter of days the box had filled up. Their customers had been so generous and quick to help out. The thought that her little shop in Merle Bay might make the difference to a woman in a desperate situation in another part of the country made her glow with pride.

'Remind me where the first ones are going?' she asked Amber.

'Newcastle, Glasgow and Bristol,' Amber replied. 'And I'm waiting to hear back from a couple more.'

'You're a star,' Katie said. Amber had volunteered to contact the women's refuges with an offer of help. Katie was pretty sure she wouldn't have been as confident at her age.

Katie held out a bag and Nula tipped the bras into it. 'I'll wash them and then they'll be ready to send.'

'I was thinking,' said Amber, clattering around getting out mugs. 'There'll be little kids at the refuge, do you think I could send some of my old books and toys?'

Nula and Katie exchanged heart-melty looks. Barney and his wife had done a brilliant job raising such a thoughtful young person.

'That's a lovely idea,' said Nula.

'But check with your dad first,' Katie suggested.

'I can't wait until I can donate a bra,' said Amber.

'All yours fit you,' Katie chuckled. 'And very nice they are too, if I do say so myself.'

'I know and plenty of growing room too,' she said, mournfully. 'If only my boobs would grow, I could donate the old ones and help other people.'

'We all develop at different rates,' Katie told her. 'Anyway, what happened to the girl who said she didn't know what all the fuss was about because they were only glands?'

'Nothing!' A faint blush crept over Amber's cheeks.

The door opened and a man and a woman came in. Nula went to serve them. It was the woman's birthday, Katie heard her explain, and she wanted a bra that wouldn't show under the new dress her boyfriend had bought her.

'Why don't you have a boyfriend?' Amber asked.

Katie was used to Amber's directness but even so, this one took her by surprise. Was it the arrival of the couple that had prompted the question, she wondered, or perhaps there was a boy at school who'd caught her eye?

'Not everyone has a boyfriend,' she replied.

Amber shrugged. 'I know but you're cool. I bet you get loads of offers.'

'Thank you. You can come again,' Katie smiled.

Amber looked at her as if to say *well I'm waiting* . . .

'I'm not the best at relationships,' said Katie carefully. 'Something happened to me when I was younger. Something bad, and it made me wary of trusting people for a long time.'

Amber blinked at her. 'I'm really sorry.'

A wave of shame rippled through Katie. In comparison with Amber's bad thing, it was nothing.

'I'm fine now, I promise,' she said. 'I've just got out of the habit of letting people close to me. Men end up getting annoyed with me because I hold myself back. It's not their fault, it's mine.'

'But how will you ever know whether you can trust someone if you never give them a chance?' Amber said sternly.

Katie laughed softly. 'You're very wise.'

'I am,' Amber said completely without guile. 'I'll tell you what I tried the other day: the one-pound trick.'

Katie looked blank. 'Tell me more.'

'OK. There's this boy at school called Ed.'

'Ed?' Katie arched an eyebrow. 'Nice name.'

Amber's blush came back, deeper this time. 'I wanted to check if he was a nice boy or not, so I put a one-pound coin on the floor by my bag.'

'Ah, a test,' Katie nodded.

'He was supposed to pick it up and ask me if it was mine. And then I'd know he could be trusted.'

'And did he pass?'

'No,' she said indignantly. 'He just took my money and walked off.'

'Oh love,' Katie sympathised. 'Well at least you know.'

She sighed. 'I still like him though. And perhaps he really needed the money. I might have to give him another chance.'

Katie laughed. 'Maybe that wasn't a good example.'

'Fair point. Let's try again.' Amber thought about it. 'OK, got it. Take Elmo, our new kitten.'

'I thought your dad wanted to call it Elvis?'

Amber pulled a face. 'I had words with him about that. So now he's called Elmo. Anyway, he slept on my bed last night. Don't tell Dad.' She scrolled through her phone and showed Katie photo after photo.

'Very cute,' Katie agreed.

'I love him so much.' Amber gazed at her phone once more before putting it down. 'And he just instinctively trusts us even though he knows nothing about us. He hasn't got anything to go on other than good vibes. He just assumes Dad and I love him and he's right. Maybe trust can be that simple.'

Katie smiled. She was with Elmo on that one; she had good vibes about Amber too, and Barney. 'Maybe it can.'

Nula's customers had paid and were on their way out of the shop.

'Thank you!' Katie called.

Before the door had fully shut, it was opened again. It was Barney, holding a copy of the paper.

'Hot off the press!' he said, kissing Amber on the top of her head and handing the newspaper to Katie. 'You're on the business pages, just past the centrefold.'

Katie's stomach clenched as she turned the pages. She gasped when she saw the size of the accompanying picture.

'It's nearly half the page!' she exclaimed.

'Oh, Katie, you look absolutely beautiful,' Nula sniffed. 'Jean would be so proud.'

356

'It is a good shot,' Barney agreed. He had taken it himself on his phone. She was leaning against the shop window, arms folded, with one foot on the step. Her hair was loose around her face and she was smiling straight at the camera. Katie recalled how uncomfortable she'd felt at the time, but there was no trace of it in the picture.

'You look amazing,' said Amber, looking over her shoulder. 'Doesn't she, Dad?'

'Absolutely. Let Katie read the article,' said Barney, rubbing a hand through his hair distractedly.

Absolutely. Katie's cheeks burned as she scanned through the words, only half taking them in. He didn't mean it; he'd had to say that because Amber had prompted him. When she'd finished reading, she forced herself to meet his eye.

'Happy?' he asked.

She nodded. 'Thank you very much. That's a very flattering piece. Well written. I like what you've said about sending ladies on their way with a bounce in their step. It's perfect.'

Barney looked pleased. 'And it'll be online as well, so you'll be able to share it.'

'I'll share it with people in real life,' she promised, 'but I don't do social media.'

'I'll post it online,' said Nula, patting her hair and fluttering her eyelashes at Barney. 'On my Facebook page. I've got hundreds of friends.'

'Oh Katie, Katie, Katie. The whole world is online, it's time you joined in,' Amber sighed. She picked up her school bag and stuffed her phone into her pocket, ready to leave. 'Not everyone is out to get you. You've got to start trusting people.'

Barney stifled a laugh and rested a hand on his daughter's back as if to lead her out of the shop. 'And here endeth the lesson.'

'Was that how they used to talk when you were growing up?' Amber demanded and they all laughed.

'We'd better go before Elmo shreds another chair,' said Barney. 'Or my darling daughter insults us again unwittingly. I suppose I'll see you on Thursday for the awards then, if not before?'

'Yep.' Katie shuddered inwardly; the closer it got, the more nervous she was about possibly having to make a speech.

'Look at that.' Barney bent down and picked something up from the floor. He held his hand out to Katie. 'Here you are: a five-pound note.'

She shook her head. 'It's not mine.'

'Nor mine,' he replied.

'You keep it.' They both spoke at the same time.

The smile he gave her made her heart flip; instinctively she knew Barney Larkin was a man who could be trusted, if only she was brave enough.

'I suppose we could always go and spend it on ice cream?' she blurted out before she had a chance to change her mind.

Barney blinked at her, surprised. 'Yeah, I'm game.'

'Same!' Amber piped up.

'Yes, great idea.' Nula flapped her to the door. 'You go, I'll lock up.'

As the three of them left the shop, Amber lowered her voice to a whisper. 'You owe me five quid.'

'It was you!' Katie's jaw dropped.

She and Barney had been set up. She laughed out loud as Amber wriggled between her and Barney and linked arms with them both.

'You two sound like you're up to no good.' Barney looked from Katie to Amber, grinning.

'Your daughter is too clever by far,' said Katie, giving nothing away.

'Just doing an experiment, Dad,' Amber smirked, 'to check that you're a nice boy.'

Barney looked bemused. 'And am I?'

Definitely, thought Katie, as the three of them headed down to the ice-cream kiosk at the beach. Very nice indeed.

Chapter Thirty-Eight

It was Thursday evening. Grace was supposed to be leaving for the *North East Gazette*'s prestigious gala awards dinner in less than an hour. Ned was coming as her plus one and was already ready. Grace still hadn't decided what to wear and had a choice of two outfits.

'I'm really not sure about this.' She inspected first one dress and then the other.

Ned looked up from the floor where he was playing tug of war with Barkly and a smelly piece of orange and red rope. They were surrounded by dog toys in various states of destruction.

'The blue,' he said, without hesitation. 'You always look beautiful in blue. Matches your eyes.'

'You charmer,' she said, feeling herself blush.

Not for the first time since Ned had arrived in Merle Bay, either. She turned to the mirror, hoping he hadn't noticed. Was it wrong, she wondered, to be enjoying compliments from another man already? Why should it be, she thought defiantly. Who had the right to judge?

'But it's not just the outfit I'm unsure about. It's . . . it's everything.'

In truth, she didn't want to go to the event at all. Her brain and her heart had had so much to process over the last week that all she really wanted to do was sit on the terrace in the dusk with Ned and watch the night fall until all she could see was the odd twinkle of distant boats on the horizon.

Ned sat back on his heels and looked at her properly.

'If you're not in the mood for a party,' he said, 'then let's not go. I don't mind in the slightest. These industry events are all the same: overcooked chicken, vinegary red wine and endless back-slapping. Katie will understand, you've had a tough week.'

'Thanks.' She smiled at him.

She'd always been fond of him. In fact, Myles used to tease her about it, saying he'd have to watch his back where Ned was concerned. Having him here reminded her that he'd always been there for her and Myles over the years. And she hadn't realised how much she'd missed male company.

'But not as tough as it would have been if you hadn't turned up.'

'Oh, get away, I did nothing.' But as he turned his face away, she saw a smile light up his handsome face. He threw the rope toy for the puppy and the pair of them went back to their game.

She held the blue dress up against her and checked her reflection in the mirror. Did it look good? Myles had once said it did. But she didn't know whether she could trust those memories anymore.

Her stomach flipped at the thought of him and Zoe and the repercussions of their 'one night only' performance. Roger Mathers had once again proved himself to be a rock solid ally and, even though he was technically on holiday, had quickly fired off letters to Zoe and Austin and Olivia regarding the distribution of Myles's estate following the discovery of a third child. He'd also sent a letter to Julia asking her not to contact Grace directly again. Grace hadn't spoken to Zoe since she'd driven away from Merle Bay on Sunday morning, but she had contacted their parents. She told them that she loved them, and she told them that Zoe had a confession to make. She wasn't going to do Zoe's dirty work for her; she could do it herself. Beyond that she hadn't had any further contact with people from her old life.

Except Ned. His arrival was the best thing that had happened to her for ages.

He'd come up on Sunday night for some business meetings in the area this week. He'd been planning to stay at a guest house and hadn't realised there was a no-dogs policy.

'It just didn't cross my mind,' he'd told her that night on the walk back to Sea Glass House, as they took it in turns to throw a ball for the puppy. 'I've only just got him, and I'm not used to thinking about anyone but myself. He's my little shadow, there's no way I can put him in kennels. I know it's a big favour, but could he stay with you? He's no trouble, house-trained and he sleeps in his crate as good as gold all night.'

'If he's your shadow, then it makes sense for you to stay too,' Grace had insisted. It was Ned's house after all, and she was staying there rent-free. 'Besides, I've missed you.'

He'd put an arm loosely around her shoulders. 'In that case, I accept.'

He'd planned on only staying for three nights, but after Katie said there was a spare seat at the table tonight and that Robyn was bringing Finn, it was an easy decision for her to invite him to stay longer.

These last few days with Ned and the puppy had been like a silver lining in the darkest of clouds. It was impossible not to laugh when Barkly was around; he was just a constant bundle of joyfulness. She'd enjoyed hearing about Ned's latest building projects, spreading drawings out on the dining table and asking her advice. She hadn't realised how much she'd been missing her job and it had been lovely catching up on industry gossip. He'd confided in her about his dreams of one day being able to retire and live at Sea Glass House and wake up to the sound of the waves. And he'd admitted that loneliness had led him to get Barkly and already they were inseparable. Gradually, she found the words to talk to him and once she'd found her flow, the floodgates had opened, and she'd talked and talked.

Ned was easy to have around, he was intelligent and witty, gentle but not afraid to challenge her views and play devil's advocate. But best of all, he'd known and loved Myles even longer than Grace. And although he was shocked to his core by Grace's revelations, he had a wealth of happy memories to share with her and she'd found herself laughing more during the last three days than she had in months.

'OK, the blue dress it is,' she said now, coming to a decision. 'I know Katie would understand if I didn't turn up, but I should go and support her. It'll be fun.'

'Thank heavens for that,' Ned grinned, pretending to mop his brow. 'I've arranged to meet a contact in the bar. I'll take Barkly out for a last wee before we go. Come on, fella.'

Grace laughed to herself as she went into her bedroom to dress; so much for Ned pretending he didn't mind if they didn't go. Trust him to have set up a meeting; he was a great believer in networking, never one to waste a good opportunity. Knowing him, he'd have some new deal in the bag by the end of the night.

Five minutes later, Grace was zipped into her dress. She wriggled her feet into her shoes and selected her silver moonstone necklace from her jewellery box.

Ned had the dog in his arms and whistled when she came out from her bedroom.

'Look at Grace, Barkly!' he said. 'Isn't she a stunner?'

'Oh shush.' She flapped her handbag at him, embarrassed.

Barkly scrabbled to get down and came skidding over the wooden floor to greet her as if she'd been gone for hours. She rubbed his ears and told him he was beautiful.

'And so are you,' said Ned.

Grace tutted at him. 'Make yourself useful and do my necklace up for me.'

Ned took the pendant from her and raised his eyebrows.

'Oh. Doesn't it go with the dress?' she asked.

He smiled and shook his head. 'It's perfect. Turn around.'

She did as she was asked and lifted the hair from her neck so he could see what he was doing.

'You were wearing this the night I first saw you,' he said softly.

His breath tickled the fine hairs on her neck and a shiver ran down her back.

'Was I?' She racked her brains, trying to cast her mind back to the first time she'd met him.

'Yep.' She felt his fingers gentle on her skin as he tried to fasten the clasp. 'It was the Annual Architects dinner in Oxford.'

She remembered that event. It was the night she met Myles. Had Ned been there too?

'You walked up to the bar on your own,' he said softly. 'The bar was busy, but the barman served you straight away. I remember thinking that a woman like you would always get the barman's attention.'

She winced. 'Am I really that loud?'

Ned tutted. 'Of course not, silly. I tried to catch your eye, but you didn't notice me.'

'How rude of me, I'm sorry. What happened then?'

'Well then,' he said, laughing under his breath, 'I was about to pluck up the courage to talk to you when you ordered two drinks. I remember my heart sinking. *She's with someone,* I thought. So I moved away from the bar. I even remember what you ordered. A white wine and a whisky.' He touched her bare shoulders. 'There, it's done up.'

'Thank you,' she murmured.

She turned round to face him. They were standing so close that she could feel his heat. She remembered buying those drinks; she hadn't realised he'd been there. 'I wasn't with anyone. I knocked back the whisky in one and then carried my wine off with me to my table.'

'Did you!' Ned threw his head back and laughed in surprise. 'I didn't see that.'

'Oh yeah,' she grinned. 'I'd just met Myles and he asked me to go and have a chat with him about a possible opening at his company. I was so nervous I decided to have a little stiffener to calm my nerves.'

'You didn't look nervous,' said Ned, his voice low, 'you looked incredible, just like now.'

Grace felt a stirring deep inside her and her heart quickened. The way he was looking at her was . . . unexpected, thrilling.

'Thank you. You don't scrub up too badly yourself.' She flicked a non-existent bit of fluff from the front of his shirt.

Her heart was racing now; his words were exactly what she needed to hear. Since finding out about Myles's 'affair' from Julia and then learning the cold facts from Zoe, she'd felt undesirable and obsolete. The way Ned was looking at her made her feel alive again, and human – no – *womanly*. She pushed her shoulders back and matched his gaze.

'I decided that I'd come and introduce myself as soon as the speeches were over. But during dinner, Myles told me that he'd met someone whom he had a special feeling about. A brilliant architect and an amazing woman. He said he was going to offer her a job. I said I'd spotted a beautiful woman, too. But then he pointed you out to me across the room and I knew I couldn't say anything, and I never did, not to anyone. A few months after that he confided in me that he was in love with you. Lucky sod.'

Grace stared at him, absorbing his words. They flooded through her like melting honey.

'Oh Ned.' Her eyes filled with tears. 'Thank you for telling me, I . . . I don't know what to say, I had no idea you felt that way.'

He took a tiny step closer to her and reached for her hands, winding his fingers through hers.

'Grace, I still feel that way.'

A tiny pulse throbbed at her throat. She gazed at his handsome face, the kindness in his eyes, the unspoken question on his lips and her chest felt so tight with anticipation that she could barely breathe. 'Do you?'

'And I'm wondering if . . . ' His voice trailed off and he swallowed. 'Maybe in time, I might still have a chance?'

She gave a tiny gasp. 'Maybe.'

Slowly he lowered his head towards her and kissed her tenderly. The sensation of his lips against hers was exquisite and a million sparks lit her up from inside. His kiss spoke of possibilities and of a future she hadn't even dared to consider.

'That's good enough for me.' He smiled, stroking her cheek with his thumb.

Her voice trembled. 'We'd better go.'

Because if they didn't leave now, there was every chance they wouldn't make it out of the door at all.

Chapter Thirty-Nine

Katie glanced down at her cleavage for possibly the tenth time. Her stomach hadn't stopped churning since about five o'clock this morning. It had taken all her courage and half a glass of wine to leave Mermaid Cottage in her form-fitting, off the shoulder evening dress. But now, sitting beside Barney in the passenger seat, she was very aware of the amount of skin on show. It was a lovely dress: sapphire-blue satin cut on the bias which shimmered when she walked, but it was a shock to the system not to be hiding her chest underneath baggy layers.

'Dad spent half an hour hoovering out the car, before picking you up,' Amber piped up from the back seat as they approached the hotel.

'That's because someone who shall remain nameless can't seem to find her mouth when she eats crisps,' he replied.

'I'm honoured,' said Katie, resisting the urge to cover her chest with her arm every time Barney looked her way. 'And I really appreciate the lift. It's very kind of you to offer not to drink so you can drive us.'

The *North East Gazette* Business Awards were being held in the ballroom of the Clifftop Hotel, a half-hour's drive from Merle Bay. Barney had insisted on picking her up after hearing that Nula and her husband had booked themselves into the hotel to make a night of it.

'Habit,' he said with a grin. 'Sophia was a party animal, so I was always the one to drive.'

'Give Mum two glasses of rosé and a karaoke machine and we all had to take cover.'

Barney laughed softly. 'Don't remind me.'

Katie's heart squeezed; the way Barney and Amber were able to drop her name into conversation without it being a taboo topic was amazing. They even managed to do so without making her feel awkward.

'What about you, Katie?' Barney slid a sideways glance at her.

'Yeah,' Amber pushed herself forward in her seat, so that she was almost between them. 'What are you like at parties?'

Katie shuddered. 'I don't like being the centre of attention and I prefer a small gathering to a large one. But I won't say no to a gin and tonic.'

'I noticed,' Barney teased. 'Especially when it comes in a tin.'

They shared a smile, remembering their fish-and-chip supper. Was it too sentimental to be thinking of it as their first date, Katie wondered. And would this be their second? Of course not, that had been business, and so was this, she reminded herself. Not to mention that his daughter was very much present.

'I've never tried gin,' said Amber slyly.

'And you won't be trying it tonight either,' he replied smartly, much to her disgust.

They pulled into the car park and Barney drove around while they all looked for a space.

Amber sucked in her breath. 'Don't know how to break this to you, Katie, but it doesn't look like this is going to be a small gathering to me.'

'And I daren't even have any alcohol just in case I end up winning and have to make a speech, not that there's much chance of that.'

The other two protested loudly about that and Katie felt very cheered, if very slightly more nervous.

Once they'd parked and Barney had locked the car, the three of them made their way to the hotel's main entrance with Amber in the middle.

'It's very posh, isn't it,' said Katie, swallowing her nerves. The butterflies in her stomach had gone into overdrive.

Even Amber's usual confidence seemed to have deserted her. She slipped her hand into Katie's and her dad's.

'I know I'm too old,' she muttered. 'Let's pretend it never happened.'

Katie and Barney smiled at each other over Amber's head and said nothing.

Barney held the door open for them, touching Katie's back lightly as she passed by. Her breath caught in her throat. Her body was hypersensitive to his presence. *Get a grip*, she told herself firmly. Her mind wandered back to what Robyn and Grace had said earlier in the week about him; about it being a mutual appreciation society. But was it really? Her legs turned to jelly when he was nearby, whereas he seemed totally at ease.

As soon as they reached the glamorous lobby of the hotel, Amber got her phone out and began taking selfies, posing in front of a large gilt mirror beside the most enormous floral display.

'I'm going to have to go and show my face,' Barney said. 'Katie, are you sure you're OK to look after Amber?'

'Dad!' Amber looked mortified.

Katie put her arm around Amber's waist. 'Amber is my guest, so I have every intention of looking after her.

Although I'm so nervous about tonight that it could well be the other way around.'

'See you later, have fun.' He kissed her cheek. 'You look stunning, BamBam. I'm really proud of you. You too, Katie.'

'Dad!' Amber groaned.

Katie's heart melted as she watched him walk away. What a lovely, lovely man he was.

Amber giggled. 'Wow, you really fancy my dad, don't you?'

The question took Katie so much by surprise that she nearly tripped over the hem of her maxi dress.

'You don't beat about the bush, do you?' she said.

'This way, ladies.' A man in uniform gestured along the corridor to the bar at the far end which was where the attendees of this evening's event were gathering.

She and Amber joined the crowd and began to make their way towards it.

'Direct to the point of being blunt, Mum used to say,' she shrugged. 'I've been the same ever since I was a kid.'

She was still a kid, thought Katie, suppressing a smile. But then Amber had experienced more of life in fourteen years than some do in forty, so was it any wonder she considered that her childhood was firmly in the past?

Anyway, regardless of her age, Amber was one of the most intuitive and astute people she'd ever met; she deserved her remark to be taken seriously. It was on the tip of her tongue to protest. But then what sort of person would that make her? A coward. A liar? She fancied Barney so much that he was constantly in her thoughts. All. The. Time.

Katie took a deep breath. 'Your dad is the nicest man I've met in ages. But listen, I'm really sorry that it's obvious and I'm mortified if I've upset you in any way. If you'd rather I didn't come and see your dad again, I completely understand.'

Amber fell silent for a moment and when she spoke again, her face was solemn. 'I'm glad you like him. I've been thinking about what would happen if he met someone. I thought I'd be really upset, but actually, I think I'm OK with it.'

A beat passed between them and Katie hardly dared speak. It would certainly put her mind at ease if she knew Amber supported having another woman in their lives.

'Are you absolutely sure?' She studied the teenager's face.

Amber nodded. 'I miss Mum. I'll probably never be over her my whole life. But the thing is,' her lip wobbled, 'she's not coming back. That life we had: Mum, Dad and me – that's gone. So, the way I see it, I can carry on being really miserable about it like I was last year. Or I can try and be happy and make a new life. Do new things and get to know new people. I think you're really cool, Katie, and I never expected to find someone cool, not in Merle Bay. Mum would want me to be happy and she'd want Dad to be happy, too.'

Katie had the biggest lump in her throat. This kid. 'Amber, you've made me so happy. I don't think I could be happier even if I won tonight's award. But there's only one woman in your dad's heart right now and it's not me.'

'What?' Amber looked aghast. 'No way! Who is it?'

'You,' said Katie.

She pressed her hand to her chest dramatically. 'Jeez, you had me worried then. Honestly, sometimes adults can be so dim.'

Katie laughed. 'Is that right?'

'Dad is mad about you.'

Katie's heart thumped and she stared at Amber in disbelief. Could that be true? But before she could quiz her any further, a woman holding a clipboard with her pen stuck behind her ear approached them.

'Katie Small?' The woman smiled as Katie nodded. 'We need you for a photograph. All the shortlisted businesses are being done. Prints will be available to purchase from our website.'

'Sure.' Katie wrinkled her nose at Amber. 'Sorry, we'll have to wait to get a drink. Will you come with me?'

Amber shook her head. 'I'll go and find the ladies room; I'm going to see if there's any free toiletries and then take some more selfies. By the way, stick your bum out behind you, it makes your waist look thinner. Top tip off YouTube.'

'Well . . . ' Katie wavered; she'd promised Barney that she'd look after his daughter, but on the other hand, she'd much rather not have an audience while she was having her photograph taken. 'OK,' she said, making a snap decision. 'But don't talk to any strange men.'

'Except my dad.' Amber stuck her thumb up. 'Got it. Laters.'

The photo session was quick and painless, and she was soon on her way back to find Amber. She bumped into Robyn and Finn in the foyer; they were posing for a selfie, their heads touching and looking very much in love.

'Look at you!' Robyn gasped, making Katie do a twirl. 'That dress looks amazing on you.'

'Do you think?' Katie felt her cheeks flush. 'I feel very exposed.'

'You look stunning,' Robyn exclaimed. 'I'm really proud of you. Oh, you haven't met Finn!'

Finn stepped forward and kissed her cheek. 'Good to meet

you. Although I feel as if we've known each other for years.'

'Likewise,' Katie said, taking in his rugged good looks and lean physique. The pair of them glowed with health and happiness.

'And this is for you!' Robyn picked up a package, beautifully wrapped in tissue paper and ribbon and handed it to her. 'It's nothing much, but I thought . . . well, open it and see for yourself.'

Katie took it from her, intrigued. It was surprisingly heavy. She tore off the wrapping and gasped. It was a mosaic made from sea glass, in myriad shades of blue and in the centre, picked out in shells, were the words 'Mermaid Cottage'.

'For the outside of my cottage, you remembered!' Katie was touched and hugged her again. 'I love it so much. Oh my goodness, I can see everyone on the high street wanting one of these. You could make a fortune.'

'Really?' Robyn's eyes danced with the thought.

'Why not?' Finn puffed his chest out proudly. 'It's genius.'

He offered to look after the mosaic for her for the time being and Katie handed it back to him after kissing them both again.

'There's something else I've been thinking about.' Robyn chewed her lip. 'But it's only an idea, I'll show you.'

She scrolled through the pictures on her phone and held the screen up to Katie.

'It's only a sketch at the moment, but . . . '

Katie stared at Robyn's artwork; it was a drawing of Auntie Small's. Above the windows was a new long sign: another sea glass mosaic on a much larger scale. But it was the name picked out along it that really stood out. 'It's beautiful, but it says *Katie* Small's?' Katie said, confused.

'That's right,' said Robyn, looking pleased with herself. 'Maybe it's time to put your head above the parapet. Just a thought.'

Katie was still digesting this when Grace and Ned arrived.

'It's the woman of the hour,' cried Grace. She kissed Katie's cheek, whispering in her ear. 'You look every inch a winner, darling girl. Barney would have to be barmy if he didn't offer to unzip this dress for you later.'

Katie glowed with the compliments and put her shoulders back. Then after more introductions and cheek-kissing, Grace suggested finding the bar to buy drinks. Katie excused herself to go and find Amber and set off for the ladies' loos.

She spotted Amber in front of the handbasin, holding her phone up, one hand pulling down the front of her dress, exposing quite a bit of chest. 'What are you doing?'

Amber glanced up, saw Katie staring at her and dropped the phone in shock. 'I didn't send it,' she protested, going bright red.

'Oh, Amber.' Katie's heart sank as approached her. She had absolutely no experience with this kind of thing; what was she supposed to say to her?

'Please don't tell Dad.' The girl's eyes brimmed with tears. 'He wouldn't understand.'

Katie wasn't sure she was any better placed. She pulled a tissue from a box on the counter and handed it to her. 'Do you want to talk about it?'

'It's that boy, Ed.' Amber's voice wobbled. 'He asked me to go out with him. I said yes. Then he asked me to send him a picture of . . . myself.' She lowered her head. 'I don't want to, but if I don't, he won't go out with me.'

'How dare he?' Katie was livid on her behalf, on every girl's behalf who'd ever been made to feel that their worth solely depended on their looks or the shape of their body.

'If he doesn't go out with you because of that, then he's doing you a massive favour.'

Amber twisted the damp tissue between her fingers, looking less like the confident young woman who normally breezed into Katie's shop and like the young girl she really was. 'But I'm new and just want to fit in. Everyone does it.'

Katie opened her arms and Amber collapsed against her. 'They don't. Do you think your dad would have done it when he was your age?'

'No.' Amber gave the tiniest smirk. 'But did they have phones back then?'

'Funny girl.' Katie gave her a squeeze and released her. She placed her hands on the top of Amber's arms and held her gaze. 'I'll let you into a secret that not many people know about me. When I was only four years older than you are now, a man tricked me into having my photograph taken. I was naked. Those photographs blighted my life for ten years. Then a few weeks ago I was sent one of them again by someone who should have been my friend. If you send a picture of yourself on your phone, you have no control over where it ends up. Don't make the mistake I did. Protect yourself and respect yourself. Ed doesn't deserve a smart girl like you.'

'I suppose.' Amber puffed out a breath of resignation. 'And he didn't give me back that pound coin.'

'There you go, you see?' Katie smiled and handed her a fresh tissue. 'He's not to be trusted.'

Amber dried her eyes and checked her face in the mirror. 'OK. Done. You know what would really help get over my heartbreak?'

'No, what?' Katie herded her out of the bathroom and back towards the bar. In the distance she could hear an announcement for people to make their way to the ball-room for dinner.

'My first gin and tonic.'

Katie gave a snort and held open the door to the ball-room for her. 'Nice try.'

Chapter Forty

An hour later, dinner had been served and a slick team of waiting staff were gliding around the room delivering trays of coffee and mint-filled chocolates. Katie and Amber were the only sober ones on their table, not that that had stopped them enjoying themselves. However, Katie's anxiety levels were creeping up as time wore on, particularly as the dias behind them was now being prepared for the speeches.

So far, the evening had been fabulous and everyone at her table was in high spirits. Ned was lovely and obviously cared a lot for Grace. Katie and Robyn had swapped knowing looks all evening, noticing how the two of them had gradually moved their chairs closer together. It was about time Grace had something or someone nice in her life; she deserved all the happiness in the world. Katie was going to keep her fingers crossed that Ned would become a regular visitor to Merle Bay.

Ned was a born storyteller and had had them all in fits of laughter with his tales. The one about the nude spa in Germany where he'd inadvertently opened the fire escape door which had then closed behind him, leaving him stark naked in the car park, would probably still be making her giggle for weeks. Amber's eyes were out on stalks and Nula had been left gasping for breath. She and her husband were good fun, if slightly tipsy. Amber had decided to forget Ed and was currently fluttering her eyelashes at the handsome young waiter who'd been assigned to their table, and Robyn and Finn were practically glued to each other like honeymooners. Katie was happy for them, naturally, but seeing the three couples around the table did highlight her own single status.

Automatically, she looked across to the next table where Barney was sitting with the VIP guests and newspaper bosses, but his seat was empty, and she felt a bolt of disappointment. He'd caught her eye several times during dinner and each time, she'd glowed with pleasure as they'd smiled at each other.

'Are you OK?' said a voice by her ear.

She turned to find herself looking into Barney's eyes. He crouched down to her level.

She nodded. 'Getting nervous.'

Barney glanced at Amber. She was concentrating on Ned, who was teaching her a trick with a coin and a paper napkin. He cleared his throat. 'I just wanted a chance to talk to you before they announce the awards.'

She raised her eyebrows. 'Do you have insider info? If so, put me out of my misery, I'll have bitten my nails down to stumps if I have to wait much longer.'

He caught hold of her hand and pretended to examine each finger. 'They look fine to me. And sorry, I can't reveal what I know.' He raised an eyebrow. 'Or even *if* I know.'

Katie's heart skipped a beat; he was so close she could smell his delicious aftershave. This man – if he only knew what he was doing to her insides. She had a sudden urge to grab him by the lapels of his jacket and press her lips to his.

Her mouth had gone dry. 'So, if you can't tell me I'm a winner, what can you tell me?'

His eyes met hers.

'I can tell you that I . . . I . . . ' His voice trailed

away, and she watched as several emotions flittered across his face. 'That I'm glad Amber needed a bra. Oh shit. Forget I said that.' He grinned sheepishly. 'But you know what I mean.'

'I do,' she giggled. 'And I'm glad, too.'

Behind them, feet clattered up wooden steps and onto the dias.

'I'd better get back to my seat,' he said, straightening up. 'Somehow I've been roped into live tweeting the awards as they're presented. Although everyone on my table is tweeting too, so I don't know why I'm bothering.'

'And I'd better start practising my runner-up face.'

'You're my winner.' He brushed his fingers against her skin, making her shiver. 'Can we talk later?'

'Of course,' she said huskily.

When he was gone, she let out a shaky breath. He could have asked her anything and she'd have agreed. *Can we run into the sea with our clothes on later?* Why not! *Can I kiss you under the stars later?* You bet. *Can I run my fingers down your naked spine later?* Yes please . . . She gave herself a shake, feeling ridiculous and slightly hot.

Barney's boss, Paul Sullivan, the managing director of the newspaper, began his speech, thanking everyone for their part in the evening's organisation and congratulating all the businesses for making the shortlist. Everyone applauded. Barney, she noticed, had taken a couple of photos and was tapping away at his phone screen.

Amber sneaked closer to Katie and whispered, 'I hope you win.'

'Thanks, BamBam.' She clapped a hand to her mouth, realising what she'd said. 'Sorry, I didn't mean to use your nickname, it just came out.'

'It's OK. It feels nice. Like, someone cares.'

Katie's eyes pricked with tears. She nudged Amber playfully. 'Course I care, you're my favourite ever teenager.'

'And now we come to our first award of the night: the award for Best Community Project . . .'

'Yours is the final award,' Grace hissed, consulting the order of events. 'Then we get a disco. Good luck, love.'

Nula held up her crossed fingers and Robyn blew her a kiss from across the table.

'Thanks, everyone.' Her heart was thundering so loud she was scared she might not even hear who the winner was in her category. Her tongue was sticking to the roof of her mouth, so she drank half a glass of water. Oh no, now she needed a wee. Panic began to rise inside her, but it was too late . . .

'Next up is our award for the Best Independent Retailer of the North East,' Paul began. 'We are extremely lucky in this part of the country that we have so many wonderful retail businesses. The shortlist for this category is crammed with talent and is one of the most hotly contested. From flowers to food, shoes to stationery, women's wear to wine, we are spoiled for choice. And the winner is . . .'

The room began to spin, noise roared around her, applause and music, faces smiling. At her table everyone was on their feet, bouncing around, hugging each other, shouting words of congratulations.

'Katie!' Amber's face loomed in front of. 'Get up! You've won!'

Her words broke the spell and suddenly Katie was back in the moment. She grabbed Amber and kissed her and then hugged Nula and Robyn and Grace before leaping up onto the dias and accepting her award.

She was ushered to the podium where she stood at the

microphone, shaking so much that the skirt of her dress rippled under the light.

From up here it was difficult to make out faces, but Barney stood up briefly to take her picture and their eyes met. He gave her such a lovely smile that it was all the encouragement she needed to begin the short speech she'd prepared.

'I'm so breathless with excitement I can hardly speak!' she laughed and the whole room laughed with her. After pulling herself together, she took a deep breath and launched into the speech which she'd spent most of this afternoon practising in the changing-room mirror.

'I want to start by thanking our wonderful customers at Auntie Small's who've voted for us. It means so much to us, not just to have won this award, but to serve you and welcome you into our little shop in Merle Bay every day. Thank you to my fabulous friends, especially Grace and Robyn, without whom I might not have been brave enough to come here tonight, or wear this dress for that matter.'

'Bravo!' shouted someone from the back of the room.

The audience erupted into laughter again and Katie felt her spirits soar. Far from being scared, now she was up here she felt on top of the world.

'Thank you to my parents Brian and Josie who couldn't be here tonight, and much love to my assistant manager, Nula, my 'work mum' who is looking radiant at our table this evening. But above all, I want to thank my aunt, Jean Small, for creating a wonderful retail environment, where people are more like family than customers. And of course, thank you to everyone in Merle Bay for taking me to their hearts and for their continued support after my beloved Aunt Jean passed away.

'There's a saying that a good bra is like a good friend: it will lift you up, support you and always stay close to your heart. At Auntie Small's we hope you'll find—' Katie halted, aware of a commotion at Barney's table. 'Both,' she finished, uncertainly.

Below her Barney's voice was raised. People were showing each other their phone screens and muttering to each other. Applause rippled around the room but gradually, whatever was happening at the *Gazette*'s table seemed to be spreading across the rest of the audience. With a sixth sense of impending doom, Katie's legs started to quake.

Barney appeared below her, leaning on the edge of the dias. 'Katie, you need to leave the stage.'

She stepped forward and bent down towards him. 'What's happening?'

He rubbed his neck. 'Someone's posted a picture of you. On Twitter.'

'Oh no.' She felt sick. 'Is it, am I . . . naked?'

He nodded grimly. 'The caption says *patron saint of perky boobs reveals all.*'

The room had erupted now, and everyone was on their phones. To the side of her, Paul Sullivan was doing his best to take back control, but no one was listening.

'It's not what it looks like,' she said, her voice shaky with shock.

Barney turned away from her to seek out Amber. Ned was looking after her and had his arm around her shoulders.

Katie was torn between diving off the stage and locking herself in the toilet and trying to explain the whole story to Barney.

'Katie!' Robyn and Grace joined Barney below her and elbowed him to one side.

'What am I going to do?' Katie cried. 'Everyone knows, everyone is looking at their phones. She's posted the picture on Twitter. She must have had digital copies.'

Robyn grabbed her hand. 'Breathe. Breathe with me.' She blew out noisy breaths and Katie joined in.

'Listen,' Grace said urgently. 'This is your time to come out of the shadows, Katie. Remember what you said the other day? The photos only have power over you if you let them.'

She nodded, still dazed.

'You have no reason to be ashamed,' Robyn insisted. 'You were a child. But now you're a strong independent woman, yes?'

'Yes,' said Katie, gathering strength from them. 'Yes, I bloody am. Thanks, girls. Pass me some water please, I'm going back up there.'

Robyn grabbed a glass of water off their table and once Katie had had a drink she marched back to the podium where Paul Sullivan was still trying to speak to a nonresponsive audience.

'May I?' she said.

'Sure, maybe they'll listen to you.' He stood aside looking relieved and waved his arm in a be-my-guest sort of way.

'Ladies and gentlemen,' Katie announced. 'Patron Saint of Perky Boobs speaking again.'

The effect of her words was instant, and a velvety silence fell across the room.

'Thank you. I want to tell you a story about a hardworking teenager, daughter of working-class people. The first in her family ever to apply to university. A girl who worried so much about the financial burden on her parents of going to university that she innocently took up the opportunity to do some modelling. It was a scam. A scam which resulted in naked photographs being circulated around her school. A scam which cost her all her savings, her place at university and her future career as a lawyer.'

She paused. Everyone in the room was staring at her. Terrifying. But for once she didn't want to hide away, she wanted to speak up. Not just for herself but for every woman who'd ever been made to feel ashamed of her body.

'That girl is me. For years I've hidden myself away both physically and emotionally. I have been ashamed. Of my body, of what I deemed to be a failure to reach my goals. I have done everything in my power to forget about those photographs, put the past behind me and move on. But the scars will always be there.' She took a shaky breath.

'Recently I've made some new friends. We meet on the beach and we collect sea glass and without planning to, we have become each other's confidantes and cheerleaders. Through these two I've learned to love myself again. I've learned that I have nothing to be ashamed of. Every body is beautiful. Every body. Mine and yours. Your body tells the story of your life. We love, we grow, we get ill, we lose loved ones, and our bodies are there recording every bump along the road. No one loves their body one hundred per cent; we can all find flaws if we look hard enough. So how about we look with different eyes: with unconditional love for ourselves? Nobody gets to old age unscathed. Your body is your own personal journal of your life. Wonderful, unpredictable, awe-inspiring life. So, own it, be proud of it, celebrate it. Because every body matters. Thank you.'

She walked from the podium towards the steps, emotion surging through her, her eyes awash with tears. She was vaguely aware of the applause, of the entire room giving her a standing ovation.

At the base of the steps, they were all there: Amber bouncing on the spot, Robyn and Grace in floods of tears, Nula covering her face with kisses telling her how proud she was, how proud Jean would have been. Katie could hardly breathe for joy and relief and the sheer elation at having faced her demons and made short work of them.

But Barney, where was he? How would he feel about her now? A woman who'd exposed herself in front of a camera and who had been in charge of his daughter all evening. Her eyes roamed the group frantically and found him. He stood at the table, arms braced on the back of his chair, his gaze pinned to her. Her heart raced as she tried to fight through her mental fog to read his expression. A room full of people but his opinion was the only one she wanted to hear. *Barney, please understand*, her eyes pleaded with his.

And then he was coming towards her, pushing through the crowd until he was there, reaching for her. She slipped her hand into his, hope blossoming in her chest. It was going to be all right; he was smiling, touching her. *Thank goodness, thank you, thank you Lord*.

'Excuse us,' he said loudly. 'Award-winners are required for photographs. I need to borrow Katie for a few minutes.'

'Course you do,' said Grace with a wink.

'We'll keep an eye on Amber,' Robyn said, beside herself with joy.

'Let's go,' Barney murmured in her ear.

Together they made their way towards the exit, weaving past tables of people who reached out to congratulate her and smile their good wishes. And then they were out of the ballroom and running along the corridor until the noise of the event was almost inaudible.

Barney stopped suddenly and Katie stopped too. They turned to face each other, laughing and breathless.

'Katie, I think you're fantastic.'

She blinked at him, weak with relief. 'Really, even after seeing that photograph?'

'Really.' He stepped closer. 'Even more so, since seeing it.'

She raised an eyebrow and he groaned. 'That came out wrong, sorry.'

She laughed. 'I think I know what you meant.'

He met her eye. 'I never dared hope that I'd meet someone so incredible. I wasn't even sure I'd meet anyone ever again, to be honest.'

'Oh, Barney.' She placed her hand on his face. This man who genuinely didn't get how amazing he was.

'And then there's Amber to consider. Any poor woman getting involved with me gets two Larkins for the price of one.'

'Absolute bargain,' she murmured. She was staring at his mouth; she could almost taste him. She drew closer and then closer still, touching his shirt, feeling the heat of him pulsing through the fabric.

'And then I met you.' His hands reached to her waist, pulling her in until their hips met and the closeness of him sent her senses wild. 'And Amber met you and I began to hope that maybe I had found someone after all. And as the weeks have gone by, I became more and more sure that you'd be good for us.'

Her heart leapt. 'You think I'll be good for Amber? Even now?'

He nodded. 'But mostly me. I think you'll be very good for me.'

His kiss when it came was exquisite. Tender and tantalising, sensuous and incredibly sexy.

His hands found hers and he brought them to his lips. 'Is it mad to say that I'm falling for you?'

She shrugged, her body suddenly fluid and languid. She slid her arms around his neck and grazed her lips against his. 'I don't think so, but you're the journalist – don't you have a moral code to tell the truth in your stories?'

'Good point, in that case it must be true,' he murmured. 'But I'm sure I just heard the most beautiful woman in Merle Bay say that our bodies tell stories.' He kissed her again, this time with more passion and a promise of more to come. He ran his hands down her sides until they rested on her bottom and she shivered with delight. 'I can't wait to learn the story of this one.'

She felt lightheaded with love; yes, love. She knew without hesitation that this was the man she'd been waiting for. A man who'd hold her tight, but never hold her back, who'd fight her corner, but never try and take over. 'It started with a kiss,' she began and then melted into his embrace one more time.

'Are you two going to slobber over each other all night?' a voice cut in. 'Or can we go home?'

Amber! Barney and Katie leapt apart like they'd been electrocuted and Amber hooted with glee.

'Are you ready to go home or would you rather stay?' Barney looked at Katie with such warmth that she could barely think straight, let alone form a sentence.

'Stay. I mean go. Just . . . give me two minutes,' she said. 'There's something I've got to do first.'

'I warn you,' said Amber, 'it's messy in there. The disco has started, and your friends are strutting their stuff.'

Katie found Grace and Robyn dancing together, singing the words to 'Sisters Are Doin' It for Themselves' at the tops of their voices with their arms in the air.

'And here she is,' Grace yelled above the music. 'Our queen! Come and dance, we requested this one!'

'It's our anthem, we've decided,' Robyn shouted.

'I love it!' Katie laughed and threw her arms around her two dear friends. 'Actually, we're going now.'

'We?' Robyn's eyes widened.

Katie nodded. 'Barney and I are—'

'Whoo-hoo! Go Katie,' cried Grace, too excited to even let her finish the sentence. 'He's gorgeous!'

'But before I go I wanted to say . . . ' Her voice cracked and she was laughing and crying at the same time. 'You're the best friends a girl could wish for and I'm so, so glad I found you. Thank you for everything.'

'Same here,' said Robyn. 'You two have helped me more than you'll ever know.'

'Me too,' Grace agreed. 'In fact, I've asked Ned if I can stay for at least another year. I can't possibly leave the Sea Glass Sisterhood now; I wouldn't know what to do without you.'

The music had reached the chorus again and for the next couple of minutes, all three women abandoned themselves to the dancefloor.

At the end of the track, Katie kissed them both again and said her final goodbyes.

'Sorry, sorry!' She was panting as she ran back down the corridor towards Barney and Amber.

'Ready now?' Barney held a hand out to her.

'Yes,' she smiled. With him by her side, she was ready for anything.

And hand-in-hand, Amber on one side and Barney on the other, they stepped out into the night together. *Watch out, world*, she thought, *Katie Small is small no more.*

EPILOGUE

Eight months later

Extract from the *North East Gazette*

Million Pound Redevelopment Project Brings Sparkle to Merle Bay!

By Editor-in-Chief Barney Larkin

Merle Bay's biggest construction project in generations, The Boat House Workshops, opened its doors to the public today at the harbour with a celebration which included a sea glass art demonstration, boat rides and food samples from new café Finn's Catch of the Day.

Renowned architect Grace Byron, who recently moved permanently to the area with partner Ned Ashcroft, bought the row of dilapidated boatsheds from the county council last year.

Byron commented: 'Working on this development has been a real labour of love for me and a genuine collaboration between myself and the people who know Merle Bay best. Together we have created four commercial spaces which I hope will bring revenue and employment to the area, but more importantly, a place for the community to come together.'

The McGill fishing business has the largest unit, continuing the family business of three generations. Finn McGill's new café next door is set to bring a whole new wave of foodies to Merle Bay with his menu of local dishes, designed to appeal to the smaller budget. The Sea Glass Sisterhood is in workshop two and is the one closest to Grace's heart. Working with women as part of their cancer journey, Robyn McGill is using art as therapy, providing a safe place to share their stories and to do something creative at the same time. Robyn will be dividing her time between teaching people to make mosaics from foraged sea glass and fulfilling commissions for her sea glass murals, which are proving a big hit with both the retail and hotel industry. Grace will base her architectural practice in the smallest of the units, which she shares with Katie Small's charity, Small Things Matter, which is an offshoot of her award-winning lingerie shop and currently run by volunteers.

'This is a great day for us and a proud day for me,' said the mayor. 'The hidden treasure of Merle Bay has always been regarded as its sea glass. But this development proves that what makes us special is the talent, the resourcefulness and community spirit of our people.'

Finally, the founder of Small Things Matter, Katie Small, shares her views: 'The Sea Glass Sisterhood began life here in Merle Bay, on the beach in fact. It started when three women discovered the power of female friendship and what can be achieved when we open our hearts, speak the truth and help piece each other back together. And in case you're wondering what it is that can we achieve? The answer is, absolutely anything.'

The Thank Yous

Five years ago, at a party, I met a lady called Joolly Smith who lives by the sea in Northumberland. She told me that she and her friends go sea glass hunting on the beaches nearby. Finding these sea-worn pieces of glass in all colours and shapes is like finding treasure. I was instantly hooked. Not only does this give them an opportunity to chat and set the world to rights to the soundtrack of the waves, but the sea glass they find has led them to learn all sorts of creative skills, such as jewellery, art and mosaics. At the time I remember thinking that this would make a great setting for a book. And this is that book! My heartfelt thanks to Joolly, without whom, I would never have had this idea, and thanks too for meeting me in Amble to tell me more about your life on the northeast coast.

Thank you to Liz Smith who helped me devise an itinerary for my research trip through Alnmouth, Alnwick, Bamburgh and Holy Island and for all your helpful pointers along the way. This book is all the richer for your input.

This book touches on some sensitive issues and I wouldn't have had the courage to tackle them without the generosity of my friend Becky Lee. Becky shared her experience of dealing with a BRCA gene diagnosis and subsequent surgery with me. Becky, I am in awe of your resilience and strength, and I am very grateful for your help.

Thanks too to fellow author, Jane Gibson who also talked me through her health scare and the surgery which followed, I'm indebted to you for your time.

Thank you, Steve Thompson for answering my questions regarding wills. All inaccuracies are mine!

Thanks to my writing chums from BookCamp who as always, are there to cheer each other on when deadlines are looming: Rachael Lucas, Isabelle Broom, Cesca Major, Jo Eustace, Cressida McLaughlin, Katy Colins, Alex Brown, Pernille Hughes, Holly Martin, Kirsty Greenwood, Emily Kerr, Liz Fenwick and Basia Martin.

Thank you, Isabelle Broom for MAKING me go to Corfu with you to write our books and also for coming up with the name of the underwear shop in Merle Bay (Auntie Small's).

Thanks to my daughters, Phoebe and Isabel for making it easy for me to develop sparky, fun, lovable young female characters in my books. I'm very fortunate to have you in my life.

Thank you to Tony, my husband for always supporting me, even when it means I'm disappearing every five minutes to write the next book. Love you always.

There are two charities I should mention: Knitted Knockers is a real charity, I spotted an advert in a lingerie shop window and thought it was a fantastic project. You can find out more about them at www.knittedknockers.org. The other is Smalls for All which was the inspiration for Katie's charity Small Things Matter. You can find out more here www.SmallsForAll.org

This book, as ever, is a team effort. My immense thanks to my editor, Harriet Bourton, and the whole Orion team for the shine you add to my stories. Thank you to my agent Hannah Ferguson for being my cheerleader through a difficult year.

And finally, thank you to my wonderful readers for buying my books, I wouldn't be able to do this job without you!

With love
Cathy Bramley

Credits

Cathy Bramley and Orion Fiction would like to thank everyone at Orion who worked on the publication of *The Summer that Changed Us* in the UK.

Editorial
Harriet Bourton
Rhea Kurien
Lucy Brem
Sanah Ahmed

Copy editor
Sally Partington

Proofreader
Clare Wallis

Audio
Paul Stark
Jake Alderson

Contracts
Anne Goddard
Humayra Ahmed
Ellie Bowker

Design
Rachael Lancaster
Joanna Ridley
Nick May

Editorial Management
Charlie Panayiotou
Jane Hughes
Bartley Shaw

Finance
Jasdip Nandra
Afeera Ahmed
Elizabeth Beaumont
Sue Baker

Production
Ruth Sharvell

If you enjoyed *The Summer That Changed Us*, read on for an utterly delightful, exclusive short story from Cathy Bramley. . .

Special Delivery for Merle Bay

Chapter One

Alice yawned as she came down the stairs of Porthole Cottage. She was used to getting up early; Merle Bay had been relying on her to deliver the mail for three decades. The strong cup of tea she'd drunk while getting dressed had worked wonders and already the gritty-eyed feeling was beginning to disappear. At the bottom of the stairs, she stopped in front of the mirror and dragged a brush through her hair. It was still blonde, just about, although the silver threads had begun to take over. She pulled it back into a ponytail. It wasn't the mostly flattering look, she conceded, now she had more than one chin, but the sea breeze would make a bird's nest of it in five seconds flat if she left it loose.

The cottage was in semi-darkness but, through the windows, Alice glimpsed a clear sky which was lightening to a fresh china blue. Outside, above the roar of the sea, she could hear the sounds of the little seaside town waking up: the rattle of vehicles over the cobbles; the tinkle of the masts from the boats moored up just the other side of the harbour wall – pleasure boats, most of them, not like the working boats she used to hear when she was a little girl; and, in the distance, the occasional rumble of shutters being pulled up as the shops further up the hill began preparing for the day ahead.

She collected her red Royal Mail jacket from its peg by front door and headed into the warmth of the kitchen.

Graham was in his pyjamas and dressing gown, still ensconced in the chair in front of the warm range where he'd spent most of the night. Chin on his chest, hands clasped over his round tummy, he was snoring softly. At his feet was a wicker basket lined with one of his Alice's fleeces. And snuggled into that was their exhausted cat, Silky surrounded by her seven new kittens, born during the long silent hours of darkness.

Graham stirred as her footsteps squeaked across the tiled floor. 'Crikey, must have nodded off.'

'I'm not surprised, you've barely slept a wink.' Alice slipped her arms into her jacket and kissed the top of her husband's head. 'Everyone doing ok?'

He stretched his arms overhead, eased his shoulder muscles and gave a sleepy groan.

'We're all as right as rain, aren't we, chaps? I'll call the vet later on, just to be on the safe side.'

Alice crouched down for a closer look and her heart tightened with love. Silky was a long-haired stripy tabby with the most striking amber eyes, the fluffiest tail and petite pink paws. Her babies would be beautiful too; despite looking more like plump mice than kittens, they were already adorable. Alice could see their unique markings and couldn't wait for them to open their eyes.

'Clever girl,' she murmured, running her fingers lightly over the litter and finally stroking Silky's beautiful head. 'What a night, eh?'

He chuckled. 'Certainly memorable. It's miraculous when you think about it.'

Silky opened her eyes and began grooming the nearest of her offspring. Alice and Graham smiled at each other like proud grandparents.

'From no cats to eight!' Alice said, shaking her head.

Silky had stalked regally into their lives one day last year seemingly from nowhere and had settled down in front of the range as if she'd been doing it all her life. After asking around and not finding her owners, they'd decided to adopt her. Although by then, this was a moot point because Silky had already decided to adopt them.

The timing of her appearance had been perfect, Graham had been recovering from heart surgery and had been a terrible patient, forever trying to do too much and hating being 'confined to barracks' as he'd put it. Even Alice who'd happily do anything for anyone had felt her patience slipping away. She'd thanked her lucky stars that Silky had turned up to distract him; he'd spent many a happy hour googling best cat beds, best toys and best diets for cats. They'd planned on having her 'done' but with everything else that had been going on: Graham's health, Alice's sister, passing away, then Graham taking early retirement, the moment had gone and before they knew it, Silky had started putting on weight. A trip to the vet had confirmed it: pregnant.

Alice caught sight of the kitchen clock and straightened up, bracing herself on his shoulder as she stood. 'Look at the time! I'd better be off.'

He took her hand and kissed it. 'I hope you aren't too tired for work after such little sleep?'

She shook her head. 'I'm fine. Besides, you did all the hard work.'

He'd sent her to bed at one o'clock after the third kitten had been born without incident, offering to keep a basket-side vigil alone.

Graham smiled. 'Not me. Silky did that, I just cheered from the sidelines.'

She felt a swell of love for her husband and ruffled his thatch of silver hair; they'd been married for thirty-eight years and she regularly congratulated herself on making such a good match. He was such a kind, thoughtful man. Since he'd retired, he'd taken on all the housework duties, he cooked the evening meal and would run a hot bath for her on cold or rainy days ready for when she came in. She knew how lucky she was.

'But you were there all night so take it easy today,' Alice insisted, kissing his bristly cheek. 'Keeping an eye on Silky and her family will give you quite enough to do. You can all rest together.'

'I was going to make a fish stew,' said Graham, frowning. 'And put some washing on if it stays dry.'

'I can make dinner when I get home.' Alice pushed the laptop across the kitchen table towards him. 'Why don't you find out how to look after kittens, how long they need to stay with their mum, weaning them, that sort of thing.'

'Good idea!' His eyes lit up; Graham loved a project. 'I might design an advert too: kittens for sale to a good home etcetera. That ought to keep me out of mischief.'

She smiled fondly. Sixty-two years old and still he had the same boyish enthusiasm he'd had when she'd met him. 'I love you, Mr Jennings.'

'I love you, Mrs Jennings.' He held his face up for another kiss and she obliged, then, taking her lunchbox out of the fridge, she left them to it.

They'd been in their twenties when they met. He'd been a newly qualified teacher and she'd been helping her father to run the village post office. He'd come in to buy fireworks to take to a bonfire party with his new school colleagues and she'd helped him choose rockets, Roman candles, Catherine wheels, traffic lights and several packets of extra-long sparklers. To his total embarrassment when she totted up the total, he hadn't had quite enough money and so when her father wasn't looking, she'd given him a discount. He always joked that there'd been fireworks going off in his heart ever since. These days she prayed there wouldn't be any more fireworks; a gentle steady heartbeat would suit her just fine.

Alice climbed into her car and after demisting the windscreen for a minute or two, set off for work. The Royal Mail depot was half an hour away inland and she headed out of the village, waving to old friends as she drove by.

There were fewer familiar faces with every passing year as people moved away to get work in the larger towns and cities of Northumberland. Alice couldn't imagine living anywhere else, but she sympathised with those were forced to do so. Merle Bay had had a thriving harbour at one time with fishing boats jostling for space to unload their catch. Now the fishing industry was on its knees with one thing and another and gradually, the number of families earning their living from the sea had dwindled. The younger generation were no longer able to join their fathers, uncles, and grandfathers in the family business. A way of life, gone. The only full-time fishermen left in the area these days were the McGill brothers, Finn and Callum. She remembered them as boys going out on the boat with their dad as soon as they were old enough. But judging by the sort of letters she'd been delivering to the boys this last year, she doubted the business would last long enough for Callum's children to join him. He had two already and another baby on the way. Finn and his wife Robyn hadn't got a family and it didn't look like they ever would; Alice had seen Robyn's letters too, poor lass.

Alice dreaded delivering bad news. She felt like those policemen on TV who arrive blank-faced at the door to announce there'd been an accident. She had a sixth sense about which envelopes contained bad news and a wisp of sadness would follow her around like a ghost for the rest of the day. She always had an urge to go back and check up on them. You got to recognise the stationery after a while. The Northumberland General hospital used a very specific creamy paper visible through the window in the envelope, whereas letters from the doctor's surgery were always hand-written envelopes. Alice knew all sorts of things about all sorts of people, but she'd never pass on her insider knowledge.

If she knew who hadn't paid their phone bill, she kept it to herself, if she noticed someone was getting reminders from debt collectors, she wouldn't tell a soul and as for speeding fines and court summonses, mum was the word. But these were in the minority. On the whole her post bag was full of joyful messages: Happy birthday! Well done! Thank you! I love you! The weight of her post bag was a constant reminder that, at heart, people loved people and found endless little ways to show it.

An hour later Alice had swapped her Mini for the Royal Mail van and was heading back to Merle Bay laden with the village's mail. She hummed merrily as she navigated the narrow lanes to the outer reaches of the village away from the sea. The houses were bigger and more spread out here, the drives were set back from the road and she rarely saw a soul. There was a time when Graham had wanted to live here but Alice had been born in at Porthole Cottage and couldn't imagine not being able to hear the sea when she woke up. And Graham, being Graham, had acquiesced.

For the next ninety minutes she was in and out of the van, making swift work of her deliveries so that she could head back to the coast. The heart of the Merle Bay was the favourite part of her round; she knew everyone, and everyone knew her and delivering mail took twice as long as it should because of the number of conversations she got drawn into. It was the best part of the job.

She pulled into the car park of the old schoolhouse and parked her van. She'd be on foot from here unless there was any mail for the cliff top houses which was unlikely; they were second homes, rented out as holiday lets for the season and rarely received mail. The old schoolhouse was a quaint Victorian building, as pretty as a gingerbread house. It had been converted into a gallery and café about fifteen years ago, which was still new as far as Merle Bay was concerned. Alice didn't think it was particularly profitable – not many people in the village had a spare three hundred pounds to buy an original painting of a seascape. And why would they need to anyway when the view out of their bedroom windows gave them a new scene every day? Not that she didn't want them to be profitable, of course she did. What they needed, what lots of the businesses in Merle Bay needed, was more tourists and wealthy visitors.

Still, she thought, hoisting her post bag on to her shoulder, there wasn't a lot she could do about that. She stuffed several thick envelopes through the letter box of the gallery and set off down the lane towards the village with a considerably lighter bag.

Pinfold Lane ran parallel to the high street and consisted of hotchpotch of dwellings from large Victorian villas to terraced cottages and a rather unsightly block of flats added during a moment of madness in the 1960s which everyone in the village agreed had been a mistake. Alice made her way along one side, bidding passers-by a good morning and popping post through letterboxes as she went.

Mel Carroll opened her front door just as Alice was wedging a fat plastic wrapped brochure through her letterbox. Mel's dog, a brown tufty terrier called Hero bounded out of the door, darted past Alice and promptly cocked his leg up the gate post.

'Whoops, excuse us!' Mel yelped with a laugh, her glossy brown hair swinging as she held tight to the lead. 'Looks like someone was desperate! Sorry about that, Alice.'

In her late-thirties, Mel added a touch of glamour to the area. Even when she was in jeans, trainers and a plain white shirt, she turned heads. Her colouring was slightly exotic too – her grandmother was Maltese, Alice recalled.

'And it looks like someone might be planning a holiday,' she replied, unwedging the brochure from the door and handing it to Mel. The unmistakable Disney logo covered most of the front of it and Micky Mouse grinned from the corner.

'Shh!' said Mel, glancing over her shoulder and closing the door behind her. She shoved the package into her tote bag. 'I'm glad I caught you before it dropped onto the mat. It's going to be a surprise for the kids for Christmas.'

'How exciting!' Alice's eyes widened. 'Don't worry, your secret's safe with me.'

She thought a lot of Mel; her partner, Dan, had left her earlier this year with three children to look after and a hair salon to run. As far as Alice could see she was managing brilliantly without him. She'd never warmed to him anyway. Shifty-eyes and a sneer for a smile. Yes, Mel had had a lucky escape in her opinion.

'So, book in early for this Christmas, if you want me to do your hair,' said Mel, her eyes sparkling. 'Because I'm heading to the US of A.'

'Good for you, love.' Alice nodded with approval. She bent down to fuss over Hero, who'd calmed down now he'd done his business. 'Those children of yours are very lucky to have a mum like you.'

Mel's smile wavered. 'Between you and me, I'm spending money I can't really afford. The salon has gone really quiet at the moment.'

'Hang the expense,' said Alice, who ever since Graham's health scare was a firm believer that life was too short to worry about that sort of thing. 'It'll be a holiday to remember for all the right reasons.'

'True,' said Mel darkly.

The two women shared a knowing look as they headed out of Mel's front path together. Last Christmas Eve, Dan had gone on a bender and was discovered by the coast guard under the carcass of an abandoned fishing boat on Boxing Day. Mel had been beside herself with worry, and the children bewildered and disappointed at their less-than-merry Christmas.

'Do you know anything about the new arrivals?' Mel nodded across the street to where the 'To Let' sign was still nailed to the gate post outside number thirty-four.

'No? Someone has moved in then?' Alice was put out. How had she missed that? She hadn't even known old Mr Lewis's cottage had been sold.

'I didn't see anyone arrive.' Mel scanned the windows for signs of life. 'But there was a light on upstairs when I woke up this morning and I don't recognise that car.'

Alice studied the unknown vehicle parked outside. It was a beaten-up navy BMW, several years old and very muddy. She smiled at Mel with a twinkle in her eye. 'Give me half an hour and I'll know everything.'

Mel nudged her with a giggle. 'What are we like? Between you and me, I think we know every bit of gossip there is to know in this village. Drop into the salon later and fill me in.'

She raised a cheery hand and they went their separate ways: Mel heading down to the seafront to walk the dog and Alice continuing with her door-to-door deliveries.

She loved her job, absolutely loved it. She knew some people thought she was nosy, but she wasn't, she was simply interested. She cared about her community and relished being the one to bring good news: holiday brochures like that one for Orlando, birthday presents, Valentine's cards, even bouquets of flowers these days. Graham sometimes worried that her post bag was getting too heavy for her, but Alice had no intention of retiring just yet. It was hard manual work, but not difficult and rarely stressful; there was the occasional early special delivery she had to rush to make, but by and large every day was the same, just the way she liked it.

Before long, Alice had reached the bottom of the street from where she had a perfect view of the sea, sparkling a deep sapphire blue today, the merest hint of white horses breaking its surface.

Her phone beeped as she crossed over the road, preparing to deliver the post to the opposite side and she fished her phone out of her jacket pocket. Pictures of the kittens from Graham and one of Silky sitting up and grooming herself, as elegant as ever. She smiled and tapped a quick message back. She hoped they'd find homes for them all, or at least six of them. She was sure Graham could be persuaded to keep one. She forced herself to focus on the post bag, picked up her pace and a few minutes later she was outside number thirty-four Pinfold Lane. There were two letters for the new occupant, one postmarked London and one from the local council, both addressed to Mr B. Larkin. She pushed open the gate and wondered what the B stood for.

Chapter Two

Barney Larkin stood in his bedroom, towel wrapped around his hips, shivering slightly after his tepid bath. He'd only given the estate agents' details a cursory glance and had completely forgotten that this place didn't have a shower. He peered into the holdall of his crumpled clothes for something suitable for his first day as editor of the **North East Gazette**. He felt a flicker of apprehension in his gut and then remembered the last time he'd started a new job: current affairs editor for **The Times**. Then he really had had an attack of the heebie-jeebies. But then he'd had Sophia to bolster him.

'They'll love you,' she'd murmured, straightening his collar and kissing him, her lips soft and sexy against his mouth. 'You've got this, Barney.'

He pulled the towel off his lower half and rubbed his thick wavy hair roughly as if scouring himself of the sweet memory.

From downstairs came the crashing and banging which always accompanied his daughter's morning routine and he grinned to himself. Amber might look like a gazelle, all big brown eyes, silky hair and long slim legs, but she had all the grace of a baby elephant, especially when she was hungry. But at least she was up and about, which meant he had at least one less battle to face.

His own stomach rumbled then, reminding him that he needed to get a move on if he was even going to have time for a coffee before leaving. He was going to need a hell of a lot of caffeine to keep him awake him this morning. He'd been sure that he'd sleep like a log after the events of yesterday: moving from London – previously the centre of their world, to Merle Bay – the very edge of it. Not to mention packing up so much of their family history into boxes and putting it into storage while he tried out a new life for himself and his daughter. But despite being physically and mentally drained, his brain had had other ideas and he'd lain awake running through the short speech he planned to give his new team later. And those bloody seagulls squawking overhead at daybreak – they sounded like someone was torturing them. How anyone around here could sleep through that he had no idea.

He grabbed a newish pair of jeans and the least creased of his shirts and after throwing them on, headed downstairs.

The cottage had been professionally cleaned before their arrival and the faint aroma of artificial citrus smell still lingered. But no amount of cleaning could disguise the air of neglect that the place gave off. Barney knew it had been uninhabited for months and judging by the décor, it hadn't seen a paint brush or any new carpet for several decades. In an ideal world, he'd stay in today and get the place straight, but the world wasn't ideal. No one knew that better than Barney.

He strolled into the kitchen and dropped a kiss on his daughter's auburn hair. He caught a whiff of her almond shampoo, the same one that Sophia used to use, and he couldn't resist inhaling deeply for a second.

'You know sniffing me is weird, right?' said Amber, crunching through a mouthful of granola.

'Says you,' he replied, nodding at her bowl. 'Eating bird seed without milk.'

She always did that. It worried him that she wasn't getting enough calcium. It was important for girls at her age; he'd read it somewhere. Something to do with puberty. He looked at her face in profile: rosy cheeks, a couple of tiny pimples on her temple but otherwise perfect skin. Amber was even-tempered, comical and loving. How would they fare together, he wondered, navigating her transition from girl to grown-up?

'That's even weirder, Dad,' she said firmly.

'What is?' he said indignantly. He wasn't doing anything.

'That melty face stare.'

He laughed and apologised, turning his attention to the mess in the kitchen instead. The kitchen in their house in Putney had been all stainless steel and glossy doors, one long run of sleek units. Evidently Mr Lewis's tastes had been rather more 'unfitted'. The elderly Formica-topped cupboards, the sink unit, the dresser and the oven, which would have looked at home in a World War II replica home, were all of the freestanding variety.

'Can you remember which box the coffee machine was in?' Barney asked, rummaging through the chaos cluttering the small table.

'Hallway,' she said without up from her phone. 'In the box marked emergency supplies underneath a half-eaten bag of tortilla chips.'

'Half-eaten?' He frowned, distinctly remembering putting a full bag in there along with a bag of giant chocolate buttons and a bottle of coke. He'd didn't have time to fiddle about now. He'd have a cup of instant now and set the coffee machine up later.

'I got the munchies in the night,' she said defensively and then grinned. 'Now that *was* an emergency.'

'Sorry, love.' He rubbed a hand through his hair, feeling bad that they hadn't eaten properly last night. They'd assumed there'd be a McDonald's en route, or at least a fish and chips shop. But by the time they'd crawled northwards on the motorway along with several thousand other Sunday motorists, it had been after ten when Barney's knackered BMW had made it to Merle Bay and everywhere had been closed. 'I'll do something nutritious for dinner.'

'Yay,' Amber said flatly. 'Oh, and thanks for saying I look nice in my school uniform.'

He looked at her sheepishly. 'You look great. And thanks for getting up by yourself.'

He put the kettle on, tipped an enormous quantity of instant coffee into a mug and looked around for his cigarettes while he waited for the water to boil. His heart sank. For one, glorious moment he'd forgotten that he'd given up smoking.

Please, Dad, Amber had begged him. *Everyone knows you can die from smoking. And if you die, too . . .*

She hadn't finished her sentence; she hadn't needed to. That had been last Friday when he'd told her he was nipping to the shop to buy cigarettes. He hadn't smoked since. His daughter wasn't a demanding teenager, and after everything she'd been through – they'd been through – the least he could do was to try and stay alive for her.

'Yeah, well have you seen the bus timetable?' she said holding her phone up for him to see.

He smiled to himself. She'd been here less than twelve hours and already she'd downloaded the app for the local transport.

'Absolute joke,' she continued. 'There's like one bus a day out of this place if you're lucky.'

He added a splash of milk to the mug and winced as he sipped his scalding hot coffee, too impatient for a caffeine hit to wait.

'You'll have to be ready on time then, won't you?'

'Or get an Uber,' Amber suggested. She looked horrified for a moment. 'Do they have Ubers in the wilderness?'

He laughed. 'We're just by the sea, kiddo, not in the middle of the Serengeti.'

'Oh my God. What about Deliveroo?' She eyed him, properly worried. 'We'll never eat again.'

He felt a pang of guilt and made a vow there and then to start cooking real food. He had a brief flashback to the tiny portions of pureed organic vegetables Sophia had filled the freezer with in order to make sure their baby was properly fed. He forced himself to relax and cut himself some slack. In the grand scheme of things if the worst consequence of losing his wife was an over-reliance on takeaway food, then he declared that a win.

'I'll give you a lift into school today, then hopefully by tomorrow your bus pass will have arrived.'

He glanced at the time on his phone. Five minutes and they should really get going. He'd been told not to come in until eleven today, but it wouldn't hurt to get there early.

'Can't believe you're making me go to school on my first day here.' Amber slid her brown eyes to his. 'I need to work my way up to it, settle in. Unpack my stuff and you know . . . transition from one home to another.'

Barney was torn. Amber made some valid points as usual. If only she wasn't so good at arguing, he thought grinning to himself. On the other hand, she'd make a brilliant barrister if she ever decided to pursue a career in law.

'I promised the head teacher you'd be there,' said Barney, trying to sound authoritative. 'And you've already missed the first week of term.'

Amber rolled her eyes. 'The only thing I'll have missed is the assembly on bullying, drugs and dodging the local paedos. And seeing as I've spent the first fourteen years of my life in London, I think I'll just about cope with whatever this tiny town can throw at me.'

'That's reassuring then.' He pulled a face. 'I think.'

She pushed her chair back from the table and dumped her bowl in the sink.

'Dishwasher,' Barney chanted on autopilot. Amber raised a wry eyebrow. 'Oh, I forgot.'

There wasn't a dishwasher, or a washing machine, or a microwave . . .

She swilled her bowl and spoon under the tap and set them on the draining board.

He pulled her into a bear hug as she passed him on her way out of the room. 'You are okay, aren't you, BamBam?' he asked softly, pressing a kiss into her hair.

His heart squeezed at the sound of the nickname Sophia had given her after the baby in the Flintstones cartoon with the cute face and penchant for getting her own way.

She lifted her face to his. 'Yes, Dad,' she said patiently. 'It's you I'm worried about.'

He blinked at her. 'Me?'

She waved an arm. 'I mean, from big cheese editor of a national newspaper to editor of . . . whatever it's called. Do they even get news up here?'

He was touched that she cared. He dotted a finger on the top of her nose and released her. 'News is everywhere, wherever there are people—'

'There's a story,' she chanted, heading into the hall.

Barney laughed. It was his first boss's catchphrase and he had adopted it years ago.

'Dad?' Amber hissed, crouching down suddenly. 'There's someone on the other side of the door.'

Chapter Three

The door to number thirty-four opened wide and Alice stepped back startled, envelopes still in hand.

'Hi. Sorry. Didn't mean to make you jump.' A man in his mid–thirties smiled at her.

'Rather you than a boisterous dog.' She assessed him quickly and decided he looked friendly. It was those hazel eyes: the open gaze, the crinkles at the corner. A nice build too, broad and chunky, like he could give good hugs. A bit like Graham's natural build before his sweet tooth got the better of him.

'I'll take that as a compliment.' His smile broadened and she realised she was openly staring at him.

'Your post, Mr Larkin,' she said, blushing as she handed over it over. 'One's from London and the other is from the council.'

Why was she telling him this? Firstly, he could see that for himself, secondly, it made her look as if she'd been snooping and she hadn't. Well, not intentionally. She'd been more interested in his name than who was sending him mail.

'Thanks.' He took them from her, scanned them quickly and tore up the flap of the council one with his fingertip.

She took the fact that he hadn't gone straight in as a sign that he was open to conversation. She liked people who took the time to chat to her. Another mark in his favour.

'What do you think of Merle Bay so far?' she asked, sorting through her bag to get number thirty-six's post ready.

He pulled out a plastic card from the envelope and glanced at it before replying.

'We only arrived last night in the dark, so I'm yet to explore the village.'

It was a town really, but Alice didn't want to appear pedantic as well as nosy.

'We?' She flicked an inquisitive glance through the open door and into the hallway behind him. Just boxes, no other signs of life.

'My daughter, Amber and me. I'm Barney, by the way.'

Only the two of them. Alice's curiosity antennae were waving about wildly.

'Alice Jennings.' She put her hand out and he shook it. Firm grip without being a tight squeeze, neatly trimmed nails. She felt herself go all fluttery and girlish. 'I've lived here all my life so I'm a bit biased, but it's a nice friendly place. I'm sure you and Amber will like it.'

'I hope so,' he said, with the hint of a sigh. He cleared his throat. 'So, I guess you know everything there is to know around here?'

'Not everything!' she said indignantly, feeling heat rise to her face. What was going on with her today? She thought she'd finished with all that hot flush nonsense. 'I didn't even know Mr Lewis's house had been sold.'

'It hasn't,' Barney answered. 'We've rented it for six months.'

'An extended holiday?' Alice's postbag was weighing heavily on her shoulder and now that the sun had risen a bit higher in the sky, she was getting warm. She should press on with her round, but nobody new had moved in for ages and she was enjoying talking to him.

His smile dropped for a second and Alice had a sense that there might be a story there.

'Sorry,' she said hurriedly. 'None of my business.'

'We've moved up from London for my job,' Barney straightened up. 'I don't know the area well and wanted to rent before settling somewhere.'

'Good thinking,' she agreed. 'Not a decision to take lightly. And to answer your question, nothing ever happens here. Well, not much.'

He grinned. 'I don't believe that for a second. Everyone has at least one good story to tell.'

'Actually.' She leaned a hand against his door for a moment to take the weight off her left ankle which ached sometimes. 'We did have a dead whale wash up on the beach a couple of weeks back.'

A teenaged girl appeared at the door dressed in school uniform, her eyes wide with alarm. Alice recognised the uniform; she used to go to the same school. Although in her day skirts were passed the knee, this one looked very draughty around the nether regions.

'That's so sad.' The girl's face crumpled.

Alice nodded grimly. 'Choked on plastic apparently.'

'You've got to write something about that, Dad.' She looked at her father who nodded thoughtfully. 'That whale could have been a mother, she might have had babies.'

'And even if it hadn't had babies,' said Alice, who wasn't a mother and didn't like feeling a less important human because of it, 'whales are a vital part of the sea's ecosystem. We need them to keep the food chain working properly.'

'Does that happen often?' Barney regarded her intensely.

'Twice this year in this area,' Alice said. 'Are you a writer then?'

He nodded. 'I'm the new editor at the North East Gazette.'

'Ooh, how exciting.' She perked up. Having a journalist living in Merle Bay could only be a good thing. It would help put them on the map. Wait till she told Mel . . .

'Humans are the worst.' The girl's shoulders sagged, and Barney pulled her to him, rubbing her arm.

'On a more cheerful note,' said Alice, feeling guilty for bringing the mood down on their first morning. 'My cat, Silky had seven kittens last night and they are the most beautiful things I've ever seen.'

'Kittens!' The girl's head whipped around and she gazed beseechingly at her father. 'Dad, could we have one? I'd love to have a pet, it would make us feel more at home. Please?'

'I was thinking of a dog if anything,' he said rubbing his chin.

'Yes!' Amber punched the air. 'Two pets!'

'Whoah, hold on.' He laughed softly and sighed, turning to Alice. 'Will they be for sale?'

She nodded. Now she felt guilty for putting him in a difficult position. 'But no need to make a decision today, they won't be ready to leave their mum for a few weeks anyway. Amber, why don't you come and see them after school one day? I live at Porthole Cottage.'

'Can we?' Amber looked at her dad for approval.

'We'd love that,' said Barney. He laughed as his daughter threw her arms around his neck and kissed his cheek. 'But first, we need to get you to school and as luck would have it, your bus pass has just arrived.'

He handed her the plastic card from the envelope.

'Cool,' Amber grinned, 'now I won't have the embarrassment of being dropped off by my dad. Social suicide.'

'And these letters won't deliver themselves,' said Alice. She turned to go and raised her hand in a wave. 'Have a good day.'

'Bye!' said Amber cheerfully. 'Save us the best kitten.'

'Nice to meet you,' said Barney, 'and remember where to come if anything newsworthy should happen.'

They went back in the house and shut the door shut behind them.

Alice laughed to herself as she continued her round. Newsworthy? Nothing exciting really happened in Merle Bay, that was one of the things she loved about it.

Alice pressed the doorbell but didn't hear a reciprocal chime. Battery must have gone. She looked at parcel she was trying to deliver. It was in one of those 'Do Not Bend' envelopes. She could get it through the letterbox but only if she ignored the instructions. What if it was a school photograph or something and folding it ruined it completely?

She was at Callum and Claudia's house in the tiny narrow street near their boatyard. If the worst came to the worst, she could always drop the envelope in there. Although, of course, the brothers would be out fishing now. But that didn't matter, it wasn't a special delivery so she could just leave it. She'd try once more. She bent down and forced the letterbox open a tiny bit.

'Hello! Anyone at home?'

'Yes!' came a distressed voice from the other side of the door.

Alice's heart thumped. 'Is that you, Claudia?'

'Alice? Oh, thank God, help!'

She pushed hard at the letterbox now until she could see the floor in the hallway. Her eyes swept to the left and saw feet in fluffy slippers. Her stomach lurched with fear.

Claudia sobbed. 'I've fallen down the stairs. My ankle . . . and the baby.'

'Ok, hold on, love.' Alice swallowed. 'Everything's going to be alright.'

'Back door,' Claudia said weakly. 'It's open.'

There was an alleyway two doors down. Wasting no time, Alice darted along it, went around the back of the house and climbed over the picket fence. She pushed her way through a washing line full of sheets and let herself in through the kitchen door. All the time her head was spinning. Should she phone Claudia's husband? An ambulance? When was the baby due? Would it be all right? Was Claudia seriously injured?

Breathe, Alice, breathe, she murmured to herself. Probably something and nothing.

She ran into the hall, already out of breath. She shed her post bag and dropped to her knees in front of Claudia who had her eyes squeezed shut and was giving a long low moan. She was on her back, her head and shoulders resting on the lowest stairs, legs splayed out on the floor. Her left foot was at an odd angle and was already swollen. Her tummy looked impossibly huge under her t-shirt.

Tears sprang from Claudia's eyes. 'I'm so scared.'

'I'm here now, no need to worry.' Alice brushed Claudia's hair away from her forehead. Her skin was clammy to the touch. She'd done a first aid course years ago; she just wished she could remember some of it.

'Your ankle hurts, you said, love. Anything else? Your back, your . . . tummy?'

'I'm not bothered about me,' she sobbed. 'I'm worried about the baby.'

'I'll call an ambulance.' Alice could feel terror building inside her. Her fingers fumbled as she found her phone and called 999. With the phone pinned under her chin, she ran into the living room and grabbed a cushion and fluffy blanket, pieces of Lego scattered as she knocked over a box of toys.

'Ambulance please,' she said, when the operator answered.

While the person on the other end tried to establish what had happened and Alice tried to keep her voice calm, she slid the cushion under Claudia's head and covered her with the blanket.

'And she's pregnant,' Alice added, shooting Claudia a reassuring smile.

'Ok, Alice, when is the baby due?' asked the operator who'd announced his name as Peter.

'A couple of weeks, I think,' Alice replied wracking her brains to try and remember when Claudia had said she was expecting. There was no use trying to ask her; her face was screwed up tight in pain and she was panting heavily. 'It's her third,' she added as if that might be important.

'There's an ambulance on its way,' Peter said. His calm professional voice was exactly what Alice needed to hear. 'It'll be with you soon.'

'Good,' said Alice, not liking the what she was seeing. Claudia seemed to be getting more agitated by the second. She reached for her hand. 'Help is on its way, love. Any minute.'

Suddenly Claudia screamed loudly. She pushed Alice's hand away, tore off the blanket and tried to yank her leggings down.

'Peter, I'm getting a bit worried here.' Alice's mouth had gone completely dry.

'Push,' gasped Claudia. 'I need to . . . arghhhh!'

'Bloody hell,' Alice yelped, helping her to remove her leggings and knickers. 'I think it's coming. Peter, what am I supposed to do?'

Just then Claudia grabbed Alice's arm, knocking the phone out of her hand. She gave a long guttural grunt and then stopped to pant.

Alice stared down between Claudia's legs. The baby's head was sticking out.

'Oh God!' Claudia breathed, staring at Alice with wide frightened eyes.

'Hello? Hello? Can you hear me, Alice?' came Peter's tinny voice from her mobile phone. For a brief second Alice wished she'd paid attention to Graham's lesson on how to put the sodding thing on hands-free, but it was too late for that now.

'The head has been born,' Alice cried, picking up the phone. She was panting almost as much as Claudia now. She knelt between Claudia's legs and put one hand underneath the baby's head. She could feel its nose and mouth.

'I'm going to kill my husband,' Claudia gasped, gripping Alice's hair.

Alice picked up the phone again and Peter gave her more instructions, telling her to check for the cord around the baby's neck. But Claudia was building up to another push and Alice couldn't focus. Surely the ambulance should be here soon? She couldn't do this alone. **Hurry up, hurry up, hurry up**.

'The phone is on the floor now, Peter, please don't leave us,' Alice said, laying it on the carpet.

'You're doing really well, love,' said Alice to Claudia. She held Claudia's hand tightly, the other hand supporting the baby's tiny head.

Claudia's face was running with sweat. She puffed her cheeks out and Alice mirrored her breathing. Claudia gave one almighty push. The baby shot out and Alice caught it and it was the one of the best moments of her life.

'Welcome to the world!' she whispered tenderly.

The infant was red and slippery and covered in goo, but Alice thought she'd never seen anything so wondrous in her life. She swallowed the lump in her throat.

'It's here!' she shouted for Peter's benefit. 'The baby's out.'

'What is it?' Claudia asked, reaching for her little one. 'Boy or girl?'

Alice checked.

'It's a girl. You've got a beautiful baby girl,' she said shakily. 'Congratulations.'

Alice passed her the baby and picked up the phone gingerly. 'What should I do now?'

'Well done, Alice,' said Peter, 'help is almost with you. Is the baby crying or breathing?'

'Um. Hold on.' As Alice looked over at the mother cradling her baby, it let out an almighty scream. Alice could have wept with relief.

'It's crying,' she said, barely able to keep from crying herself.

'Gently wipe off the baby's mouth and nose. Then dry the baby off with a clean towel. Then wrap the baby in another clean dry towel . . .'

Not wanting to climb over Claudia, Alice ran into the kitchen, opening drawers until she found a stack of clean tea towels. She wrapped the baby as instructed and covered Claudia with the blanket again. Outside she heard the sound of the ambulance siren getting closer.

'Thank you,' said Claudia, her eyes shining. 'I don't know what I'd have done if you hadn't turned up.

'Thank you.' Alice brushed away her tears before kissing them both. 'That's the most special delivery I've ever made.'

Chapter Four

Two days later, Alice had finished her shift and was sitting with Graham having a cup of tea when there was a knock on the door of Porthole Cottage.

'I'll get it,' she said, springing to her feet.

'Ok, love,' Graham chuckled. 'It's probably someone wanting your autograph.'

Alice was still euphoric. Everyone in Merle Bay was talking about what a hero she had been. She'd had flowers sent to her, she was stopped in the street and even felt a bit of a celebrity!

It was Claudia was the hero, Alice thought, doing what she'd done with so little fuss. Nevertheless, she'd been delighted when she heard that Claudia and Callum were calling the baby Elizabeth Alice. The little mite was doing well, all seven pounds two ounces of her and already she had both her parents and her two siblings wrapped around her tiny little finger. The paramedics had checked Claudia and the baby over, but nothing was amiss, and Claudia insisted that as they'd managed at home this far, there was no need for them to go into hospital.

She opened the door and a newspaper was thrust at her: the *North East Gazette*.

'Surprise!' Amber cried, waggling the paper at her. Behind her stood Barney, hands in pockets, smiling warmly. 'You've made the front page!'

Alice's hand flew to her throat. 'What?'

Amber put the newspaper into Alice's hands and looked guilelessly over her shoulder. 'Can I see the kittens?'

'Sure,' said Alice, standing aside. 'Straight through into the—'

Amber didn't wait to hear the directions, darting past Alice down the hallway.

Alice looked at the front page of the newspaper. Two thirds of it was taken up with a picture of her and Claudia, both holding the baby and beaming proudly.

'Good grief,' she exclaimed, reading the headline. 'Alice's Special Delivery for Merle Bay' by Editor, Barney Larkin.

'So, you were saying,' said Barney, grinning cheekily. 'Nothing ever happens in Merle Bay, does it?'

'Well,' Alice said, returning his smile. 'A journalist once told me that everyone has a story to tell. I don't think I'll ever top that. In fact, I don't think I even want to!'

The End

Loved reading *The Summer That Changed Us*?
Make sure you don't miss out on more feel-good,
comforting and heart-warming reads by Cathy Bramley!

Merrily Ever After

Could the best Christmas present be a brand-new family?

Merry has always wanted a family to spend Christmas with, and this year her dream comes true as she says 'I do' to father-of-two Cole. But as she juggles her rapidly-growing business, wedding planning and the two new children in her life, her dream begins to unravel.

Emily is desperately waiting for the New Year to begin, so she can finally have a fresh start. She has always put her family first, leaving little time for happiness and love. When her beloved father Ray moves into a retirement home, she discovers a photograph in his belongings that has the potential to change everything.

As past secrets come to light, will this be a magical Christmas for Emily and Merry to remember?

Coming Autumn 2022

Pre-order your copy now

Can she find her perfect fit?

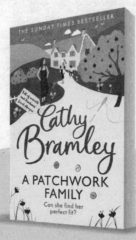

Gina Moss is single and proud. She's focused on her thriving childminding business, which she runs from her cottage at the edge of The Evergreens: a charming Victorian home to three elderly residents who adore playing with the kids Gina minds. To Gina, they all feel like family. Then a run-in (literally) with a tall, handsome American stranger gives her the tummy-flutters...

Before a tragedy puts her older friends at risk of eviction — and Gina in charge of the battle to save them. The house sale brings her closer to Dexter, one of the owners — and the stranger who set her heart alight. As the sparks fly between them, Gina carries on fighting for her friends, her home and her business.

But can she fight for her chance at love — and win it all, too?

'A book full of warmth and kindness'
Sarah Morgan

It started with a wish list.
Now can she make it happen?

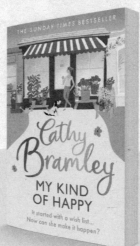

'Flowers are sunshine for the soul.'

Flowers have always made Fearne smile. She treasures the memories of her beloved grandmother's floristry and helping her to arrange beautiful blooms that brought such joy to their recipients.

But ever since a family tragedy a year ago, Fearne has been searching for her own contentment. When Fearne makes a chance discovery she decides to start a happiness wish list, and an exciting new seed of hope is planted...

As Fearne steps out of her comfort zone and into the unknown, she starts to remember that happiness is a life lived in full bloom. Because isn't there always a chance your wishes might come true?

Praise for Cathy Bramley:
'A warm hug of a book'
Phillipa Ashley

Can two complete strangers save Christmas?

Christmas has always meant something special to Merry - even without a family of her own. This year, her heart might be broken but her new candle business is booming. The last thing she needs is another project - but when her hometown's annual event needs some fresh festive inspiration, Merry can't resist.

Cole loves a project too - though it's usually of the bricks and mortar variety. As a single dad, his Christmas wish is to see his kids again, so getting the new house finished for when they're all together is the perfect distraction.

But this Christmas, magic is in the air for these two strangers. Will it bring them all the joy they planned for . . . and take their hearts by surprise too?

After all, anything can happen at Christmas. . .

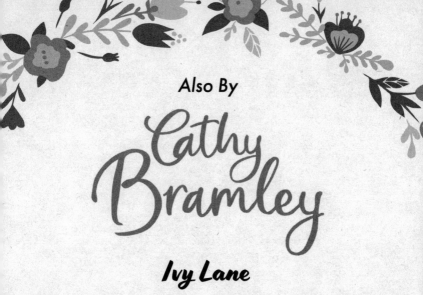

Also By

Cathy Bramley

Ivy Lane

Tilly Parker needs a fresh start, fresh air and a fresh attitude if she is ever to leave the past behind and move on. Seeking out peace and quiet in a new town, will Tilly learn to stop hiding amongst the sweetpeas and let people back into her life – and her heart?

Appleby Farm

Freya Moorcroft is happy with her life, but she still misses the beautiful Appleby Farm of her childhood. Discovering the farm is in serious financial trouble, Freya is determined to turn things around. But will saving Appleby Farm and following her heart come at a price?

Conditional Love

Sophie Stone's life is safe and predictable, just the way she likes it. But then a mysterious benefactor leaves her an inheritance, with one big catch: meet the father she has never seen. Will Sophie be able to build a future on her own terms – and maybe even find love along the way?

Wickham Hall

Holly Swift has landed her dream job: events co-ordinator at Wickham Hall. She gets to organize for a living, and it helps distract from her problems at home. But life isn't quite as easily organized as a Wickham Hall event. Can Holly learn to let go and live in the moment?

The Plumberry School Of Comfort Food

Verity Bloom hasn't been interested in cooking ever since she lost her best friend and baking companion two years ago. But when tragedy strikes at her friend's cookery school, can Verity find the magic ingredient to help, while still writing her own recipe for happiness?

White Lies And Wishes

When unlikely trio Jo, Sarah and Carrie meet by chance, they embark on a mission to make their wishes come true. But with hidden issues, hidden talents, and hidden demons, the new friends must admit what they really want if they are ever to get their happy endings...

The Lemon Tree Café

Finding herself unexpectedly jobless, Rosie Featherstone begins helping her beloved grandmother at the Lemon Tree Café. But when disaster looms for the café's fortunes, can Rosie find a way to save the Lemon Tree Café and help both herself and Nonna achieve the happy ending they deserve?

Hetty's Farmhouse Bakery

Hetty Greengrass holds her family together, but lately she's full of self-doubt. Taking part in a competition to find the very best produce might be just the thing she needs. But with cracks appearing and shocking secrets coming to light, Hetty must decide where her priorities really lie...

A Match Made In Devon

Nina has always dreamed of being a star, but after a series of very public blunders, she's forced to lay low in Devon. But soon Nina learns that even more drama can be found in a small village, and when a gorgeous man catches her eye, will Nina still want to return to the bright lights?

A Vintage Summer

Fed up with London, Lottie Allbright takes up the offer of a live-in job managing a local vineyard, Butterworth Wines, where a tragic death has left everyone at a loss. Lottie's determined to save the vineyard, but then she discovers something that will turn her summer – and her world – upside down...